PRAISE FOR NEVER ASK ME

"Abbott writes in an authoritative way about the protocols, many of them maddening, of adopting a child. He also has a real understanding of the emotional roller-coaster couples going through the process must endure."

—New York Times Book Review

"No one exposes the dark, fraught underbelly of suburban America quite like Abbott, and his propulsive latest, depicting the relationships between families tied together via an overseas adoption process, is a proper humdinger."

—Boston Globe

"Cunning and complex."

—Publishers Weekly

"[A] suspenseful novel by a master of the psychological thriller." *—Booklist*

"NEVER ASK ME produces almost unbearable tension and suspense.... Readers will be kept guessing all the way to the end and most assuredly will be flipping back to some of the previous journal entries [to predict] the future events that Abbott deftly lays out for us as only he can."

—Book Reporter

PRAISE FOR JEFF ABBOTT

"Abbott uses his skills as a master storyteller to convey a complicated and ambitious tale that seems straightforward but is full of twists and red herrings. He also keeps the story moving without falling into clichés or over-the-top revelations. The mystery works because of the terrific characters and the beautiful road map he unveils while navigating the reader through a complex landscape. Those who enjoy unpredictable stories can never go wrong diving into the world of Jeff Abbott." *—Washington Post*

"Like a stage magician, Abbott often seems to be doing one thing when he's actually doing something else, and when we realize what he's been up to, we can't help but shake our heads in admiration." *—Booklist*

"Abbott is a master of misdirection." *—Library Journal*

NEVER ASK ME

JEFF ABBOTT

GIC

GRAND CENTRAL
PUBLISHING

NEW YORK   BOSTON

Grand Central Publishing
Hachette Book Group
1290 Avenue of the Americas, New York, NY 10104
grandcentralpublishing.com
twitter.com/grandcentralpub

Originally published in hardcover and ebook by Grand Central Publishing in July 2020
First trade paperback edition: January 2021

Grand Central Publishing is a division of Hachette Book Group, Inc. The Grand Central Publishing name and logo is a trademark of Hachette Book Group, Inc.

The publisher is not responsible for websites (or their content) that are not owned by the publisher.

The Hachette Speakers Bureau provides a wide range of authors for speaking events. To find out more, go to www.hachettespeakersbureau.com or call (866) 376-6591.

Library of Congress Cataloging-in-Publication Data

Names: Abbott, Jeff, author.
Title: Never ask me / Jeff Abbott.
Description: First Edition. | New York : Grand Central Publishing, 2020.
Identifiers: LCCN 2019049270 | ISBN 9781538733158 (hardcover) | ISBN 9781538733141 (ebook)
Subjects: GSAFD: Suspense fiction.
Classification: LCC PS3601.B366 N48 2020 | DDC 813/.6—dc23
LC record available at https://lccn.loc.gov/2019049270

ISBNs: 978-1-5387-1701-1 (trade paperback), 978-1-5387-3314-1 (ebook)

Printed in the United States of America

LSC-C

Printing 1, 2020

For Vince and Chele Robinette
with admiration and thanks

NEVER
ASK ME

1

JULIA

Ned Frimpong waits for Julia Pollitt on the porch, six minutes away from the terrible moment. They're up earlier than teenagers normally are, the sun just rising above the hills of Lakehaven. When Julia walks up to his front porch from two houses over, Ned is frowning at his phone and flicking his finger across the screen, saying, "Oh, that Megabunny just cost me points."

"Don't you ever tell anyone we're doing this," she says. She gives him a smile.

He smiles back. "My lips are sealed. I have so much Megabunny shame." He glances at the phone screen. "Oh, there's a Shocker-squirrel."

"Those are good, right?" she says, pulling out her phone, opening the game, and frowning at her screen. "Lots of points?"

He opens the front door, leans in, calls, "Mom, Julia and I are heading out to play our game. Back in a bit." He doesn't wait for an answer but shuts the door. "Oh. Do you want coffee?"

She just started drinking coffee black, the same way Ned takes his, but she can't play the game and carry a cup of coffee at the same time. Not gracefully, at least. "No thanks," she says. She's waiting for the game's little digital creatures to appear on her screen so she can capture them with a flick of her thumb. She and Ned are up early, like fishermen, because with daylight the neighborhood will be full of little cartoon monsters appearing on their phone screens, and they're both trying to move up a level in the game.

"There will be tons of them at the park," Ned says. He turns that way; Julia follows.

She thinks that if they didn't both have their phones out they could walk to the park holding hands. Ned walks slightly ahead of her, staring at his screen.

"This is a slightly embarrassing addiction," Julia says. "We're too old for this."

"I was at the mall last week and I saw grandmothers playing Critterscape," he said. "Bonding with their grandchildren. Nothing to be embarrassed about."

"Telling me grandmas are playing this is not upping the cool factor," Julia said. She sees a rare Critter wander onto the neighborhood map; a flick of her finger on the screen launches a cartoon net, and the little digital animal is hers. Hundreds of points added to her total, sparkling animation playing across her screen; she smiles.

"Hey," he says. She turns to him and he's holding a key. She looks at him again, and there's that shy-yet-knowing smile that has been part of the change in looking at him, from childhood friend to something more.

"What's that?" she asks.

"Privacy," he says. "Someplace where we can go when we're ready."

She opens her palm and he drops the key into her hand. She puts it into her pocket. He keeps his smile in place, then turns his gaze to the phone like it's no big deal that he gave her that key, and she walks alongside him, playing it cool as well.

They walk in starts and stops—stopping to attempt to capture the prizes that Critterscape lays over the digitized homes and yards of Winding Creek Estates. A jogger plods past, then an older neighbor walking her two retrievers. Julia wishes she'd taken Ned up on his offer of coffee. She wouldn't have to feel she was focusing on the game and maybe they could talk. About everything that was—and wasn't—happening between them. She watches him stop in front of a house, fingers moving across the screen's keyboard.

"What are you doing?" she asks. Tensing. "You're not...?"

"No. I'm just sending a message to someone else in the game." His gaze is steady on her.

She forces herself to relax. "I just want to catch Critters." She starts walking ahead of him. After a few moments, he catches up to her with an apologetic smile.

They walk down Winding Creek Trail, the main street in the subdivision; it dead-ends into a park, one with a sprawling playscape for little kids and a large pool, home of the Winding Creek Salamanders, the neighborhood youth swim team.

Julia sees someone sitting on a bench, the person's back to them as they enter the park, heading toward the pool. A woman. Long hair, stirred by the wind. Even from behind she seems familiar.

"Frustrating," Ned says, staring at his screen. "My last two Critters have run away. Life is cruel. I swear some algorithm kicks in right when you're about to level up."

The woman on the bench isn't moving. Just sitting there. Julia thinks she recognizes the coat.

"Is that your mom?" Julia asks.

"No. Mom was at home. I mean, I think she was." Ned stops for a second, as if he doesn't want to continue. He's staring at the figure on the bench.

Julia keeps walking. "Ms. Roberts?" she calls. "Hey."

The woman doesn't turn around at her voice.

"Mom, are you trying to steal all our Critters?" Ned calls to her. He comes up behind her, touches her shoulder. She slumps to the side. Ned freezes, but Julia keeps walking and rounds the bench. And then she sees Danielle Roberts's face, purpled, dead, dried blood on her lips and her chin. At her expression Ned pushes past her to his mother.

Ned screams first, the sound raw and broken, grabbing his mother and shaking her like he could will her back to life. Julia pulls him off; he shoves her to the ground and collapses next to her. He sobs, starts screaming the word "Mom" over and over again.

Julia reaches over to touch the woman's throat, but it's terrible, discolored, and instead Julia searches for a pulse on the cold wrist.

Nothing.

It takes Julia three shaky jabs at her phone screen to exit the game, and she forgets to breathe as she texts her mother.

NEDS MOM IS DEAD IN PARK

2

GRANT

Grant Pollitt stands in front of the tree on the greenbelt that leads down to the creek, beyond his backyard. When he was little, he used to hide his treasures in a small hollow near the tree's roots, until his mother worried that same hole might harbor copperheads or water moccasins.

He stands there, trembling, a little scared, and not sure why.

It's been a very weird morning.

First the email arrives, sent to him from a friend. The email contains a picture of his favorite football player, arms lifted in triumph after a win. The email reads trust me, Grant, you want to click on this. It makes him suspicious, because a virus could hide inside a picture or a link, right? But it has his name in the caption and the email wasn't from some unknown person; it was his friend Drew's address. He bites his lip. He has heard other pictures could be hidden inside digital photos. Maybe this is Drew's way of sending him the kind of pictures your parents don't like you to have. He feels guilty, but Drew would know if he doesn't click it because he couldn't fake his way out of not knowing. He clicks it.

His browser opens. A new picture appears. It's a photograph of a woman caught whirling in the misty rain; behind her stands the Eiffel Tower. She's wearing an expensive raincoat and laughing. People around her are clapping and watching in admiration. At the bottom of the photo are the words:

Some days lies fall like the rain. Go look in your tree.

That's...incredibly odd, he thinks.

He texts Drew. Did you send me an email with a picture of JJ Watt?

The answer: Uh no why would I do that and I was asleep thanks for waking me up

Never mind, Grant texts back. This wasn't the kind of joke that his buddies Drew or Landon or Connor typically pulled on another friend. He scans the computer for viruses. None.

Go look in your tree.

It can mean only one tree. Maybe it's Julia, pulling a prank on him. Julia isn't interested in computers, though, and hiding a picture inside a picture—she wouldn't know how to do that. It wasn't the kind of joke his parents played, either, trying to turn everything into a learning opportunity or a challenge he could write about on his college essays.

He goes downstairs and into the kitchen. Mom is making coffee, tapping her foot as if the coffee maker were delaying her.

"Good morning," she says. She runs a hand through the mess of his bedhead hair. She's always trying to fix his hair. He loves her, but he wishes she wouldn't do that. Sometimes Mom looks at him as though surprised he's there.

"Hey," he says, giving her a quick hug and thinking: *This is silly. I should tell her about this email.* But then, it's so odd, so strange, that it's like having a special secret. So he doesn't, and she says: "I think your sister went out playing that Creaturescape game with Ned."

"Critterscape," he says. He gets orange juice from the fridge, pours a large glass.

"Whatever. Do they just walk around the neighborhood?"

"It's exercise," he says, not looking at her.

"That's what her dance class is for. Do you know what's going on between them?" Mom asks.

It's like she can't help herself, Grant thinks. Like if Julia confides in him he will break that confidence just because Mom asks. "I don't know," he says.

Mom bites at her lip, unsatisfied.

"I have to go down into the greenbelt," he says.

"Why?" Mom is always a little suspicious of the greenbelt. Kids go down there into the heavy growth of oaks and cedars and swim in the wide creek and walk the convoluted trails and sometimes smoke weed or drink. He hasn't done the forbidden activities. But he knows other kids who have.

He realizes then he should have waited until she wasn't around or had gone upstairs and then just gone to his tree. Now she is interested, in that Mom way.

"Biology class specimens," he says. He's a freshman and biology is the bane of his existence.

"In winter?"

"Yes, Mom, in winter, biology still goes on."

Her phone buzzes with a specific ringtone that indicates Julia is calling. The ringtone's melody is that of a song Mom wrote about Julia when she was very young and fighting cancer—a neuroblastoma—and Julia hates that it's a ringtone but doesn't want to hurt Mom's feelings. Grant keeps meaning to tell Mom to change it. Mom picks up the phone, stares at the screen.

Her face goes pale. She makes an odd little noise, like a gasp or a cough interrupted.

"Mom?"

She keeps staring at the screen; it's like he isn't there. "Mom?" he repeats.

"Stay here. Stay here. Keep your phone close."

"What is it? Is Julia all right?"

"Yeah. No. I've got to go to her. Stay here."

Mom grabs her coat from the mudroom and hurries out to the garage. He hears her car start and then silence for several seconds, as if she's forgotten how to drive, and then the garage door powering up. He stands at the kitchen window, sees her Mercedes SUV jerk down the driveway, going way too fast. Julia's done something stupid, he supposes, and she's gotten into trouble. Last year she was Little Miss Perfect; now she's in some vague rebellion that makes no sense to him. He wishes she would make up her mind.

He wonders where Dad is. He goes to his parents' room. His

father is lying under the covers, snoring softly. Another late night working, Grant figures. He closes the door softly.

Go look in your tree.

He goes out the patio door, crosses the backyard, and opens the gate. The greenbelt is just beyond. It's fed by Winding Creek, a middling tributary of Barton Creek in West Austin, which runs across a slice of Lakehaven. There's a hiking path by the creek. He walks off the trail, listening to the hiss of water as he heads down toward the creek, and his old tree is to the left.

A rock covers the cleft near the tree's roots. The cleft was his hiding place: small, cozy. Grant would put pretend treasure maps there, or Legos, or hide little objects he had stolen from his parents—a penknife, coins, his father's car keys once when Kyle had an endless succession of overseas business trips. He wasn't even sure why he took small, worthless things and hid them away: he always brought them back home, put them in plain sight, and sometimes smiled to himself when Dad or Mom would find the missing item and say, *How did I miss seeing that?*

Now inside the cleft, where he hasn't looked in years, is a plain brown envelope. His breath catches in his chest.

He pulls it free. It's thick, with GRANT written across it in block letters with black ink. He opens the envelope.

Inside is money. Cash. Crisp twenties. Bound, organized, like it just came from a bank. He counts it, stunned.

It's a thousand dollars.

Left for him in a tree.

He looks into the envelope again and sees there's a note inside. He unfolds it and reads it.

Grant: You have been told a huge lie. I will only tell you the truth. Keep this money hidden and please tell no one about it. It's a gift from me to you.

Grant stands up. This is insane. Someone spoofing an email address to lead him to money hidden behind his house. He's never seen this much cash in his life. And it's his now. It makes no sense. Why?

Grant feels like someone is watching him. He stands. He scans the dense growth of oaks and cedar along the creek, the hiking trail. Sees no one, listens to the quiet of the wind in the trees.

He clutches the envelope close to his chest, feels the weight of the cash.

Then, on the morning air, he hears the approaching scream of police sirens.

3

IRIS

Iris Pollitt sits in her car, in her closed garage, hands on the wheel, thinking: *Danielle is dead. Really dead.*

And then she thinks: *Good.*

It's the worst thought she's ever had, a horror, unworthy, and she shoves the thought away. She wants to cry; she wants to vomit. Instead she takes several deep breaths and starts the car. Music plays, the nineties channel on satellite radio, or the "Mom Channel" as Julia calls it. Britney Spears is singing "...Baby One More Time," and Iris turns the volume down into silence.

Now she hears only the sound of her own ragged, gasping breath.

Go. Go there. Your kid needs you. Mom mode. Now.

She's in such shock she's forgotten to open the garage door, and she jabs the button, thinking herself lucky she didn't rocket into the closed door. She waits for the door to power up and reverses up the driveway, fast. Going past the kitchen window, she sees Grant staring out in surprise, in curiosity.

What do you say when you get there? What do you do?

She should have woken Kyle, made him come with her. She didn't even think of that. She is moving through this morning as if she is in a dream and she needs to be *awake*.

Iris floors the Mercedes GLS. She doesn't think about Danielle being dead—she can't. She keeps that terrible thought at bay and instead retreats to thinking about her to-do list, which now won't get done today: organizing the final fundraiser for the Lakehaven High Music Festival (featuring band, orchestra, and choir); dropping off donated supplies at the fundraiser for a less fortunate school on the other side of Austin (a project of Julia's, both to do good and to bolster Julia's résumé for college applications); then a meeting with the choir parents board tomorrow, where she'll outline the spending for the school musical and the end-of-year senior chorister trip to Houston, where the kids will see a touring Broadway show and have a private session with the show's understudies to learn about musical theater. It's a lot; it's a job where she doesn't get paid, except that then her kids have better programs and her husband thinks she's doing something worthwhile and not pining about her vanished career all day.

Thinking about her day as if it could still be normal doesn't keep the horror at bay. Tears now in her eyes. Oh, Danielle. Why?

Danielle is dead.

And my daughter found her.

Suddenly, in her mind, an old and precious memory: Danielle surprising her at the front door, with a smile: *I got the email. They've matched a baby for you. A boy.*

And Iris screaming in joy, and Danielle embracing her.

She blasts down Winding Creek Trail. Past one neighbor walking a pair of dogs, past a jogger. The houses are morning-quiet. All that quiet, that sense of security, is about to go away for a long time. She feels the world shift. She has to be ready for her family.

Iris skids to a stop inside the park entrance. Ned kneels by the bench, sobbing, Julia embracing him from behind, still holding her phone. Two men she doesn't recognize, but both dressed for jogging, are standing near them, watching. One has a phone pressed to his ear, speaking quietly. The other, a tall redhead, just stares, pale and unsure.

The enormity of it all slaps her in the chest, the stomach.

Iris stumbles out of her SUV, her hand at her mouth in horror, and runs toward them. "Julia!" she screams.

"Mom!" Julia looks like she's seen the end of the world. "We found her…we found her on the bench." Julia doesn't let go of Ned, her face twisted, tears on her cheeks. "She was sitting here…She's cold."

"Don't look. Kids, don't look." It's too late for that, but she doesn't know what else to say. She tries to pull them both away, but only Julia goes. Ned lets out this keening cry and lies down on the ground, his hand clenching his mom's leg. It breaks Iris's heart. She kneels, puts her hand on the small of his back because she doesn't know what else to do.

"I tried to get him to move," one of the joggers says quietly. "He won't go."

Iris forces herself to look at Danielle Roberts. The dead woman wears a dark wool coat, jeans, loafers, a dark-gray sweater. Expensive ring on her finger. A massive bruise discolors her throat; blood cakes her mouth, her chin.

"Iris?" the jogger on the phone calls to her. He knows who she is, of course; she isn't sure of his name in the charge of emotions. She forces herself to flip through her mental catalog of contacts and remembers him. He's Rachel Sifowicz's husband. Matt. They have two kids, a senior in high school who plays football and an eighth-grade girl in band. Rachel had to cut back on volunteering when Matt was briefly unemployed after being laid off. Odd rambling thoughts fighting for footing in the slippery slope of her overwhelmed mind.

"Matt," she says. "Call the police."

"I did. They're on their way. I'm on the phone with the emergency operator. They said don't touch anything."

"Did you find her?"

"The kids did," he says. "We heard them screaming and ran here. Is she…for sure?"

Ned found his own mother. Dead. Iris feels faint. She swallows down a tickle of bile. She forces herself to check Danielle's wrist; she can't bear to touch that discolored throat. No pulse.

"Yes," she says. Mom mode. She has to get into mom mode. For both of them.

She looks at the other jogger, a brawny redhead. She doesn't know his name. "Help me with him," she says, and he nods.

"Ned," she whispers. She puts her fingertips on his chin and turns his face toward hers. She has known this boy since he was a toddler. His face is gaunt, his mouth quivering, brown eyes hollow with grief. His breath smells like mouthwash. His dark hair is under a cap. He looks at her like he no longer understands the world.

"Ned, come away." She can hear the police sirens approaching; he hears them, too, and he shakes his head. Everything is about to change. He can't let it, she sees; he cannot accept this new world.

"Ned," she repeats. "Ned."

He whispers, "Mom can't be dead. She can't be."

"I know, I know. The police are here. Let them help her."

"Why would anyone hurt her?"

"I don't know, sweetie. I don't know. Come with me. Come with us."

She sees a shadow start to pass over his face, as if he is asking himself the question and considering the answers, and then he presses his face into Iris's shoulder. She begins to stand, and he resists, but then the redheaded jogger gently raises the boy to his feet, and Iris guides Ned toward the police car that has just pulled up. The weight of him against her shoulder is the weight of this new, awful reality.

She hears words being spoken—Matt, remaining calm; the officer, taking command of the scene; Julia brokenly starting to tell them what happened—but she focuses on Ned, on steering him away from the horror, on holding him up, on comforting him. Another police car arrives.

Ned shudders under her arm.

Iris looks back at Danielle, an empty shell on a cold bench.

She can never tell now.

Iris hugs the grieving boy closer to her.

4

TRANSCRIPT FROM INTERVIEWS FOR *A DEATH IN WINDING CREEK* BY ELENA GARCIA

Elena Garcia: How long have you lived in Winding Creek?

Matt Sifowicz: Nearly seventeen years. We bought early. I mean, some people don't buy until their kids are school age. And all the prices do here is go up. So we bit the bullet and got in when our son was a baby. Would have cost me an extra forty thousand if we'd waited until he was in kindergarten.

Garcia: People really buy here for the school district.

Sifowicz: And everything that comes with it. The football team, the music programs, the robotics and business incubator programs, the college placement, the real estate investment…That is what sells Lakehaven.

Garcia: And low crime. Presumably.

Sifowicz: You have to realize, we've never had a murder in this neighborhood. Tools being stolen from a garage is a rare kind of crime in Winding Creek. Maybe one or two burglaries, or stuff being taken from cars in driveways. The most common is trespassing, people who don't live in the neighborhood going down to our greenbelt to tube in the creek, drink beer, smoke pot. Sometimes they start campfires, which is a threat to the whole greenbelt and every home in the neighborhood.

Garcia: So Winding Creek—the actual creek and the surrounding greenbelt—is on private property.

Sifowicz: Yes, owned collectively by the home owners in the neighborhood. I'm on the HOA board. Four hundred houses. Average sale price now is eight hundred thousand. That's twice what some people bought theirs for fifteen years ago. This is a good place to be.

Garcia: How did you feel the Pollitts were viewed here in the neighborhood?

Sifowicz: Pretty well. They were popular. Iris is kind of a force of nature. Everyone knows her.

Garcia: What was your first thought when you saw Julia Pollitt and Ned Frimpong in the park?

Sifowicz: I was jogging with a coworker who also lives here, Steve Butler. I'm VP of sales at a software company and Steve is our VP of product development. It's easier to stick to the training regimen when you have a partner. Steve suggested a run that morning. We were approaching the park when I heard Julia Pollitt screaming. Steve heard it, too. We looked at each other and ran straight for the park. I thought she was being assaulted. We entered the park and saw them by the bench and saw the body. Ned Frimpong was trying, I think, to resuscitate or embrace his mother, and Julia Pollitt was trying to pull him away from the body. She had her phone out.

Garcia: She texted her mother instead of calling 911, yes?

Sifowicz: Yes. I think that might be normal for a panicking teenager. I took care of calling 911 and told her I was.

Garcia: Did you know Danielle Roberts?

Sifowicz: Well enough to say hello. My wife knew her better. All the school moms, well, they seem to know each other. If they volunteer a lot.

Garcia: How so?

Sifowicz: The moms, and yeah, some of the dads, well, they run the programs. They raise the funds for all the extra things that make our schools special because the state takes a ton of

Lakehaven's property taxes to build and support schools in less fortunate areas. I'm OK with that, by the way. But it is a huge amount of money shifted from Lakehaven schools—last year it was over one hundred million dollars—and parents here have very high expectations. Stratospheric, even.

Garcia: What with having bought their homes here strictly for the school district.

Sifowicz: Absolutely! They make sure the teachers have any extra thing they need. Iris is kind of that supermom volunteer who is on every committee. My wife is an insurance agent. She doesn't have time to volunteer the way Iris does, but I think she was amazed at Iris's energy. But that's Iris. Or was.

Garcia: You were there when Iris Pollitt arrived.

Sifowicz: Yes, and of course, I didn't know the truth. None of us did.

Garcia: The truth?

Sifowicz: Well, yes, all that's come out since. So much deception, so many lies. It's shocking. This is a nice neighborhood.

5

KYLE

"Dad?"

Kyle Pollitt awakens with a bolt. Sweat on his ribs, feeling fevered. He blinks away the awful image from his dream—blood droplets on an expanse of white—and sees his son, Grant, standing over him, pale. For a second Kyle thinks he's still in the dream and has said something in his sleep. Something terrible that Grant would never understand. Kyle blinks again and realizes he's awake.

It was only a dream.

"Dad?" Grant repeats.

"Yes. Hey, buddy. Good morning." Kyle blinks, wipes a hand across his face.

"Something bad is happening. Julia went somewhere with Ned and then Mom ran out of here and told me to stay here and there's tons of police sirens in the neighborhood."

"OK. OK." Kyle gets out of bed, wearing only his boxers, and pulls on exercise pants and a long-sleeved T-shirt with Lakehaven Track printed across the front—Julia runs cross-country. He picks up his phone and texts Iris: YOU OK?

No answer.

They look at each other, hearing another set of sirens approaching in the distance.

"You stay here," Kyle says.

"Why?"

"Because I said so." Kyle steps into sandals, the closest shoes at hand, although it's cold outside, and searches for his car keys.

Grant watches him gather his stuff. He sees his father's hands tremble, slightly, as he stuffs keys and wallet into his gray pants.

"Dad?"

"I'll text you in a few minutes." Kyle finds his car keys and hurries out. He drives his BMW toward the sounds of the sirens. He sees people, neighbors, walking along Winding Creek Trail, toward the sirens.

Toward the park.

Fresh sweat breaks out on his ribs, his palms. He feels sick.

He arrives. There are multiple police cars: Lakehaven and, just arriving, Travis County Sheriff's Office. An ambulance. Lights flashing on all of them. A crowd starting to form. Near one of the cars he sees his wife and his daughter. Unhurt, but in the middle of it all. He swallows past the thickness in his throat.

The police officers are setting up a perimeter and they keep him back. He calls to Iris; she hurries over to him, holding Julia tightly.

"It's Danielle Roberts," Iris says. "She's dead."

"What? How?"

"I don't know how she died. Julia and Ned found her." Iris's gaze is steady on him.

The words nearly stagger him. Kyle tries not to show it, and so he folds his arms around his wife and his daughter. Kyle's tall, and over their heads he sees Danielle's body sprawled on a park bench. Officers are starting to process the scene. He stares at her. And then he sees it, below her feet, under the bench, near her shoe, because one of the deputies has started taking pictures and aims her camera right at...

A cell phone. Lying on the ground, under the bench.

Phones have records in them. Of calls made and calls received.

He tightens his hugs on his family.

What has he done? Panic roars in his chest, like a clawing, living beast.

This isn't happening, he thinks.

"Dad, I can't breathe," Julia says into his shoulder.

He releases her instantly, instead putting a reassuring hand on her shoulder.

"The police want Julia to give a statement. At the station, away from all this," Iris says.

"All right," he says.

"I'll take her. You stay with Grant."

"All right." He most decidedly does not want to go to the police station. "Who did this?"

"I don't know. It's not like we have muggers hanging out in that park." Iris's voice is shaking, her lip trembling.

"It has to be random," he says. "Everyone loved Danielle. Where is Ned?" he asks.

"With the police. They're talking to him. Trying to establish her movements."

Movements. What a clinical word, he thinks. Her movements. Where she was, who she talked to. Who she saw. Tracking her phone. He feels cold terror inch up his spine. *I want out. I want out*. Words, echoing in his head.

"I'll go with Julia. You've had a shock," he says. Knowing full well what Iris's answer will be.

"No. I'll go. I was here." And there he hears it, the barest bit of accusation that she had to come and comfort their traumatized daughter while he lounged in bed.

"All right. Whatever you think best."

And then Julia starts crying. Really crying. Brokenhearted crying.

"We'll tell them you'll talk to them later," Iris says, embracing her.

"No, no," Julia said. "Whoever did this has to be caught. I want to help the police."

Kyle can see Iris is in full mom mode. Protective, determined. Is he in dad mode yet? He is so shaken right now. "We'll both go."

"Is Grant home alone?" Iris asks.

"Yes."

"Well, go home. Whoever did this could have fled into the greenbelt, been hiding…" Iris says, and she's off, theories pouring out of her. "I mean, he could try to break into a house to hide."

"Grant is fine."

"I'll feel better if you go home," Iris said. "I got this."

None of us do, he thinks. *No one has this. It has us.*

He puts his hands over his face, feels the nub of his wedding ring against his cheek. He can't bear to look at his family for a moment.

"Are you OK?" Iris asks.

Kyle lowers his hands. He realizes it's a normal question. They've known Danielle for years. "Yes. It's just a shock," he says. "No one expects this."

Her gaze meets his and then he glances away.

A police officer comes over and Iris tells him they're willing to go to the station now. The detective, the officer says, will join them there shortly.

"Ned," Iris says. "He shouldn't stay alone at that house."

"Where is Mike?" Kyle asks, looking around. Mike is Danielle's boyfriend, a big, brawny bear of a man. One of Kyle's best friends.

"I guess they haven't found him yet or contacted him," Iris says. Julia has calmed a bit, wiping the tears from her face.

"I can give the police his number. If Ned isn't up to it."

"I need to get out of this circus, Mom, please," Julia says. A van from a local television station has just pulled up.

Iris hurries her toward the car after telling the police officer they're heading to the police station and will wait there for the detective.

Kyle stands there, stuck. He feels like he should stay. But he has things he must do, right now, *now*. He may not get a second chance.

6

EXCERPT OF TRANSCRIPT OF TCSO AND LPD INTERVIEW WITH EDWARD FRIMPONG (MINOR)

Conducted by: Travis County Sheriff's Office detective Jamika Ponder, Lakehaven PD detective Carmen Ames, and TCSO juvenile counselor/advocate Juan Castillo.

Present in observation room: Iris Pollitt, a family friend requested by the minor.

Detective Ames: I know this is very difficult and I am so sorry. We just want to establish what happened this morning. Detective Ponder and the Sheriff's Office will be the lead investigators on this, and you can tell them everything you know.

Ned: Yes, ma'am.

Detective Ames: Can you tell me your full name?

Ned: Edward Roberts Frimpong. But…everyone calls me Ned.

Detective Ames: OK, Ned. Your mother is Danielle Roberts.

Ned: Yes.

Detective Ames: Ned, where is your father and what is his name?

Ned: Gordon Frimpong. He's originally from Ghana, but he lives and works in London. In international banking. I haven't seen him since last year, but I talked to him last week. His number is in my phone if you want to call him.

Detective Ponder: Right now I just want to talk about what happened this morning. I know this is terrible, and I'm so sorry. Do you think we can do that?

Ned: Yes.

Detective Ponder: If you need to stop, you just tell me, OK?

Ned: Yeah.

Detective Ponder: Julia Pollitt met you at your house this morning to walk around playing this Critterscape phone game?

Ned: Yes. We texted last night about it. We were both trying to up a level. So Julia said she would meet me at my house at seven and we'd walk around and play for an hour.

Detective Ponder: And Julia got to your house at what time?

Ned: Around seven.

Detective Ames: Julia said in her statement you called back into your house to your mom as you were leaving.

Ned: I thought Mom was home. In her bedroom. She often wakes up and reads in bed for a bit before she gets up.

Detective Ponder: But you had not seen her that morning.

Ned: No. The automatic coffee maker had made a pot, though. So she had loaded the coffee and the water at some point last night. She…she…

Detective Ames: Are you OK, Ned?

Detective Ponder: We can take a minute.

Ned: I just don't understand why this happened. Do I have to go live with my dad now? I'll be eighteen in a few months. Can't I stay here?

Castillo: Ned, we'll talk about that later. You'll be taken care of, I promise you.

Detective Ponder: When was the last time you saw your mother?

Ned: Last night when I went upstairs to my room. She was down in the den. I told her good night. She had a look on her face like she was upset.

Detective Ponder: What about, Ned?

Ned: I don't know. She was on a phone, texting, and I noticed it wasn't her regular phone.

Detective Ponder: Do you know who she was texting with?

Ned: No.

Detective Ponder: Did she normally carry extra phones?

Ned: Yes. Well, no. I mean, she had before, just not in a while. She had a phone for her legal work and one for personal. But this one was neither. I thought maybe Mike got it for her.

Detective Ames: Mike Horvath.

Ned: He's my mom's boyfriend.

Detective Ponder: Do you know where he is? We haven't been able to reach him.

Ned: He travels a lot, but I thought he was in town this weekend. He also lives in the neighborhood. Over on Compass Circle.

Detective Ponder: Had Mr. Horvath and your mom had any problems lately?

Ned: No. I don't think so.

Detective Ames: Here's a tissue. You take your time.

(Sounds of snuffling, crying)

Ned: She hadn't said anything bad to me about Mike. I thought they were fine, but maybe she wouldn't tell me if they fought. I don't know. Why was she in the park?

Detective Ponder: We don't know yet. And once you went to bed last night, you and your mom were in the house for the rest of the night?

(Pause)

Ned: Yes.

Detective Ames: Are you sure? You seem a little hesitant.

Castillo: Please don't badger him.

Detective Ames: I'm not badgering him.

Detective Ponder: Thanks, Carmen. Let me take it.

Ned: It's OK. Yes. I was home for the rest of the night.

Detective Ponder: Did you hear anyone arrive at your house? Or leave?

Ned: No. I was there. But I had my headphones on. I was bingeing a show on my laptop. Then I turned off the lights at midnight and went to sleep. I have the ceiling fan running. The noise puts me to sleep. I didn't hear anyone come or go.

Detective Ponder: Did your mom normally go to Winding Creek Park? Like, go for walks there?

Ned: I don't think she's ever there except for the neighborhood fall party and the Fourth of July party.

　　(Sounds of sobbing)

Castillo: Let's take a short break.

　　(Resumes)

Detective Ponder: Did your mother go for walks around the neighborhood often? Like if she was upset?

Ned: No.

Detective Ponder: And you didn't hear her leave?

Ned: I said no. I didn't.

Detective Ponder: OK. What time did you wake up this morning?

Ned: Like six thirty. I work a shift at Target later today...Oh, I've got to call them.

Castillo: We'll have Mrs. Pollitt call them for you.

Ned: You get more Critters the earlier you go, in the park, and the game was offering bonus points before noon today, and so that was our plan. Play the game, go have a doughnut together at Donut Shack—it's right by Target—then I'd go to my shift. I told Mom last night that was what we were doing. Oh, I forgot. I went into the garage this morning to get my charger out of my car. Her car was there. So that's why I thought she was there, too, I guess. I for sure didn't think she'd gone for a walk.

　　(Sounds of crying)

Castillo: Can he have a minute?

　　(Break, interview resumes)

Ned: I just don't understand who could hurt my mom. She didn't have any enemies. Everyone loved Mom. No one hated her. Ask Mrs. Pollitt. They've been friends forever.

Detective Ponder: We found an inexpensive phone under the park bench. This is a photo of it. I'm showing Ned Frimpong a picture I took of this phone.

Ned: That looks like the phone she was using last night. Who was she calling?

Detective Ponder: I can't share any information about this with you right now.

Ned: Tell me! Was she calling the person who killed her?

Detective Ames: We don't know yet.

Ned: I'll find out. I'll find out who it is. She can't…She can't be dead. She's my mom. My mom can't be dead.

(End of interview)

7

KYLE

Kyle has, very quietly, destroyed the phone. He did it with a hammer, and on a towel, spread out on the master bathroom floor. Trying to make sure that Grant doesn't hear. *Dad, what are you doing? Why would you destroy your phone—wait, whose phone is that?*—all questions he cannot bear to answer right now. Kyle wraps up the shattered screen and the SIM card and the other components and dumps them all in a plastic grocery trash bag, then puts them in another bag. Then he folds up the towel and puts it back in the bathroom closet and hurries out to the garage, putting the hammer back in its little outlined spot on a board where all his tools are mounted. He wonders if he should rinse the hammer or wipe it down, if there can be traces of phone components on it the way there could be traces of blood on a weapon. He decides not and leaves the hammer in its place. He cannot imagine his kids or Iris finding him, on this dark day, washing off a hammer, doing something so odd without a real explanation.

You just have to get through today.

After a moment's hesitation, he puts the bag in the trash can. It sits next to a matching recycling bin. For a moment he wonders if it's better to hide the broken phone in the recycling. Will the police be less likely to look there? No, of course not. He is overthinking this, overthinking everything, and that is its own danger. He'll say or do something suspicious, and he can't. He mustn't.

He would like to take the phone's remains to a dumpster some-where, but businesses have cameras in parking lots or in alleys now, and he doesn't want to be captured on film getting rid of any-thing.

That is something guilty people do.

He goes back inside the house. Grant is sitting at the kitchen is-land, drinking orange juice, looking at his own phone. He glances up at his father. "Who died in the park, and why didn't you tell me? Kids are talking about it on Nowpic."

"I didn't want to upset you. It's Danielle Roberts."

He sees the shock pass along his son's face.

Grant is not a crier. Kyle always thinks it's because Grant learned as an infant at that dismal orphanage outside Saint Peters-burg that crying got him no extra attention; it was never a solution. His mouth now, though, quivers and he starts to breathe in sharp huffing pains, and Kyle hurries to him, thinking, *I'm losing my grip if I thought this was the right way to tell him*, and folds his son in an embrace.

"Did she have, like, a heart attack in the park?" Grant manages to ask.

"No, son. No. Someone killed her."

"Why?"

"I don't know. I guess the police will find out."

Under his arm, he feels Grant suddenly stiffen. His son disen-gages from the hug, wanders over to the sink. Then he throws up the gulps of orange juice he's downed. Kyle, uncertain, puts a re-assuring hand on Grant's back while Grant rinses his mouth with water and spits into the sink.

"I know this is a shock."

"I wouldn't be who I am without Danielle. I'd be someone else. Some Russian kid no one wanted. Or adopted by some other family."

It's all true, but Kyle doesn't know what to say to this. The ripples Danielle had set in motion in all their lives. "They'll find whoever did it," he repeats.

"Where is Ned? And Mike?"

"Ned is talking to the police. I don't know about Mike. I should try to call him." That's a thing an innocent person does, try to help. He gets out his phone—his usual phone—from his pocket and calls Mike's number. He stands at the window. He can see Danielle's house; there are no police cars there yet. Surely they'll be arriving to secure her home, to look for evidence. The thought chills him. *What does she have in there?*

He gets Mike's voicemail. "Mike, it's Kyle. Call me as soon as you get this." He imagines then that the police or Ned have already tried to reach Mike. "I'm so sorry." He shouldn't have said that, in case Mike's listening to his voicemails in order and the police are probably not leaving him a message that his girlfriend is dead.

Stop second-guessing. Act normal. Forge ahead.

He adds: "Call me, Mike, please." And hangs up.

"Where's Mom?"

"At the police station with your sister and Ned." Danielle's house. What's in her house that could point back to him? He goes to the large window in their living room. The house is two homes away from theirs. She moved into that house when Ned was in middle school, years after Grant had come from Russia as a squirming baby in their arms.

You have to get in before the police do. Lakehaven is a small department. They don't often deal with murder, and he guesses from the Travis County sheriff's cars that arrived to secure the park that they'll be the lead agency. And TCSO is big and capable. But he can't go inside there, not now, with the police about to arrive. Nothing would make him look worse.

You have time. You're her friend and neighbor. Make up an excuse.

He puts on his running shorts, shoes, and a pullover.

"Are you going for a run?" Grant asks, disbelieving.

"Yes. A short one." Kyle heads out the back door, along the greenbelt. His phone chimes. He glances at the screen. Mike Horvath. He steels himself. "Mike," he answers.

"What's going on?" Mike's deep voice, booming.

"Where are you?"

"I got up early this morning and went fishing on Lake Travis with Peter." Peter was Mike's son, a senior at Lakehaven. "Why are the police looking for me? I got two voicemails before yours..."

"I am so sorry. Danielle..." He can't say the words, even as he's hurrying toward her backyard.

"What? What is happening?" Mike's deep voice, lightly accented, rises in fear.

"Danielle is dead. She was found dead in Winding Creek Park this morning."

Mike makes a noise of sheer shock and pain. It's half gasp, half scream. "That can't be right."

"I'm so sorry."

"It cannot be. Where is Ned?"

"He's with the Lakehaven police. Iris is with him."

"Is Ned all right?"

"Physically he's fine. They're talking to him about who might have wanted to hurt her."

"Hurt her. Wait. Are you saying she was murdered?" Mike's accent, a weird mix of his childhood in his native Slovakia and then long years in Canada, thickens in a way Kyle has never heard before.

This was not how he wanted to tell his friend. "Yes. I am so sorry, man."

Mike Horvath takes several long, gasping breaths. "Why was she in the park? She never goes there."

"We don't know."

"I have to talk to the police."

"The station is off Old Travis. On Raymond Road."

"I'll find it." Then another long pause. "They don't think Ned hurt her, do they?"

Is that a possibility? Why would Mike think that of his girl-friend's son? Ned Frimpong likes to play video games. He watches a lot of English soccer. His grades are average, not great. He had gotten drunk last year at a party with some older kids who'd been expelled from Lakehaven High and the Lakehaven police brought him home and Danielle took his car away for a month. That was his worst offense, at least that Kyle knows about. Kids like that don't kill their mothers. Do they?

Kyle uses the cover of the dense growth of trees along the winding greenbelt to move down to Danielle's house. "No, I'm sure not," he says.

Mike, sounding now like he is crying, hangs up just as Kyle goes into Danielle's backyard. He knocks on the door; he's got a story ready in case someone is there, but no one is.

He tries the knob, using the hem of his shirt. It's unlocked. He listens for the ping or soft hum of an alarm system being activated, but there's only silence. He walks across the den; he heads into her first-floor bedroom.

If there is anything to tie them together in this house, it will be there, he thinks. He has to know. He is nearly drunk with fear at the idea of the police arriving at any second.

He hurries into her closet. Organized on a shelf are boxes—ones for hats, more for sweaters, even though the weather has turned cool by Austin standards. He searches the boxes. Nothing. There are also photo albums there, placed in plastic storage bins. He takes them out, looks through them.

Where would she keep anything that could hurt him? He puts them back on the shelf, thinking.

He pushes aside a rack of coats—she had more coats than a woman in Austin might expect to, given her travel to cold climes such as China, Russia, and the Baltic states. And behind them, hidden simply by their bulk, are a couple of jewelry boxes. He opens one. Snakes of silver bracelets intertwine. He digs through them. Maybe she hid it in a safe-deposit box. He opens the second jewelry box. Rings, here, bracelets. A string bracelet, the kind children make in school. He recognizes the weave of colors—Grant made this for Danielle in art class, for helping his parents find him in Russia. A child's THANK YOU, carefully written in red and purple crayon. His breath catches.

And beneath it, a flash drive.

This. Here.

He pockets the flash drive—then hears what sounds like the

slow crawl of tires on pavement. Her closet is near the front of the house. What if the police are arriving? He tucks the flash drive deep into his shoe, under his foot. Unlikely to be patted down there. He puts everything back where he found it. He tries to remember if the closet light was already on. He uses his shirt to wipe the light switch, the jewelry boxes. He heads out of the master bedroom and is halfway across the den when something heavy slams into the back of his head.

Kyle staggers. Strong hands grab him and put a cloth bag over his head; he can't see.

Then he feels the weight of a gun barrel pressed against his neck. He freezes.

"You're not going to give me trouble, are you?" a voice says. Low, hissing, harsh.

And then blow after blow to his head, shielded only by the cloth bag. He feels blood on his face, a hard cut on his ear, a hammering blow beneath his eye. Dazed, he feels himself draggged across the den, the gun pressed against his head, out the patio door, across the yard. The gun. This person is going to shoot him. Kill him. He climbs to his feet, but he's rushed along and then he's standing in the cool of the creek.

His brain is spinning, his ears ringing with the blows. The barrel of the gun is a burning constant against his throat. "Please!" Kyle says, crouching into the water, cringing. He feels a hand groping his pockets, the top of his socks. It finds nothing. He freezes. But the fingers don't dig into his shoe.

"Why are you here?" the voice says again, a harsh forced whisper.

"I just wanted something of hers. Something to remember her by. Please." He can feel his own blood on his face. He's never been hit like this in his life.

Four hard punches, brutal and unyielding, smash into his face. The cloth bag protects him, but not much. He falls into the creek, stunned, the bag still over his face.

"If you talk about this," the voice says, "I'll kill one of your kids."

Kyle can't speak. He can hardly make out the words due to the cinematic guttural whisper, but he nods.

Then there is only the sound of someone moving through the woods and the water against him. Everything hurts. He's too scared to take off the bag; the faces of Iris, Grant, and Julia dance in front of his closed eyes. *Whoever that is, he knows who I am. And that I have children.* Finally he does, and there's blood in the bag. Blood from his nose and mouth and ear. He can hardly breathe for fear. The cloth bag is from the Lakehaven Library. He doesn't know what to do with it. He can't leave it in the creek. It might be found.

He remembers Grant's tree, his old hiding place in the greenbelt. He goes there, stuffs it into the cleft at the roots, and decides he'll come back later. His face, his jaw, are seriously aching now.

He needs a story. An explanation. Because the truth is not an option. He's going to have bruises; his nose and lip are bleeding. The back of his head aches; he feels a bit of blood in his hair.

He decides on a plan. He scrabbles up the creekside, slips, falls, crawls back up. Mud and blood on his hands, his face. He makes his way toward home, piecing it together, hoping the story will work. The flash drive is still in his sock, maybe ruined from the creek water, maybe not.

Everything has gone horribly wrong.

Before he goes into his house, he peers in the space between his house and the neighbors', and he sees the Sheriff's Office cars pulling into Danielle's driveway to secure the house. They have no idea that they're too late.

And as Kyle reaches his own back door, bloodied and bruised, ready to embark on the latest series of lies, afraid for his children, he wonders: *Who was in Danielle's house with a gun, and why?*

8

GRANT

In his room, Grant debates where to hide the money. He can't believe his luck in Dad leaving him alone for a few minutes. He wonders how Mike and his son, Peter, are taking the news of Danielle's death. He's close to Mike, who is like a genial uncle who lets you get away with mischief. He probably shouldn't call him right now, but maybe Mom will let him call Mike later.

Grant has left the thousand dollars in the manila envelope. He knows his mother has looked under his mattress for weed and pills (he's heard parents talking about prescription drug abuse, and they had a school assembly about it); he doesn't do that stuff, but she might look there again anyway. He doesn't really hide stuff in his room. The bottom drawer in his bureau is full of swimsuits, and it's winter, so he decides Mom is not likely to paw through there anytime soon. He stuffs the envelope of cash under the stack of swimsuits and arranges them so that none of the paper shows. He closes the drawer.

How would he explain this money to anyone? He doesn't have a job. He couldn't save up that much. Will people assume he stole it? He's trying not to think of how he might spend it. New Nike shoes, video games galore, asking that pretty girl in his English class to the movies and not have it be an outing full of a half-dozen friends.

But he can't spend this money. It feels wrong. But if he doesn't spend it, Mom will eventually find it, and then what?

He goes back to the computer.

He opens the email that contained the message. He can't email his friend's spoofed email back. Drew will get it, not his mysterious benefactor.

He looks back at the picture of the young woman dancing in the rain in front of the Eiffel Tower. Then he sees it. In the corner, a Gmail address, integrated into the picture, but written very small. A random-looking series of numbers and letters, not something a person would ever accidentally type or use as a regular address.

Left there to see if he would notice?

Grant goes to Google's image search page and enters in woman in rain Eiffel Tower. They learned to use this feature in his history class.

There is a large number of matches—apparently photos of women and couples with umbrellas near the Eiffel Tower are romantic. He finds the image six rows down and clicks on it. It's a stock photo, from a company based in France. He knows that stock photos are the kind of photos companies buy to use in ads or brochures or websites. There are several similar pictures, with the same young woman standing near the tower, with a variety of colored raincoats and umbrellas. In a few of the photos a handsome man accompanies her; they laugh, they hold hands, they walk. A variety of licenses are available for the photos, in different sizes and resolutions.

Why send him this, a meaningless photo designed to be used in an ad?

Lies come down like rain, the message said.

Well, it was a picture of people in the rain. Lies like rain.

Grant writes a new message to the Gmail address: I found the money and the picture of the Eiffel Tower. Who are you? What do you want with me?

And then he presses send.

9

FROM IRIS POLLITT'S "FROM RUSSIA WITH LOVE" ADOPTION JOURNAL

2002

So the consultant/lawyer I talked with about foreign adoption, Danielle Roberts, suggested that I keep a journal to chronicle our process in adopting a baby from overseas. It can be a long, hard road (look! My first cliché!), and journaling, she said, could help me through the ups and downs. "A writer like you probably already keeps a journal, don't you? To write down images and phrases, right?" she said, and I nodded. And she said, rightly, that our new child might really like to read this one day, to understand what Kyle and I went through to get her or him, and that Julia would value it as well—she may not remember any of this when she's older. And that we would want to remember every detail.

I got into doing a journal when Julia was so sick, and hopefully this will be a help along the same lines. Sometimes it's calming just to get the thoughts down on paper.

So, pen in hand, I start. This will be harder than writing a song.

How did we decide on adoption? Four miscarriages, then Julia, and then the doctors told me no more pregnancies. Not meant to be. We love Julia, of course. But we wanted another child.

Kyle said we should adopt an American child. And for a week, we discussed that. We didn't want to adopt a child older than Julia. With a newborn the birth parents have ninety days to change their minds and take the child back—and away, forever—from you. After having dealt with Julia's illness, I couldn't risk it: a mother with regrets changing her mind or a father asserting his rights. Although that seems so unlikely in these situations, you never know. I wanted distance between us and the birth parents. Distance to give safety, distance to give perspective. Thousands and thousands of miles.

Distance meant certainty.

When we first moved to Lakehaven, I got to know some women who had adopted internationally. I listened to what they had to say, the pros and cons, and a mom (her name is Francie) who had three adopted kids from Russia, a girl and two boys, swayed me. They were really cute, happy, well-adjusted kids. Francie said it was a lot of paperwork and a lot of bribes(!), but otherwise the process would go smoothly and there was no chance of a birth-parent interference. And I'm Swedish on my mom's side, and Kyle's grandmother's family are descended from Czech settlers who came to Texas, and we thought, right or wrong, a Russian child might look more like a blood relative. I know that shouldn't matter, but it did, to me.

So, Francie, with the three adorable Russian kids, contacted the service she used to manage the process—they're called Global Adoption Consultants—and that is how I met Danielle Roberts, your guardian angel (or she will be). I was lucky. They were based in Austin, the only agency here.

Danielle and I met for coffee for the first time to talk. She was striking, dark haired, in a business suit, elegant. Nice watch, nice rings. I notice stuff like that—I think it matters how a person presents themselves. (Warning: you will be a well-dressed baby.)

I bought us both vanilla lattes, and we caught up on my friend Francie and her three gorgeous children. Francie had sent Danielle an email about me, and of course Danielle asked me about writing songs for NSYNC and Britney Spears, and she did that thing people do where they sing the lyric at you, and I smile and nod and say "yeah, I wrote that," and thankfully she didn't ask if I was still writing songs and I was suddenly nervous the Russians would charge me more because a couple of songs I'd written had been hits. The musician gets richer than the writer—that's the way of the world.

And then I said brightly, optimistically: "So, I have a thousand questions."

"Don't ever ask a question," Danielle said. Her face was serious, almost grim. The friendly smile had vanished.

"What do you mean?" I asked. "I can't ask you questions?" Panic blossomed in my chest. This wasn't going to work.

"You can ask ME anything. Always." She leaned forward, like she was telling me a secret. "But when you set foot in Russia once we've been matched with your baby, you do not ask any questions. You do not challenge the Russians. You do not argue with them. You tell your husband not to explain things to them. You keep your mouths shut, you hand everyone you meet a little money or a gift, and you come home with your baby."

I was silent. And then I nodded.

"Not every family is suited for this ordeal," Danielle said.

"I keep calling it a process."

"That's sweet but inaccurate. It's an ordeal. It will test you and Kyle"—I was impressed she remembered his name, since he wasn't there; we'd decided I would screen the consultants first since he was traveling so much—"in ways you can't imagine. I understand you're already blessed with a daughter. That will be held against you, eventually. They'll argue an infant should go to a family without children. Or they'll realize you are"—WERE, I thought, WERE—"a successful songwriter and the bribes will rise. Someone will try to be an obstacle to you, and when that happens, you must do as I say. If you can't follow my instructions, then I will be wasting your money. And you'll get your heart broken. And I don't want to do that. If you want this baby, truly want this baby, then you'll do as I say. Do you really want this child?"

Well...did I? I hadn't expected this question. I closed my eyes for a moment and took a deep breath. I loved Julia more than I had ever thought possible. When your child is sick, really sick, it either focuses you or breaks you. With me, it gave focus. But at the same time, it expanded my capacity for love, just as Julia's birth had. Growing up, it was just me and my mom. I was loved. I thought I knew what love was when I met and fell for Kyle. And then again, even more so, when Julia was born. I didn't know I had so much love in me; it just had to be unlocked. Kyle and I had so much more to give. The answer was clear. I was almost shaking, and I steadied my voice.

"Never ask me," I said, "how much I will love this baby."

10

IRIS

It's been a long day. The second longest day of her life.

When she and Julia get home from the police, they find Kyle a complete mess: face bruised, blackened eye, cuts on his temple and ear, nose swollen, lip cut. He's cleaned himself up, but he looks like he went two rounds in a boxing ring and lost.

"I fell down the slope. I did a faceplant all the way down into the creek," he says. "I was running."

"You went for a run?" Iris can't keep her voice from rising in anger. "I asked you to stay here with Grant…"

"Grant was fine," he says. "We all deal with this in different ways, all right, Iris? All right? I feel bad enough as it is."

Julia stares at him. "Dad…" And he encloses her in a hug, being Dad, being there for her now.

"Where is Ned?" he asks.

"He's at Mike's house."

Julia makes a face. "I know why he's there. I just hope Peter's not being a jerk to him." Peter is Mike's son, a moody, quiet senior who prefers the company of computers to people.

"I'm sure Peter's being good to him," Iris says.

The four of them seem lost today, sitting in the den, looking at each other. "Are you sure you don't need to see a doctor?" Iris says, pointing at Kyle's face.

"Please let's not make a production of this," Kyle says. "We have enough to deal with today."

So they retreat from one another. Julia doesn't want to talk about it—at least with them—and she cuddles up on the couch with her mom. Iris puts on Julia's favorite comfort movie, *The Wizard of Oz* (the high school did it for their musical last year, and Julia was an Emerald City resident), and they watch it together. Grant goes up to his room; Iris thinks he's preoccupied. Or he's having trouble processing this shock. She feels like Julia, having suffered the more direct trauma, needs her more right now. Kyle tries to get Grant to join him in the media room, to watch ESPN, but the boy's curled up on his bed and politely declines.

The phone rings. A lot. Friends and neighbors calling, eager for information, some wanting gossip, others wanting to give comfort. The day bleeds away. Kyle looks in the mirror often, and Iris watches him.

She's not sure she believes his story. But why would anyone punch her husband in the face?

Kyle doesn't meet her gaze. He naps while they finish the movie. Julia tries texting Ned as the credits roll and gets a half-hearted answer, but now Julia's full attention is on the phone, on Ned's few words. Iris goes to the front window and watches the police officers go in and out of Danielle's house.

Kyle has offered to cook dinner, which Iris both appreciates and resents. She could have used the meditative quiet of making something simple, and she wants to be the one to comfort her hurting family. She watches Kyle putter with pots and pans and jars: he's making spaghetti with a meat sauce, salad, and garlic toast. He glances at her and takes out a wineglass, pouring her some of the Chianti he's opened. It feels wrong to enjoy wine with Danielle dead, but they both could use a drink.

"Thanks," Iris says. She takes the wine and walks to the window. Mike and Ned are now at Danielle's with the police. She'd offered Ned a place to stay, with them, but she feels she said it the wrong way. As though he heard in her tone that she didn't want him to say yes. Ned thanked her but said he would stay at Mike's house. So she texted another volunteer-minded mom in the neighborhood, who set up a meal schedule online and linked it to the

Winding Creek Faceplace page. Already it's full, people wanting to help. Ned and Mike are set for dinner tonight; the Harpers are bringing them chicken casserole. She hopes they will eat. She will take them dinner tomorrow night. She wonders if she can hover then for a moment, find out what the police have said and are saying to Mike and Ned, learn something.

Julia has folded in on herself. She's up in her room, on her phone. Texting, but not Ned, not for the moment. Her daughter has achieved a weird kind of celebrity in the past few hours. Julia says that Ned's friends have rallied around him, although they're mostly boys who don't seem to know what to do other than tell him how sorry they are and ask what they can do for him. But Ned told them Julia was with him, and now Julia tells her that kids she doesn't even know well are texting her for details.

"Julia!" she calls up the stairs. Julia, after a few moments, appears.

"Will you bring me your phone?"

"Why?"

Because I asked. Because I'm your mother. But instead she says, "I want a log of everyone who is contacting you about this. It could be of interest to the police." But she really just wants to know what's on her daughter's mind.

"Why would the police care?"

"Because they might. I saw that on a *Law & Order* episode."

"That's made-up stuff."

Iris holds her hand out for the phone, end of discussion. "I'm not going to read your messages."

"Yeah, right. I haven't answered anyone except to say I can't talk about it. I'm not an idiot, Mom."

"I know you're not."

Julia comes down the stairs and, with a sigh, hands her mother the phone. It has been a horrifying day, but this moment of normal teen resentment feels like a reassurance that Julia, despite the trauma, is going to be all right. Won't she? Won't she get over what she saw?

Iris takes the phone, and Julia sees her mother's hand trembling. "Mom."

"I'm all right. I'm just worried about you."

Julia hugs her. "I'm fine."

"No, you saw a horrible thing you'll never unsee, and I wish I could change that."

"Mom…"

"I mean, if you feel you need to talk to someone, someone not me or Dad, a therapist…"

"Mom."

"I just want you to be OK."

Julia doesn't say anything to this. She folds her arms and goes past her, into the kitchen, to Kyle. Iris walks away, scans through the messages. Julia isn't hyping up what she saw or playing the victim or milking this for attention: nearly every response is crisp, curt, mature. *I can't talk about this, so please don't ask me. Please pray for Ned. We need to be there for Ned.*

She frowns at a few of the messages from Julia's friends. Sorry we teased you about liking Ned. I wasn't trying to be gross by asking about his mom and what happened. Please text me back and let me know you're okay.

Iris walks to the kitchen, stands at the corner of the open space. She watches Kyle fold his arms around Julia, Julia lean into his shoulder. They've always been close. Iris feels a pang in her chest, her stomach.

"I just want you to be OK," Iris repeats.

"I know that is what you care about."

"What does that mean?"

"Me being OK. So I can do well on my tests and in my classes and get into a good college and have a bright future. You don't want that derailed."

"That's not what I meant, sweetheart. You've had a trauma."

"I'm worried about Ned right now, Mom. Not myself."

A long, silent pause between them. *You sure are focused on Ned these days*, Iris thinks. She's not sure how she feels about that. She likes Ned. She knows what she should do is not care, not fight it, so Julia won't dig in her heels. Let the infatuation run its course. It might even end the friendship, and she'd be fine with that.

"That's so good of you," Iris says. "To worry about him so."

Then Iris hugs her daughter and Julia hugs her back.

"Of course," Iris says. "Let's just take a break from the phone. For an hour. Just an hour." *Where is this in the parenting books or blogs? Helpful checklist when your child discovers a murdered body.* Julia steps away and starts to help her father prepare dinner. Iris retreats as Kyle glances back at her with a look she knows: *Really? Now?* He returns to the stove, murmuring to Julia. Iris sips the wine, goes back to the window.

Somewhere in the Travis County Morgue, Danielle lies in a metal drawer, awaiting autopsy. Cold. Gone. Over. But when they were leaving the station, Iris heard Carmen Ames taking a call, jotting a note, quietly saying, "Crushed windpipe? Crushed with what?" then listening. Ames had her back to them and Julia didn't seem to register it, but Iris did.

That might explain the discoloration in the throat, the blood on the lips. She hopes it was quick and Danielle didn't suffer, but she probably did. A shattering blow to the throat, fighting to breathe and unable to, then the darkness. A strangulation without the hands closing around the throat. Iris shudders. Takes another sip of wine.

Did she see any potential weapon on the ground? She didn't. Something heavy or blunt but narrow enough to strike the throat. Rock, pipe, wrench, bat? Or was the fatal blow delivered by a fist?

A blow. And her husband looking like a punching bag in the time between the body being found and Iris getting home from the police station.

Kyle is lying to her. Lying to them all.

Of course he's not lying. He fell. He fell, just like he said.

Their home phone rings again, as it has done all day, and she lets it. They all let it. The phone machine announces the caller—a friend, another mom who is on school committees with Iris—and then the inevitable message begins: calling because she just heard, it's so terrible, did Julia really find the body, what can she do for Iris's family, for Ned, bring dinner maybe, just let her know, please call back when she has a minute. Listen, rinse, repeat. She stopped writing down who had called her at message number fifteen, three hours ago.

Grant comes downstairs. He looks haggard, tired. He was close to Danielle; she adored him, the baby they'd brought back together from Russia. She's been so worried about Julia, she hasn't worried about Grant.

"You hungry, baby? We'll eat soon," she says to him. He's always hungry; he's a fourteen-year-old boy.

"Not particularly. Can I go see Mike? I want to be sure he's all right. I mean…not all right—he can't be—but…" They're all stumbling for the correct words.

"Mike might not be up for company right now," Iris says. "I'm taking them dinner tomorrow night; do you want to come with me?"

Grant nods. Then he sits down on the couch, across from the window. From the kitchen they can hear the soft murmurs of Julia and Kyle talking.

"Mom?"

"Yes?"

"Who do you think killed her? I think we should talk about theories."

A cold finger of fear flicks her spine. *Theories.* She curses every network and streaming crime drama she's ever let him watch. Of course, Grant is the type to think about who did it rather than deal with the emotional fallout of a murder. "I have no idea." She makes her voice clipped.

"You must have an idea."

"Grant."

"The police will think it's Mike. They always suspect the boyfriend. But why would he kill her in the park?"

She starts to say *I don't know* but then she stops herself. He's not a dumb kid. "Well, I guess there are a few reasons. She might have been there to meet someone. Someone she didn't want in her house. She might have been forcibly taken there. Or maybe she was killed at home and the killer put her on the park bench."

"He didn't try to conceal her. He wanted her found."

She gulps at her wine. "I guess."

Grant has a look on his face like he'd like to kill the killer himself. "The killer had to be comfortable with killing her in the open. Someone could have seen. Even super early on a Sunday morning."

"Maybe. Maybe they were both in the park and he didn't intend to kill her."

"He."

"I think it's probably a man. But, hon, this could have been a random thing. Maybe she saw someone breaking the law in the park. Maybe a guy tried to kidnap her, to assault her, and she fought back."

Grant frowns. "If I were looking for a victim, I'd go to a park in Austin, where there's foot traffic at night, not way out here where the park's normally empty."

"I can't guess what might be in the mind of someone like this."

"But we have to," Kyle says. "I mean, what if this is a stranger and he comes back?" He's walked in with his own glass of wine, takes a long sip. Iris sees him wince at the alcohol on his swollen lip.

"You don't need to scare the children," Iris says, tight-lipped.

Grant stands. He has the look on his face Iris recognizes, when he wants to say something but can't decide whether or not to say it. He opens his mouth, then shuts it. "People are texting me," he said. "About what happened. I haven't answered. Not a one."

"That's probably wise," Kyle says.

"I can't ignore my friends forever."

"Just tell them you can't discuss it," Iris suggests.

"That works so well with teenagers," Julia calls from the kitchen. "Tell them that the police say you can't talk."

"Is that to make him look cooler?" Iris asks.

"We don't care about that right now, Mom. If he invokes the police, people back off. We need one message as a family." Julia comes into the living room, sounding like a public relations executive instead of a teenage student.

They all look at her in surprise. Iris thinks she should have scrolled through more of the messages to learn how Julia deflects people.

Iris catches Kyle gazing out the window, so she does as well, and then so do their children. The family stands there, in front of their living room window, all four of them, staring out at the police cars parked at their dead neighbor's home, watching the officers and investigator teams moving in and out of the house, forcing it to give up its secrets.

Julia breaks the silence. "We have to be there for Ned. Like we're his family."

"You're right," Iris says. "Of course."

"Ned has to be our priority. Helping him." Julia's voice grows stronger, and Kyle and Iris exchange a glance.

"And Mike," Grant says.

"Yeah, whatever, once his alibi clears," Julia says. "I know you think he's awesome, Grant, but he has to be the prime suspect. The boyfriend or husband always is."

Iris glances at Kyle. *Would anyone ever believe you could kill me? Yes, I think they would. We never know what someone is capable of. We kid ourselves that we do, because it makes life easier.*

11

IRIS AND KYLE

They're getting ready for bed. Iris brushing her teeth, Kyle stepping out of his jeans and sweatshirt, pulling on a T-shirt. He collapses into the bed. He feels both exhausted and wired, which is terrible; it might be a sleepless night. His whole body hurts: his face, the scrapes on his legs from being dragged down to the creek. He could drink more wine; he could take a pill to calm himself. But he doesn't. He doesn't deserve quiet. He stares at the ceiling.

He has had time to think, to calm down, to grow angry again. Someone beat him up. Someone threatened his children if he talked. But that same someone could have killed him and didn't. That same someone could have knocked him out and left him for the police to find in Danielle's house as they arrived. But hadn't.

Someone else was in her house at great risk. Why? If that man was Danielle's murderer, then he hadn't wanted to commit a second murder so quickly.

Looking for something, the same as Kyle was?

The flash drive he's found at Danielle's is hidden in another shoe. He doesn't dare put it in a computer here.

"Is something going on between Julia and Ned?" he asks. He needs a break from his own thoughts, and he senses this is a ripe topic.

Iris spits, rinses. "Other than being friends? I'm not sure. I asked Grant. He shrugged."

"He wouldn't know."

"He would," Iris says.

"Why? They're not close."

"That's a terrible thing to say about your kids." She climbs into bed, holding her laptop. He looks at it like it's the enemy. She ignores this look and opens it. "Julia and Grant fuss at each other, but they're siblings. Don't be silly."

"They're going through a phase, then, of not getting along," he says, refusing to cede ground. "What are you doing?"

"I'm reading the latest news account." She's silent for a minute, studying the screen. "No arrests, no suspects. They released her name."

They are both silent then. Thinking of Danielle.

"Everyone on the neighborhood Faceplace page is freaking out," she said.

"Murder does that," Kyle said.

"Some dads and moms are talking of forming a neighborhood patrol where they are just going to walk around at night like they're a security team. People are posting that they've spotted strangers in the greenbelt. A group wants to put up cameras everywhere. Another group wants to turn us into a gated community, and the Carter girl said someone tried to open their back door early this morning."

"They'll find who did it," he says quietly. Then he adds, not looking at her: "Why do you think Danielle was in the park at that hour?"

"Went for a walk, maybe."

"That early? Because she'd been dead for a while, right?"

"How do you know that?"

"I don't. I'm just guessing. You said her wrist was cold."

Iris doesn't answer.

"I mean, it's not like it's Zilker Park or Pease Park," he said, referring to two large public parks in Austin. "This is in our quiet little neighborhood."

"I think," Iris said, "she went for a walk, and there was someone there doing something they shouldn't be, maybe kids from another neighborhood—you know they've had problems with that—or someone who came into the park from the greenbelt, and maybe Danielle confronted them or she saw them smoking dope and they killed her."

"For smoking dope," he says in a flat voice.

"Well, I don't know, doing something worse, then." She isn't looking at him. "No one could have wanted her dead." But now she glances back at him as she sits on the edge of the bed.

"It's weird," he says, "when someone does something unexplained. Like going for a walk in the park at five o'clock in the morning, or whenever she did."

"You were very late coming to bed last night." There. She says it. Now their gazes meet.

"Is that a problem?" he asks. "I told you why when you woke up as I got into bed. I was working. I couldn't sleep."

"Did you see her walk by your office window?" His upstairs study faces out onto the street; if Danielle walked to the park, he might have spotted her. She might have looked at his study window, being the one light on in any of the houses along the road. She could imagine Danielle walking, head down, intent. She had been an intense woman. Walking toward her doom.

"No," he says, but he waits ten seconds to say it. "If I had, I would have told the police."

"I wonder if anyone's security camera picked her up walking by their house," Iris says. "Or anyone else walking to the park."

He doesn't answer that. "The police won't tell us that. And she could have walked up there via the greenbelt."

"Is there anything you want to tell me?" Iris asks, very softly. She touches his bruised face. "It's OK. You can tell me anything. You know that."

He stares at her for so long she thinks the worst. Then he says, "No, there is not. Is there anything you want to tell me?"

"No." She slides under the sheets, closes the laptop. She kisses her husband's forehead, touches his swollen lip with her finger, and then returns to her own pillow. She closes her eyes and he closes his.

She listens to the silence in the darkness and her own breathing and presses a fist against her mouth as she watches the shape of her husband in the bed, wondering what he's thinking.

Wondering what he's done.

12

GRANT

Midnight.

Grant has set his email on his laptop and phone to ping if something arrives. When he hears the soft noise he's half-asleep, but he sits up in the darkness.

It's from the obscurely named Gmail account. From the Sender—this is how he thinks of this person now, with a name tied to activity.

He opens it.

There's another picture this time, but included in the email, not a link to another website. A small house bundled in snow. The house is wooden, painted a soft green that seems almost hopeful for spring against the white of winter. He doesn't know this house. There's a cat sitting in the window—a small black cat—and he doesn't know the cat, either.

There's a message from the Sender below the picture.

Lies can surround a home and bury it in coldness. Be the cat, looking out the window. And look again in your tree.

A reference to lies again. Lies in rain, lies in snow. What does this mean? He searches Google Images again ("green house in snow"), but he doesn't see the exact same picture in the results. Maybe this isn't a stock photo.

He writes back: I don't want any more emails from you.

The response is nearly instant: It's hard to hear the truth for the first time in your life.

Grant stares at the words. Who is telling me lies?

Your family. They've lied to you for so long. Especially today. The money shows I'm serious. This isn't a prank. This is your life.

Grant writes: Stop emailing me.

The Sender's answer: if I stop talking to you then I might have to start talking to the police about what your daddy did. The bad, bad thing he did.

Grant freezes. You're a liar, he writes. But he doesn't press send. What if he makes the Sender mad? What if...?

Then he hears the soft click of the back door, which is directly under his room. He looks out the window and sees his sister heading out into the darkened greenbelt.

13

FROM IRIS POLLITT'S "FROM RUSSIA WITH LOVE" ADOPTION JOURNAL

2002

My earlier entries have outlined all the paperwork we did—financial reports and assessments, the six home studies performed by a consultant, with results sent to Russia, the endless background checks. I was supposed to list every house I'd lived in, when my mom and I moved around a lot—yet I found them all, although my mother thought adopting from a foreign country was vaguely unpatriotic. (You'll read this one day, baby, and I want you to know your gammy loves you; it's just how she was.) I listed them on the form, the original, which I kept in pristine condition, working my notes up on printed copies because I lived in mortal terror I'd make a mistake on the submitted form—and that means I'd never get to meet you or be your mom. Our family's finances were exhaustively chronicled—I even had to list the small trust set up for Julia by Kyle's parents when she was born. I'm surprised they didn't ask how much loose change was in Kyle's pockets or between the sofa cushions.

Everything notarized, everything "apostilled" (my new word, which rules my life—apostilles authenticate the seals and signatures on birth certificates, court orders, or any other document issued by a public authority so that they can be recognized in foreign countries). The Russians, and Danielle, insist on all this. The stakes are high: if we take one misstep in authentication, we could lose our chance to have you...wherever you are.

Everything proper and done right.

I have a binder of notes, of forms, of checklists. It is like having a second job. You'll appreciate this when it's time for school reports. (Ask me for help, not Dad.)

SO I'd finished going through today's paperwork TO BE YOUR MOM when Danielle's unexpectedly at our front door, telling me THEY'VE FOUND YOU for us. (My penmanship is a little shaky right now. I just realized they don't teach cursive anymore. Will you be able to read this? Oh, the thoughts I have on a day like today.)

But they don't say "We found your child." They say "We have sent you a referral." This is what I know about you:

You are a boy, Alexander Borisovich Stepurin. Danielle had warned us to not specifically ask for a certain gender, and we truly didn't care, but I am secretly a little pleased. I always wanted a girl AND a boy, but I never said it aloud. This is a good omen.

You are nine months old.

You live at the Volkov Infants Home near Saint Petersburg.

The Russians have sent us a medical record of you. (Danielle has already told us this might not be legit. Sometimes they haven't disclosed to prospective parents long-standing medical issues, or illness, or surgeries you may have had, yet of course everything we send them has to be both perfect and verifiable—don't get me started.) We have your Apgar score, your measurements at birth, your test results for HIV, hepatitis B and C, syphilis—all negative. According to Russian medical specialists, you have "no pathology" with your eyes, your ears, nose, or throat. You have had your vaccines. The ultrasound of your brain is normal. But there are a whole range of specialists who have never examined you: cardiologist, for example. Or oncologist. I think of Julia and her neuroblastoma, and that to go through that again would be so hard. The section marked "relationship with other children" is blank, and I panic for a moment, until I think it's because of your age, not for a worrying reason that you can't get along with others.

And a video of you on DVD. We don't get to keep this. It has to be returned. That bugs me—is this a test of our trustworthiness?

Would the Russians know if this video was copied to a computer? I think about it, but I don't want to risk it.

And a photograph.

And on the back of the photograph is written, in carefully block-printed English: ALEXANDER BUT WE CALL HIM SASHA.

The clock is ticking.

We have seventy-two hours to say we want you, Sasha.

I studied the photograph of you as Danielle drove us to the children's hospital in Austin. A doctor she knows will review the video of you to try to identify any concerns or problems or issues that could affect our decision.

Danielle said to me: "Normally, the doctor would review it without you there, but Dr. Gupta said he could look at it with you and Kyle since you might have questions. As a favor."

I stared at your picture. You were not a fat baby, but that might not be unusual in a Saint Petersburg orphanage. Your eyes were open wide, and you seemed vaguely startled by the camera. I hoped the flash didn't make you cry. Wispy blond hair crowned your head. You looked good. A little serious. I wished you were smiling in the picture... You think they would have sent me one with you smiling. You looked handsome.

You looked like you should be my child. And Kyle's.

Danielle asked, as she drove, "Iris? Are you all right?"

"Yes," I answered. "I think he's the one."

"Iris, deep breath. You'll want to watch his video and see what Dr. Gupta says. If there are signs of problems, we want to know now. Don't be swept away by emotion."

"It shouldn't matter. He doesn't have to be perfect."

"I know. It doesn't matter, as long as you know what you're signing up for. Do you hear me?" Danielle wasn't being my friend right now. She was being the adoption consultant whom we pay to be blunt and direct and to leash in our emotions so this process/ordeal goes like clockwork.

"All right," I said. "It's just a picture. I wish he were smiling."

"These babies don't always have a lot to smile about," she told me, and her words were like a curtain falling.

I didn't want to think about whether anyone at the orphanage has ever cradled you when you were sick or comforted you when you were sad. I knew they must; don't they? But you are one of dozens of infants under their care. Maybe hundreds. The thought crushed me. You needed someone to love you. You needed me. And I knew Danielle was right, but for a moment I just wanted her to shut her logic-spewing mouth. Keep her true words to herself. Just let me wish you will be mine. Sasha. Alexander was a fine and noble name, but I had a name picked out for you, one I haven't stuck on you yet. One I dared not say aloud, so I didn't break the spell.

(Do you see how nuts your mom was? One minute I was a process-oriented paperwork machine, and the next minute I was riding unicorns and thinking if I say the name I want to give you aloud, it would work some kind of magic.)

Danielle was quiet the rest of the drive.

Kyle was already at the children's hospital when we arrived, pacing in the lobby like a nervous father awaiting delivery. We didn't bring Julia with us—she was too young and she was with Kyle's mom, Margaret, your nana. We embraced, and I showed him the photo. We studied it together, each holding a side of it, while Danielle summoned the elevator.

"Oh," Kyle said. "He's a handsome boy." His hand squeezed on mine.

Dr. Gupta was around our age, a college friend of Danielle's whom Global Adoption Consultants had a contract with to evaluate these infant videos. He smiled, was pleasant but not too friendly. Even a bit cool. And I realized why: he may have to tell us there's something wrong with this baby we want.

Danielle, in case we were entirely mentally scrambled, reminded us how this would work. Dr. Gupta and we would watch the video together. Then he'd watch it alone. If he saw a problem where he wanted another doctor to consult, he'd call the doctor or set up a time for the other physician to watch the video.

We sat and watched the video on his computer screen.

It started with Sasha—I don't know what else to call you; how can I give you a different name when I don't know if you will be ours?—in his crib. On his back. He was skinny. He was not marked or bruised. Adult hands reached toward him, gently extended his arms, his legs. A finger tickled his ribs, and he gurgled then—a smile, finally. I felt the bolt through my heart.

Now he was lying on a blanket on the floor of another room. Sasha turned over onto his stomach. Held up his head. I glanced at Dr. Gupta, silently studying. No sign of emotion. Not taking notes.

Fingers snapped near ears; Sasha turned. A light was gently shined into his eyes; Sasha blinked.

Now Sasha sat up. He crawled toward some toys, but a bit uncertain. I got the feeling he'd never been in this room before, never seen these toys. Did he know he was performing? Auditioning for a new life with a loving family on the other side of the planet? Put on a stage by someone who didn't want him for someone who did, who could feel the ache of wanting him in her arms? He crawled. He stood unassisted. He looked up with lovely blue eyes at whoever filmed him, and I pretended he was looking at me and Kyle.

And then the video was over. I hoped it would be much longer. Hours of Sasha, and sequels. But no. Danielle had warned me it would be brief.

"This is like shopping," I said, very quietly, and I felt a tug of shame.

"No," Kyle said. "No, honey, it's not. We're not looking at two, or five, or ten babies. We're just looking at HIM. Doctor?"

"I don't see any developmental or physical issues, based on the film," Dr. Gupta said. He probably says "based on the film" after every sentence. "I'd like to watch it again."

All these qualifiers felt wrenching. I wished Julia were here. She has been a little ambivalent about a baby coming to live with us; I'm not sure she understands. I'll show her the picture and the video later, but how will I explain if we don't get you? "Sorry, your little brother was canceled. We're hoping for a second try."

We went and got a coffee while Dr. Gupta reviewed the video again and read through the medical file. He joined us in the cafeteria and gave me back the DVD. He showed us the report from the Russians.

"So much depends on the language they use, the nuance, if they're trying to hide or mask a condition," he said. "But he looks like he is hitting his milestones for development at his age. His gross and fine motor skills, his eye contact, all are good."

I read through the medical report as well. No serious illnesses, no disability diagnosed. Doesn't mean it's not there, just not diagnosed. But doesn't he look fine? And act fine?

Dr. Gupta told us he would write the medical report that afternoon, and he thought this was a healthy child (hurray). Despite his reassurances, I felt my anxiety rise.

"You're a songwriter, yes?" he asked me as he stood. "'Shaking Up My Soul' and 'Sudden' were two of yours?"

I saw Danielle blush slightly.

"Yes," I said.

"Ah. My daughter is interested in songwriting. She's in a band. They've gotten a few gigs around town."

I nodded. Austin: where everyone is in a band or knows someone in a band. A favor, for a favor. "Well, I'd be happy to talk to her."

"Oh, that would be great. I can get your email address from Danielle."

I just nodded, and Dr. Gupta walked off.

"Sorry," Danielle said. "I thought you wouldn't mind, and that way he let us watch the video with him. You won't have a sleepless night wondering what his opinion will be."

I glanced back at the Russian report. Under a section for known history before being at the orphanage, it reads: mother admitted to hospital, gave birth, left him at hospital; mother was young and healthy, this was her second pregnancy, and she had given birth once before.

Sasha would have a blood sibling. I wonder, Why give Sasha up? Did she give up her first baby, too? Where was the father? Was he involved in the decision, or did she make this wrenching choice all alone? Did this father care? Or was he entirely out of the picture? Did they love each other? Did it matter? No, it didn't.

Never ask me. That applied to this young woman, too. She'd made her choice.

"If we accept Sasha," Kyle said quietly, "we just send an email, right?"

"And a signed form. A scanned version and then the paper version. I'll handle that," Danielle said.

"And then we go to Russia to see him?" I asked.

"The government has to accept your acceptance," Danielle said, and I didn't have to look at Kyle to see his eye roll as we continued down the endless path of paperwork. "Then they will send us an invitation date to go to Russia and meet Sasha."

Kyle took my hand. I gripped it like we were drowning. "Kyle?"

"We have seventy-two hours," he said. "Let's use them."

"What if they don't get the email in time?" I said, thinking of every possibility that can go wrong. Like an email could take seventy-two hours.

"Iris, it will be fine," Danielle said. "Go home. Think about it. If Sasha isn't a match for you, that's OK. Wait and make the right decision."

That night, Kyle and I were in bed. Julia had fussed and cried all afternoon and she wore me out. This moment would change our lives. We knew it. We would always remember it.

"I'm going to say something, and don't be mad," Kyle said.

Why does he ensure I'll be mad by saying that? But I do what's expected and say, "All right."

"We might pass on him."

"Why?" The word burst out of me.

Kyle paused. "He doesn't have much energy. Compared to an American child."

"Well…" I didn't know what to say to this. This criticism is so Kyle, who is in constant motion. We've been on the same team since we decided to adopt, and now that the moment of decision is here, he's backing out? I want to punch him.

"What the hell do you mean, energy? That can-do American spirit? That rugged individualism? He's nine months old!"

"I'm just saying he's not going to be like Julia. She's had every advantage. Food, love, attention…This boy has not had that foundation."

"Uh, yes, we know," I want to say. We knew this going in. But now he's seen a child that could become ours. Now he's scared.

"She also had cancer," I said. "And we got her through that. We can do this for him. We give Sasha a foundation. We love him and take care of him and we do our best and that's all we can do for any baby, born here or not."

Kyle was silent. Thinking.

I pressed ahead: "What, so we shouldn't adopt him? Thousands of kids get adopted from overseas and don't have the same head start American kids have." I hated this conversation. In that moment, I hated Kyle. Why was he doing this? Was he just humoring me through the hours of paperwork and fretting?

"That's true," he said in his totally reasonable voice. "I'm just playing devil's advocate, babe. So we make an informed decision."

Which to him meant logic and to me meant looking at that video and seeing a child who could be mine. "Kyle, if you don't want to do this, the time for that was weeks ago. Months. Before I got invested. Maybe you can turn your emotions off like a light switch, but I cannot."

He looked stunned. "Babe, that's not what I'm saying."

"What if Sasha is perfect? And we say no? We reject this boy, why would they even consider us for another one?" I could hear my voice rising and I forced myself toward quiet, so I wouldn't wake up Julia.

"Honey…"

I got up, got my lyrics notebook, and stomped out to the den. Kyle knew better than to follow me right then. I needed to be alone. I uncapped the black Flair pen and stared at the blank page. I had not opened my lyrics notebook in months. MONTHS.

I wrote:

Sasha

The first time I saw you, you were a million miles away

I heard the vaguest beat in the back of my head, a melody trying to come free. I wanted every word to be a punch.

A child I've never held but a child I already love

I scratched out that line. I was breaking one of my songwriting rules, in that I never scratched out lyrics while drafting. You could still use or reinvent an awkward line.

So why did I scratch out an admission of love?

Do I love this boy, or do I just want to win the process?

It sounded like a question a Russian would ask me in an adoption hearing. Never ask me, I told Danielle, how much I would love this baby.

I cried. I hate crying. I looked a mess. No one was here to see me. I watched his far-too-short video again. And again. And again.

I fell asleep. At some lost point in the long night, I felt strong arms lift me and carry me back to the cool of the bedsheets. I rolled into Kyle's chest, and my arm went around him. I felt his kiss on my forehead. I didn't want to talk to him, and I fell back asleep.

The next morning I overslept. I heard my quitter husband in the kitchen; I glanced at the clock, thought: he's going to be late for work. I stumbled to the breakfast nook, intent on silence and coffee, and there, on my place mat, was the acceptance form, with Kyle's signature.

He looked at me, full of apology and hope, and I cried again. I embraced him. I made sure I wasn't dripping tears or snot when I picked up the pen to sign, and he called Danielle to tell her.

"What do you think of naming him Grant?" I asked. "If we get him." I'm afraid to jinx it by assuming all will go well. Grant was my maiden name. I didn't have a lot of family names to draw on. My father walked away when I was young, and it was just me and my mom. As a lyricist, I didn't necessarily love that both Grant and Pollitt end with a t sound, but it is what it is, and I thought: a family name matters for this child. We named Julia for Kyle's much-loved grandmother. It would be a first step to knit him into our family.

Kyle smiled and nodded. "That's a great idea, babe. Grant. What about a middle name?"

"You pick," I said, not really meaning it, believing that he'd pass and defer to me.

Kyle gave me his thinking frown. "You might not like this. But we could keep his Russian name as a middle name. Alexander. One syllable, four syllables, two syllables." That was all for my benefit, as a songwriter who chooses words for variety and length. "Grant Alexander Pollitt."

He said it grandly.

A rush of joy passed through me. I thought it a very fine name, and I cried again like the mess I was, and then I dried my tears, because now that we've named you, nothing, neither hell nor high water, was going to keep you from me.

14

JULIA

Julia slips out the back door, closes it silently. She stops on the back step, takes a deep breath, listens for the sound of a parent's chasing-her-down footsteps. Silence. Grant's room is directly above and she glances up at the window; a light is on. She knows Grant is probably in bed, headphones on, watching Critterscape videos on YouTube or bingeing a TV show on his tablet. But she doesn't move, because if one of them finds her, she wants to say she just is getting fresh air.

The silence stretches out, and she hurries across the yard. She stares into the darkness of the greenbelt, the thick growth of the oaks and mesquites and...then she feels the weight of a stare.

Someone watching her.

You're imagining it, she tells herself, but the feeling persists like a rising fever. She shoves the fear away. It's just the horror of the day, creeping around her mind and her vision and jangling her nerves. She activates the flashlight on her phone and steps into the greenbelt. Stops. Listens.

Maybe Danielle was walking in the greenbelt. Maybe. And someone out there took her.

She shines the light forward, and there are only branches and trunks and the well-traveled path, worn by her neighbors and their dogs and kids' bicycles over the past twenty years, and she walks down it.

She sees the man then. She nearly screams. He's tall, wiry, early forties, dark hair with a touch of gray. Nice clothes, expensive jacket. He switches on a flashlight.

"Oh," she says. "You scared me." She's still scared—she doesn't know this man.

"Sorry. Some of the neighborhood dads and moms organized just to walk around, make sure no one suspicious is lurking. I got assigned this stretch of greenbelt leading to Ned's house."

"Oh," she says. "Ned's not there. He's at the Horvath house."

"Yeah, I saw the police took over Ned's house," the man says again. "Let me guess, you're heading over there to see him."

How does this man know about her friendship with Ned? Well, probably she and Ned were mentioned multiple times on the Winding Creek Neighborhood Faceplace page.

"I'm Julia," she says.

"I know," he says with a neighborly smile. "I'm Marland. Friend of Ned's. I take it your parents don't know you're out."

"Please don't say anything. I just want to check on Ned. In person." She tries not to blush.

"It's not my business," Marland says with a slight smile. "I can't imagine how horrible his day has been. He's lucky to have a friend like you."

She nods and goes past him. "Are there other people patrolling on the greenbelt?"

"Just me along this stretch. We want to keep the curiosity seekers from Ned's house. There are others up by the park."

"Thanks. Bye." She nods again and hurries on, glancing back at him once. It strikes her as odd he called it *Ned's house*, like a teenager would…not Danielle's house. Odd that an adult described himself as a friend of Ned's rather than Danielle's. She hopes no one else is along the greenbelt, to snitch on her to her parents.

She passes several more houses, exits the greenbelt, cuts between two homes, and she's on another street. If she stuck to the greenbelt, she'd still get to Mike's house. It would just take longer. She crosses the street and heads to the backyard. There's an iron fence fronting the greenbelt here, a low mesh barrier on the ground, to dissuade the snakes and field mice, and a gate, usually locked. She climbs over the fence and approaches the back door of Mike Horvath's house.

She hears Ned's and Mike's voices inside, talking softly.

"...Not going to London. Or Ghana."

"I'll talk to him." Mike, calm and quiet.

"He said I have to go!" Ned's voice, rising.

"Of course you should finish school here. You'll always have..." and then Mike's deep voice fading, moving away from the door that leads into a back mudroom connected to the garage, and Ned's voice, pleading, fades as well. She waits. Then she knocks gently.

The door opens. But it's not Ned. It's Peter, Mike's son, a year older than her and Ned. He's dressed as per normal for him: a hoodie with some obscure computer symbol on it, faded khakis, high-top sneakers. Dark blond curling hair, a frown. His eyes are red-rimmed, and she realizes he's been crying. She has been worried about Ned and Mike but not Peter. Peter's just sort of...there. Sometimes she's felt the weight of his gaze on her and she thinks: *If Peter could be a little more social, dress a little nicer, find some topics of conversation beyond computers, he'd have a chance with a girl.* He could be, she has thought, an interesting project. Not for her, but for a friend.

"Hi, Peter," she says evenly. "How are you?"

"I'm all right," he says. He moved down from Canada with his father; there had been whispers about school problems, which was why he'd had to stay an extra year. "I'm sorry for what you went through this morning," he says. Not looking at her.

"Thanks. Is Ned here?"

"Yes. Sure. Come on in." He mumbles a lot, and she has to strain to hear his words.

She steps inside, and Peter Horvath closes the door behind her. He doesn't yell or announce her name but gestures at her to stay put and leaves. Then Ned comes into the mudroom, and she folds her arms around him, like a simple embrace could make it better, but it is all she can do. He isn't crying now, but she feels the tremble on his jaw, of his body. She tries to imagine if it had been her mom killed, and the image won't even come. The idea is like something shielded in darkness, not visible, beyond her thoughts. Her fingers go into his dark hair, stroking his scalp gently, and he gives a little sigh. For a moment she wonders if she should kiss him; she has wanted to for a long while. But not today. Not so close to this awfulness. She doesn't want them linked in his mind. But then she thinks: *I'll always be the girl who found his dead mom with him. What does that mean for us?* Then she shoves the thought away.

"Mike is upstairs," he whispers. "Peter won't tell."

"Am I not supposed to be here?" Their faces are very close together.

"He wants to grieve in private," Ned says. "He's falling apart. People were over here earlier to see us, just neighbors, and Mike lost it. I think he just needs time alone."

"Oh. Of course. I just wanted to see if you're…" What, all right? He wasn't. He wasn't OK or all right or keeping it together. "I just wanted to see you," she amends quickly.

"Thanks." He steps back from her, suddenly speechless. He was a guy, and he'd let her see how vulnerable he could be, and so he was probably going to all guy up right now. She wants to hold his hand, but she doesn't.

"My father wants me to move to London and live with him. Or even go back to Ghana, go to school there, live with my grandparents." The words spill out in a flood. "I won't do it. I don't want to leave Lakehaven. My friends. You."

"You can live with our family," she says. "To finish school. There's no way Mom or Dad wouldn't agree to that."

"Sure they might. Your mom doesn't like me."

"Of course she does."

"She just doesn't. She didn't like my mom, either."

"Ned. If she didn't like you, she wouldn't have come with us to the station."

"She did that for you, not me."

"Ned…" But she doesn't want to argue with him. Not now,

on the day his mother died. "We wouldn't have Grant without your mom. My mom always said that." She puts her hand on his shoulder.

"I'm not going to London or Ghana. Mike said I could stay with him and Peter, but Mike doesn't have any rights. My dad has all the rights, and he'll be just enough of a jerk..." Now the tears shine in his eyes. "Mike's got a friend with a private jet. He's flying Dad here from London. He'll be here in the morning. I have to figure out what to do."

"You know, maybe we can talk to your dad. He can't want to disrupt your life further."

"He wants to take care of me. Now. Now he decides to be my dad." Ned's voice rises slightly. "I haven't seen him maybe but ten times in my whole life." Ned gives off an awful, choking laugh. "But Mom's dead, and so he knows he has to...*he has to*...step up, because, like, the world is watching."

"Let us talk to him."

"He won't care what Mike or your parents say. But he is going to have to drag me onto a plane. I will kick and scream and someone in the airport will film it and it will go viral and..."

She pats his shoulders, trying to calm him. "Let's not worry about that right now."

He nods. He swallows. He looks her in the eye. She thinks for a moment he might kiss her, and maybe a kiss would be a solace. "I have to pick out a coffin."

The words are a punch in her gut.

"I mean, that's what Mike said. The police will release her body at some point, and then we'll have a funeral, and I have to pick out her dress and her coffin and what songs they play. Even though she wasn't much for church, we'll have it at a church. I guess I have to pick the church, too. At Christmas, if we went, we went to the Episcopal one." His voice is soft. "I can't even think straight. I can't."

"What can I do to help you?"

He tilts his head slightly, studying her. "I keep thinking. The cops found a phone near her feet. And I saw her arguing on a phone last night, telling someone she wanted out. But it wasn't her regular phone."

"What could your mom have wanted out of?"

His voice lowers. "The relationship with Mike. Her business. An upcoming adoption? Or maybe she'd gotten involved with someone other than Mike." He makes the last part a whisper. "I don't think Peter can hear us, but he was in the kitchen. Mike's upstairs."

"Do you think she was cheating on Mike?"

"I don't know. She seemed happy. But preoccupied. Whoever she was in touch with on that phone, that could be who killed her. They won't show me the number."

"Have you mentioned this to Mike or Peter?"

He shakes his head. "Not yet. I can't...I can't stay here thinking that Mike could have hurt her."

"This is Mike. He never would hurt her."

"People do terrible, unimaginable things sometimes," Ned says in a low voice. "And then the neighbors are always surprised."

She doesn't know what to say, but she decides it is better not to say anything and make it worse. She watches him. She has known him since they were small and his mother found her brother for them. Most of her life, through childhood and the awkward middle school years, he'd been her constant friend, annoying at times, sweet at others. But everything feels changed between them ever since they stopped looking at each other as just friends but as something more. There are cuter boys at school, boys who aren't too shy to flirt with her and let her know of their interest, but Ned is Ned and he is a little dangerous. She sees it in those dark eyes, with their stare that promises something more. The kid who always charms the teachers but skirts the rules, who smiles at the parents while the flask is hidden in his backpack, who manages to sweet-talk his way out of setbacks and troubles. *That boy always lands on his feet*, she'd heard Mike once say, and she thought Ned hadn't considered a world where he might trip or stumble.

He murmurs something, so quiet she can't hear.

"What?" she asks, leaning close, whispering.

"Do…do you think what I've done…had anything…?" And then his voice stops, turns to a ragged breath.

"No. No, Ned. It couldn't." She grabs his forearm, squeezes it. "It couldn't."

"What if…?" he says. "What if…?" And Julia realizes these are the two most poisonous words ever.

She takes a deep breath. "But you have to stop doing it. For a while."

"I'll get in trouble if I stop."

"No. It'll be fine."

Slowly he shakes his head.

She cannot argue with him, not at the end of this awful day, so she doesn't. But she squeezes his hand.

"I think I just want to go to bed," he says. "Like, for days."

It's not a time for big decisions, but they may not have a choice. "Let me take care of this problem for you," she says. "I'll talk to the guy for you."

He shakes his head. "It doesn't work that way, Jules."

But she's already decided. She just won't tell him. "All right," she says. "I won't do anything. We'll get through this. Are you sure you'll be OK?"

He shakes his head. "I can walk you back to your house," he says.

"No, I'm fine. There's a patrol out there. I saw a friend of yours on the trail, near your house. Keeping an eye on it. Guy named Marland?"

Ned's eyes grow wide. "Tall guy? Older?"

She nods.

If she didn't know him well, she wouldn't see him gather himself this way. But she does see it.

He's scared. Of this man who was so friendly to her on the greenbelt.

"What?" she asks. "Who is he?"

"I'll walk you back." Ned goes into the kitchen, then the den, and she hears him telling Peter he'll be back in a few. Then they head out, back to her house, skipping the greenbelt, sticking to the streets. They cut through a yard to the trail, but Marland is gone. For a moment Ned stands there.

"Who is he?" she asks again. "Is he...the guy?"

"Don't tell anyone you saw him. I beg you. I'll be in so much trouble, Jules. Please. It...it has nothing to do with Mom. OK? Please."

"All right." But she's not one bit sure about keeping this odd promise. Something is terribly wrong. She goes into her house silently, Ned waiting until she's inside, and as she shuts the door, she sees Ned turn and run into the darkness, eager to be gone.

15

GRANT

Grant can't sleep. He guessed that Julia would duck out, at least to go check on Ned in person, and he watches from his upstairs bedroom window as his sister sneaks into the greenbelt. She'll walk right past the tree where the money was left for him, and he wonders if he should stay at the window, waiting for her return.

Or go out to the tree and see what's there now. What if it's more money?

What are these lies he's been told? What is the bad thing his father's done? He doesn't want to believe it has to do with Danielle. It *can't*. That's his dad.

Be the cat, looking out the window.

Does that mean the person leaving stuff for him in the tree can see him right now? He goes back to the window, the room lit up behind him, and stares out into the night.

Then he thinks about it: How does the Sender know about his tree? Who knew? His family. Did either of his parents tell people about it? Maybe they told Danielle? *Oh, guess what Grant does. It's so funny.* Who would remember that? Who would care? He's sure he hasn't mentioned it to anyone.

He needs to find a way to catch the Sender. If they've left him something in the tree again, they might do so a third time. He could catch them then.

But he's scared to go out in the night and check the tree right now. Danielle went out in the night and died. Julia just went and he did nothing, but he can guess where she's going. Mike's house, to see Ned. He wonders how Mike and Peter and Ned are doing. Instead he goes to the computer.

He opens the Sender's email and reads it again. He hates email. It's so much worse than texting. Maybe this is an older person who doesn't text? His friends have complained about grandparents who won't bother to learn texting. So he has these few clues to go on: the pictures sent to him, the Gmail address, the spoofing of Drew's address to send him the original mail.

You don't have to wait for the Sender to tell you who he or she is. You could find out. His parents were always telling him this—to take the initiative, to be a leader. It looks good on college applications, and it's simply never too early to worry about that.

How do you trace an email?

He knew who he should ask, but he feels weird asking him. Peter Horvath, Mike's son. He's a computer geek. He's a senior and Grant's a freshman, so their paths don't cross much, but he knows Peter. And he knows Peter is not into the activities his father, Mike, is into: fishing, football, basketball. All of which Grant loves. Peter and Grant have never had a private conversation and he has no idea what state Peter is in—his father's girlfriend was just murdered. But maybe he would help.

Mom has already told him and Julia they're not going to school in the morning. He assumes Peter won't as well. He does have Peter's number in his phone. He texts him: Hey. It's Grant. Really sorry about Danielle. I hope you all are doing ok. I mean of course you're not ok. I mean...I'm just really sorry.

He doesn't expect an answer, but he gets one quickly: Thanks. Your sister is here right now with Ned.

I figured, Grant texts. How are you?

Numb. Not sure how to help my dad. Probably more than you wanted to know.

Grant wants to text *you have a great dad*, but that seems like too much. Just be there for him, I guess, he texts instead.

Yeah. Thanks for checking in on us.

Grant takes a deep breath and writes: I wonder if you can help me. Something weird is going on, but not related to Danielle. It might take your mind off all this sadness if you need a distraction.

He waits and he waits, and finally an answer comes: What?

Grant hesitates—he has to be very careful with what he shares with Peter—and then he writes: I think I need a hacker.

And presses send.

16

IRIS

The next morning, Iris awakens groggy with sleep and has a strange thought: that she's dead and she only just now realizes it. For a moment she believes this and then she breathes hard, which jolts her to full wakefulness. She pulls the covers over her head, feeling sick. She slept very badly.

Kyle is still asleep, snoring softly. She knew he tossed and turned much of the night as well before slipping into quiet slumber. She watches him sleep. She thinks about when they first met. She didn't really notice him and then she did, running daily with a club at college past her Houston apartment, and he was all she could think about. The intensity of his gaze, the strength of his stride. She actually waited on the sidewalk for him to run past and asked him out for a coffee as he ran past; he was a shy college senior and she was a year out of college and already starting to write for bands. But he'd stopped and jogged back to her, smiling awkwardly, and she said, *If not coffee, then a bottle of water so you can hydrate*, and he'd laughed and asked her for her number and the next day they'd met for coffee. That young man is still somewhere inside Kyle, not yet eroded away. She touches his hair; he doesn't awaken. His face is bruised from his fall on the greenbelt. She studies the marks as if they're a map.

I love you, she wants to tell him, but she doesn't.

Then she gets up and goes to the kitchen. She brews coffee and opens her laptop, half hoping that the Lakehaven police will have made an arrest, solved the case, and delivered justice. No such luck. Danielle's murder isn't even the lead on the front page of the Austin news website she reads. She's overshadowed by a plane crash near Munich and a political scandal that blew up overnight; Danielle, older woman dead in a park, is halfway down the page. She reads the article. There's not much there, mainly a few details about Danielle's work as a lawyer who coordinated international adoptions. Her friend Francie, who convinced Iris to adopt from Russia, is quoted as saying what a wonderful person she was.

Very little on the kind of person she was. On the secrets she kept.

There is a mention that her teenage son and a friend found her. No mention of Julia by name. Small mercies.

Iris opens the neighborhood Faceplace page. The fear and panic are unabated. Iris reads each post, each comment. People are scared. Jumping at shadows, devolving into arguments about how to best protect themselves, one group still promising to wander the neighborhood like an unofficial patrol and others objecting to the whole idea, and it all gives Iris a headache.

She starts to write STOP IT ALL OF YOU in all caps in a comment bubble and then stops herself. Deletes it. She cannot get involved in this fray. She must stay above it. Instead she posts a link to the dinner schedule for Mike, Peter, and Ned, asking that if anyone else wants to volunteer, they should sign up, and to please read what others on consecutive nights are bringing so the guys don't get fajitas or spaghetti three nights in a row. Like they would care. But she still says it, because the idea of it done wrong bothers her. She doesn't say anything regarding Danielle, Ned, or her daughter. She does say that there may be a separate dinner list once Gordon Frimpong, Ned's father, arrives from London. She'll find out where he's staying. She doesn't think it's likely he'll stay with Mike and Peter; surely by then the police will let Ned return to his mother's house.

Iris pours herself a large mug of coffee. She answers the emails and texts she's gotten, in order, systematically. She writes some empty, reassuring phrases, using them again and again, cutting and pasting, being careful though to always have the recipient's name right.

When she's done, she listens to the silence in the house, and then there's a knock at the front door. She peers through the peephole. It's Mike Horvath. She knew she would have to see him, but she didn't expect it this soon. And why wouldn't he call first? Because they're grieving and shaken and not thinking straight, she tells herself.

She pulls her terry-cloth robe tight around her, reties the belt to keep it snug, and opens the door.

"Mike. Come in. I am so, so sorry."

They hug. She can feel Mike trembling a little. He steps back from her.

"Thank you," he says. "Ned is sleeping, finally. He did not sleep all night. I could hear him pacing the floor, watching television. Finally he slept. I cannot stay long, I want to be there whenever he wakes up."

"Let me get you some coffee."

He follows her into the kitchen and sits at the granite island when she gestures toward a barstool there. Mike's a big man, six three, broad shouldered, built like a rugby player, not conventionally handsome—not like Kyle—but with an appealing face. His accent—he grew up in Slovakia, and then his family moved to Canada when he was a teenager—is one she has always found charming. He arrived in Austin two years ago as an investor in start-up technology companies, a recent widower, bought a house in the neighborhood because he liked the greenbelt and the quiet and the high school for his son, Peter, who Iris considers an antisocial oddball but a basically good kid.

And then he met Danielle, and they seemed well suited for each other.

"I am sorry to bother you so early," he says in his deep voice. "Especially after what you and Julia went through yesterday. How is she?"

Iris loves Mike a little for asking *How is she?* instead of *Is she*

OK? because no, she's not OK, she won't be, not for a while, and that is part of the awfulness of this. "She's not great. But she's mostly worried about Ned. And you. How are you? And Peter?" She wonders if Peter ever noticed his father was dating someone and chides herself for her unkindness.

She sets the coffee down in front of Mike.

"Iris," Mike says, "I have loved twice in my life and both times she has died." He says her name *I-ris*, a very clear break between the syllables, the *I* always longer than it needs to be. It irritates her usually, but not now. He looks very directly at her, as if she will have an answer to his grief. "I should know what to do, right? I don't."

She takes Mike's hand. "I am so sorry."

"To lose her this way...I cannot understand it."

"They'll find who did it."

"I can't worry about myself right now." He sips at the coffee. "I wanted to see how you all were, but I need your help with Ned."

"What?"

"His father is coming from London. An investor friend of mine with a private jet there is getting him here this morning."

Iris tries not to make a face. She dislikes Danielle's first husband, Gordon, a man she met once or twice, briefly, when he came to Austin to visit his son. He's a banker, as well, with an international practice covering Europe and Africa. Iris does not understand how he could have a child and leave him behind in another country, put his job before his kid. It's beyond her. But right now she tells herself to be generous. Of course Gordon is coming here. He must.

"Does he need a place to stay?"

"No. He will stay at Danielle's house. But he wants to take Ned back to London."

She hadn't even thought of that in the insanity of the last twenty-four hours. Ned can't just live alone in his dead mother's house. The house will have to be sold. Presumably, being a lawyer, Danielle had a will. She thinks how Julia will react. "Of course Gordon does," she says.

"Yes, and I am sure Gordon means well, but Ned is in no emotional shape to leave everyone he loves and knows. He is upset."

"What does he want to do?"

"He tells me that Julia has invited him to live with you. We could not sleep last night and he told me this."

"Oh. Well. He has another year of school. Sure," Iris says, trying not to think of what she's agreeing to, trying to keep her voice steady, while another voice in her head, a screeching howl that is ugly and unkind, says, *No, no, no, no. You cannot endure that.*

"Well, so you offered?" Mike asks.

"Well, honestly, we hadn't discussed it with Julia."

"So I thought." Mike clears his throat. "I am willing to be appointed his guardian until he's eighteen. I don't know how American law works on this front, though. And Gordon has to agree."

"Gordon is his dad. I'm not sure any court is going to interfere with his rights as a father."

Mike takes a long sip of coffee, his gaze steady on her. "Well, perhaps we can reason with Gordon. He is trying to do what he thinks is right."

"Maybe he's right."

"Let's be honest. Ned barely knows Gordon and has been to London only a few times."

"That's a lot of change, but kids are resilient."

"Yes. Look at Grant, adjusting from Russia to Lakehaven. That must have seemed a million miles apart."

"He doesn't remember Russia," she says.

They are quiet for a moment, Mike sipping coffee. Iris says: "The ugly truth is now this neighborhood will always be, for Ned, where his mother died. Not just died, but was *killed*. He might do better with a fresh start."

"He is very concerned about leaving his friends."

"And he'd miss out on in-state tuition for a public university if he leaves. I think he wants to go to UT or A&M."

Mike lets ten seconds pass, studying his coffee. "I am not sure he has thought about his college career much in the past hours, Iris. And Gordon will want him to go to university in Britain now, I would think."

"Oh." She's done it again, said something thoughtless when she didn't mean to. "You're right, of course. We're so focused on Julia's college applications for this year that I'm stuck in that mode. I'm sorry." She is talking about college applications to a man whose girlfriend died yesterday. She wants to crawl under a table and stay there. "I don't know what to say. I think we're all in shock."

"You never know. That issue about university is a good point and perhaps one that will sway Gordon," Mike says diplomatically. "A banker understands costs."

"I'll talk to Kyle and see what we can do to convince Gordon." She squeezes his hand again.

He puts his hand atop hers. "Thank you. I thought you might give the eulogy at the memorial service."

Iris wants to say *You did not just suggest that to me*. Instead she keeps her expression blank.

"You just knew her for so long. Friend and neighbor. And she made such an impact in your life with Grant."

"I might not be able to keep my composure," she says slowly.

"But you are a poet, with your songs. And you speak to groups of parents all the time."

"It's not the same. You should. She loved you." Did Danielle love him? Iris doesn't know. She hopes she did. That there was happiness, and contentment, between Danielle and this gentle bear of a man.

"I can't do it," Mike says. "I don't want to lose it in front of Ned and Peter. If you cannot, then perhaps Kyle."

This keeps getting worse. "Doesn't Danielle have family?"

"Her dad left them when she was young, and her mother died about eight years ago. Cancer."

"Oh. Yes." She'd sent flowers; it was the decent thing to do.

"And she was an only child and not close to any other relatives. All of us here in Winding Creek were her family."

"Of course," Iris hears herself say.

"If you'll talk to Kyle about the eulogy and about Ned's situation, I would appreciate it."

"Yes."

"And, Iris?"

"Yes?"

"Do you have any idea who would have wanted to hurt her?" His voice is a low rumble, and she hears a cold threat in it. Not to her. But he's mad. He's hurt. He wants to hurt whoever did this. She understands.

She meets his gaze. She's never been afraid of Mike, but now she is, a little. A smart, capable man with a good cause can be a dangerous thing. "I can't think of anyone who wished her ill. Surely this has to be random. She was in the wrong place at the wrong time."

"I wonder," he says. "The police questioned me. I understand why. I was fishing with Peter, yes, but she could have been killed before we went out on the lake. As if…as if I could kill her and then go spend time with my son." Now she sees how close to losing it he is.

"Oh, Mike."

"We did not spend the night together. I was at my house, since I was going to get up early to fish, and she was at hers."

"Mike, I know you couldn't hurt her," she says, because it's what one says, she supposes, in this situation.

"We don't know what people are capable of. You, or me, or Kyle," he says. "In Czechoslovakia, under the heel of the Soviets, children informed on their parents. Parents on each other." He meets her gaze again. "People are good until they are not."

Iris swallows past the lump in her throat. She hears footsteps on the stairs and sees Grant coming down in his old pajama pants and last year's Austin City Limits Festival shirt that Kyle bought him, worn and thin. For the first time since he found out about Danielle, Grant smiles, for just a moment, and comes down and hugs Mike, who awkwardly hugs him back.

"*Chlapec*," Mike calls him, a Slovak word for "boy" or "lad," his hearty nickname for Grant. "How are you? You taking good care of your sister and mama?"

Grant nods. "I am so sorry about Danielle," he says quietly. "I know how much you loved her. I loved her, too. I wouldn't have my family without her."

Mike leans down, puts a hand on his shoulder. Iris can see tears in his eyes. "You know she loved you, yes? She helped bring you to this better life. Your happiness was a reminder of the good job she did."

Grant starts to cry, and Iris's heart shifts in her chest. But she stands there frozen while Mike pats her son's shoulder and comforts him.

"What are you going to do now?" Grant asks.

"What do you mean?"

"Are you going to go back to Canada?"

"I will stay here. This is my home now." He looks up at Iris. "My friends are here, the ones I like to see every day. Like you."

Grant wipes the tears from his face.

"Don't cry, *chlapec*. When we are feeling better, we will go fishing, OK?"

Grant nods.

"I did not mean to upset you. I'm going to go check on Ned, but maybe I'll see you later. I just want to know you are all right. And Julia, and your mom and dad."

Grant nods again. *Mike is better with him than Kyle is*, Iris thinks, and then she shoves the thought away because it feels deeply disloyal. But it's true.

"We're bringing you dinner tonight," Iris says. "What do you and the boys want?"

"Anything is fine. We don't feel like eating so much. We appreciate everyone helping with the dinner schedule."

"I'll bring some wine, too."

Mike says, "If I get drunk, I'll break all the windows." His voice has gone low and soft again. "I want to find who did this."

Grant is silent, and he glances at his mother.

"That's what the police are for," she says.

"Why does someone take a woman's life like it is nothing, when it is everything?"

His words silence them.

Mike rubs the top of Grant's bedhead hair and gives Iris a quick hug. "I don't want to be gone if Ned wakes up," he says. "I'll see you both later, yeah?"

Iris walks him to the door and watches him go, heading down the road and turning into a cul-de-sac. He doesn't look back.

"Oh. I forgot to tell him. Peter is coming over later to help me with a project," Grant says. "For computer science."

"Peter probably needs to be with his dad. Why would you ask him for help now?"

"I had asked him before," Grant says. "He said he'd still help me. He needs to take his mind off Danielle."

"All right, but if he changes his mind, don't make a big deal about it," Iris says. She glances in the pantry to make sure she has enough for an impromptu lunch or snack. Teenagers eat constantly. She needs to go to the store anyway, and now she dreads it. It's a running joke that anytime she goes to the grocery she will see five people she knows. But they're running low on peanut butter, and she needs to get the makings for the dinner she's promised for Mike and the boys. "All right," she says. "When is Peter coming over?"

"Around ten this morning, if that's all right."

"Don't talk about Danielle," she says. "Unless Peter wants to."

"I don't think he will."

Iris hugs her son. "I know you're worried about Mike. He'll be fine."

She feels Grant tense under her grip. Whatever she says right now seems wrong, but silence feels worse, so she keeps talking. "What do you want for breakfast?"

"Mom, I love you," he says into her shoulder.

"I love you, too, baby," she whispers.

"You aren't going to leave me, are you?"

She knows what he means. She won't die. "No, no, no," she says, like a spell, like a wish, like a promise.

17

FROM IRIS POLLITT'S "FROM RUSSIA WITH LOVE" ADOPTION JOURNAL

It was a long flight to Russia. I imagined, sitting on the plane, the miles of land and water and ice we were flying over to come to you. To find you. To make you ours.

We didn't bring your sister. She was too young, it was too cold—early December—and we would have our hands full with you. We didn't get to bring you home this trip. That would require a second trip. Julia stayed with your dad's parents.

Danielle was with us. Not sitting with us on the plane. She was back in economy. (I booked us first class, since we weren't traveling with a kiddo this time, even though Kyle said it was a waste of money that we could use to bribe whomever we have to bribe in Russia.) I felt bad we were in first and she was in economy, but she said she was fine. Not every consultant does this, but Francie told me this was the extra service that made her work special. She must have buried this cost in her fees, because we weren't billed for her ticket. Which I guess means she worked on other adoptions while we were there, which is fine. I knew she was staying a few days beyond us coming back to America. It would be great to have her there with us. It would make things go easier.

Kyle read during the flight and listened to an instructional audio on beginning Russian. We'd already been cautioned repeatedly on what we can say and what we can't say. We'd been warned especially to speak English and let the translator do her work in

Russian so there are no gaffes or misunderstandings. Kyle told Danielle he was studying Russian, just to use at the hotel, and she smiled and told him practically everyone at our hotel would have a command of English. He murmured softly to himself, repeating the words he learned. I put on my own headphones to block him out and listened to the last three albums by an artist who asked me to write a song for him, thinking of you. Of writing a song for my new baby, just like I did for your sister.

We changed planes in London—it was about a four-hour flight to Moscow. We had a short layover. Kyle studied his Russian. Danielle was on her phone a lot, looking worried. Was something wrong? Maybe she was trying to iron out some detail. Maybe it had nothing to do with us but with another client. I was constantly telling myself to calm down. I was calmer giving birth to Julia, which makes no sense—birth is way harder than this.

I got up to go to the restroom, and when I was washing my hands, a woman stepped up next to me at the sink.

She looked at me in the mirror. Our gazes locked.

"Go home," she said in lightly accented English. Quietly. It was a whisper.

This was not what anyone expects to hear from someone at an airport sink. I said, "What?" I thought she must be talking to someone on the phone. You know, with an earpiece in.

"Go home, Mrs. Pollitt. Go home and write a song."

My hands were dripping. I froze. "What?"

"Go. Home." Now I heard a little blade of threat in her tone.

She turned and walked away from me. My reactions kicked in, and with my wet hands I grabbed at her. "Who are you? What do you mean?"

She pulled free, staggered out of the women's room. A couple of entering teenage girls glanced at us, curious, surprised.

"Hey! Hey!" I yelled. "Who are you?"

A female security guard headed toward us, stern look. The woman said to her, "This woman accosted me in the bathroom. I don't know her."

"She told me to go home!" I yelled, because no one was going to tell me I couldn't come get you, Grant, and I wanted to know what was happening. The security guard interposed herself between me (crazy yelling person) and the woman (quiet now and acting frightened).

So you can imagine how it went.

They talked to her, she lied and said she'd said nothing to me, but she thought I was drunk or high in the bathroom, as I seemed confused and clumsy. (Note, baby, my hands are still wet, so well done her for that bit of improvisation that made me look bad.) For me, yelling had not helped. Because a normal person would not be this upset at some weird random comment and I was.

I told them we were heading to Moscow for an international adoption, and suddenly Kyle and Danielle were both there. Then they escorted me back to our gate, the Russian air crew and the Russian passengers watching the proceedings with interest—there's not much else to do at a gate if you're bored with your phone. People watched me. The warning woman (I don't know what else to call her, so that's her name now) was gone.

And I realized, repeating this story for the fourth time, I sounded like an idiot. A fool. She said my name, but she denied knowing who I was. I had no way to prove it. Why would this harmless-looking woman, who was quite good at acting frightened, say something like this to me? I saw, when they asked her for ID, that she had a Russian passport, but I couldn't see her name.

Kyle was trying to calm me and was looking at me like maybe he was not the one hesitating about the adoption, that I was, and it had somehow manifested itself in me hearing this woman say these words to me. Danielle reassured them that I was fine, reassured the gate agent who came over to inquire what was the matter. I realized with a shock: I needed to act sane to board the flight. Would she be on our flight? I was suddenly scared she was and that I wouldn't be allowed to board.

And then what? Danielle would have to say to the Volkov Infants Home, "Oh, sorry, the mother-to-be freaked out in the airport in London." And maybe they would give Sasha to someone else.

I apologized repeatedly, and then I hushed because I've realized taking the blame on myself and shutting up is the smartest thing to do. Deep breath after deep breath. The warning woman was gone, but her face was locked in my mind: brown hair, a tiny mole on her lower cheek, eyes of grayish blue, and a slightly crooked front tooth. The security people, reassured I wasn't a threat to anyone or to myself (after my profuse apologies), took their leave.

Danielle said, "You don't want there to be an incident report in the airport."

I was stunned. "What, you mean the Russian authorities could still find out about this? That woman spoke to me. I'm not lying."

"Of course you're not," she said. "I believe that you heard what you said."

That wasn't the same as believing that she said it, but I dug my nails into my palms. "Danielle. Why would someone not want us to fly to Russia? Is there another family interested in Grant?"

"No, of course not. That's not how it works." Danielle was pale, shocked, flustered.

"Maybe this is a stunt to rattle us. Make us pay more bribes," Kyle said.

"It's not a stunt. I've never heard of such a thing." Danielle shook her head. "Is it at all possible you misheard this woman?"

"No!"

"At. All. Possible?"

And what answer can I give to that? Of course it's possible. I felt like my husband and my friend were stepping back from me, looking at me with new eyes, worried about me when it's me who worries about other people. I took a deep breath. Centered myself. Thought of you. Thought of you in that cold orphanage, of how little you smiled.

I could do this.

"I'm sorry," I said, and I repeated it like a prayer.

"If you're not up to this..." Kyle started to say in that patron-izing voice I loathed, and I shook my head. I grabbed his hand and squeezed it so he'd shut up.

"I'm exhausted," I said. "I'm overwrought. I'm just so sorry." I could feel the weight of stares on me, and I didn't know if my fellow passengers were British or Russian, if someone was watching me to see if I obeyed the warning woman.

Why would anyone care what I did in Russia? What we did?

Who didn't want us to have a baby?

Why did someone hate us?

Kyle leaned over and whispered to me, "This can't be like in the cancer center. I love you, but get ahold of yourself."

My mouth quivered a little. I'll tell you about that one day, but it was me standing up for my child, insisting on information and care for her, not wanting my baby to be a number but a human fighting a terrible disease.

I just can get... real determined.

I clutched Kyle's hand and then they called us for our flight. We were in first class again, so I glanced over my shoulder and saw the warning woman, the left edge of her face, hiding behind a tall businessman, far back in the crowd, waiting to board, watching us.

Watching me. And then she was gone when I blinked, and I wondered if she was even there.

18

GRANT

Peter Horvath arrives right after the local television stations have set up their vans outside Danielle's house. They're two houses down on the cul-de-sac, and with the Sheriff's Office in command, Peter has had to park farther down the street and show a driver's license to the deputy on duty.

Grant watches from an upstairs window.

He thinks the camera crews and reporters are parked in front of Danielle's house because they don't know better. They don't yet know that Danielle's boyfriend lives a couple of streets over, on a different curve of the greenbelt, and that is where Danielle's son is. The reporters will knock on doors, looking for quotes or comments, and someone will mention her boyfriend lives here in the neighborhood. Like a dummy. Grant's a kid and he knows better than that.

And he wonders, maybe the police don't tell them, because when a woman dies they look at the men in her life. Her teenage son. Her boyfriend. Her boyfriend's son.

I'll have to talk to the police about the bad thing your dad did.

Just words. Words that don't mean anything. And when he knows who this person is, he can tell his parents and they will fix it. Won't they? All he knows is if he goes to the police with the accusations, it's like turning on his dad. And he knows his dad would never hurt Danielle.

The deputy waves Peter through.

Mom, with her mom radar, has already arrived at the front door. She opens it before the doorbell rings. Grant stands at the bottom of the stairs.

"Peter," Mom says. "Sweetie, how are you?" She hugs Peter, although Grant can tell Peter does not like to be hugged.

"Hi, Mrs. Pollitt," Peter says. Today he's in an MIT hoodie, jeans, Vans shoes. He looks tired. "I'm all right."

"How are you holding up?"

"Fine," Peter says. He always talks so softly, like he's worried he'll make a ripple in the world.

"You don't have to be fine with us, you know," Mom says, and Grant wants to say, *Mom, just give him some space.*

"I have to be strong for Dad and Ned," Peter says. "I mean, I've never known anyone who was murdered before. How am I supposed to feel other than sad?"

"Angry," Grant says.

"Maybe later," Peter says, and something in him saying that makes Mom hug him again, and Peter endures it again.

"You really don't have to help Grant with homework," Mom says.

"It's a good distraction." He's bad at keeping a steady gaze; Peter looks down at his scuffed-up shoes. "They talked about getting married, you know," Peter says.

A heavy silence falls on Grant and his mother.

"That just makes it all so much worse," Grant finally says. His mother shoots him a glance, and Grant knows he's said something he shouldn't have.

Peter just nods. "Ned and I won't be stepbrothers now. It would have been nice to have a brother."

"You and Ned will always be close."

"Will we?" Peter asks with a shrug, and Grant can see the answer is no, probably not. Their lives will spin off in different directions now.

Peter says, "We should get to work, Grant. I don't want to be away from my dad too long, in case he needs me."

Grant leads him up to his room and sits on the edge of the bed, gesturing at the chair in front of his computer desk, where Peter sits. He doesn't seem like a kid as much as an adult who emerged a little too early from the cocoon.

Grant has been thinking about what to say. He doesn't want Peter to see the email message from the Sender that mentions Dad. So he just shows Peter the first email he received, spoofed from his friend Drew's account, the stock photo of the woman in the rain, and the message about lies.

Peter says nothing, looks at it all.

"I want to find out who sent this to me."

"I can only tell you where it may have come from."

"This person—I call him or her the Sender—has to know things about my life," Grant says. "That Drew is my friend. That J. J. Watt is one of my favorite football players. That I have a tree where I used to hide stuff. Who could know that?"

"Are you on social media?" Peter asks.

Grant nods.

"OK, is Drew one of your friends on Cheeper or Nowpic or Faceplace?"

Grant nods again. He can see where this is going.

"You belong to a fan page for the Texans?"

Grant nods again, his stomach sinking.

"The tree—I don't know about how someone might find that out. Did you ever talk a lot about it?"

"No. Julia might have told someone. Or my parents. But it's not like it was some big thing in my childhood. Just a thing I did."

"Did you ever write about it?"

"Like a school paper?"

"Sure."

"No."

"Did your mom? In one of her songs?"

Slowly he nods. "Yeah. In a song a couple of years back. It was on an album. It wasn't a hit." Mom hadn't had a hit in years, but they didn't talk about that…She still got asked to write songs to fill out albums. Grant knew that wasn't the way to talk about what she did when she wrote, but it was true. Grant clears his throat and sings softly, "You keep your little secrets hidden from me/like they were treasures in an old oak tree/like the one down by our creek/where we'd play hide-and-seek/and you'd always find me…" He has a nice voice.

"Amazed that wasn't a hit," Peter says, and with anyone else it might sound mean, but with Peter it sounds plainspoken.

"The melody was the best part," Grant says.

"But that answers the question. She might have talked about it. She's written about you and Julia, right?"

Grant nods.

"So someone who was determined to learn about you could know these pieces about your life and what they mean. It could still be someone who's never met you. Was there anything in the tree?"

Grant's not ready to share the news about the cash. "There was nothing there."

Peter shrugs. "Then probably it's just someone trying to convince you that he knows about your life to be credible when he's accusing your family of lies."

The cash changes that, Grant thinks, but instead he says: "But how would he get Drew's email?"

"Email spoofing is super common," Peter says. "In this case the…Sender could find Drew's email any number of ways once he realizes Drew is a friend of yours. Then he could edit the email headers in the message to look like it came from Drew. Now, in the picture, he's got another email address…this Gmail address, with the random-looking numbers and letters. Did you see that?"

"Oh, yes," Grant says, as if he hadn't noticed it before.

Peter stares at him. "Well, have you tried emailing him at this Gmail address?"

"No," Grant lies. He doesn't look at Peter, staring at the screen.

"That's smart. You don't need to engage with this person. Sometimes these people are dangerous. Now, you clicked on this photo. It was a hyperlink that opened your browser and took you to a site, yes?"

"Yes. That's where the photo of the lady in the rain and the message about lies was. That's a stock photo, by the way." He notices that Peter is staring at the photo.

"Yeah, scammers use stock all the time," he says. "OK, when clicking on J. J. Watt took you to the site, the site could still display the lady-in-rain picture and the message, but it could have also installed malware on your laptop. That could be anything from monitoring when you're online to leaving a back door open where the bad guy can come in, see what's new on your computer, download it, and leave. You could have a little beacon hidden on your laptop now that tells the Sender everything about your laptop; it would barely be a blip in the bandwidth; you'd have to know to look for it."

"Can you find it?" He feels sick, someone peering into his life.

"Yes. I should tell you, if you connect or share with your parents' or sister's computers, your family's network could have been compromised, too."

"All right. Can you check mine? And can you see if you can find who sent me the email?"

"I can maybe find out the IP address, and then I can contact the company that owns that IP address. But I don't know if I can get a name. We'll see. It involves me using some trickery on them." Here Peter finally smiles a little. He looks a lot better when he smiles. More like Mike.

"How long will that take?"

"I don't know. We'll see. Will you let me know if you hear from them again? And don't click on any more pictures from friends."

"I will. And I won't. Thanks, Peter."

"I'll bring your laptop back soon," Peter says. "I want to thank you for something, though, Grant. You hanging with my dad. I appreciate it."

"You're not mad?"

"I hate fishing. He knows it. He goes with you and he has a good time. It's been hard since my mom died. I'm glad he has you for stuff like that."

"You went fishing with him yesterday, though."

"I make an effort. He fishes and I just sit there and we talk about school and what I'll do with my life and what I've learned about computers, although he'd rather talk sports or business. And now Danielle is gone. He really thought she was the next chapter in his life."

Grant feels a heaviness in his heart.

Peter clears his throat. "Dad loves me, even though we're opposites. I know that. We don't get to pick our kids. Well, your parents did." And Peter gives an odd little laugh.

"Yes," Grant says, smiling. "Although it was kind of random. It wasn't like they shopped among the cribs and picked me."

"Oh. I don't know how it works," Peter says. He slides Grant's laptop into his backpack. "I know you don't want to be without this, so I'll check it as quickly as I can."

"Thank you," Grant says, and he means it.

Peter nods. Then he says, "Keep an eye on your sister."

"What?"

"Do you think Ned's ever going to get over finding his mom dead? That's the kind of stuff that messes up a guy forever. I mean, forever. Everyone probably needs to back away from Ned for a bit."

Grant doesn't say anything. "Does Ned really like Julia?" he asks suddenly. "She really likes him, but she doesn't know how to help him."

Peter frowns. "He wouldn't tell me if he did. But mostly I think Ned likes Ned." He holds up his backpack. "I'll let you know what I find out."

"And don't tell Ned what I asked. Please. Julia will kill me."

"I won't. Don't worry." Peter gives him a rare smile, but it's reassuring.

"We're bringing you dinner tonight, Mom and me."

Peter laughs. "I won't have a report that quickly. Sir."

"I didn't mean...Sorry. I'm nervous about this."

"You should tell your parents," Peter says.

"Not now. Especially if it's just some stupid prank." But the money tells him it isn't.

"Yeah, when stuff calms down."

Peter heads downstairs. Mom gives him another awkward hug and he leaves.

"Did you finish your project?" Mom asks. Mom loves nothing more than hearing a project that's due is done. Even when their lives are in chaos.

"No. I will, later." Grant doesn't want Mom to notice he doesn't have his laptop. Too much explaining to do.

He goes upstairs and lies down on his bed. His mind is spinning. Everything Peter said about email spoofing and social media over-sharing and all that sounds entirely plausible. Why does he feel like the danger is close? Like he's being watched, right now?

Your family's network could have been compromised...Does that mean the Sender knows what's on Dad's computer, too? Is that how he knows what Dad did that was bad?

A cold finger of fear runs down Grant's spine. Peter will find the bad guy. He's just afraid of what the bad guy knows. *How can a kid like me*, Grant wonders, *take on a guy like that?*

He walks outside to the greenbelt. No one is along the trail. Are people scared now? He walks down toward the tree. He looks up in the nearby branches, wondering where he could hide a camera. Something to catch his mysterious benefactor in the act of leaving another object.

He kneels by the opening and sticks a hand in. He feels some-thing soft and silvery under his fingertips. He pulls out a bracelet, grimy with dirt. It looks to be silver, and along the band is a series of green stones. Emeralds? Or fakes? He doesn't know.

He holds the bracelet up to the light.

He kneels again and looks into the cleft of the tree. Nothing else is there.

He stands and returns to the house, glancing back at his tree. Money. Jewelry.

What is the Sender trying to tell him?

19

JULIA

From her bedroom window, Julia watches Peter Horvath leave. Something is up with Grant. Peter Horvath, the man of fewest words, helping a freshman with a comp sci project? She doesn't believe it. Like she doesn't believe Dad's story of a tumble down the creekside beating up his face, either. Something awful, something poisonous, has seeped into the air of the Pollitt house since Julia found Danielle's body. Like death itself, trying to find a new home.

She shakes off the morbid feeling as she watches Peter walk away.

Julia sits down at her computer with two objectives: find out who this Marland is that Ned is afraid of and take care of his business dealings while he's coping with the death of his mother. It feels like a step forward that she can never take back. This is not who she is; she is the good girl who should go tell her parents everything she knows, including about this Marland guy in the greenbelt. But if she does that, Ned's life is derailed and done, probably forever. Any mistake follows you forever. He was stupid, and he needs her to save him from his mistake.

She can do this. *You'll be smarter about this than he was*, she thinks.

First she searches for Marland in the Travis County Appraisal District. She knows to do this because she's heard her father mention doing it before, to see what homes in the neighborhood are worth, and it surprised her you could find out where someone lived so easily. There are several Marlands, but none own property in Winding Creek. Maybe his wife owns the property and doesn't use his surname? Or he was lying about being a neighborhood dad. But he knew about the proposed patrols—how? The neighborhood Faceplace page was supposed to be strictly private. If he hadn't heard there, then maybe Ned had told him, or he knew someone else in the neighborhood.

Ned was afraid of him. She searches Ned's friends list on social media; no Marland there.

So she goes to the Critterscape website. She knows Ned's log-in and password. From there she can see his game activity, and most important…his messages inside the game.

Deep breath. *You can do this.* Last week, when he had confessed to her what he'd done, she had first thought, *You're a complete idiot*, and then thought, *Well, this is sort of genius.* He has always had a swagger, a confidence, derived from thinking that the world of his video games could edge into the real world, where you got endless retries in your life.

She goes to the message center, where Ned—as CritterMaster99, his log-in—can exchange messages with other Critterscape players.

Ned has far more messages than one usually would.

She reads through them:

Looking for 5 Shockersquirrels?

Hey I need some Dangersaurs for later.

Need 10 Dangersaurs, 5 Sleeperdoodles, and 5 Boomdogs.

And so on and so on. She checks his "Critter" inventory—he only has a few of the digital creatures, certainly not enough for these proposed trades. But that's not what they are.

She calls Ned. He answers on the first ring.

"Where are you?" she asks.

"Mike is driving us to the airport to get my dad," Ned says. He sounds broken, miserable.

"You're going to send me a text," she says. "And you're going to tell me what the code names are for each of the prescriptions inside the game."

Silence. "I asked you not to mess with this." He can't say more because he's in the car with Mike.

"If you don't fulfill these orders, you're going to get into trouble. Is that why Marland is around? He's the guy who's supplying you."

"Please. My mom is dead and I can't deal with this right now."

"OK. Then I can tell everyone who messages you you're out of the business. That's one solution, Ned. Please, take it. You have to stop this."

In the background she can hear Mike saying something reassuring, clearly having no idea what the discussion is.

"Not now. Do nothing until we talk, OK? I don't want you to mess up my project."

"Good luck with your dad," she said, and she meant it. He hung up.

She waited and the text came: Shockersquirrels: Xanax. Boomdogs: Percocet. And so on, every Critter tied to a prescription drug. She made a list on a piece of paper and then went back through his messages. He had around seventy looking to buy in "Critter trades." No mention of drugs or money. Everything was coded to terms used in the game.

She felt sick. How could she get him out of this ring or scheme or whatever it was without destroying his future by going to the police? He'd told her last week because he'd needed a way out, he'd said. His words rang in her ears: *I can't tell my mom. This would kill her. And I can't let my friends deal with this guy. He's dangerous. How do I shut this down?*

Why would you even do this?

He said I could make a lot of money.

He who?

This guy I met. He had the supply; he needed the customers. The game would keep us from getting caught the way dumb kids dealing usually get caught via texting. He got me all the drugs once it took off. All I had to do was play the game and take the orders.

This guy was Marland, she suspected.

And they were supposed to talk about how to extricate him from this mess while playing Critterscape, in the early morning when no one was going to be around.

But you told me, Julia thinks, *and now you're my responsibility*. She couldn't let Ned twist in the wind this way. How did you shut down a drug ring without involving the police?

There had to be a way.

Do you think what I was doing had anything to do with...?

What if Danielle had found out? And confronted this Marland guy? And then...?

The strength goes out of her legs; Julia feels dizzy. No. That wasn't the reason. It couldn't be. And if it was, then Ned was in terrible danger.

But he had said nothing to the police. Nothing. He had a way out of this mess; his father would just take him away, to the safety of London or Ghana. Safety in distance. If she went to the police, she risked implicating Ned in a crime that would ruin his future, and maybe hers, and she had no proof of anything else. She could put her own family in danger. Marland didn't know her, except that she was Ned's friend.

But how had he known that?

She hasn't reported him to the police. She knows about this and she is silent. She could be named an accessory. She had gone on the internet. Keeping her mouth shut was called aiding and abetting, a misdemeanor, and if you were convicted of it you couldn't get federal financial aid for college. Assuming a college didn't immediately rescind your admittance. She was waiting to hear from Rice, Vanderbilt, Cornell, and Brown. She couldn't risk not getting in. She couldn't risk going to the police; it could ruin both their futures. No college. No career. Everything she'd done to prepare to apply for top schools wasted because of one mistake a friend made and because she decided to help him.

She has to somehow stop this. Extricate Ned, send him on his way overseas with his father, and forget this ever happened.

She acts before she loses her courage. She sends out a message under Ned's account: due to unexpected tragedy I am unable to continue play or trading. Thank you all. Good luck in the Critterscape. This is my final communication. She sends the message and then logs out.

Done. There. How hard was that? Her friend saved. Now she

just has to wait. This Marland guy will step into the breach, if he was some kind of dealer trading in prescriptions, and find some other kid, and he was welcome to it.

She imagines her mother's voice rattling in her head: *Make good choices. Be a good girl.* Was that possible to do all the time? Make every choice right in the heat of the moment or when you didn't have complete information? She was helping a friend out of the worst mess of his life at the worst time of his life. Wasn't that a good choice?

She feels uneasy. But now she's done what she's done and all with good intentions, and she believes that will be enough.

Ned could go collect his father, and then he would thank her. She'll catch him some rare, cool Critter in the game, in case he's mad, and he'll get over it. Mom would say quit worrying so much about what a boy thinks, but Ned isn't just a boy; he's special. He's worth fighting for.

Julia opens Critterscape on her phone, logged in under her own account…wondering if the game is going to feel ruined for her now, since they were playing it when they found Danielle on the park bench. The digital world appears: a delightful little glade, with a road that mirrors the street were her house is, and instead of murdered neighbors and troubled handsome boys and annoying parents, it's all sparkles and whimsy. Little creatures appear—a dancing pink dinosaur, a purple cat, a wood elf—and she uses her Critter nets to capture them, to rack up points, to add to her Critter zoo. For a few moments she forgets the nightmare. Then a little hand appears in the corner of the screen—she has a message from another player.

She clicks on the hand.

The first message is the one she sent out from Ned's account, to all his friends, including her. The second message is one she hasn't seen.

She doesn't have a ton of friends in the game, but she doesn't recognize this player name: MagickMan. She pages through her friends list: no, he's there. They've never exchanged game gifts or Critters, and she doesn't remember adding him. He shouldn't be on her friends list. But he is. Ned must have added him. He has her password.

She opens the message.

I think you wrote that message from our friend, Julia.

Her breath catches in her chest. Her game name is Pollittesse; you'd have to know her personally to know Pollittesse is Julia Pollitt.

She messages back: Who is this?

The blinking palm tells her this player is active and writing her back. Then the message:

You two don't just quit on me.

She stares at the phone, cold. You two. Like she was part of this. She's not. She writes in the message screen: Leave him alone. He can't do this anymore.

You're going to fix what you just did. I heard you're applying to some really demanding schools. What if they got an email about what you and Ned have been up to?

She shudders. She nearly drops the phone. I had nothing to do with this, she writes.

Anyone who can shut down the business is part of the business. You're an accomplice, Julia. Now what are we going to do about that?

20

IRIS

Iris wonders.

Kyle's lying to her. She can tell. Kyle is not a good liar. He's a big-hearted guy, not a man who easily deceives. And she doesn't believe that he fell down in the rough of the greenbelt. No alternate explanation makes sense. But she doesn't quite believe him.

Either someone attacked him or he got into a fight, a physical fight, with someone. All in the wake of Danielle's death.

Something is wrong. Obviously. Something is wrong all over the place.

Maybe he's just shaken. They're all shaken. None of them are right.

Kyle goes out to the backyard and Iris watches, where he can't see her. Then into the greenbelt.

She follows him outside. At a distance.

She watches him go off the trail, down toward the creek. She hangs back. He goes to a tree and kneels by it. Sticks his hand in. It's Grant's tree, the one he used to hide things in. It had made her so nervous because he'd be down there alone and there were sometimes water moccasins and she had a horror of him getting bitten. Now Kyle is using it. And peering into the tree now, as if he is expecting to find something there and he isn't.

She ducks back to their house so he won't spot her. What is he hiding? Why?

Her phone chirps with a text: Girls, we need to meet and mourn. Iris, we want to know if you're ok. In an hour at Trivet, don't dress up, let's just be there for each other.

Iris considers, then texts back: I'm OK and I'll be there. Love you all.

She could confront Kyle. And knowing him, he'll just seal up tighter. But whatever is wearing at him, he'll get tired of carrying it alone and he'll tell her.

Unless it's really, really bad. Like he knows something about Danielle. Like he did something about Danielle.

And that she doesn't want to know.

She showers, puts on a dressy, dark sweater and navy slacks. Back in the den, Kyle is sitting, watching television, a blank look on his face. Their gazes meet. She could say, *What were you hiding in Grant's old tree?*

But she doesn't. He looks away from her to the TV. His face has clearly taken more than one punch and they just aren't going to talk about it, and what does that say about them right now? She makes a noise in her throat, and he glances back at her.

"Wherever you fell in the greenbelt," she says, "maybe it ought to be marked. Like a sign that it's slippery or dangerous. I don't want it happening again to you. Or anyone else."

He nods. "I'll send an email to the greenbelt committee. I don't think we have to worry about it happening again."

She nods back, and for a moment she thinks, *Well, he really did slip. He really did fall. I can just tell myself that.* He stares at the television.

She goes upstairs to check on the kids. Julia's lying on her bed, holding a pillow. "I have to run an errand. Are you going to be OK for a bit?"

Her daughter looks at her with a mix of grief and terror, and something twists in Iris's heart. "Baby. What's wrong?"

"What's not wrong?" Julia says, putting her face in the pillow. Iris sits by her on the bed, puts a reassuring hand on her back.

"I know this is all so horrible. It will get better in time."

"You were her friend," Julia said. "Right?"

"Yes," Iris says, without adding *once*.

"You'd do anything for a friend, wouldn't you?"

"Nearly anything," she says. She pats Julia's back. "What friend is needing your help?"

"I don't know how to help Ned."

"You're there for him. You listen to him. You help him with his grief. You help him see that he can get past this. That's what a friend does."

Julia takes a deep breath. She seems like she's going to say more, but she doesn't. She only says: "We can get past this."

"I have to see my friends I had with Danielle. Are you going to be all right?"

"Yes," Julia says. "I need to finish reading a book for English. I'll do that, but it's hard to concentrate."

"Try, though," Iris says, then immediately regrets it. Julia says nothing more, and Iris eases the door shut. They need to ask a professional about how to help Julia. Down the hall she knocks on Grant's door. He's sitting on the bed, studying something on his iPad.

"I have to go out for a bit. Do you need anything?"

He stares at her like he's not sure how to answer, but finally he says, "No."

"What's wrong?"

His face is neutral. "You wouldn't ever lie to me, Mom, would you?"

"Lie to you." Iris says the phrase as though hearing it for the first time and it possibly being in a foreign language. "Why do you think I've lied to you?"

"I'm just asking. You wouldn't. I mean, lie about more than something like Santa Claus."

"Santa is real. I can't help what the rest of the world thinks." This is an old joke between them, but Grant doesn't smile. "No, baby, I wouldn't lie to you."

"All right," he says. His look is still neutral, but he keeps his gaze locked on her as she closes the door.

Her family, she thinks, will get through this. They'll figure it out. She goes down the stairs, a bit shaken, telling herself: his asking that, it didn't mean anything.

* * *

Iris backs out of the driveway, "Mom Channel" playing softly; the news crews are gone from in front of Danielle's house. She has a hunch and turns onto Mike's street, and yes, there they are. They found out where Ned was staying and that Mike was her boyfriend. She could strangle whoever told them. But they probably found it through social media, like Kyle suggested. She drives past; they don't look at her, not that they would know who she is.

She realizes if they're still there, this is a gauntlet she might have to run when she brings their dinner tonight.

She drives into Lakehaven, down Old Travis, turning into one of the larger shopping centers in the town. Trivet is a small coffee shop in Lakehaven, but it has held on in the face of chain-store saturation. Book clubs meet there, church groups, writer groups. It's owned by a pair of Lakehaven grads and is an institution in the town.

And it's where the moms who Danielle helped often meet. They call themselves the Mommy Club.

It surprised Iris how much international adoption occurred in Lakehaven. But she can count twelve families who have adopted from overseas. The reasons vary. Some feel a religious calling to bring a child home. Others can't conceive. Others already have children and decide to add one more. But once every couple of months (it has gotten more difficult as the children have gotten older), Danielle and her flock of moms she helped get together at Trivet to share stories, support one another, laugh. Iris knows many parents through her volunteering, but she thinks of this group as her real friends.

Susan, Georgina, and Francie are already there. Susan, a University of Texas professor of biochemistry, two children adopted from China. Georgina owns a jewelry store in Lakehaven, mother of six, one child adopted from Ghana. Francie, co-owner with her husband of an investment firm, three children adopted from Russia, older than Grant.

They're all there. They rise as one as she enters and embrace her in a group hug. Iris tells herself she must hold it together. Can't

cry. Francie starts crying, and Iris fights the urge. They're not crying for her. They're crying for Danielle. The last time they were
together was Halloween, several weeks ago, following their tradition of trick-or-treating with their international crew of kids, this
time in Iris and Danielle's neighborhood, even though most of the
kids were too old for it now. Iris remembers her and Danielle, bundled up against the unseasonable cold that night, walking together
to catch up to their friends who had already come by. Glasses of
wine and chocolate as they walked behind a knot of kids.

That seems forever ago.

The embrace breaks, and they sit. Susan gets Iris a mocha, her
favorite. Iris lets their talk wash over her. No one asks her, "How
are you?" or "How awful was it?" or any such thing. They know
it was awful. They know she's a wreck. That need not be discussed.
She sips at her coffee, and for the first time since she saw the body,
she feels herself relax, just the tiniest bit.

"Ned," Susan says.

"He's not good. It was horrible for him and Julia. His father is
coming in from London as we speak. It's awkward. Gordon hasn't
had nearly enough contact with him, and now he's his only parent."

"Ned is not going to be an easy kid to suddenly parent," Francie
says.

"What do you mean?"

"He's just a boundary pusher," Francie said. "Danielle found
some weed in his room, not much. And he's been with a crowd
Danielle didn't love—a couple of kids that got expelled from Lakehaven last year."

"I didn't realize," Iris said.

"Danielle didn't talk about it," Francie said. And Iris thinks,
Well, not to me.

"He might go back to London with his father," Iris says. "I
don't think he wants to go."

The three make various noises of dismay. "He can stay with us,"
Susan offers. "Through his last year of high school. We can do that.
I'll tell Roger. Surely his father doesn't want to take Ned away
from everything he knows."

Iris marvels at how Susan can make such an offer. Just take in a kid, sure. "Distance might be good," Iris says after a moment. "I was there when the police first talked to him. In an observation room. Ned said he was going to find out who killed her."

"What, like solve the case?" Georgina says with a wide stare.

"I guess."

"But this was a random attack in a park, right?" Francie says.

"Maybe not," Susan says. "The police should look at her client list, her acquaintances. Or people who didn't get a kid."

"You mean people Danielle rejected?"

"Not everyone passes muster with the home study or the background check. Danielle mentioned a weird couple a few months ago. It didn't work out, and they blamed her."

Iris hasn't thought of this, her mind a steady whirl of just dealing with Danielle's death. "But them falling short is not her fault."

"Blame the messenger." Susan straightens her eyeglasses. "You know how emotionally volatile her business could be. All those people left hanging when Russia cut off foreign adoptions, and I know some of them told her they'd have kids if she'd 'acted' faster. Like she could control Russian government policy or pride."

"Ned said she was arguing with someone on a phone he didn't recognize as hers." Ned said that in his statement. She shouldn't repeat it. But she has. She glances around, but no one's near them, except a boy on a laptop, but he has on big heavy headphones and is paying them no mind. Iris can, just barely, hear the thrum of his music.

"So she had a new phone."

"Another phone."

They all ponder the meaning of this.

"A boyfriend," Francie says. "A secret boyfriend."

"She wouldn't cheat on Mike," Iris says.

"I never got the Mike situation. They didn't seem a good match," Susan says.

"Mike adores her," Francie says.

"I'm sure he does. I'm talking about how she felt about him." Susan frowns.

"Mike is wonderful," Iris says, feeling she should defend Mike, who's taking care of Ned right now. Susan watches her, as if she wants to say more, but she doesn't.

"So, an unhappy client or a mystery man." Georgina sips her coffee.

"Why would she be on a phone her kid doesn't recognize with an unhappy client?"

"It'll be a man at the heart of this," Susan says. "It always is."

They sit, quiet, not disagreeing with her. Wishing it weren't so.

"We could find out," Francie says.

"The police are on it." Susan frowns.

"It might be a new phone…if someone was hassling her. Maybe she switched phones," Iris says. Carefully. "To avoid their calls."

"You think that couple that got turned down?" Francie asks. "She said the dad just lost his temper entirely, ranted and raved. He scared her. She didn't tell me their names. She didn't want to violate confidentiality."

"We could find out," Susan says, warming to the idea. "I mean, we can ask around. So many of her clients came to her by word of mouth."

"But why would they kill her now?" Georgina asks. "Why not then, when they were at their angriest?"

"I think," Iris says, "that this couple should be checked and eliminated, by the police."

"Surely they're going through her computer and her client list," Susan says.

"Still. We should find that name." Iris stands. "I'm making Ned and Mike dinner tonight, but I'll start on it after that."

Francie takes a deep breath. "Let us try to find out who this couple is that scared her. You've got your hands full."

Iris sits back down. Maybe the reason Danielle died has nothing to do with her family. The relief, the terrible guilty relief, hits her. She's shaking, visibly quaking, and then the tears start, and Francie is murmuring apologies and holding her, and then they're all holding her, crying, mistaking the reason for her tears.

21

KYLE

Iris has gone to have coffee with the Danielle Fan Club. Kyle is wrapping his head around the fact that the bloodied library bag he hid in the tree is now gone.

Taken. Someone has taken it.

He tries to convince himself that maybe some wild animal in the greenbelt smelled the blood and dragged it out of the tree.

Sure. That could be it. Right?

Maybe Grant is still using the tree. To hide stuff, and he found it. This is worse. Is his son going to take it to the police? It has Danielle's name on it. It has blood (his) on it.

He goes up to his son's room. Grant is lying on his bed, watching something on his iPad.

"Hey," he says.

"Hey."

"Everything all right?"

"Why does everyone keep asking me that?" Grant says.

"Mom's going to be home soon to cook dinner for Mike and Peter and Ned and his dad," he says. "You want to help her? You could take food to Mike." He knows his son admires Mike, enjoys spending time with him. It's as if Kyle earned nothing with all the diaper changing and the sleepless nights. He started working so much when Grant turned six, he frittered all the good-dad karma away.

"Sure, I'll help her," Grant says.

Kyle has no way to ask him about the library bag. His gaze dances around the room, wondering where Grant would hide it. But then he thinks, *This is ridiculous. Grant would tell us if he found something like that. Wouldn't he? Of course he would.*

"I have to run a quick errand," he says. "I'll be back before Mom is home. Will you all be OK here?"

Grant nods.

"Don't answer the door," Kyle says. "If it's the press."

"Yeah," Grant says.

"Anything you want to tell me?"

Grant's eyes widen slightly. "No, Dad," he says.

* * *

Kyle has to push the library bag out of his mind. If someone has found it and taken it to the police, they have no way of knowing it's his blood. No reason to test him for a match. Right?

But who would know to look in that tree? Grant and Iris, maybe Julia remembers it.

Or someone saw you hide the bag there and took it.

Not someone who loves you and might protect you.

Someone who was watching you.

He knows he can't be paralyzed by fear, so he must deal with the problem at hand. Now that he has the flash drive, Kyle is terrified to look at it.

He thinks he read somewhere that inserting the flash drive will create an entry on his computer's log that the particular flash drive had been inserted. He isn't sure how the log entry could be permanently erased. So. How is he going to do this?

He goes to an ATM and withdraws a few hundred in cash, all in twenties. He then drives over to South Austin to a Best Buy where he has never shopped and, using cash, buys a cheap laptop with a USB port. He sets up a false name as the user account on his new laptop. Sitting in the car, he slides the flash drive into the computer.

The data inside isn't what he thought it was going to be. The drive contains files but nothing about him or his family. There is one large spreadsheet, tabbed into months, from over fourteen years ago. This is old news. They appear to be a list of dates, numbers, and dollar amounts. The full amount comes to more than $200,000.

Kyle stares at the screen.

This might be perfectly legit. A normal record of payments made to her. All of the payments have a word next to them: either Lark or Firebird. In the next column are amounts of money, each ranging from a few thousand to nearly $800,000.

The figures next to Lark are smaller; the payments to Firebird are larger.

This is an old record of payments, but he has no idea what it's for.

He opens another folder. Pictures. Pictures of kids she's placed from Russia, smiling American families. Organized by surname. He goes to the subfolder marked POLLITT. Afraid of what he might see, unable to look away.

He opens the folder. Photos of all the miles of completed paperwork, organized, he presumes as an unofficial backup. This he skips through. Then pictures. Of him and Iris, boarding the first of their flights that took them to Russia. Danielle had taken these pictures. They're smiling, in a determined way. Not celebratory. It's too early to celebrate having Grant.

Pictures of them in Russia. Looking tired but thumbs up. Danielle told them to be quiet, to not be too "American"—this meant loud and assertive—to be controlled. This was a business trip.

Pictures at the orphanage. He felt the hair on the back of his neck rise. The buildings, choked in snow, the branches of the trees cloaked in white. In one photo a guard dog lopes around a corner, looking, hunting for trouble. An orphanage with guard dogs. Why? What were they keeping in? Who were they keeping out?

A picture of him waiting in the snow. No Iris around. Him staring at the building, a father waiting for his son-to-be. Pensive.

He remembers to breathe.

He skips through the other photos. Pictures of them outside

the courtroom. Pictures of Iris holding a naked Grant, about to put him into the clothes they brought for him. Pictures of them in the courtroom, before the judge came in—Danielle wouldn't have dared take a picture with the judge present—Iris and Kyle sitting at attention, posture erect, trying to look deserving and capable. Sober and parental. Like they could be trusted with Grant's life.

He moves through the pictures: leaving the courtroom, Grant in their arms now. Smiling as they boarded the plane. Waving his little hand goodbye to his motherland. Grant looking sleepy and confused. Iris weighed down with bags of clothes and bottles for the long series of flights to take them back to Texas.

The next picture stops him and he ejects the drive, not wanting to see it.

Drops of blood, on pristine snow.

22

TRANSCRIPT FROM INTERVIEWS FOR *A DEATH IN WINDING CREEK* BY ELENA GARCIA

Elena Garcia: So much has happened in the days since you arrived in the United States after your ex-wife's death. I'm sorry for your loss.

Gordon Frimpong: Thank you.

Garcia: Let's talk about your relationship with your son, your relationship with Danielle.

Frimpong: Yes. You have to understand, I followed Danielle's requests regarding our son. She didn't want me around, and I had my own life to lead. People are so judgmental until I have a chance to explain.

Garcia: I'm not judging.

Frimpong: I just found it very strange that it was written about in the news accounts that I had not spent much time around my son. What did that have to do with Danielle getting herself killed? Nothing.

Garcia: "Getting herself killed" is an unusual way to put it. Like you think she was responsible.

Frimpong: Well, pardon an infelicitous turn of phrase. Danielle was a wonderful woman, and no, I'm not blaming her. I'm still in shock. It's turned all our lives upside down.

Garcia: How did you meet?

Frimpong: I had banking clients in London who had a cousin in the United States. This cousin wanted to do a foreign adoption from Ghana, which is my homeland. Danielle handled it. It went very well. She was in London on a connecting flight to Moscow and she had an overnight. I was based in London then. They asked me to take her out for a drink or dinner if she felt up to it. I'm ashamed to say I viewed it as a chore, but I met her and we hit it off. She was a delight.

Garcia: And then you dated for a while?

Frimpong: Less than a year before we married. Obviously we rushed a bit into things. The romance of it all. But she got pregnant with Ned and my parents are very old-fashioned and I didn't like to let them down. So we got married, and I went into it very optimistically but it didn't work out. No regrets though, as we stayed good friends—I would like to stress that we were always good friends—and we got Ned.

Garcia: So she returned to the United States?

Frimpong: She had kept working in the US. The travel was a strain on our marriage. But her clients were in the US and mine were all in London or Ghana. Working in Austin was never an option for me. And our work was so important to us both.

Garcia: Had you been in touch with them recently?

Frimpong: I'd gotten an email from her the week before, just updating me, expressing some concern about Ned and his lack of focus in school. He was running around with some kids who'd gotten kicked out of Lakehaven for drinking and drugs and ended up in private school. We emailed more than we talked. I sent checks for Ned's support; I invited them often to London, or to visit my parents in Ghana, but they usually said no. I got to see him about once a year, either in the summer or at Christmastime. I know Ned resented me. I wasn't around, and when I wanted him around was when he wanted his holidays with his friends. I couldn't win with him. I should have done more, but one gets so busy with life.

He wanted his own life so he can't resent me for having
mine. Clearly if I had been there, he would have stayed on a
more productive path than the one he was on. Danielle let
him down. She was too permissive.

Garcia: So what do you think happened?

Frimpong: A murderer stalking this neighborhood park seems
unlikely to me. I don't think she ran afoul of someone who
was just out hunting a victim, like a serial killer. I think she
made an enemy.

Garcia: Who? Or what sort of enemy, rather?

Frimpong: *(pauses)* She told me once that she saw people at
their greatest and at their worst. Their greatest when they
got the child she'd helped them adopt. I can imagine those
were golden moments for her.

Garcia: And the worst?

Frimpong: That, she didn't explain. But she told me in an
email that a former client and neighbor had her worried. I
assume she meant Kyle and Iris Pollitt. I'd met them before
on a visit to Austin; their children were friends with Ned.

Garcia: Define "worried."

Frimpong: I feel that perhaps, at some level, she thought she'd
made a mistake in getting them a child. Even though it had
been years.

Garcia: That's a very strong charge. Are you saying she suggested to you that Kyle and Iris Pollitt should not have been
given their son?

Frimpong: I think Danielle would not stand by if one of the
kids she helped get adopted found himself in a dangerous or
unstable situation.

Garcia: Did she tell you that was the situation?

Frimpong: Did she have to spell it out? We weren't married
long, but we were married and I knew her well. I knew how
careful she was in speaking about a parent. But imagine
you're her and you decide one of your client families was
wrongly approved. What do you do? I can tell you Danielle
wouldn't have stayed quiet.

Garcia: Are you suggesting she would have taken steps to in-
volve the authorities in removing a child from a former
client?

Frimpong: I am.

Garcia: Did you get along with the Pollitts?

Frimpong: What does that matter?

23

JULIA

Julia watches the press camped in front of the house. They've returned because Gordon Frimpong, upon arrival, has said he and his son will stay in his son's home. The house is, after all, not a crime scene, despite that it might hold the clues to whoever killed Danielle and why, and the investigative team has done its work.

The chicken enchiladas are in a casserole dish, hot against her palms. Her mother has taken over a dish to Mike and asked her to take dinner for Gordon and Ned. Julia takes a deep breath and walks from her house to Ned's house, going around the press, ignoring them. One reporter peppers her with questions about having found the body and she ignores the woman. Julia knocks on the door.

Ned answers, and the press call out to him a barrage of questions. He ignores them, and she hands the foil-covered casserole dish to him. Then she turns to face the reporters. "What's wrong with you?" she asks. "His mother is dead. If he has something to say, he'll say it to people who aren't standing in the street. I know you're just doing your job. Isn't there another way to do this? And by the way, I'm a minor, and my parents and I don't give you permission to air what I'm saying to you." She turns back and goes inside.

"Wow," Ned says.

"Hey," she says. She wants to tell him about what she's done in the game and about Marland threatening her, but then she sees his father looming in the dining room that connects the foyer and the kitchen.

"Hello, Julia," Gordon Frimpong says. "I am so glad to see you. It's been a long time. What a beautiful young woman you've become." He has a deep voice. Tall, a wiry but strong build; she guesses he was a looker when he was younger. He still is, if you're into older guys. She can see echoes of his face in Ned's. Stylish glasses. Expensive sweater and slacks. He doesn't look like he's exhausted from a flight overseas or jet-lagged. He looks like someone ready to question her.

"Thank you," she says. "I'm sorry to see you again under these circumstances."

"It is terrible," he agrees in his courtly voice. "But how fortunate Ned is to have you as a friend." He takes the enchiladas dish from Ned, carefully balancing the salad bowl atop it.

"I'm also making you dessert. Cookies. Nothing fancy. They're still in the oven. My dad will bring them over."

"Ah. And how is your little adopted brother? Grant, yes, the one from Russia?"

Even when she doesn't always get along perfectly with Grant, Julia is sensitive to any suggestion that he is somehow not her true brother. "Yes, my brother is well," she says.

"This is so thoughtful of you all. What do you say, Ned?"

"I was about to thank her, Papa," Ned says. Ned gives her a quick wink, which his father can't see. She doesn't wink back.

"Forgive me, Julia. I'm rather a solitary old lion, and I tend to think of Ned as a small child when he's nearly a man." He goes into the kitchen, and Ned rolls his eyes and he and Julia follow.

"I think there are a few less reporters than there were before," Julia says, thinking that it's best to find a sliver of something positive right now.

"I'm not really familiar with enchiladas, but this smells delicious." Gordon places the dish on the granite counter. It's beyond strange—this isn't this man's kitchen, and Danielle is dead and gone. All the food in the refrigerator is stuff she bought and will never eat. The suddenness of her passing hits Julia like a fist.

She takes refuge in talking about the food. "It's not too many jalapeños. Mom knew you weren't used to them."

"How very thoughtful," Gordon says, and she wants to say, *Do you always sound like you talk from a book?* But she doesn't. "It's so appreciated. I hope I will get the chance to thank your mother for her many kindnesses to my son. And to Danielle."

"We all loved Danielle," Julia says. Ned looks as if the very life is draining out of him.

"Yes," Gordon says. "Well, I have some phone calls to make. There are so many arrangements to handle. Would you like to stay for dinner?"

Ned gives her a pleading look, but she says, "I can't, and the two of you should have private time together." She has a lot to say to Ned, but not in front of his father. Looking at him, she feels this weird mix of longing and anger and frustration.

"Well, if you change your mind, you're welcome." Gordon nods and goes into the kitchen, and in a moment they hear him talking quietly, presumably on his phone.

"His girlfriend back in London," Ned says quietly. "He calls her about every fifteen minutes. Short leash."

"I shut down what you were doing inside the game. For now. But I got an angry message. From MagickMan. Is that your friend Marland?"

Ned's face is like stone. "Why would you interfere?"

"He says if he can't deal with you, he'll deal with me. That you can't quit. And that means I can't quit, although it's got nothing to do with me."

The smiling face that winked at her is gone. Now he just stares at her blankly. "I'm going back to London with my father. It's decided."

She stares at him. She thought his reaction to all this would be *Oh let me handle it* and he would be full of his fire to stay here in Lakehaven.

"When?"

"After the funeral. Or whenever the police say I can go."

"Don't you want to stay here?" *With me, with your friends*, she thinks but doesn't add.

His voice is barely a whisper. "The police found a bit of blood here. In the house. They cut up some carpet. I heard them talking, explaining to my dad, when we came back here. So I think my mom was taken from here and killed in walking distance, and no, I do not want to stay here if that is true. Do you understand? It's like living in her grave."

He's leaving, but he can't be leaving you to deal with his mess. Not on purpose. Right? "What do you want me to do?"

"Nothing. Nothing at all. Just stay out of it. I'll get Marland to leave you alone. And keep your mouth shut."

But he doesn't know what to do; she can see it in his face. It's weird; she thinks of times when they were kids, when someone teased or bothered her, and Ned—not exactly a brawny physical specimen—was the one who would stand up for her. Always. She feels a hot mix of rage and anger and hurt and betrayal.

"I need to go get the cookies, or see that Dad hasn't burned them." Her tone is dulled. And Ned, right now, keeps looking at a spot near her left foot.

The doorbell rings. Ned goes to answer it, returns with Kyle, and a plate of cookies. He and Gordon shake hands. Kyle gives condolences. "I thought I'd walk Julia back through the press scrum," Kyle says.

"They didn't bother me," Julia says. But she doesn't want to linger. The silence is awkward.

"You look like you were in a fight with someone," Ned says suddenly to Kyle.

"I fell. In the greenbelt. Jogging," Kyle says.

"I could use a good run. Can you tell me what route you take?" Gordon asks.

Kyle tells him, standing at the back window, pointing to the greenbelt, his voice sounding just a shade odd. "Yes, you can just run along there...The path follows the creek. There are mile markers..."

"Well, I know metric," Gordon says.

It's not the time for a joke, and the comment feels leaden and dense in the air, and no one says anything more but goodbye.

* * *

Locked in her bathroom, Julia opens her phone, starts the game, and rereads the message from MagickMan. She sends to him: I'm not part of this. You'll have to take it over. He can't do it anymore.

You are part of this because you're part of the solution. You and I have to talk. Bring Ned if you can. Meet me at the abandoned house. Tonight. 8 PM. I'll make it worth your while.

She knows where he means. Why won't this man leave her alone? She closes the game.

24

FROM IRIS POLLITT'S "FROM RUSSIA WITH LOVE" ADOPTION JOURNAL

2002

I was trying not to be paranoid.

The warning woman wasn't on the plane.

Blur: airport, customs, nice hotel in Saint Petersburg. Kyle unpacking, not looking at me. "Don't be mad at me, Iris," he said.

"You didn't believe me." I got under the sheets, turned my back to him. I craved sleep; I wanted to look my best for Grant, for the officials, for anyone who was watching. They would not shake me.

"I did. I just wanted to calm you down, and if I went along with what you were saying, we might not have made our flight. How would that have looked? American couple misses flight to adopt child because of airport fight with weird stranger?"

I closed my eyes. He snuggled next to me. I felt his warm breath on my neck.

"I love you," he said.

"I love you, too," I said. My eyes felt hot. (Your dad is the love of my life, and it's important to me that you know that.) "I think that woman sat near us in the airport café. She might have been one of those Russians who disapprove of Americans adopting Russian babies. Remember I told you about that article I read about it?" I hadn't, but Kyle wouldn't remember and wouldn't want to say he doesn't.

"OK," he said, his lips close to my ear.

"So I think she heard us talking about adoption and decided to mouth off to me when I was alone."

"Oh. OK, babe. People are crazy."

"People are crazy," I repeated. Then we talked a little more and fell asleep curled into each other. I woke up four hours later. I got dressed and brushed my teeth. I was still tired, but I was ready to face the day.

I checked my stash of, well, bribes. Filling one of my suitcases was an array of gifts to smooth our road: expensive bags of coffee, cartons of cigarettes, makeup from a really nice store in Austin. Boxes of chocolates. Stuffed toys—cartoon characters I hoped Russian children would know, as well as safer choices: plush little otters and ponies and kittens. It was hard to know what to get for the older children—all the board games I found are in English. I didn't know if they have computer game consoles. I imagined not. I didn't have time to go shopping for more here. We were expected at the orphanage at a certain time and we could not be late. I moved the goodies into a pair of nice-looking Louis Vuitton knockoff totes, which would also double as gifts.

Kyle was showering again because even after four hours of sleep he had serious bedhead, and I went down to the ornate lobby to get coffee for us both. I needed more sleep, but that wasn't going to happen.

Across the lobby I saw Danielle. She had her back to me. Talking to a man, not our driver, Feliks, maybe the interpreter that GAC is providing—even with Danielle having an OK command of Russian, it was better to have a professional interpreter, and a Russian one.

I started to go say hello, but something stopped me. I watched them. Danielle did not smile or chat. The way the man spoke to her, waving his arms a little bit, it was intimidating. I didn't like it, and I started walking toward them.

The man was quite a bit taller than Danielle, thin, a face of sharp edges along his nose, his jaw, even his glare. Dark hair. He wore a good suit, a silver tie. Then he gave Danielle a smile, not a warm one, but apparently the argument was over. He turned and left.

I saw her hand go back to the seat behind her, as if she leaned against it. Then she turned and saw me, offered a smile. I hurried the rest of the way across the lobby.

"Are you all right?" I asked.

She nodded.

"Is everything all right?" Meaning: Is our adoption in danger?

"Oh. Yes. That man is an official. I was meeting him about another adoption case. Nothing to do with yours." Her voice shook a little, but she put on a smile.

"Danielle, don't lie to me. Did he scare you?"

"Oh, no. These guys, they fume, they demand. A bad temper is part of their style. He just caught me before I'd had coffee and so I wasn't quite ready for him." She offered a stronger smile, a shrug.

"Then let me buy you some coffee and we'll head out to the orphanage."

She nodded. There was a swank-looking lounge at the other end of the lobby, currently serving coffee, espresso, and hot tea instead of cocktails. I ordered three coffees.

Why didn't I believe Danielle? A finger of paranoia ran along my spine. I shouldn't tell you all this, but here we are and I am. I thought you should know it. I thought the paperwork was honestly the hardest part about this. But now I think something worse is happening, and I don't understand it. All we wanted now was our son. Russia picked him for us. Why did it feel like something was closing in on me? I thought this was going to be a day of joy. I'm meeting my son—we're meeting our son.

I told myself to put all this worry aside and enjoy today. It would be a great day.

Through the glass windows I saw the dark-haired man with the silver tie. He was on the street, talking on a phone. He frowned. He gestured. His face wasn't so impassive anymore. Then he turned off the phone, tucked it into his pocket. A Mercedes SUV pulled up by the curb. A huge young man got out from the passenger side, opened the door, and the man with the silver tie got in the back. They drove off.

An adoption official? I thought. In that kind of car? With a hulking bodyguard? Then I remembered I had a suitcase of "gifts" (otherwise known as bribes). I knew this was how Russia operated. But it unsettled me. That man didn't look like someone you wanted to have as an enemy.

While I waited for the coffee orders, I scanned the lobby for her. The warning woman. No. This was ridiculous. This woman, this stranger, wasn't going to ruin this glorious day for me, for Kyle, for our soon-to-be Grant. I took a deep breath. I got myself centered. I had to be Iris Grant Pollitt, supermom, songwriter, wife, woman who feared nothing and no one. I went to the entrance and looked out on the cold, gray day.

"Russia, here I come," I thought to myself. "I'm going to take a prize from you."

25

IRIS

Mike looks bad to Iris. Gaunt, tired, pale, as if Danielle's death has sunk into him like an illness. He opens the door and she walks in with the dinner, the one she cooked and split between him and Ned and Gordon, with Grant following her, carrying the side dishes. The house is quiet and dark: no sound of television, or music, or anything but the absence of Danielle.

"How are you holding up?" she asks, setting the casserole dish down on the counter.

Mike is giving a sideways hug to Grant. "I am just taking it hour by hour."

"How's Peter?"

Mike shrugs. "He has a project to work on…He throws himself into that. It is avoiding how he feels, but if that is what works for him…?"

Grant bites his lip, which Iris notices.

Mike says, "How is Julia? I am worried for her. The shock."

"She's all right. She's mostly worried about Ned."

"Ned," Mike says, shaking his head. "His father is not good medicine right now. Gordon is more interested in doing what looks right than what is right for Ned."

"Can I stay here with Mike and Peter for a bit, Mom? Please?" Grant asks.

"Well, that's up to Mike," Iris says. "He might not feel up to company right now."

"Yes, fine, of course. Just for a little while. Then I'll eat and try to sleep. I didn't sleep last night." Mike pats Grant's shoulder.

"OK, then." Iris leaves, and while walking home she gets a text from Francie: Call me. I found out who threatened Danielle.

26

GRANT

Mike makes himself a cup of hot tea in the microwave, heating the water, dropping in a tea bag, then stirring strawberry jam into the mug.

"That's weird," Grant said.

"That is how some people drink tea back home. My brother would keep the jam in his mouth to sweeten the tea. Or we put in honey."

"I'm sorry about Danielle."

"I know. Maybe, when a few days pass, I will go fishing again. You can come with me, OK? If you want."

"OK," Grant said. Mike drank his tea, and Grant helped himself to a soda from the refrigerator.

"Is your sister really all right?" Mike asked.

"I don't think so, but we all have to say we are fine. Why is that?"

"It's just what people do."

"Don't people care how you really are?"

"People mostly care about politeness. After my wife died, people would ask how I was, and even before I answered they were looking over my shoulder, bored. People are odd, *chlapec*."

"Peter said you were going to marry Danielle."

"Maybe. We talked about it a couple of times; once Peter heard us. She didn't want to get married again. I'm not sure how Peter would have reacted to me marrying."

"Didn't he like Danielle?"

"Oh, yes, of course. But it is a huge change to go from Dad's girlfriend to stepmother."

"Are you really, truly going to stay in Austin? Peter's graduating in a few months and maybe he'll want to go back to Canada and you'll go with him."

Mike looks at him with a sad, knowing smile. "Little man. Would it make you sad if I left?"

"Yes. I don't want you to go. I want us to go fishing, and—" *And all the things Dad doesn't have time to do with me because he works all the time.*

"Sometimes...I think I'll go back to Canada with Peter. Or even back to Slovakia. My money would last a lot longer there than in Austin, when I want to retire." He sits down across from Grant. "But, Grant, you have your parents here. If I leave, it really won't matter. You understand? Your father and your mother love you very much."

"Yeah," he says, but he lets the tone of doubt shine through.

"Do not be giving me the whole 'they don't understand me' stuff," Mike says. "You know that's not so."

"You listen to me, but they don't."

"We are friends. But I am friends with your parents, too, and so I will listen to you but not listen to you complain about them. You are the center of their world, you and Julia."

"Peter should hang out with my dad, and they could silently work on their endless projects and you and I could go fish. It's a better arrangement." And Grant knows as soon as he says this he shouldn't, that it's somehow unfair to both Peter and his father. But, to him, it's true.

"If everyone was exactly like their parents, how dull the world would be," Mike says, trying to lighten the moment.

Grant takes a deep breath. "I want to tell you something, but I shouldn't. Not now. Not with everything you're dealing with. Did Peter tell you what I asked him for help with?"

Mike slowly shakes his head, and Grant remains silent. Grant can hear the quiet ticking of the clock in the breakfast nook. It's an old timepiece Mike brought from Slovakia. He laughed at Grant when Grant once told him he wasn't sure his family owned a clock, what with clocks already in their phones and ovens and cable boxes.

"You tell me and make me forget my troubles, OK?"

"Someone emailed me anonymously. They told me to look somewhere I used to hide toys and stuff. In the woods. I went there and they'd left a note for me. It said Mom and Dad were lying to me."

"Lying about what?"

"I don't know." He drums his fingers on the table, nervous.

For a few moments Mike is silent. "Why send you to the tree? Why not just tell you in the email?"

"I think they wanted to show me they know about my life. You'd have to know us pretty well to remember that tree was my hiding place."

"Was there anything else in the tree?"

Grant bites at his lip. He doesn't think he should mention the money. He doesn't want the money, but he doesn't want to give it up.

Mike says, "You're not telling me something."

"There was money. A thousand dollars in cash. I didn't tell Peter this part. He's looking at my laptop to see if he can trace the email. Don't be mad. I asked him not to tell you."

Mike blinks. "What...? Why would someone be giving you a thousand dollars?"

"To prove that they're serious."

"How long ago did this happen?"

Grant swallows. "The morning Danielle was found. I mean, even as it was happening. I was by the tree when the police sirens started."

Mike drags a hand across his unshaven chin. "We have to tell your parents."

"What if they really have lied to me?"

"It's easy for some anonymous person to be accusing them of lying."

"But why would they? What reason would the Sender—that's what I call this guy—have?" Grant says.

"Your parents may know that."

"Which is why we can't say anything."

"I am not comfortable keeping this from Iris and Kyle," Mike says. "I can't."

"Please. I know Peter will be able to find out something and then we can tell them together."

"Peter says he can track the email?"

"He might be able to find their internet provider and then their address. We have to see."

"All right. So, what, you want to wait and talk to your parents about this after Peter finds out more information?"

"They could deny this. They could tell me anything and I don't know anything, so I don't know if it's truth or lie."

"Your mom and dad are not liars. You know this."

"But the Sender gave me a thousand dollars to prove their point; it must mean something." He doesn't mention the bracelet. Or what the Sender said about Dad having done something bad. It's all wrapped up together, but he can't tell Mike that part. He can't make his father look bad.

Mike is silent for ten long seconds. "I'll stay quiet until we see what Peter finds. But then we tell your parents right away."

"I didn't know what to do." His sense of relief in having told an adult is palpable. "But I'm trusting you not to say anything."

"I'm glad you told me," Mike says. "Do you want some of this food your mama brought me?"

"No." Grant wipes his hands on his jeans, feeling sweaty. He has a hunch Mike will call his parents the moment he leaves.

"You are sure you have told me everything? So he said your parents lied. Did he say anything about Danielle?"

"No. Nothing."

Now Mike's face is grim. A man who lost the woman he loved. "Are you sure? I need to know if this person knows something about Danielle."

"Nothing. I swear."

"If you tell me this, I believe you."

Grant just nods in agreement so it feels less like he's lying. "Can I talk to Peter, see if he's found anything?"

"He'll call you when he knows something. He doesn't like to be disturbed when he's working." There's something sour and sad in Mike's voice now, and Grant realizes he's made a mistake. He's held back, and Mike realizes it.

He has made Mike suspicious of people he trusts. What if Mike or Peter find the Sender and the Sender tells them the bad thing his father did?

Mike might want his own revenge.

"OK, I'll go home now, Mike," he says in a small voice. "Please don't tell my parents this. Not yet."

Mike doesn't say anything now.

Grant walks home in the fading light. He glances back, and Mike is watching him from his front door. Mike raises a hand in a wave. But he's not holding a phone in his hand, calling Mom or calling the police. Not yet.

He has never done this to his parents, turned to a different adult in an hour of need. He's never needed to. But he can't push away the thought in his head.

He thinks if Mike reads the threat against his dad in the email, he'll know it's a lie. He'll dismiss it.

Dad is one of Mike's best friends. But what if he doesn't think it is a lie? What has he done to his own father?

27

JULIA

The abandoned house. It's surprising that in a neighborhood of homes all worth well above a half million, there's one that often stands empty. In Winding Creek you say the words "that house" and people know which one you mean. Among the well-maintained yards and the immaculate porches, *that house* sits there, like a child alone every day at a school lunch table.

That house, at the end of the lane.

No one's living there now. It used to be the Carlyle house, back when Roy and Laurie lived in it, before Roy left Laurie for his assistant at his advertising firm and Laurie took an overdose of sleeping pills. It didn't kill her, but it left her in limbo, a coma that she's been in for two years. Roy and the new wife moved to Houston because he couldn't live with the silent shaming of his neighbors. He never sold the house. Is he keeping it for Laurie in case she wakes up? Or for his two kids, who will always hate him? Maybe he thinks giving them the house they grew up in will buy him their love. Or out of a sense of guilt? No one knows.

The house usually sits empty, except when Roy's nomadic brother moves in for a few weeks, sometimes for a couple of months. This often happens at Christmas and Easter. The lawn gets cut regularly by a work crew, but nothing can make the house look lived in except people actually living there. Roy's brother moves back and forth between Austin and Albuquerque, and no one knows quite what his business is.

What matters is that the house is empty, and Ned Frimpong gave her a key just minutes before they found his mother's body, back when the world was still full of promise.

He used to babysit for the Carlyles. Laurie gave him a key and Roy forgot that he had it in the wake of their overwhelming tragedy. Ned forgot he had it, too, until he needed it.

Ned appears to have forgotten her as well; he's ignoring her texts and her voicemails. Or maybe his father's taken away his phone. She's scared to go to this meeting by herself, but this is the only way to find a path out of this for her and Ned.

The house has a back deck. She goes up its steps, carefully, trying to make sure the wood doesn't creak. She doesn't want a neighbor to hear her. She opens the back door with the key and goes inside. She's there before Marland. The rooms are still furnished—a sofa, chairs, a few books on the shelf. The power is on, still paid for; she hears the gentle hum of the heater. She doesn't dare turn on a light; the neighbors would think the no-madic brother was back, but there's no car in the driveway and they might investigate or call the police. She wonders if Laurie Carlyle might ever wake up and wander back in, unaware of the time she's lost, unaware that the house sleeps as well.

She hears a noise.

Someone is already here.

She sees him in the doorway leading to the kitchen.

"Hello, Julia. Thank you for coming. It looks like Ned couldn't make it."

She doesn't say anything to that.

"Did he lead you on? Encourage your feelings? He seems the type."

What does this man know about her and how does he know it? She finds some courage and uses it in her voice. "And what would you have done if I'd brought the police and they arrested you for trespassing?"

"I'm a professional. I would have submitted myself to arrest, my lawyer would have me out in a matter of hours, and then you and I would still have to come to an understanding."

"I can't do what you want me to do. I can't be your point of contact for these drug sales."

"It's risky to approach someone else. You already know the business."

"Only because he confessed it to me and I tried to talk him out of it, mister, please," she says, her voice rising.

"But you still helped him. You couriered, what, merchandise four times for him."

"He didn't tell me that's where I was driving him until later." She was mad at him about that, but he shrugged it off, telling her as long as she hadn't seen the drugs or touched any cash, she wasn't involved. She was pretty sure now a lawyer or police officer would disagree.

"Then it's his word against yours, isn't it?"

"Please. I want out."

"I just need you for a little while. Ned's been the middleman. I need to be...not dealing directly with consumers. They'll trust a fellow student. Me, not so much. But you, you'd be golden. No one would suspect you."

"I can't. I won't tell the police on you, for Ned's sake, for my sake, but I can't be involved. I shut it down for Ned."

"You're going to restart it," Marland said in a steady voice. "You have his account password for the game."

"Fine, yes. And I'll give it to you if you'll leave me out of all this."

"What do you think happened to his mother?" Marland asked suddenly.

The shift scares her. She's alone in this house with this man. Her parents and most of the neighborhood are at a meeting about security and the Danielle investigation right now. If she screams, likely no one will hear her.

She doesn't answer him.

"It's an absolute tragedy," Marland says. He sips at his bottle of water, offers her a cold one on the counter. She just shakes her head. "I understand she was an adoption consultant. There must have been so many families she brought joy to. But, see, there's one family that would be really upset with her. Yours."

"What…?"

"I mean, Ned pulls you into this business. Even on the edge, it's bad for you if you're caught. You'd be arrested. You'd be charged. You probably can't get a lawyer as good as mine."

She waits. She tries to remember to breathe.

"What if your dad or mom found out about that and went to talk to Danielle about it? Maybe at some time when you and your brother and Ned wouldn't be around to witness it?"

The air has all gone from the house. Marland stands like something out of space and time. "You're just making this up."

He holds up a phone and turns the screen toward her. A video. She sees her front porch, a dark figure emerging from the house in her father's coat, hood up, walking to Danielle's house, and Danielle coming out in her coat and scarf and the two of them walking together. Toward the park.

"That's not real," she says.

"It is," he says. "I lucked into your dad showing himself, what with keeping an eye on Danielle so she didn't interfere. So, if I show this to the police, your father has a problem. If I don't, no one has a problem. I need a kid in this operation. You're the only one Ned confided in. Be mad at him, not me." His voice softens. "It won't be so bad. I'll keep all your earnings in an account. That account will be the front for a small company that ends up giving you a full scholarship to the college of your choice. You'll never have to touch the money; your parents will never know. If there's no money to trace back to you, you'll likely be safe."

Likely, she thinks. "There is another explanation," Julia says. "My dad would never hurt her. Or anyone. I know him. I know the man he is."

"You think you do, but people disappoint us all the time. To protect you, he'd kill. Nearly every parent would."

She thinks quickly. The whole point was to extricate herself from this mess. But everything has changed. She has to get that video from this man, destroy it and every copy he might have. And she can do that only by getting closer to Marland.

Choose and change the course of your life, she thinks.

"I want Ned's phone he used to contact me in exchange for this video," Marland says. "And then we can peacefully coexist."

"Ask Ned for it."

"His mother took it from him and Ned hasn't found it. I can't exactly be around him right now and he can't come to me."

And did you kill her before you could get that phone back? Julia's terrified. But this is her chance.

"All right," she says. "I'll help you."

28

IRIS

Iris gets home and calls Francie back. She doesn't have long to talk. There's a community meeting tonight at the Winding Creek pool clubhouse about the investigation and security in the neighborhood. Mike is speaking at it, as are the investigators from Travis County and Lakehaven PD.

"I found the family that threatened her," Francie says. "Their name is Butler. Steve and Carrie Butler."

Butler. She's heard the name before, but she doesn't remember where. *Think. Think.*

"How did you find them?"

"I remembered she complained about them in an email to me and I found it from months ago. I'll forward it to you."

It arrives in her in-box seconds later, and Iris scans it:

Yeah, this older couple was mad about being declined. Steve and Carrie Butler. They were just problematic. China and Uganda both said no and I think it took them really by surprise. They don't know what they want to do yet, but they're blaming me. My heart breaks for them but they don't get to be terrible to me. This isn't my fault. In other news Ned is about to make me tear out my hair, but life with a teenager, even so how lucky I am to have him.

"Should I give this to the police?" Francie asks.

Iris thinks. "No," she says after a moment. "I will, if that's OK. I already know the detective. It'll be easier coming from me."

Francie says, "I looked the Butlers up on Faceplace. He works for a software company, and she's a pediatric nurse. They should have been stellar candidates."

"But they weren't. Did she say why?"

"No. I was surprised she even told me their names. Confidentiality—you know that was crucial to her."

"Yes," Iris says in a flat tone.

"I think she told me their names because if something happened to her, someone else would know they had threatened her."

"But had they? Threatened her? Or just been mad at her?"

"Look at the email."

Iris reads the end of it:

Hey thanks for listening to me vent. It's fine. They're disappointed and I'm disappointed for them but not everyone that asks us for help is a good match for overseas adoption and I think that they just don't want to accept the verdict. We tried to prep them best we could, help them adjust their thinking. I'm only telling you this not to bring up my name if you cross paths with them. I'm their least favorite person right now. Just so you know. I wish them well.

"There's no other time she mentioned them to you?" Iris asked.

"No," Francie said.

"So it wasn't like they were harassing her."

"No," she said. "Well, whatever 'be terrible' means. She mentioned about her car getting keyed. But she didn't say they did it."

"When?"

"Last month."

"Francie."

"I'm just saying she never specifically mentioned them. So you'll tell the police?"

"Yes," Iris said. "I'll take care of it. They may want to talk to you, though."

"Sure."

"Thanks, Francie."

She'll track down the Butlers tomorrow. She can find them via Faceplace or her network of Lakehaven volunteers, with careful asking that doesn't tip her hand as to her interest. The Butlers might be the answer to this whole terrible mystery. But as a successful adoptive parent, she'll have to consider how she talks to a family that was turned away. Their resentment could be powerful. *Hi. I'm here to talk to you about a murdered woman you blamed for your greatest unhappiness.* She would have to be careful.

Now she has to get ready for this neighborhood meeting. All her neighbors, all talking about Danielle, all expecting her to be a voice of compassionate leadership, of calm and order, and Iris wants to run away from this awfulness and not think about what secrets her husband is keeping or why her daughter is more worried about a boy than her own family and why her son asked her the questions she's always feared: if she had ever lied to him.

29

FROM IRIS POLLITT'S "FROM RUSSIA WITH LOVE" ADOPTION JOURNAL

2002

Feliks drove us to the orphanage. The interpreter, Pavel, sat up front with him. Pavel was—pardon your mom for saying this—hot. Maybe twenty-five, blond hair, broad shoulders, square jaw. Seriously, he could get a modeling job. Back when I wrote songs, I knew people in modeling because of the models who dated the more famous musicians I knew—I could probably connect Pavel. Danielle whispered to me, "Pavel can be very charming with the administrators. He's one of my secret weapons. His mother taught English at Saint Petersburg State University, so he was raised speaking both."

If Pavel heard this, he ignored it. He laughed at something Feliks said.

I sensed Kyle studying the two men. It was weird to think what we had at stake with these two strangers. If Pavel said the wrong thing in translation, we might anger a decision maker. If Feliks made us late because he underestimated traffic, we might irritate someone who could stamp a giant red *nyet* on our application. The thought unnerved me.

I didn't like the idea of control slipping away from us.

The orphanage was down a side road off the main road in a rural area outside of Saint Petersburg, between a scattering of smaller villages. We turned down it, past a large gate and fence. It felt, God help me, a little like a prison. The building was Soviet architecture—I imagined (hoping against hope) something bright, elegant, soaring, a charming old palace built by Peter the Great now turned to the care of abandoned, adorable infants. This place had a brutalist architecture, and it was cold, forbidding, depressing. I wanted to cry. I wanted to snatch up all the babies and run from this place.

Feliks parked. Another driver sat outside, smoking, and he waved at him. You didn't think about there being a whole subculture, subeconomy around international adoption. The same agencies hiring the same drivers. Feliks and Pavel had been here before, witnesses to dreams balanced on a delicate point.

Pavel and Danielle and Kyle and I got out. You, our son, were inside there. I had my two totes full of gifts and a mental list of who's who and what I should give them, courtesy of Danielle.

We walked into the orphanage, and I inched out onto the tightrope.

Chocolates for Svetlana, the receptionist, and Irina, a guard. (Why do babies need a guard? Were they keeping the children in or keeping a threat out?) Perfume for Maria, the caseworker assigned to Sasha, and a coloring book for Maria's niece, whom we'll never see but I wished her well. The gifts were accepted with a smile, and Maria made sure that we knew the coloring book was for her niece, not child, as she was not married, and she glanced at Pavel.

We walked down the halls. Inside one room were a few older children, ten to twelve, listening to a teacher. There were the children never adopted as babies, or brought here when they were older (or adopted internally in Russia and returned for behavioral problems—many of these kids had emotional issues and found great difficulty in adjusting to a family life). They were in uniforms. I saw them for only a moment through the glass of the shut door, and I wondered what they thought when they saw our little parade, people here for a baby, this year's model, and not here for them. Why do we have to walk past them? My heart jolted for them, but I didn't stop. I kept walking.

"History class," Pavel whispered helpfully to me. "They are learning about the Great Patriotic War. What you call World War II."

I wondered if we would get a tour of the whole building, but we didn't. I wondered what the conditions we weren't seeing were. Kyle took one of the totes of gifts from me, the heavier one, and held my hand. All the anger and frustration I felt with him melted away. I glanced over at him, my heart feeling swollen. We could and we would do this.

We entered a room of mirrors. Mirrors on every wall. It was disorienting at first, and I summoned a strange image, prompted there by Pavel and his comment on the history class...If I were a Russian fighter in the Great Patriotic War and I wanted to mentally break a Nazi, well, this room would be my choice. I didn't like mirrors.

The carpet in the room was old. There was a worn-looking couch and a couple of chairs, and a shelf full of toys that looked newer.

Maria announced something in Russian, with a friendly nod, and Pavel told us a detail we already knew. "You will have two hours to sit and play with Sasha," he said. "No more, so please understand when the time is up."

I nodded. Kyle nodded and smiled. We kept smiling at Maria. She didn't notice. She was immune to smiles of hopeful parents.

Then there was more Russian, muted but rapid-fire between them, and Pavel frowned. He said something back. Maria responded, waving her hand slightly, a universal signal for "no big deal." "One moment," he said to us. "I want to be sure I remember correct English word." He checked on his phone while my heart prepared to drop.

"*Vetryanaya ospa*," he said. "Chicken pox. Sasha has chicken pox. It is going through the orphanage."

"Oh, no," Kyle said.

"You have all had it, yes? As children? You are immune?" Pavel asked.

Kyle and I both nodded. So did Danielle.

"Ah, so not a problem," Maria said, in broken English.

"Does he feel up to seeing us?" I asked. His needs came first. Would he feel like playing, or would he just want to go to bed? I didn't care if I wasn't seeing him at his best. I cared how he felt.

Pavel translated. Maria said more in Russian, and Pavel said, "She says he'll be fine. Russian children, very tough. Resilient." Pavel dazzled us (well, not Kyle) with an encouraging smile.

Maria left. I looked at the mirrors. "Are they watching us?"

"I don't know," Danielle said. She had been very quiet, watching, probably listing things I was doing that I shouldn't. "Let's not discuss it here."

Maybe I was distraught over the chicken pox announcement, but I was a little short-tempered. "I only asked…"

"Well, don't. Do you want to make an issue of it? So what if they are watching? Assume they are. They don't know you, and you're asking them to entrust one of their charges to you for the rest of your life. Stop acting offended."

I opened my mouth to snap back, then shut it. "You're right," I said. Danielle didn't acknowledge my apology.

Kyle was silent, eyes locked on the door.

Maria reentered, with a young female nurse holding a pox-covered boy, nine months old, blond, frowning at all these new people.

"Sasha," Maria announced unnecessarily.

I didn't know what I expected when I first saw you. I thought my heart would feel overwhelmed with love and joy, but it wasn't like that. It was something else, a slower burn. You looked confused and miserable, so in this moment it was no longer about what I felt, what I wanted, but what you needed. I stood and held out my hands, and the nurse, with a smile, handed you to me.

But you knew the nurse, and you didn't know me, so you squawked and fussed, and that was all right. I rested you against my shoulder and I gently patted your back (not wanting to make your itching worse) and I thought of the first time I held Julia in my arms, freshly born, and this is different yet in a way it's the same. I held you. I let you feel my heart beat and I felt yours.

I wondered why I didn't think to learn a Russian song, a Russian lullaby. Something you would know. So instead I sang "Cotton Fields," one of the first songs I ever learned, sitting at my grandmother's piano, picking out the melody. I sang it softly, the way my grandmother sang it to me, thinking of all the times it's been sung since Lead Belly wrote it: Odetta, Johnny Cash, Mother Maybelle and the Carter Sisters, the Beach Boys. But I heard my grandmother's alto, strong and vibrant and soothing, and that was how I sang it to this Russian baby who was going to be my American boy.

I didn't know if Maria or Pavel knew I've written songs for famous people. And I didn't know if they've ever heard this old song. But Sasha fell quiet and still against me, and I kissed his splotchy little forehead for the first time and I kept singing.

Danielle was watching me like she'd never seen me. It was like she was measuring me as a mother, watching me as intently as the Russians.

Kyle seemed frozen. He watched us. I wondered why he didn't reach for Sasha and show the faces behind the mirrors what an excellent father he was. Then I realized no one wanted to interrupt me quieting the baby. Sasha didn't snake an arm around my neck or put his head on my shoulder. His head was raised, taking in all this strangeness.

I took him to the mirror and let him get a good long look at his future: him, my child, in my arms. I sang softly, and now he watched me and him in the mirror, dancing our little dance. Poor sick little thing. "You don't know where those places are I'm singing about, do you, sugar pop?" This nickname came unbidden into my head. "We live in Texas, with our little girl. She's three." I said this to him but to the mirror as well. To whoever was watching and judging on the other side. "That's next door to Louisiana."

Now Sasha was just looking at me. Was this the most anyone has ever talked to him? Directly? Had he never been sung to? I put my finger on his little hand and he didn't really grip back. He seemed surprised by everything. I touched his forehead. No fever. Maybe he was on the downside of the chicken pox.

"Iris?" Kyle's voice, soft behind me. "May I hold him?"

I handed him over, checked my internal barometer of love. I smoothed his hair at the back of his head as Kyle took him. Did I love him yet? I didn't know.

Kyle took him and Sasha fussed a little, but Kyle eased down onto the floor in a cross-legged sit and reached into the tote bag. There were toys there. I knew we couldn't give them just to Sasha—collectivism is still alive and well at the Volkov Infants Home, where all the toys are shared—and he pulled out a stuffed green dinosaur, a friendly looking T-Rex with a smile, not a snarl. Sasha wasn't sure what to think of this oddity.

Kyle said carefully, "*zdravstvuj*" to Sasha, one of the ways to say hello in Russian and the one supposedly to use with children you don't know well. I think it's more formal, but maybe that's appropriate. A sign of respect for the culture. I watched Pavel for a reaction if Kyle said it correctly, but Pavel's face betrayed nothing; Danielle told Kyle not to speak Russian, but now he's done it, for no good reason, and Sasha didn't react to the word (which if you ask me needs more vowels). But he reached for the dinosaur, and Kyle gave it to him.

Then he wanted on the floor, and Kyle set him down but stretched out along the floor next to him. Sasha crawled to the tote and peered inside.

"Smart boy," Pavel said. "He knows where the presents are."

"Sasha!" I said in a happy, cheerful tone. He glanced back at me. He wobbled as he stood and he reached into the tote again and pulled out a small stuffed otter. He held it, uncertain. Did he think someone was going to take it from him?

I knelt on the floor next to Kyle, not crowding him.

And Sasha gave us both a shy little smile.

Go home, that interfering woman in the airport told me.

Nope, lady. Nope.

The two hours flew. Kyle picked up Sasha, held him over his head, which was an entirely new experience for Sasha, and he giggled and drooled (Sasha, not Kyle). But two hours was a long while when you weren't feeling good, and at the end of the time he was cranky and sleepy, unused to the unrelenting attention.

I was holding him, and now his little head was tucked into the mom-space between shoulder and neck, when Maria reentered the room (she had gone in and out during the visitation time in silent observation of us) and spoke to Pavel in rapid-fire Russian. "Time is up. I am sorry," Pavel translated. "Time for Sasha to go rest."

Kyle put his hand on Sasha's head, kissed his blond hair. "We'll see you soon, son." The final word was like a knife through me.

Maria held out her arms for our son. My limbs felt like lead, but I handed him back to her. Sasha turned away, sleepy again, and Maria was gentle with him.

I burst into tears. (Oh, I hate crying. I really hate it.) Kyle folded his arms around me. "Goodbye, sweetheart. We'll see you soon," I said, and Maria thoughtfully turned so I could see him yawn in answer.

Maria closed the door behind her. I could see that Kyle—who I saw weep only when Julia was sick and at her lowest with the neuroblastoma—was fighting for control, and behind the mirrors were the faceless administrators watching, judging, saying we were too emotional, too overwrought. I didn't know what standard we were supposed to meet with these folks. So Danielle embraced me and I let her and I sobbed.

After we composed ourselves, we met the rest of the staff. Presents were given, from the administrator down to the custodians, who asked us about American music (note to self: bring CDs next time) and were happy to have American cigarettes. Everyone smiled at us, Pavel was the target of gentle flirtations. Maria joined us, having taken our poor sick baby elsewhere, and I asked about the older children, if they could use computer games. Or computers. Or whatever they needed. We'd already spent thousands upon thousands of dollars to get to this point. What was a bit more? I felt dizzy.

"How did it go?" I whispered to Danielle.

She squeezed my hand in reassurance.

It was time to leave. I built a mental list of things to bring in five to six weeks' time, for when we came back to have the hearing and hopefully take him home.

"Do you still want him?" Maria asked me, through Pavel. Of course they asked us this. "Yes," Kyle and I chimed together, Kyle nodding forcefully, and Pavel didn't need to translate for her. Kyle added a "*da*" and Maria spoke more Russian to Pavel.

"Do you have questions?" Pavel translated for her. "About Sasha?"

We asked about his health, his development, and Maria's answers mirrored what Dr. Gupta told us in the report.

After she answered our last question, I said, "Tell Maria we'll give him a wonderful home. Tell her we're so grateful to her for the care he's received here."

Pavel nodded and spoke. Maria didn't betray much emotion. Would she miss Sasha? Or he'd be gone, and minutes later another child would arrive to take his old place. How did Maria do this?

We walked out of the building. The air was crisp with the promise of snow. Feliks was standing by the car, talking to a woman.

A woman with hair covered by a scarf, but dark-framed glasses on, glasses like the warning woman in the airport.

And suddenly I was sure, the set of her shoulders, the turn of the part of her face that wasn't hidden behind the scarf.

It was her.

The warning woman. Here. Here, where Sasha is. She followed us—from London, from our arrival in Russia, to the very spot where my child was, the child she warned me against taking. She was not going to stop us from getting Sasha.

My rage, my anger, was like a bursting flame.

I ran to her. Feliks glanced at me as I reached for her, grabbed her arm. She turned toward me. I yanked the scarf away.

It was not the warning woman.

Similar age, similar build, similar nose, but now I saw the eyeglass frames were a lighter shade of brown and her hair was dusted with gray.

She cried out in surprise and shock.

Kyle looked at me like I'd

Completely.

Totally.

Entirely.

Lost my mind. I glanced over at him and saw Maria stared at me in shock. Looking for signs of instability, of aberration, of a reason to say no, because they can say no to us and some other family will get Sasha.

Pavel hurried forward as the woman yanked her arm away from my hand, mouthing off at me in a torrent of Russian. I babbled an apology that no one heeded.

"That's one of the administrators," Pavel said to me. "Galina. She is in charge of purchasing supplies." Pavel's voice was tense with me, but his smooth-flowing Russian was conciliatory with the wronged woman.

"I'm sorry...I thought she was someone else," I said.

Pavel said something in Russian, short and brief, and the woman looked mollified. Feliks said something to Pavel. Pavel didn't translate. There was one gift left in the tote—perfume—and I gave it to Galina. She took a deep breath and nodded her thanks, but took a step back like I might snatch it from her hands. I also gave her the fake Louis Vuitton tote and she nodded, the ice slightly melted. Pavel said more, tried to laugh very softly. She didn't laugh, but she kept the gifts.

I nodded to her, just saying "I'm so sorry" again and again, and she nodded to Kyle and Danielle.

We got into the car.

The doors all slammed, and then there was just a stunned silence.

"What the actual hell were you thinking?" Kyle said, his voice like a blade.

"I thought it was the woman from the London airport," I said, my voice thin and broken. What had I done? Kyle gave off this cough of frustration, of anger, of dismay.

"One step forward, a dozen steps back," Danielle said. "They aren't going to remember you singing to that boy. They're going to remember you charging across a parking lot and grabbing an employee's arm."

"It will be fine," Kyle said. "We can bribe our way out of this."

I made a noise in my throat.

"No, you can't. Maria and the administrator write a report on today and send it to the judge. There's not a lot of sympathy in this country for anything that looks like mental or emotional instability among adoptive parents. They don't have to say yes to you when they can say yes to the next family, who doesn't accost people."

"Stop the car," I said. Pavel murmured, and Feliks stopped. I got out. I marched back up the road to the Volkov Infants Home. I walked in. I saw Galina talking with the guard. I approached her and she looked at me. I say, "*Mne ochen zhal.*" I had heard Kyle practicing it and telling me what the phrases meant, trying to interest me. "I'm really sorry." He thought that would be a useful phrase for him. Yet I was the one who needed it.

She saw in my face the whole awful mix of sorrow, worry, and fear, and she offered a diplomatic smile and nod.

I said it again. "Is OK," Galina said.

I hoped it was enough. What if they said no? What if they made us wait, offered us another child much later? Sasha was my boy, I realized with a jolt. He was my child, and leaving him here was the hardest thing I could imagine. Now there was the possibility I would never see him again because I was stupid and rash. What had I done to myself, to Kyle, to the hopeful life for this poor boy that we just wanted to love? I had a vision of him now, ten or eleven, learning about the Great Patriotic War in an ill-fitting, worn uniform, with no one to love him, a prisoner of this place until he was eighteen. Because I was a fool.

I stumbled out into the cold.

We drove back toward Saint Petersburg. Danielle decided to be optimistic, chirpy. No doubt she would call the home, apologize for me. Surely they were used to dealing with parents who were stressed and emotional.

Sure they were, and they didn't have to give them kids.

"Pavel and I have to go today to two other orphanages," Danielle said. We were flying home the day after tomorrow. We'd given ourselves an extra day in case there was an issue seeing Sasha on our assigned day, so tomorrow would be spent sightseeing or shopping. I could buy supplies for the orphanage and take them back there for Galina. Get back some of the goodwill I squandered.

I didn't see the SUV come up behind us; I was lost in my thoughts of being a screwup and wondering how I could fix this. Did the two hours I spent with Sasha prove to them my worthiness, despite my silliness with Galina?

I was sitting in the middle, next to Danielle, who was behind Feliks, and next to Kyle, who was behind Pavel, and I heard Feliks muttering, and his tone rose in alarm. And then Danielle turned and glanced out the window and said, "Hey..." and then the black SUV rammed into the side of our car. We were on a highway, at speed. Feliks hollered and fought for control. Pavel yelled in Russian. The force of the sideswipe launched me against Kyle.

The SUV—it had tinted windows—rammed us again. Feliks screamed and turned the steering wheel.

The SUV swooped in, forcing us off the road, onto the grass. We spun and started to slide down the embankment, down toward a rushing creek, its banks thick with snow. Kyle threw an arm across me to protect me. Feliks seized control on the muddy stretch of grass and wrenched the wheel, but the SUV rolled. Glass shattered and Danielle screamed and I felt the weight of Kyle's arm across me. Then we were upright again and I felt, for the oddest moment, that I was a kid on a roller coaster. It lasted a microsecond as we toppled over, coming to rest on the roof.

Then an awful shocked silence.

"Get out," I said to a dazed Kyle. "Get out. Get out."

I had a horrifying picture in my mind of the SUV's occupant walking toward us, guns in hand, led by the warning woman: *I told you to go home.*

We were all hanging upside down by our seat belts; the top of the car was crushed. Kyle swept the shattered glass still in the passenger-side window and eased out, then helped me. Pavel was cradling his arm, but he still helped Feliks, who was choking and coughing, his face bloodied from a cut caused by flying glass. Kyle eased me out onto the snowy grass and then leaned in and helped Danielle. She pulled herself free, shrugged off his hand, and staggered a few feet, then vomited into the snow.

"They drove us off the road!" I screamed.

"It was an accident," Danielle said, glancing back at me. "He was weaving on the road before he reached us." Then she was sick again. I heard police sirens. Pavel clutched his arm, and I realized it was broken.

Kyle and I leaned against each other. Someone just tried to kill us. Why was this happening?

30

IRIS

The Winding Creek Neighbors House looks more like an extra-large home at the far edge of the park than a community center—inside there was a venue for parties, a library upstairs filled with leftovers and castoffs from the neighborhood's shelves. There was a pool outside, with race lanes for the neighborhood swim team. Iris had been here for birthday parties, graduation events, even a wedding reception.

Danielle had been found dead on a bench on the opposite side of the park. People had to pass where she was found to get here tonight. Tonight was for the neighborhood to gather to discuss Danielle's murder, to plan what they should do. Normally gatherings here are lively and fun, the crowd relaxed and mingling. Now it's lots of crossed arms, furrowed brows, small groups whispering, and suspicious glances exchanged—she guesses there will be different agendas at play. When people want change in their neighborhood, chaos is an opportunity. Iris sits down in the front row of chairs, ignoring the coffee and cookies volunteers have placed on the back table. Refreshments are fine when the discussion is funding the pool repairs, but not for murder, she thinks.

Kyle's not here. He's stayed home. She told him it was a bad idea not to appear, and he told her he wasn't up for the hysteria. She gets the feeling he doesn't really want to be around people. Or answer questions about why his face is bruised and battered. Julia went out, too, probably to go be with Ned, who is not here. Neither is Peter. This isn't a place for kids tonight, anyway. When she left the house, Grant was curled up on his bed, staring at the ceiling.

What has this death done to us? It was as though Danielle's murder had affected each of them directly but differently. She feels, oddly, like she is living with strangers who wear the faces of her family.

She watches people watching her. Because, she thinks, her daughter found the body. People are curious. She doesn't meet their gazes. She feels sick. She thinks about Danielle and what she could have done differently. She glances around the room, trying to read it. People are scared and they *want something done*. Their anxiety is not comforting.

She is surprised when it's Mike who calls the meeting to order. The association president, a normally hearty, gregarious guy named Felipe, is sitting down and looking grim.

"I want to thank you all for being here tonight," Mike says. "I know…I know Danielle had many friends in this neighborhood. Ned and Peter and I have felt your kindness and your love. I want to thank you all for what you have done for us."

Mike's voice shakes ever so slightly. Iris can see a glistening of tears in his eyes as he blinks. She glances over her shoulder. Ten rows of chairs behind her and everyone looks rapt. A couple of people are crying. Iris can feel tears at the back of her eyes, but they don't seem to want to come forward.

"This has been, as you can imagine, a terrible shock for Ned. He is my priority right now; even though his father is here from London, Ned is like a second son to me." Mike clears his throat. "I hope you will all keep him as a priority, too."

The room is silent, until a woman in the back says, "Of course, Mike. We'll all be here for Ned. And for you and Peter." There is a hum of general assent.

"And please, remember the Pollitt family in your prayers," Mike says. "It was a terrible shock for Julia when Ned and she found Danielle, and Kyle and Iris have been at my side every step of the way."

Iris feels frozen to her chair, and she tries not to flinch when someone behind her—she doesn't know who—gently pats her on the shoulder.

"There will be a memorial service later this week for Danielle. I've asked Iris to speak. I hope you will all be able to attend. Please tell your neighbors who are not here tonight."

I can't give her eulogy. I can't, Iris thinks. Then she feels a surge of strength in her gut, born of desperation, and she decides she can. Only because she must.

"That is my first plea to you. My second plea is anyone who knows anything, who may have seen anything, to please come forward. Come to Detective Jamika Ponder of the Travis County Sheriff's Office or Detective Carmen Ames of Lakehaven police, they're here tonight to talk to us." Iris notices the two detectives are sitting farther down the row. Ames looks like a schoolteacher at an assembly. Ponder is leaning forward, staring out at the audience. "Because of the complexity of this kind of homicide case, TCSO has the resources to be the lead agency on the investigation."

There is silence.

"If you're scared," Mike says, surveying the crowd, "or if you don't want to publicly accuse someone, then call the anonymous tip line the Lakehaven police have set up." He clears his throat. "I'm also donating fifty thousand dollars for information leading to an arrest and conviction for Danielle's killer."

The silence is replaced by a low rumble. Iris glances around. Does someone here know something?

"Anything," Mike continues. "Any information that lets us know why this happened. Why Danielle died."

Why. Why does *why* matter so much to some people? *Why* will change nothing. Iris closes her eyes and feels a dull thump of pain in her head, the start of a headache. She hates Mike for asking this question. Who is she becoming? It's as if this murder has unmoored her, made her wonder about the person she is and the life she's led. Just as she had started to believe it would all be fine.

"Iris?" she hears Mike ask. She realizes, with a sinking shock, that while lost in thought she's put her hands over her face. She lowers her hands. It feels like the entire room is looking at her. "Did you have anything to add?" Mike says.

She should just shake her head no. Instead—*what are you doing what are you doing what are you doing?*—she stands. She turns and faces the crowd. Like she has done at all kinds of parent meetings over the years. She feels the weight of their gaze. She takes in their expressions: some are shocked, some mournful, some curious, some scared.

"Many of you know," she says, "that Danielle changed lives for so many families in Lakehaven. Her work in foreign adoptions has helped many here. Including me and Kyle, when we got our son from Russia with Danielle's help." *Shut up and sit down shut up and sit down.* "She helped children from China, from Ghana, from Vietnam, and more all find their forever families here in Lakehaven. She was loved"—*stop lying stop lying*—"that's why it's just unfathomable to me that anyone who knew her could have hurt her." She clears her throat. *Don't offer a theory shut up and sit down.* "I know we're all looking at each other, wondering how this could have happened in our quiet little neighborhood. I think someone came here and hurt Danielle." She could not make her mouth form the word *murder.* "And so, like Mike, I beg you, if you know anything, if you saw anything, if you heard anything, to please come forward." Her voice steadies, and she glances over at Mike. He nods in gratitude.

"Drugs," she hears a voice say. She looks to her left, and there's Matt Sifowicz, one of the two guys who were jogging past when Julia and Ned found Danielle. He stands up slowly. "I think this was theft for drug money. I think someone saw her alone in a park and attempted to rob her. Then they punched her in the throat and killed her."

"Her purse was still in her home. A diamond ring was still on her finger. She'd gone up to the park, we don't know why." Now Detective Ponder has risen and stands next to Mike. "But of course we're considering every possibility."

"I saw something," a woman who lives four houses down from

the circle says. Iris has seen her on the street, walking down to the mailbox, but these are newish neighbors who have kept to themselves and Iris doesn't know her name. "I was up late. I have insomnia. Shopping on an online auction site. My dog was awake and he barked like he does when someone goes past the house. I went to the window, because who's up and walking at 4:00 a.m., and I saw a man. I think it was a man. Coat, and hat pulled down. He wasn't walking a dog. And he didn't have a flashlight."

"Which way was he coming from?" Ponder asks.

"From the circle, heading toward the park."

Iris feels the world around her freeze slightly. There are six houses on the circle, another six maybe between the circle and this woman's home. Twelve husbands. One of them is hers.

"He could have walked in from the greenbelt," Iris says. "Parked on the other side of it and walked into the neighborhood that way." The moment she speaks she wonders if people will think she's covering for Kyle.

"That's true," Mike agrees.

"Did you see anyone with him?" Ponder asks.

After a moment, the woman shakes her head.

Iris wonders: Why did Danielle die in the park? Why not at her own home? Why did she go to meet someone in the neighborhood park? Who did she go see?

And she thinks: She didn't want Ned to see. She didn't want Ned to know who it was.

"Thank you for coming forward. Will you give a statement after the meeting?"

"Yes."

"And your name, ma'am?"

"Carrie Butler."

Iris stares at her. Carrie and Steve Butler: the woman and her husband who had been denied an adoption and blamed Danielle. She notices now the woman's sitting next to the brawny redhead who was jogging with Sifowicz when they heard the kids screaming and ran to their aid. The redhead takes her hand as she sits back down.

They moved into the neighborhood, Iris thinks. A few houses down from the woman they blamed for not getting them a child.

"I didn't want to accuse anyone…" Carrie Butler says. "We're new in the neighborhood and…" Carrie stops again. "I didn't want to accuse anyone," she repeats flatly.

"Coming forward with information is not an accusation. It's just information. And that's what we need," Ponder says.

Iris wonders if the man was Kyle. Could he have followed Danielle to the park, killed her, and then come home and calmly slipped into bed next to Iris? The thought staggers her.

People are asking questions of Ponder. "Should we be locking our doors?" "What do *you* think happened?" "Was she raped?" (A man asks this as though asking what she was wearing.) "Do we have any sex offenders who have moved into the area recently?" "Have there been any similar deaths in Austin, you know, like it's a serial killer?" "Do you need a list of all the repairmen and lawn services and contractors who have been in the neighborhood recently?" There was clearly a cadre of residents—mostly older people—who felt that Winding Creek was under some kind of siege and were too happy to point a finger at who they believed to be likely suspects.

When people show you who they are, Iris thinks, *believe them.*

Ponder and Ames handle it deftly, reassuring people that there is no reason to believe there is a continuing threat; no, there have not been similar murders in the area; yes, Lakehaven and the Travis County Sheriff's Office deputies are patrolling the neighborhood.

Iris glances back again at Carrie Butler in time to see Steve Butler stand. "We appreciate the patrols, but they can't have eyes on Winding Creek twenty-four-seven. We can. We are just an informal patrol of home owners. We're keeping our eyes open, being visible as a deterrent in case this guy comes back…"

Boos suddenly arise from the crowd.

"We don't need amateurs policing the neighborhood," a woman yells at Steve Butler. "You'll probably end up getting shot."

"Most of us aren't armed," Steve said. "I have an open-carry permit and so does one other home owner here. Mostly what we're armed with are our cell phones, to capture what happens."

"We have professional police. We don't need this," the woman says.

"We don't need our single moms murdered in the neighborhood either," Steve Butler fires back. "You've got a teenage daughter, Belinda. Do you feel she's safe here right now?"

Ponder is now saying that armed patrols are unnecessary; the situation is in hand. But scared people are scared people, and Iris thinks: *What have you clowns got to be scared of? I know what fear is. You don't even know the shape of it. You don't know what it can take from you.*

For a moment, in the hubbub, she thinks she feels the drift of snowflakes, windblown, against her face. The terror of her life being on the verge of ending. The way the fear tunneled into her bones, a living thing claiming her.

But it hadn't. She'd beaten it.

The discussion has descended into chaos, Ponder and Mike both calling for order, Mike pleading with Steve Butler that no one else start patrolling and no one be armed so no one gets hurt. Butler shouts that they, as concerned neighbors, will still walk the streets and no one is going to stop them.

Iris just wants out. She wonders what Ponder and Ames will make of Carrie Butler's statement.

People are starting to stand and leave because the meeting has fallen apart. Steve Butler's face has turned purple with yelling, and she sees something twisted in his eyes. A man who does not deal well with frustration.

Iris's gaze shifts down and to his left and she sees Carrie Butler looking at her, staring at her. She knows. She knows and she's not saying. And then Carrie Butler smiles at her, a smile that is cruel and calculating and cold. For a moment there is a naked hatred in that smile, and Iris gasps.

You hated Danielle. Why would you buy a house a few doors down from her?

Steve Butler's yelling at an objector in the crowd that they don't understand there is no way the unofficial watch could be a danger, that they're not going to be firing guns willy-nilly into the darkness. Do they think he's a total idiot? He's ex-army. He knows what he's doing. The families of Winding Creek have to be protected at all costs.

Mike is at the microphone, trying to restore order.

Carrie Butler continues to smile at Iris and turns away. She takes her husband's arm, leading him away from those who are arguing with him. They start to work their way through the crowd.

Iris follows them.

31

GRANT

Grant walks into the empty house; Mike is at the same neighborhood meeting that his mom is attending. There is food all over the kitchen table; people have brought pies, cookies, vegetable plates. He steals a cookie and eats it. Then he takes another cookie and goes upstairs to Peter's room and knocks.

Peter looks exhausted, rubbing his eyes. He tries a smile at Grant when Grant hands him the cookie.

"Hey," Grant says.

"Hey. You have an interesting problem."

Grant's heart sinks. "Is my laptop infected by this hacker?"

"Yes."

"How?"

"Have you ever heard of the Shadow Brokers? Or WikiLeaks Vault 7?"

"Uh, no."

"Those are two very famous releases of cyberwarfare tools, done by hackers. Shadow Brokers released some old NSA — National Security Agency — tools a while back. WikiLeaks Vault 7 release showed how the CIA uses tools to hack everything from web browsers to iPhones to Android phones." Peter looks at his screen. "But before both of those, there was an earlier leak, about ten years ago, of a program called Dangerzone. It was a CIA hacker tool to remotely scan, download, and activate functions on a laptop. But the CIA said Dangerzone was never deployed. There were problems with it; it was easy to detect. It was a prototype. You understand?"

Grant nods, thinking: the CIA?

"There's a hidden file on your system called Dangerzone. It looks like it's been updated or modified and it's been on your system for a while."

"Spying on me."

"Yes. It could have activated your laptop camera, so someone remotely could watch you through it. Or your microphone, so they could hear you. I don't know if it could infect other systems. Probably it could hide on a flash drive and install itself on the next computer."

"Why would the CIA want to spy on me?" His camera? His microphone? Has someone been seeing and hearing what all goes on in his room, his den, his kitchen, wherever he has the laptop? The thought is chilling, what a stranger could know about his family and what they've done and said.

"Well, I doubt it's the CIA," Peter says. "The program, although kind of a dud, was released by a hacker group. Someone took it and updated it and fixed it. What I don't get is why not change the name? Why leave it 'dangerzone' when that's likely on a list of released hacker tools a cybersecurity expert would know to look for?"

"How do I get it off?"

"I think we have to go to the police."

"No, Peter, I can't."

"Grant." Peter's stare on him is no longer the disinterested gaze of the too-cool-for-school loner. "Have you been threatened?"

"No," he says quickly.

Peter studies him. "I'm going to call the police now."

"No, you can't, please, please," Grant says.

"So you have been threatened?"

"No. I asked you to figure out where the email came from…"

"That. Yeah." For a moment Peter seems to forget about calling the police. "So here's what I did. I sent an HTML-formatted email with an image of you in it as a reply—I found a picture on my dad's computer from the last barbecue we had at your parents' house. You're making a face at the camera. I copied the image to a server where I have administrative access at one of Dad's companies. I sent it to the Gmail address. And I waited. That image is a little trap."

Grant waits, hoping for an explanation, not sure what it all means. Peter smiles again.

"So our friend the Sender opens the email and the image loads. The Sender's web browser sent a 'GET' request to my web server, trying to pull that image of you. I can check the logs to see the IP address of the Sender because he opened the email—the address of their computer on the internet, not their physical address. You understand?"

Grant nods again.

"So the email got opened. We were lucky. The Sender wasn't using a virtual private network to obfuscate his or her location."

"So where is the Sender?"

"I looked up the IP address. Whoever is sending you these emails is in Saint Petersburg, Russia."

"Who is it?" Grant whispers.

"I used an IP registry to see what company in Saint Petersburg owns the IP address. They've not responded yet. They may not. I hear the Russians are not always cooperative. I told them that the person had been contacting a minor, though. That might make a difference. Assuming they even bother to read an email sent in English."

Grant feels as though he's been punched in the gut. "I was born near Saint Petersburg…Why would anyone have a CIA spy program on my computer and be sending me this stuff?" Grant's voice shakes. *I'll have to talk to the police about the bad thing your dad did.* What if his infected computer had infected Dad's laptop? He'd copied something off Dad's laptop not a month ago. And maybe Dad had something incriminating on his own computer, and now this person knew about it…

"Have you or your parents ever gone back to Russia?" Peter asks.

"No."

"Did your parents have an enemy there?"

"No." But…he doesn't really know that, does he? An enemy? Who has an enemy?

"One other explanation. The CIA has been known to hack bad guys and mislead them into thinking the attack came from Russia. I can't imagine why, but that's the other possibility. Do your parents have any ties to the CIA?"

Grant stares at him, trying to wrap his head around the question. "But, Peter, the Sender can't be in Russia. Someone is leaving stuff for me here, now, in the tree. Money. Jewelry. A hacker in Russia can't do that. So it has to be a trick." He tells Peter about the money and the bracelet. He pulls the bracelet from his pocket.

Peter stares at it as if fascinated. Then he hands it back to Grant. "Be careful with that. It looks real."

"Why would someone do this?" Grant said.

"Don't know. But let's set up a trap for them," Peter says. "Never mind all these high-powered computers. If someone tied to this is here in the neighborhood, let's just catch them in the act."

The laptop pings. A new email arriving, from the Gmail address.

"The Sender is emailing you again," Peter says.

"Should I open it?"

"Live fast," Peter says.

Grant opens the email: Ask them for the journal. Ask them for the truth.

32

IRIS

Iris always faces a challenge when at a school event or neighborhood gathering: people want to talk to her. It's hard for her to move quickly across a crowd. There's another fundraiser to discuss, a choir activity requiring parent chaperones, a meeting. Grant and Julia used to roll their eyes and complain about this. Now she gets stopped by people wanting to know how to help Ned, or help Julia, or just ask how she is holding up, or to thank her for the kind words she said about Danielle.

Stepping outside, she sees the Butlers get into a car and drive off. Fine. She'll give them time to get home. She says her final goodbye and drives back to her house, watching the shadows in this neighborhood that she always thought was her refuge from the world, her safety net.

Then, having figured out which house is the Butlers' since she knows the neighbors on each side, she walks down and knocks on their front door.

Carrie Butler answers the door. She doesn't seem surprised to see Iris.

"Mrs. Butler?"

"Mrs. Pollitt," Carrie Butler says.

"You know who I am."

"My husband told me your name after your daughter found Danielle."

"May we talk?"

"What about?"

"That you knew Danielle before you moved here."

"What does that have to do with anything?" Her voice is reedy, thin, but even. Not rattled.

"You got turned down for adoption and you blamed her."

"Come in," Carrie Butler says. "I can straighten this out."

In the silence she could hear a television being muted.

Then the husband, Steve, standing in the foyer's doorway. He's holding a gun. Not aimed at her, but pointed at the floor.

"Mrs. Pollitt." He nods.

Iris stares at the gun. He sets it in a drawer of a table and slides the drawer shut. "It's for the neighborhood watch. I have duty tonight until 2:00 a.m."

"I know you mean well," Iris says, "but you walking around with a gun is going to make people nervous."

"I saw Danielle. So did you. Someone killed her in an incredibly vicious, painful manner. I am not going to let that happen again."

"You didn't give a statement to Detective Ponder tonight." Iris looks at Carrie.

"I'm going in tomorrow to do that."

"Will you mention your previous business relationship with Danielle?"

"I feel there's a misunderstanding," Carrie says. "Danielle was helping us again."

"What?"

"It's true we hired her a while back and our applications were rejected." Steve Butler clears his throat; his pale skin reddens in embarrassment.

Iris thinks: They might not have met an income requirement. Or it might be that they were older than most families that were trying to adopt. All sorts of prejudices, varying from country to country about which kinds of Americans could adopt, but it was down to Danielle to be the unfortunate messenger. It was a side of her job Iris had never appreciated, saying to someone, *No, you're not getting a child. I'm sorry.* Crushing all their hopes and aspirations and their future in one heartless moment. What had that been like? What would the reaction be? Accepting heartbreak, or hatred?

She looks for an answer in their faces. Steve is flushed; Carrie seems defiant.

Steve clears his throat again. "I had financial difficulties. I had a gambling problem. It was nothing Carrie did, the responsibility was all mine. I thought once we had a child again, I would stop. I had it backward, of course." Carrie takes his hand. "It became clear to the authorities in China and Uganda from our financial records that there was an issue, and that's why we were told no. I've been going to therapy and I'm no longer gambling. I've got a good job with a software company—I work with Matt Sifowicz; that's why we were out running together—and we're stable now. So Danielle said she'd help us. She had a lead on a couple of likely adoption possibilities for us."

"I didn't know she had taken you back on as clients." The old email from Danielle was half the story.

Unless the Butlers were lying.

"Why would you?" Carrie says. "It's none of your business. Did Danielle normally discuss clients with you?"

"No. And she didn't discuss this with me. She told a friend. Because she said in an email that you had been terrible to her."

"So much for confidentiality," Carrie says. "We were angry. We apologized. She accepted. It's what grown-ups do."

"We don't have room to complain," Steve says quickly. "Not every consultant would have worked with us after two nations said no. We knew she was the best. We were lucky to have her. I didn't react well to our rejection and I vented to Danielle. She was right to step away from us. That I apparently scared her or upset her, I'm genuinely sorry for."

Are they telling the truth? Iris wonders. "And you bought a house near her because…?"

"Are you suggesting we bought a house because we wanted to *annoy* her if she didn't take us back on?" Carrie says. "Wow, just wow."

"We wanted to be in the Lakehaven school system, and we didn't want to wait until prices went up even more," Steve says. "This happened to be the house we found. You can understand that."

Slowly Iris nods. Time to play another card. "Is there anything I can do to be of help? About being an adoptive parent? There are groups, resources. And Danielle's not here to tell you." She cuts off her words.

"We don't need parenting tips," Carrie says. "We lost our kids. Our son, John, and our daughter, Addie. In a car accident in Dallas, when they were fifteen and seventeen."

Iris feels a tremble rise up her legs. "I'm very sorry. I'm so sorry." What was she doing here, preying on these people?

"We wanted to give our love to a child. What was left of it," Carrie says, and Iris thinks, *She's a walking ghost. She's hoping a child will bring her back to life.*

She cannot imagine what these people have gone through. "Yes. I understand."

"Can you? You still have your teenagers. A boy and a girl. Just like we did."

Iris knows no words are adequate. And no words will help ease this woman's pain. "I'm truly sorry for your loss."

"Thank you. I mean, we'll have a child soon. And that child will be safe. We won't lose a child again," Steve Butler says, and now she can see something in his gaze, pain so dark and unknowable, something she doesn't want to look at. He wipes at his mouth and then she sees it.

Bruises on his knuckles.

A mottling of purple, above and beneath the bone, like someone has struck a pipe against his hand.

She stares at Steve Butler. Wouldn't it be a good cover story to be one of the first to find the body, while jogging with a coworker who's an established presence in the neighborhood? And then have your wife claim to have seen a mysterious man come from the direction of your home to Danielle's? She wonders whose idea it was for the two of them to run that morning.

She thinks of the bruise on Danielle's tender throat, the broken windpipe, the bright blood on her mouth.

Iris wants out of this house. Now. *Now.* "I'm so sorry for your loss," she says again. Trying not to look at the bruises. "I'll leave you to your evening."

"I'll see you out," Carrie says, rising.

Iris steps into the night, Carrie following.

"She mentioned you to me. As one of her success stories," Carrie says.

Iris turns to face her. "We love our son very much. We're grateful to her."

"That man I saw that night, I really can't be sure which house he might have come from. The color of his coat…it was dark; it was hard to tell. But he was about your husband's height and build. He skipped the meeting tonight, didn't he?"

Iris stares at her.

"Memory is such an imprecise thing," Carrie says. "Tricky. If someone says something bad about one's family, it can spur one to sharper, more certain memories, can't it?"

It was a threat. Iris smiles, because she understands threats, and says, "Welcome to the neighborhood. I know we'll be great friends." *Because you don't want me as an enemy.*

She walks home and she doesn't look back at Carrie Butler. She sees a sheriff's car parked in the distance, between the Butler house and her house. Probably to keep an eye on Steve Butler and his troop of volunteer watchdogs.

Kyle is in the driveway, putting out the recycling and trash bins. Tomorrow is pickup day.

"How did it go?" he asks quietly. He doesn't know about the Butlers. He means the meeting.

Iris doesn't know how to answer at first, but then the words spill out of her: "If I had been a better friend to her, maybe I would have known what was happening with her. Maybe she needed someone to confide in and that should have been me. To protect our family, I should have been a better friend to her. I know I failed her."

And then the tears come, hot and sudden, and Kyle encloses her in his arms and she weeps for all that has been lost.

33

FROM IRIS POLLITT'S "FROM RUSSIA WITH LOVE" ADOPTION JOURNAL

2002

Black SUV, that's all the few witnesses said. One driver saw it racing away. There were cameras along the highway and the roads, and perhaps they would pick up a damaged SUV making its way into town in the minutes after our crash. We were taken to a hospital and all pronounced fit, except for Feliks, who had a concussion and cuts on his scalp and forehead, and Pavel, who had a broken arm.

I kept thinking about the warning woman in the airport: "Go home."

Why did anyone care if we got a baby here?

What did we do to anger someone?

The police are polite but not hopeful. Kyle calls the embassy and they send a young woman to translate for us.

"Do you think you were targeted? Was the car following you?" the embassy woman translated as the police asked us questions. One of the officers looked at us as though we were hysterical Americans, imagining a conspiracy.

"Yes," I said and "No," Danielle said.

There was discussion then, and one of the officers shook his head sadly.

"There is a lot of drunk driving on that road," the embassy woman said. "It is regrettable."

"We are adopting a Russian infant and I think we were targeted," I said, and Danielle said something in Russian to the police.

"Not everyone approves of foreign adoption," the embassy worker said, "but we've never had parents targeted."

"Well, you do now," I said, and Kyle put a hand on my shoulder and I shrugged it off.

No one saw a license plate of the other car, and so we would have to rely on the police checking body shops or the security cameras on the streets catching the damaged vehicle.

We went back to the hotel. The two hours with Sasha had been so wonderful, even with him sick. With my embarrassing scene at the orphanage and the crash, the day felt ruined. I wouldn't let it. We met our son today. I would not let these unfortunate moments cloud this day.

"What the hell is going on here?" Kyle said as we sat down at the lobby bar. We ordered glasses of red wine. My nerves felt shattered.

"That woman in the airport doesn't seem so unbelievable now, does she? We were warned to go home. And then this."

"Maybe we go home," Kyle said, looking at me. "And we don't come back."

So much for "See you soon, son."

No Sasha to become Grant. No. No. I would not be scared off and I could not believe Kyle, my brave, smart Kyle, would consider backing down.

"Absolutely not," I said.

"I'll let you talk," Danielle said. She gulped her wine down.

"Wait. If we back out, do we get any of the money back?" Kyle asked her. I took refuge in a long sip of French pinot noir.

"From the Russians? No. I'll do what I can with GAC given the situation. But you have no proof you've been targeted. None." Danielle's voice wasn't strident, but she seemed out of her depth. "Look, it wasn't that long ago that Saint Petersburg was considered the crime capital of Russia. Foreigners were often targeted. You want to find a rich foreigner? Go to an orphanage and follow a car from there. Or someone at the orphanage doesn't like the gift you gave them and calls a friend and tells them when you're leaving. People have been run off the road before and robbed. The idea that anyone objects that you two specifically are adopting a child is garbage." Danielle set down her glass, exhausted. "I'm sorry. We've just never had this issue." She looked at me. "I know you love that child, Iris. I could see it. All I've wanted to do, for you and every family, is to bring you together. To give these kids a future and to give you a child to love." Her voice broke.

For a moment I stopped thinking of her as the nagging coach on what I should say or do or the adoption consultant we've paid thousands of dollars and I see her at my front door, beyond excited with the news that the Russians found a baby for us. Us falling into each other's arms in relief and joy, sisters in battle. I must get my mind right. I took her hands in mine.

"We are not giving up," I said. "That boy is meant to be with us and he's going to be with us."

"I won't have you in danger," Kyle said.

"Look, someone identified us, maybe because of my work"— Kyle flinched, as he sometimes did when I mentioned that I used to work for some very famous people—"and decided to make an example of us. Because we'd get press coverage of it. Maybe they want to not scare just us, but any foreign families wanting to adopt Russian children."

A horrified look crossed Danielle's face at this idea. "I need to make some phone calls." She left us.

In our room Kyle and I collapsed on the bed. We held each other. The lobby called later and told us two journalists from the major newspapers in town wanted to talk to us. We declined.

"Five weeks," Kyle whispered to me. "We have to hold on for five weeks until he's ours. Then we never have to come back to this place."

"Promise me he'll be ours," I said to him, and Kyle nodded and kissed me with resolve.

34

IRIS

When Iris comes downstairs the next morning, Peter Horvath is drinking coffee at the kitchen island while Grant eats his cereal.

"This is an early start," Iris says. The boys were awfully quiet; she didn't even hear Grant let Peter in the house.

"Grant asked me to take him to school," Peter says. "He didn't want to take the bus today."

"Do you feel up to school, babe?" Iris asks Grant. He nods.

She wonders if Kyle will go to work. He should, she decides. They can't just sit in limbo.

"Ned is going, too." Peter's gaze meets hers.

Iris stares. Surely Ned should take at least a week off. Peter shrugs.

Peter says, "I've never told you how cool it is that you write songs."

"Oh, well, used to. I don't really write anymore." The last time she heard one of her songs out in public, it was at the grocery store, piped into the aisles, and she embarrassed herself by singing along as she shopped for breakfast cereal.

"I have my mom's CDs from the nineties, and I went through them and found five songwriting credits to you."

Iris flushes with pleasure. "Oh. Well. How nice."

"You're, like, the coolest mom in Lakehaven," Peter says, and for a moment Iris wonders about this boy who has kept to himself so much, who hasn't seemed to mind when his own father spent extra time with Grant. He's an odd duck but a sweet kid, and she feels a swelling of gratitude that Peter is shepherding Grant through this difficult time.

"I wish I knew how to write a song," Peter says. "I'd like to write about what it's like to come to America." He laughs. "All the way from Toronto."

"Just write it. You learn by doing," Iris says.

"Did you ever want to write about bringing Grant from Russia?" Peter asks. "The way you wrote about Julia being so ill when she was little?"

The smile freezes. For the barest moment. "Oh, gosh, no. I don't know that he would want me to."

"I wouldn't care," Grant says, not knowing if he would care or not.

"Who would sing it, honey, except me?"

"Danielle once told me," Peter says, "that she encouraged all her clients to keep an adoption journal. I bet one written by a songwriter would be fascinating reading." He sips at his coffee. He glances at Grant. Iris notices that Grant is staring at her.

Iris keeps her smile steady. "I did not do that. With the tidal wave of paperwork, I couldn't manage it."

"Where in Russia did you get Grant?" Peter asks. "Moscow?"

"Saint Petersburg. Well, near it."

"Have you ever wanted to go back?"

"Never," Iris says. "I mean, if Grant wants to go, of course we'll take him, but he's never wanted to go. It would be best to wait until he's an adult."

"I've changed my mind," Grant says. "I'd like to go back soon. Like, maybe my next school break."

"Not during winter," Iris says, laughing weakly.

"Would that bother you? If I wanted to go back?" Grant asks.

She sees he's serious. "It would be fine with me. But you've never wanted to go back there before."

"Do you want to go back to Russia, Mom? Like a tourist?"

She measures her answer. "I don't think so. I don't much like snow."

Now he gives her a long look, the kind she gives him when he's dodging a question. "Was there anything weird about my adoption?"

"All adoptions are weird," Iris says. "What's brought this on?"

"Danielle has made me think of all that. What it must have been like for her, and for you and Dad, to go so far away to get me. You never talk much about it."

"It was a process. It doesn't matter. What matters is you are our son and you are deeply loved."

"You're my mom," Grant says. "My real mom. But my biological mom and dad…I'd like to know about them. I could have asked Danielle, or her contacts there, about them."

Peter looks uncomfortable, trapped in this family conversation, and he stares deep into his coffee mug.

Iris pours herself a cup of coffee. "Once adoptions stopped from Russia, Danielle didn't do business there anymore," Iris says. "I don't know if she still even stayed in touch with anyone there."

"Did you ever meet my mother or my father?"

"No, honey. It's not allowed. Why would we want to meet them?"

"What if my mom gave me up because she was a drug addict? Wouldn't you want to know?"

"I don't know what she was," Iris says steadily, "but we were told she was healthy when she gave birth to you. There was nothing in your health history to suggest otherwise."

"So why didn't she want me?" Grant's voice rose.

"I don't know, Grant. Maybe she couldn't afford to keep you. Maybe she believed an American couple would adopt you and you'd have a better life." Iris keeps her voice mom-steady. "We can't know. But I'm so grateful to her for making her choice. I'll be forever grateful to her."

"Have you ever lied to me about anything that happened in Russia?"

"No. We have not." Iris makes her voice steel.

Grant digests this. "I would like to see Saint Petersburg."

"It is a lovely city. Have you ever been, Peter?" Just trying to change the subject, to get the pressure off her. "Your dad is such a world traveler."

Peter shakes his head. "Dad loathes the Russians for what they did to Czechoslovakia back in the day. He won't go there, won't invest there. He says there's too many criminals in power. Did you enjoy your time there?"

"We saw so little of the country. It was mostly meetings with bureaucrats and going to the orphanage and buying stuff and meeting with the judge."

Grant says, "Mom, we've got to go."

Both the boys head toward the backyard.

"Wait, where's your car, Peter?"

"Back at my house," Peter says. "It's faster to walk there through the greenbelt."

"OK. Be careful. Have a good day."

"Peter, go. I'll catch up," Grant says. Peter walks on through the yard, the gate, into the greenbelt.

Grant stares at his mother. "Have you ever lied to me?"

He doesn't sound like a child. He sounds like a young man, stepping into shoes he can't quite fill.

"About what?"

"I thought it was a yes or no question."

"No, I haven't lied to you."

"Did you really not keep a journal?"

He knows. "I didn't have time."

"You're a songwriter, Mom. You express yourself in words. Did you keep a journal?"

"Where on earth is this coming from?"

"You're shaking," he says, and she knows he's right.

"You accusing me of lying is upsetting," Iris says through clenched teeth.

"OK. I love you," Grant says, and he turns and goes out the door. Into the greenbelt.

She can feel him slipping away from her now. The greatest fear of her life, her children turning their backs on her.

How does he know about the journal? Who told him?

She heads up to his room.

35

JULIA

Ned texted Julia early and asked her for a ride to school. He also asked her for help in organizing his mother's stuff, at least giving him an idea of what to do with it. He hasn't paid attention to her unanswered texts, but she decides Ned is key to getting Marland off her back. So she buries her anger and walks to his house, her mind racing after hearing Marland's threats. If her parents were involved in Danielle's death—it was the question she couldn't imagine asking, but there it was—it had to be dealt with.

Danielle had something on them, something bad from the past.

Maybe it was about Grant's adoption. A bribe? A broken law? Something worse. It had to be worse, she thought. Why would Ned ask her to come over and help organize things? Either he wants to talk, or he takes her loyalty and friendship for granted.

Packing up his mother's stuff seems rushed to her, but she takes it as a sign that Gordon is desperate to get his son out of Austin, back to London. Away from all this. Gordon must know his slightly wayward son has gone fully wayward. Never mind if there was an extradition treaty with the UK. Gordon could get his son to Africa, where there were countries without extradition treaties. Ghana would extradite, but Ned was a minor. Gordon could hide him.

So it was up to her. Maybe whatever hold Danielle had on her parents was here in this house, and it was up to Julia to find it.

Make Gordon's fear and anxiety work for her. Pretend she wasn't hurt by Ned's abandonment and Marland's…insistence that she step into Ned's role.

Ned greets her like everything's sort of normal between them— is he for real, she wonders, or is he just in a grief-fueled daze?— and he walks her to his mother's large closet.

"I can't use any of this," he says. "I thought maybe a church or a resale shop…What do you think?"

"Sure," she says. She doesn't want to say anything else to him. It's easy for him to act like he doesn't know what Marland has said, and maybe he doesn't.

She surveys the closet. It's a lot of professional wear, and she knows nothing about that, but this will let her search the closet. Wouldn't it be likely, if Danielle had hidden something in the house, she would have done so in a room her son rarely ventured into? "I can organize it for you, count the number of items." She tries to put a hint of enthusiasm into her voice.

"Before you came over," he says, "I sat on the couch and just stared off into space for ten minutes."

"Ned." She's so angry with him and at the same time she feels sorry for him. He's never going to get over this, she realizes. He feels guilt about what happened to his mother. That is not something you shake. And here's his father, telling him to bundle up his mother's life, pack it up and give it away, and he's just doing it.

"I'm sorry I didn't answer your texts last night. My dad just kept talking at me. I don't know what to do about anything," he says. "I'll talk to Marland about leaving you alone, Jules." His voice is small.

It will make no difference, except then he can claim that he tried. "That's fine," she says. "I've got it handled. You have enough to worry about."

"You do? Oh, good." Now he's absolved from responsibility. She can almost see the relief in his face. "Papa is sleeping in the guest room, so you can lay out clothes on the bed if that helps. Papa is working on her office."

Danielle's office is another interesting place where secrets could be hidden. But she can focus on only one room at a time and so she starts here.

She begins by organizing the suits first—a couple of them have dust on the shoulders. Then a long lines of slacks and jeans. With the pants, she starts checking the pockets and she goes back and checks the suit jacket pockets as well. Nothing. She starts on the blazers. Nothing. She notices some discarded clothes on the floor, roughly tossed toward the laundry hamper, and those will need to be washed or dry-cleaned before they're donated. She organizes them and then starts to work through the clothes already in the closed hamper. She picks up one—a navy blazer—and a phone falls out from its inner pocket, onto the floor.

Julia kneels by it.

Hadn't Ned said he lost a phone and Marland told her he wanted Ned's burner?

Danielle had it. And had hidden it. Tucked in a jacket down in a hamper.

She turns it on. It still holds a charge, a slight one. There is one number in the phone.

It's the same number she's seen before. Marland's number.

This burner was what Marland wanted in exchange for that video of her father walking at night with Danielle.

Julia remembers to breathe. She goes to the text app and looks through them. Ned had been using Critterscape to communicate with his customers, but not with Marland. She opens the text app and reads the last and final text:

Listen to me, you punk. You are going to leave Ned alone and never contact him again or I'll have the police on your ass so fast your head will spin.

There is only one person who could have written a text like that—a parent. It screams *parent who found my son's burner phone he used to communicate with a drug dealer and rather than turn over my son to the police I'll just break off the business relationship how do you like that?*

There was one response: bitch don't threaten me

Julia stares at the message. She hears Ned calling for her, and she shoves the phone into her boot, smooths the hem of her jeans over it.

"Yeah, what?" She steps out of his mom's closet.

"I don't know that I can do this right now. It's all too soon."

"You have to deal with it eventually," she says.

Ned holds up a document. "I found this in her files."

"What?"

He looks guilty for a moment, and she feels the weight of the phone against her ankle. The text would kill Ned, the idea that this so-called harmless prescription pill dealing he'd engaged in had led to his mother's death, that Danielle had threatened Marland and he'd killed her to ensure her silence.

Ned holds a folder with more papers in it. "I wondered... well, Papa asked me if she had a will."

Julia hasn't thought of that. Wills were something for adults to worry about. "I'm sure she must have," Julia says. "She was a lawyer."

"Yeah, well, yes, she did, and she left everything to me. The problem is... the house isn't in her name." His voice is a whisper.

Julia waits.

"It's held in the name of a company. Firebird Investments." He shows her the papers in the folder. "My dad started making phone calls. They don't call back. Their website is super basic. No one knows who this company is. It's like in a movie—it's like a front company."

"Why would she buy a house and then not have it in her name?"

"I guess the answer is that someone bought it for her."

"Bought. Her. A. House. For real."

"Yeah."

"Who would buy your mom a house?" Most of the homes in Winding Creek had been moderately priced when first built, but the property values in Lakehaven skyrocketed as Austin grew and money poured in from Californian and New England buyers. Now the homes cost well over twice what they had fifteen years ago. She knew that because she'd heard her parents talk about whether or not to sell once Grant started college... The money would help finance his education, but where would they buy a house in Austin at a reasonable price? It was a dilemma.

"My dad looked up Firebird Investments. They don't seem to exist. I mean, they're not at the address used in the home purchase papers. At least not now."

Mystery upon mystery. But she thinks, sickeningly, that the solution to the murder lies in her boot. "I need to go outside. I need some fresh air."

"What's the matter?"

"I'm going through your dead mother's clothes first thing in the morning and it's overwhelming," she says snappishly, when she didn't mean to use those words or that tone. Ned's mouth trembles, but she cannot stand to see him cry right now. It would undo her grief and her rage. So she pushes past him and goes out into the yard. The day is cloudy, perfect for mourning, and she sinks to her knees in the grass.

What is she going to do? The weight of her bad choice presses down on her like a giant's fist.

If she shows this phone to the police, Ned will be exposed as a…drug dealer. There are no kinder words. Sure, he wasn't trafficking heroin, but what he was doing was illegal. Earlier she'd done an internet search, and yes, there were examples of nice suburban kids getting busted for drug dealing at high schools and colleges, and guess what, often they went to prison. She knows about the ring. She hasn't reported it. With a murder complicating this, she knows she is in serious trouble.

So, not an option. Also not an option: letting Marland get away with Danielle's murder. She doesn't know if he did it. But the police don't know about him, and here he'd threatened her directly. He had to be a suspect. But the moment she accuses him, even if she does it anonymously, the police will start to search for the connection between Marland and Danielle and Ned, and Marland, who was so oddly obsessed with her being involved, will tie her to all this. And college will be over for her, for Ned. What would the admissions officers make of their entrepreneurial spirit? She starts thinking of the first line of her apologetic essay:

I really learned the meaning of friendship when I kept my mouth shut and then interacted with the dealer of my friend's prescription drug ring.

She bursts into tears. A shadow falls across her and she looks up. Ned's dad, standing there.

"Are you all right?" he says in his low tone.

"Yes," she says. "No. But I'm supposed to say yes."

Gordon sits down next to her. "None of this is easy."

"No. Harder for you and Ned, of course."

She can feel the weight of the phone in her boot. If she sits the wrong way, the phone might slide out, and what would she say? *Oh hey, sorry. Just stealing this phone of your dead ex-wife.* It was concealing evidence. If she did nothing, she broke a law; if she took it to the police, even if she made a deal where she wouldn't be charged or prosecuted, it would still all come out. She wouldn't be in jail, but she likely wouldn't be in college. Could a deal with the cops be kept secret, truly secret, where a college couldn't find out? They were minors. But it was such a huge risk. Her whole future at stake. It was nice to sit here and listen to Gordon's deep voice and be caught between two horrendous decisions but not make one yet.

"How well did you know her?" she asks suddenly.

Gordon's eyebrows go up, and although he and Ned are so different, they have those same eyebrows. "Well, I married her."

"But not for that long. I mean. Forgive me, but…"

"No, you're right. It was a short marriage. But both of us thought it would be forever. We thought we could overcome all the obstacles. The distance. The cultural differences. I quite loved her."

"I'm sorry it didn't work out," she says.

The smile widens. "I'm sorry, too, because I think she made a good life for herself and I should have shared in that, helped her build it."

Julia nods. "It must have been hard to leave Ned, though."

"I didn't realize how hard it would be." He clears his throat and looks away. "Sometimes new fathers are not very bright. Danielle convinced me I wouldn't really miss him. That my work would consume me again, and they'd visit me…and it so rarely happened. Once I was gone, it was like I was dead." He lets that last word hang in the air. "I had to beg to see Ned. And I couldn't understand why. Here was a woman who made a career out of connecting children to parents, and yet she stood in the way of me connecting with my son." He clears his throat again. "Ned doesn't want to hear that, I suspect, and I don't want to say it to him. What does it matter now? He and I are responsible for our own relationship."

Julia isn't sure she buys into this poor-pitiful-me routine; he could have chosen a job closer to his son. And if he kept him here, well, then wouldn't Ned have to deal with Marland? It would be easier for her.

The words come more quickly than she expects. "He's your problem now."

Gordon looks surprised at her tone. "He's not a problem. He's a kid."

"I have to go." She has what she came for and she doesn't feel the need to be nice. What a curse that is, the niceness that is expected of her. "If he still wants to go to school, I'll take him."

"I know Ned is grateful for your friendship."

"I don't know that," she says, more angrily than she intends.

"You seem upset," he says.

The question comes to her and she doesn't hesitate to ask it. "What did your ex have on my family?"

"What?" He seems genuinely surprised.

"She had some leverage over my parents. I suspect it had to do with Grant's adoption, but I don't know that for sure."

"I have no idea. She met your parents after we divorced."

"She never mentioned it?"

"No. Why would she?"

Because you had a child together and if something happened to her, she'd want you to know the truth.

She's said too much and she realizes it. "All right. I'll get Ned to school."

She has the phone. She has proof of a threat against Danielle. But if she shows it, the explanation will derail Ned's life and her future and...maybe it's a card she won't have to play. Maybe she can get Marland out of her life with a threat.

She sees Ned standing at the front door, his school backpack on his shoulder, as if life is normal again.

"Ned, you ready to go to school?" she calls, and her voice is surprisingly calm.

36

GRANT

"Are you all right?" Peter asks Grant. He's waited on the trail for Grant to catch up.

"The Sender said she was a liar and yes, I think my mom is lying to me."

"If she is, it's for a good reason."

"Is it? Is it?" Grant's voice rises. "I know that we're supposed to think our parents are useless and lame and know nothing, but I love my mom and dad." His voice cracks. This is not the kind of stuff he ever dreamed he would say to a senior, even an unpopular one, but he does it and he sees in Peter's face that this is all right. "I don't know why they would lie."

"Because they love you. What people do for love..." Peter trails off.

"If we find out who is doing this, then we'll know why it is happening," Grant says.

"I brought a camera to conceal." Peter holds up a small handheld camera from his bag, along with black masking tape. "Basically, we're gonna aim this at the tree. There's a flash drive that it will record to as a backup. It has a motion detector, so it won't keep filming all the time."

"Where did you get all this?"

"I asked another hacker who's a hobbyist photographer. It's his equipment."

Grant walks Peter along the trail and points at the tree as they approach it.

"So that's the famous tree." Peter studies the angles. Then he places the camera in the low branches of a nearby tree.

"Check to see if something was left for you," Peter suggests as he works. "After all, they sent you another email."

Grant kneels by the tree and checks. "No, nothing. Seems dumb now that I ever hid things here."

"We all need a place to keep our secrets," Peter says.

"Where do you keep yours?"

"Oh, I don't bother with secrets. No one truly has a secret in a world where we can be hacked."

"You don't believe that."

Peter shrugs, makes a final adjustment to the camera, and camouflages it with a branch. "OK. Let's go send your email and see if your stalker takes the bait."

* * *

As Peter drives them to the high school, Grant sends the email from his phone: Hey. You keep saying stuff about my parents. I'd like to see some proof.

And a sudden reply, as if the Sender was reading emails when Grant's message arrived: Your parents have the proof.

37

FROM IRIS POLLITT'S "FROM RUSSIA WITH LOVE" ADOPTION JOURNAL

2002

The next day my shoulders and back and legs ached, delayed soreness from the crash. I took aspirin. Kyle, also aching, with a wrenched arm, didn't sleep well either but finally drifted off and started snoring. I felt like I should hide out in the hotel room, but I couldn't. Danielle wasn't answering her cell phone or her hotel room phone, but I knew she had other orphanages to visit. She was staying in Russia longer than we were. I went downstairs and asked the concierge for recommendations on where I might buy infant clothes, diapers, and toys for older kids. The concierge helpfully gave me a list in English, with a map, and offered an interpreter to go with me, but told me the higher-end stores often had a shopping assistant who spoke English.

I will not be scared off by these criminals, these punks, I told myself. I ate a quick breakfast at the hotel's buffet and headed out. By myself.

I went first to a large chain drugstore to buy a huge amount of diapers, lotions, and such and had the store deliver it to the hotel. There. Galina will have to forgive me for grabbing her arm, I thought. Then I went to a store that sold infant clothes, which I bought in a variety of sizes. Also delivered back to the hotel. Then to another store for toys and such. I bought hardboard storybooks and more stuffed animals (these kids needed something to hold) and two computer game consoles for the older kids, along with games the English-speaking sales clerk told me are "good" and "cool."

No one noticed me or paid attention to me.

I had the toy purchases sent to the hotel. I tried Danielle on her phone. No answer, no text. I felt a worry creep up my spine. No text from Kyle either. Was he still asleep? I texted him, told him I'd gone shopping. I could head back to the hotel, but I knew I couldn't sleep, and Saint Petersburg is supposed to be a lovely and interesting city.

I will not be bullied. Or scared.

Snow started falling. Normally I would find this charming, but it was so cold, so penetratingly cold, I wondered how any civilization arose here. I am going to take Sasha—Grant—away from all this and to the bright Texas warmth.

I walked down to a café that wasn't too crowded and looked spotlessly clean. I sat alone at a table in a corner, consulted the Russian-language app on my phone, figured out how to order, butchered the request but still managed to get a cup of hot tea with honey stirred in for sweetness and a slice of cake, called *muraveynik*, which means "anthill." It tasted like crumbled cookies covered in milk caramel, joined with sour cream, shaped and baked into its unappetizing namesake. But the *muraveynik* is delicious—sweet and dense—and the tea warmed me up. I decided having high blood sugar was a plus, so I toyed with having another cup of tea and sampling the honey cake, another Russian staple. I wondered if Grant would crave cakes such as these—surely they got a sweet now and then at the orphanage; where would I find genuine Russian recipes for them?—when the warning woman from the airport slid into the seat across from me.

I didn't scream. I didn't panic. I stared at her and she stared at me. Then she smiled.

"The anthill is not considered a fancy cake at all. Every family has their recipe. My mother puts chocolate chips in hers." Her English was excellent, her accent light.

"If I'd taken your advice and gone home, I never would have gotten to try it," I said. My voice shook and I swallowed some tea, hoping she wouldn't notice. "So what do you have to say to me now? Why do you care what my husband and I do? Did you know we were run off the road yesterday?"

For a moment she frowned. Then she said: "How much have you spent on getting this baby?"

"A lot and it's none of your business."

"And your daughter was very sick. Also very expensive. You must be wealthy."

"My husband has a good job."

"Does he, now?"

I didn't like where this was going. "What do you want?"

"I want you to pick another child at that orphanage. It's not too late. There are so many other children there who need love."

"Why? Why not Sasha?"

"If you pick another child, you decline Sasha, you will be amply rewarded. A quarter million dollars in an account for you, offshore. Tax free."

I just stared at her. "Who the hell are you?"

"This offer is good for today. You can call and tell the orphanage that you did not bond with Sasha, that you'd like to try another child. There are so many. So. Many."

I started to speak, and she held up a gloved hand, like an impatient teacher cutting off a student's meandering reply. "I will answer no questions. This is the deal. Just think of all the money you've spent on your daughter, and this adoption, and you'll be able to put at least one of them through private college if you just do as I ask. It will be the easiest money you've ever made."

"Why?"

"I said, no questions."

"I could say no to adopting Sasha and then you will not pay me."

"The moment you say no," the warning woman said, "I will call you with an account number in a Cayman's bank, and you can verify the amount. I won't cheat you."

"Why do you want my baby?" I hated the tears in my voice.

"He's not your baby. Not yet. He won't even remember that you played with him yesterday. You just say no. Your husband and your adoption consultant may be surprised, but they won't talk you out of it. You're a strong personality, Iris. I admire that about you."

She slid a cell phone to me. "It's a burner phone. There's one number programmed in it. You call that number, day or night, and I'll answer. I understand you have to think about it. I understand you have to sell this to Kyle. Or simply tell him you don't want the child. He seems like he would defer to you. But it really is for the best." She stood up.

Once, after my dad abandoned us, some girls cornered me on the playground and teased me about having a deadbeat father who had taken off. I wasn't a kid who got into fights. But they were pushing me and shoving me between them, like I was nothing, like they had the right, and I don't even remember it, but I bloodied two of their noses and gave the other a black eye. And I went crying to the teacher, ashamed of what I'd done, so many tears, until they sent me home, and on the drive home, Mama telling me how embarrassed she was, didn't I have manners, didn't I know better. A smile cracked my face, and those mean little bitches never bothered me again or even looked at me sideways or said a word to me that they didn't pick carefully.

I wondered in that moment if I could deck her, knock her silly with a playground punch, make her tell me why. But she looked back at me with an unflinching gaze.

I took the phone. "What happens if I say no to your offer?" I said.

"Say no," she answered, "and find out." Then she turned and walked away.

I slipped the burner phone into my purse. I walked back to the hotel. I never did try the honey cake. Kyle had woken up and I slid into the bed next to him and lied about what I'd done, who I'd seen. I kissed him to stop his questions.

I can write stuff like that now because after today this journal isn't for you anymore. It's for me.

I didn't tell Kyle about the warning woman or the phone in my purse or the money in the offshore account. I just told him I loved him and listened to him talking about teaching Sasha to play football and baseball and that he'd get him a telescope so they could look at the craters on the moon together, the giant red spot on Jupiter, and then we called Julia and talked to her on the phone so she could hear our voices, and we listened to her giggle and I thought of that woman and that money and the choice she told me I had to make.

I didn't tell Danielle, but I called Pavel at his apartment and asked him for a favor while Kyle was in the shower. I asked him to call Maria and ask how many children total are at Volkov. He called back and told me one hundred fifty-seven.

I'm sure they all deserve love. A chance. A shot at happiness. A hundred and fifty-six candidates. Maybe the child that is truly perfect for us is one of them.

Or maybe we've already found the one who is.

38

KYLE

Kyle has gotten dressed for work in a nice suit but is lying atop the made bed in the master bedroom. He just lay down for a second and he has no energy to rise. As if the world is pressing down on him.

He closes his eyes to think. He is surprised that Julia is going to school, given what happened on Sunday, but she missed Monday and now it seems she's going. Ned, too, but maybe it will help Ned to have his friends around him. Kyle is pretty sure no schoolwork will get done this day.

Iris is in Grant's bedroom. A mother is in a teenage boy's room for this long for only one reason, and that is to search it. He wonders if Grant found the bloodied library bag he hid in the tree and that is what Iris has found. She has been in there for a long time, and he just hopes she doesn't come out with a bag of weed (very un-Grant-like).

He goes to her desk in the mudroom. On the shelf above her computer is a series of notebooks, her lyric books that turned into songs for NSYNC and Britney Spears and Christina Aguilera, and once, improbably, for Chris Isaak. She doesn't write anymore, and when he pulls three of them down, he can see the edge of a dark-blue journal. He pulls it out, glancing up to make sure he's alone.

He pages through the memories, the drama, of their time in Russia. He hasn't looked at it in years.

Then he sees it. At the bottom of a page, toward the end. He sees it and he knows what Iris has done.

The doorbell rings. He hopes it's not the press again.

He closes the journal, steadies his breathing, and replaces it behind the lyric books. He brushes the light layer of dust from his shaking hands. He answers the door as Iris comes downstairs. He can't look at Iris right now. It's the Lakehaven detective, Carmen Ames, and the Travis County detective, Jamika Ponder.

"Good morning," he says.

"May we come inside, sir?" Detective Ponder asks. No "good morning."

He nods and lets them in.

"Did you get in a fight, Mr. Pollitt?" Ponder gestures toward his face.

"I fell in the greenbelt while running the other day."

"Yes, sir, when did that happen?"

"Why would that matter?" he asks, and the second he does he knows he's made a mistake.

"Just curious," Ames says.

He glances between the two of them. It's not exactly good cop/ bad cop. Ponder is in charge. He saw that on the news and Iris said she ran the meeting.

"Sunday. I went for a run."

"Right after the body was discovered?"

"Well, yes," he says awkwardly. "But that's how I deal with stress."

"Your friend is found dead by your daughter. Your wife accompanies her to the police station. Your young son is here alone. And you go for a run."

"Yes," Kyle says, putting some firmness into his voice. "Is that a problem?" He senses Iris stepping up behind him, listening. He still can't look at her, not now. He will crack if he looks at her.

From a large backpack Ponder holds up an evidence bag…containing the crushed remains of some electronic device. Black, with a silvery-green edging. "Do you recognize this, sir?"

"It looks like broken electronics." He keeps his voice amazingly steady. This is worse than the journal.

"Crushed and pummeled," Ames says. "It's a phone."

"Where did you find it?"

"In your trash can late last night, sir."

"Don't you need a warrant?" Iris says, but no, they don't. Not to search his trash.

"What we got was an anonymous tip that said you might be getting rid of a phone identical to the one found near Danielle's body. That phone had only one number in its log," Ponder says. "Is this your phone?"

"It's not mine." Someone else knew he had the phone and someone else knew he might destroy it after Danielle died. His chest feels thick with shock.

"Is it your son's? Or your daughter's? Or your wife's? Mrs. Pollitt, do you recognize this phone?"

Kyle knows he should shut up. He should call Kip Evander, a local lawyer he knows well. Kip specializes in personal injury, but he's done criminal defense a few times, and it would look better to call a lawyer friend than a defense specialist. The thought that the police will think the phone belongs to someone in his family is crushing. "No," he says. "I mean, yes, I destroyed the phone. But it wasn't my property."

He's played this wrong. He knows that now. But he has to protect Iris, and in turn, his children. All of them. Sometimes you take the bullet even when it's not meant for you. Would he be so willing had he not read Danielle's handwriting on that page?

"Whose phone was it?" Ponder asks.

"Honey, I think we should just not say any more until a lawyer is present," Iris says.

He wants to turn to Iris and tell her how much he loves her. And that it will be OK. He'll make it OK.

The detectives wait to see what he says to her, and when he stays silent, Ponder asks again: "Whose phone, Mr. Pollitt?"

"Danielle's," he says. "She bought it."

"Mr. Pollitt, why did you have a phone belonging to Ms. Roberts?" Jamika Ponder asks the question almost mildly.

"Danielle gave it to me." He glances over at Iris, who's now standing protectively next to him. She stares at him. He stares back. *It will be all right.*

"Why did you not tell the police about this? Why didn't you come forward?" Ames asks.

"Her giving me a phone had nothing to do with what happened." His mind races. Who could have placed that call?

"We'd like to make that determination," Ponder says.

"Why did you have a phone from Danielle?" Iris asks, and her voice is flat, cold as a stone striking brick.

Kyle doesn't answer.

"Where were you Saturday night, Mr. Pollitt?"

"Here. Working late in my home office."

Ponder glances at Iris. "Is that so, Mrs. Pollitt?"

"Yes. Of course."

"Mrs. Pollitt, you said earlier you went to sleep around midnight. Was Mr. Pollitt in bed by then, too?"

Ponder can't miss the look between Iris and Kyle. "No, he wasn't, but I had set the security alarm already. If he turned it off, it would have beeped, and that always wakes me up. So he was in the house. He couldn't have left it."

"Was he in bed with you when you fell asleep?" Ponder asks again.

Iris shakes her head. She's staring at Kyle like he's a stranger. "No, but I just told you he can't turn off the alarm without waking me." She seems angry that Ponder isn't accepting her word for this as a given scientific fact.

"Did you talk to Danielle that evening, sir?"

"Briefly. She called me on the phone she'd given me. She was incoherent. She just said she wanted out, but she wouldn't tell me what that meant."

"We'd like to bring you in for further questioning, Mr. Pollitt."

"I understand. I'd like an attorney to be present. Iris, will you call Kip and have him meet me down at the police station?"

"Kyle, Kyle." Iris shakes her head. "What are you saying?"

"I'm not saying anything more," Kyle says. "Do you need to put handcuffs on me?"

"You're not under arrest."

"Oh. Yes. Of course." He's knows better, but right now his brain feels scrambled.

"Kyle...what the hell is this?" Iris's voice rises.

Kyle meets her stare with his own. "You are everything in the world to me. You and the kids. Know that. I want you to call Kip, and I want you to look out for our kids. Everything will be all right."

The detectives lead him out the door—it feels like his world has completely dissolved in less than one minute—and Kyle wonders if the life he knew has just vanished forever.

39

JULIA

The words Julia doesn't say to Ned on the drive to school: Well, your drug-ring buddy Marland is blackmailing me into working for him while you skulk off to London and are entirely off the hook, and though you're my best friend, I'm not going to let you destroy my life.

But she has to outthink both Ned and Marland. Get that video of her father and Danielle walking toward the park. Get it and destroy it. Without being forced to be Marland's accomplice and middleman to a bunch of prescription-downing Lakehaven kids who represent a revenue stream for him.

She has to act like everything is vaguely normal. Which it isn't.

"Are you sure you want to go to school?" Julia asks. She's driving, Ned in the passenger seat.

"I don't want to sit at home all day with my father," he says. He stares out the window. He just seems oblivious to her anger at him.

"With people at school, it's hard for Marland to get close to you."

Now he looks at her. "Get close to me?"

"If he wants to threaten you. To keep you quiet. Or hurt you."

"What?"

"He's a drug dealer and you broke a deal with him," she says. "In the movies this is where you get your leg broken."

"What movie? Plus, this is real life, and a Lakehaven kid getting roughed up would be bad for business."

That's true. He glances away from her.

"Why did you want me to drive you to a delivery?" she asks. Marland knows she did.

"I wasn't just delivering. From one kid I got physics notes, too."

"Ned." The anger in her voice makes him turn toward her. "Was it so I'd like you more? Feel closer to you, like we were partners in crime?"

"I liked being with you. You liked the danger. Admit it."

"You've made me an accomplice."

"No, I haven't. You're fine. Act like you know nothing. And Marland will just have to run it with someone else."

His denial is complete. It's like a door has closed.

But she has to stay close to him. So she changes the subject.

"Ned. You need to prepare yourself for the stares, the questions, the hugs of support from people who don't even know you…"

"I know." He's a little short with her. But if she tells him that Marland is blackmailing her, she'll have to say it's because of a video with his murdered mother and her father walking off in the darkness together. And she's afraid Ned will lose it. Either go after her father or go straight to the police.

And she's afraid of what the video means. She keeps shoving that awfulness back in the corner of her mind, where it paces and dances and won't stay still. Get the video, keep her and Ned out of trouble, because if one of them talks they both go down, save Dad. She can do all that. She's her mother's daughter.

Ned and Julia have first period together, Euro history, and the door is decorated with pictures of his mom at school events: supporting Ned in freshman basketball (the one year he played, before he hurt his knee and gave it up), standing with a large group of other moms at a Lakehaven football game, volunteering at a booth at the language festival (Ned was in Spanish club), pictures of her and Ned. Even a picture of her and Ned and Gordon, all smiles, when Gordon visited during the school year and got to see Ned perform with the choir.

Ned stares at the tribute.

"Are you all right?" Julia asks.

"No," he says. "I'm not." He opens the door and Julia follows him. The other students are quiet, but several come up and embrace him. These aren't kids Ned is close to, but in Lakehaven, a staggeringly high number of them have known one another since elementary school, and so there is a familiarity, a comfort. Ned doesn't cry. Julia does.

And then Mrs. McPherson calls the class to order, tells Ned how sorry she is, if he needs to excuse himself from class, it's fine, and that they'll continue with their discussion of the assigned reading. Julia loves Mrs. McPherson. She is her favorite teacher. Mrs. McPherson keeps it a normal class, mostly, and Julia sees the gratitude in Ned's face. The smile she used to wish she could see. The Ned she thought she knew.

They don't have second period together, and they part ways, then reunite for third, which is varsity chorale. They sing after the choir director tells Ned how sorry she is and remembers the times Danielle volunteered to hand out programs before the concerts, or helped with the costumes for the spring musical, or chaperoned the kids during the all-region choir auditions. People don't much feel like singing after this, but they do, and the choir director sensibly has them focus on the more somber songs for the upcoming spring concert. Julia, with the altos, glances at Ned again and again, surrounded by his fellow tenors, but he doesn't look her way. He just looks numb now, and she wonders if he wants to go home.

Fourth period she has AP physics and he has Spanish—and this is finally where some idiot asks her what it was like to find a body and she freezes him with a stare, glad that Ned is not there—and then their lunch period. By the time she's gone through one of the lines to get a salad and bottled water, he's sitting at a table, surrounded by Julia's friends, who texted her after the murder, the same ones who teased her for becoming sweet on Ned, and now they're butterflying around him like he's a blooming flower.

She puts her salad and bottled water down across from him. "Go. Now," she says, and the girls almost seem ready to argue.

"Now he's interesting? Go," she says again, and that time it's enough. They wander off.

"Are you saying your friends didn't think I was interesting before?" The old smile of the old Ned, back for a moment.

"I am. Are you tired of people asking you how you are?" She pokes at her salad to spare him the penetrating gaze she wants to give him.

"A little. I might go home now. My dad cleared it with the school, if I felt overwhelmed. I'm about two-thirds whelmed." He pauses. "I don't want to cry in front of everyone."

"It's too soon. You came back too soon."

"It's better here. I can't stay in that house with my dad. It's smothering. This is easier, believe it or not. How are your parents?"

"My...They're fine. I mean, not fine. They're coping."

She's looking at her salad and then another wave of sympathizers comes by. There are kids like that, who want to attach themselves to drama. Rumor has already spread that he's moving soon to London. She thinks: *He's not interesting; he's a mess. He gave me a key and he smiled at me and he made me think we had something and I've got this horrible problem because he's thrown me to a wolf.*

Ned is polite to the students, who move on after rote expressions of sympathy. He looks down at his plate. He's barely touched his two slices of pizza.

Now he looks up at her. "Julia. I think I know who did it." He says the words like they're painful.

She just stares at him. She feels drunk with fear. Then she moves around her salad with her fork, and she says: "Then you have to tell the police."

"You're not going to ask who it is? That's like the reaction of 99.9 percent of the human race." His voice is very small.

"What I care about is you and what you do," she says. "I don't want you to do something stupid." *Who, who, who?* she thinks. *He can't mean my dad. He can't.* So who could he mean? Marland? If it's Marland then the guilt has to be crushing Ned. If he never deals the prescription drugs then Marland never enters his and Danielle's life.

She can almost see Ned summoning the words. "Look. All I have to do is get him talking on tape…" And then his phone pings, a ringtone she's never heard before.

"That's my dad," he says, almost in relief, and picks up the phone. Looks at the screen.

And she sees something change in his face. Now he looks at her.

"What…? What is it?" she asks. Dread in her voice.

"Dad said he saw the two detectives who were at the meeting come to your house and take your dad away in a police car."

"That can't be," she says.

"My dad ran over to the driveway and asked if they were arresting your dad and they said no."

"They're just interviewing him, then."

"At the station? Why at the station?"

"Ned…who do you think did this?"

He looks at her. "What do you know? Why are they talking to your dad?"

Something must show in her face, some expression, because he stands up quickly, shoving back the chair he was sitting in, and the other students, watching them already, notice.

"I don't know, Ned. You just said you think someone else did this. *Who?*"

"Why are the cops talking to your dad?" he asks, in a louder voice, and she can see that other students have heard him now. But he doesn't wait for an answer. He turns and runs from the cafeteria.

It's the longest walk of her life, leaving her lunch table, the weight of a hundred stares on her back, and going to find someplace private where she can text her mother.

40

IRIS

Kyle has gone with the police. Iris has called Kip Evander and asked him to go to the police station. It's not an arrest. It's a questioning. Just questions.

About secrets her husband has kept from her.

And her son. This is a house of secrets.

And if she's going to save her family, she needs to know them all.

Iris was in Grant's room when the police came, kneeling on the floor, looking at neatly bound stacks of cash hidden under the swimsuits he's grown out of and she meant to donate to a resale shop. Where did this money come from? She could text him, but she doesn't want to give him hours to formulate a lie. And she can't bear to tell them, over the phone, that their father is being questioned by the police. Wait for them to get home from school.

And then here are the police, talking about a phone shared between Kyle and Danielle and an anonymous tip.

There was a phone and apparently Kyle destroyed it after Danielle was dead.

She finds it hard to believe they were having an affair. She believes she would know the signs. She knows Kyle. And she cannot imagine some odd passion arising between the two of them. It just does not seem likely.

But do we ever know someone? She shakes the thought away.

She watches Kyle leave with the detectives and Gordon hurry over, asking questions, and then she sees Gordon walk back slowly to Danielle's house after the cars are gone and just stand on the porch. Safest to assume he'll assume the worst.

How long will it take the neighborhood to find this out? Someone other than Gordon will have seen Kyle in the police car, even if not in handcuffs. He was taken away, even if not under arrest. This neighborhood is living on the knife's edge, and someone will talk. Someone will accuse him. And there was a time she would have worried about what that would do to her and the kids, but the brief flare of worry in her chest fades into a smoking ember.

The Butlers. If someone called in an anonymous tip against her family, it had to be the Butlers. Steve with his bruised knuckles and Carrie with her whispered threats. And now Iris is certain: Carrie Butler has implicated her husband as being the unseen figure walking the streets the night of the murder, the boogeyman to scare Winding Creek.

They are hiding something. They could have lied about their patched relationship with Danielle. They could have killed her, and they could be framing her husband.

She walks down to the Butler house. Neither car is in the driveway, but the garage door is closed. They keep to themselves.

Detectives Ponder and Ames were both at the neighborhood rally. They heard Carrie Butler talk. They know she saw someone. Now this, searching in their trash and finding something unimaginable.

Why did Kyle have the phone? Were they...?

Iris cannot imagine them together and then she does, Kyle's strong back, moving, Danielle's vapid face contorted in pleasure, writhing under Kyle, squirming under her husband. Sure. It could happen. Kyle's been off, the accident on the greenbelt—maybe there was no accident. Maybe someone beat him up. But if someone knew about the affair, why not go to the police immediately to say, *Hey, take a look at Kyle Pollitt?*

It didn't happen. It never happened.

She stands before the Butler house.

They hate you. They didn't get a baby, and you did, and they hate you and Kyle. And they hated Danielle. She could see the hatred for Danielle under their honeyed explanations. Sure. But that she and Kyle had gotten a child when Russia still offered them, well, it was crazy to hate them for that. The Butlers' shortcomings as potential adoptive parents were their own issue.

But people weren't logical when it came to babies, or happiness, or the lives they think they should have and don't. She wasn't.

Never ask me how much I would love this baby. Her words to Danielle that had managed to find a sticking spot deep in her brain.

What would the Butlers do? Imagine the unimaginable: Kyle and Danielle have an affair. Somehow the Butlers find out about it. Could they have blackmailed Danielle into taking them back on as clients? Would she place an innocent child with them for their silence? Maybe she agreed and then changed her mind and Steve Butler aimed that massive fist at Danielle's throat and...

She walks up the Butlers' empty driveway. She rings the front doorbell. Waits. There's no answer. She knocks on the door. No answer. They've gone to work. Steve works for a software company, he said. Is Carrie working a nursing shift, or has she gone to run a few quick errands?

She turns to leave and then she thinks: *This might be your only chance. If there's something inside that incriminates them... or Kyle... there's no one to do this but you.*

Iris turns back to the door. She lifts the two potted plants that stand sentinel by the front door. Empty beneath. She walks, nonchalantly, around the house. There's no backyard fence; the Butlers back up to a curve of greenbelt. If anyone jogging or walking along the trail should see her in their backyard, well, she'll wave like the good neighbor she is. She keeps her gaze locked on the house, moving from window to window. All the curtains and blinds are drawn. She reaches the patio and knocks again. Maybe the Butlers, being somewhat antisocial, just don't answer the front door but a back-door knock will get their attention. Nothing. She searches the wood above the back door, tries the potted plants. Under a brick with the words STEVE AND CARRIE hand painted on it, she finds a key.

Iris decides if an alarm system starts beeping the moment she enters, she'll just run. She has no excuse to be here.

The door unlocks and she's in, stepping into the house's silence. She doesn't call out. She leaves the door open because if she gets caught, she'll lie and say the back door was open; she noticed it while walking on the greenbelt and came to investigate, in case her neighbors and new friends were in trouble.

She reminds herself that Steve put that gun in a drawer in the foyer. It may not still be there. Or it might be, if she needs it.

The back door opens onto a breakfast nook and kitchen, which are both empty. She notices the carafe of coffee is partially full, but the heat light is off. Dishes in the sink. She stands and listens to the silence. No distant sound of running water or television hum. No one's here.

Iris moves quickly through the house, nearly staggering with the idea that she's done this, but also energized by it. *You want to mess with me? My husband? My family? Bring it.* Then she thinks of Steve's awful face when she came here, the sickening false smile of Carrie's.

She isn't sure what she's even looking for. She goes to their cordless phone, perched on its charger and answering machine. She glances through the call log. She doesn't see Danielle's number. Or any number she recognizes. She listens to the messages. A dentist office calling about an overdue bill, a couple of telemarketers cut off by the answering machine's time limit, an aunt Judy calling and urging Steve to please call his mother, a real estate agent calling for Firebird Holdings, asking if this was the right number. Iris recognizes the real estate agent's name...She'd cold-called their house as well last week, asking if they were interested in selling. It wasn't uncommon. The influx of corporate relocations to Austin meant it was a seller's market, and all the new people from California and New England arriving in Austin needed houses.

But who was Firebird Holdings? There is a small built-in desk, with a built-in file cabinet, and she goes through the folders: phone, cable, lawn service, insurance.

There is no mortgage file. They bought this house right near

Danielle. That always struck her as too much coincidence to swallow. Now a real estate agent calling here, asking for a different owner?

Do the Butlers not own their own house?

She shakes the thought away. This can't matter. She searches the desk but finds nothing of interest. No signed confessions. The computer—an older iMac—takes up much of the desk. She tries to access it; it asks for a password. She knows nothing about the Butlers other than they want a child and were denied. And that they'd lost two children. Carrie had mentioned their names. John and Addie. She tries both names, then the two names together. It doesn't work.

She gives up on the computer and goes into their bedroom. She searches the dressers, the cabinets, the closets. Nothing...until she finds a phone. A cheap plastic phone, like the one found in her and Kyle's trash.

What? The same cheap burner phone, with its silvery-green plastic edging, that Danielle gave to Kyle? She could visualize the odd shards of green in the bag Ponder had shown them. But why would Danielle give a phone to a pair of rejected parents who she had then mended fences with?

After a moment's consideration, she checks the call log. Just one number in it. She memorizes the number and puts the phone back where she found it. It is hard for her to leave it; what if it could prove some relationship between the Butlers and Danielle? But if she takes it, they will know someone has been in the house. The phone is here. Carrie is not the only one who can make an anonymous tip.

The last time she'd seen a phone with one number programmed into it, it had been slid across a teashop table in Saint Petersburg, a woman asking her to do the impossible.

Iris goes upstairs, wondering again if Carrie had maybe just run to the grocery store or to a morning workout. She's terrified of being caught here. But she goes. Upstairs is an office with a small desk, a computer, and a bookshelf full of computer and business books—Steve's study. Pictures of two children, one with Steve's red hair, are carefully framed and cover most of the wall. The next room is a guest bedroom, with pictures of Steve and Carrie and their children. The Butlers are smiling; she hardly recognizes Carrie. Their children are laughing. This was a happy family, once.

The last room is a nursery. It looks as if it is immediately ready for a baby.

She feels a chill inch down her spine. Her palms grow sweaty. The Butlers don't have a baby yet. They've been turned down, and even if Danielle was helping them again, there are no guarantees. When one nation says no, it's easier for another nation to say no.

But they have a nursery.

She checks the closet. Linens, with the fresh smell of having been laundered. Unopened toys. Stuffed animals with the sales tags still attached. She studies it all for a moment and then she closes the door.

Carrie Butler claimed to be upstairs when she saw the mysterious man go past. So she was either in her husband's study, the guest room, or…this room. The rocking chair is close to the window. Does Carrie Butler sit here, waiting for a baby, staring out at the night? Was she sitting there when someone went by? Or is she lying?

She hears the rumble of a garage door opening.

Iris runs down the stairs, exits the house, closes the door to the patio, and hurries out to the greenbelt. She walks along the trail to her house, hoping she was unseen by whoever arrived home.

And then she walks back to the Butler house and rings the doorbell.

Carrie Butler answers the door, dressed in workout clothes, hair pulled back into a perfect ponytail.

"Iris."

"Is there something you want to say to me?"

"You mean other than 'good morning'?"

"You talked about seeing someone on the street the night Danielle died."

"And?"

"Do you think it's Kyle you saw that night?"

"Hard to say. It could have been."

"It wasn't him. Why are you doing this?"

"Doing what?" Her smile is toothpaste-ad perfect, bright, infallible.

"Coming after my family."

"I've done no such thing."

"Danielle couldn't get your personal failings past the foreign adoption services and so...you move onto her street?"

"We told you, that's a coincidence. We wanted a home in Lakehaven and this house became available. What does it matter?"

"You hated her. You blamed her."

The smile doesn't waver. "I'm sorry if I left you with that impression."

"Do you have emails proving that you resumed your business relationship with Danielle?"

"She'd come over and we'd talk."

"The police got an anonymous tip about my husband," Iris says. Confessing this to anyone, especially a gliding snake like Carrie, is agony, but she suspects Carrie already knows this.

"How unfortunate," Carrie says.

"Are you trying to get a child now? I mean, without Danielle to help you. Had she started this process?"

"Excuse me? How would that be any of your business?" Now there is a tremble on her lips.

"You tried before. I'm just asking." *And you have a completed nursery in your home.*

"We have a family member, a distant cousin of Steve's, who is expecting. She's unmarried and not prepared to care for a child. She wants us to raise the baby."

"I'm happy for you," Iris hears herself say. So they didn't need Danielle. And they're getting a child. A baby is going to arrive here soon. With a tidy explanation.

For a moment her response seems to mollify Carrie.

Iris says, "But you have to know, whoever you saw, it wasn't Kyle. It wasn't."

Carrie looks at her as if she holds their lives in her hands. It's a terrifying moment, a strange, odd grin.

"Did you and Danielle laugh at us? Talk about me and Steve being unfit?"

"No. Never. I had no idea you wanted kids. I didn't even know you. Danielle never mentioned you to us."

"I find that hard to believe, since you were one of her success stories."

Iris felt dizzy with the realization that her…not knowing this neighbor, not learning about them, was going to have a horrifying effect on her family's future. How different would it have been if she had reached out? *Oh, you know Danielle, too? Yes, she can be a headache.* Iris could hardly breathe with the shock.

"She never talked about you. Not after you moved in."

"She mocked us. I know."

"Not to me. You being mad at her has nothing to do with me or my family."

"I watched you all once. I followed her, saw her meeting with a group of women at that coffee shop off Old Travis. I understand they're all mothers she helped. Of course she talks about me. How did you find out about me?"

You followed her. That sounds healthy. "She mentioned your name to another mom. Not to me."

"One of her successful moms."

"Only because she was afraid of you."

"She misunderstood us being so upset. We would have done anything to get a child. Anything. You know what that's like."

Despite herself, Iris nods. She is suddenly afraid of this woman. Steve is all bluster, but Carrie is the knife in the shadows. There's something unconnected in her gaze, as if more than one voice plays in her head and she's trying to decide who to listen to.

"We. Would. Be. Wonderful. Parents." Carrie Butler's dazzling smile was back. "We already were. That's clear to most people. I don't know why that was not clear to Danielle. Or you."

"I'm sorry for everything you've been through," Iris says. "I hope everything works out with your new baby. I just want you to leave my family alone."

"If you don't want people to think that your husband's guilty,

Iris," Carrie says helpfully, "stop acting like he's guilty." She closes the door.

Iris stands there. Somehow, the answer to Danielle's murder is with these people. She knows it in her gut.

Her phone pings. Julia, texting: have the police arrested Dad? Ned knows.

41

EXCERPT OF TRANSCRIPT OF TCSO AND LPD INTERVIEW WITH KYLE POLLITT

Detective Ames: This is Detective Carmen Ames, interviewing Kyle Pollitt on January 8 with TCSO Detective Jamika Ponder. Also present is Mr. Pollitt's lawyer, Kip Evander.

Detective Ponder: Mr. Pollitt, can you tell me where you were on the night of January 6?

Pollitt: Yes. I was at home with my family. We had dinner together, the kids went off to do schoolwork or play video games, my wife went to go read the novel for her book club, and I watched a basketball game on TV. Then I went up to my office to work for a bit.

Detective Ames: You keep an office on the second floor of your home?

Pollitt: Yes.

Detective Ames: And does this office face the street or your backyard?

Pollitt: The street.

Detective Ames: So you can see the street, and the sidewalk, from your window.

Pollitt: Yes.

Detective Ames: And presumably be seen.

Pollitt: Well, yes, but normally I have the shades drawn.

Detective Ames: Did you have them drawn that night?

Pollitt: I believe I did.

Detective Ponder: We have a witness who says they were open and they could see you in your window at one point.

Pollitt: They might have been open…at one point. I honestly don't recall. There's not much to see out on the street at night. It's a very quiet neighborhood.

Detective Ponder: Did you see Danielle Roberts that night?

Pollitt: No.

Detective Ponder: Did you talk to her on the phone that night?

Pollitt: No.

Detective Ponder: Did you have a special phone with which to contact her?

Pollitt: Yes. She gave me a phone.

Ames: Do you recognize this destroyed phone?

Pollitt: I'm not sure how I would recognize something so pulverized.

Ames: Do you recognize it or not, sir?

Pollitt: I don't.

Detective Ames: This phone was found in a bag in your garbage the day after the Roberts murder.

Kip Evander: I'd like to know why you searched my client's garbage.

Detective Ames: We received a tip.

Evander: From whom?

Detective Ames: An anonymous tip.

Evander: So someone could have placed this broken phone into the Pollitt family's garbage can and then called you and here we are, with these ridiculous accusations. I want to thank you both for the early Christmas gift.

Detective Ponder: Is that what happened, Mr. Pollitt? You're being framed?

Pollitt: I don't understand what this phone has to do with anything.

Detective Ponder: We found a matching phone, a cheap one that Danielle Roberts used, at the site where her body was found. It had only one number called in it. She bought both phones at a local drugstore—prepaid ones. Sometimes in movies, they call them "burners," because you use them up and throw them away.

Pollitt: I'm familiar with the concept.

Detective Ponder: You know, even with a cracked SIM card, we can determine if this phone you destroyed was the one phone she called.

Evander: You have no reason to suspect my client in this crime. A phone proves nothing.

Detective Ames: Your client had a long relationship with the deceased due to her work, and they had known each other for a long time.

Evander: So? She knew lots of people. She had lots of friends.

Detective Ames: How would you characterize your relationship with Danielle Roberts, then?

Pollitt: She was a family friend. She was a neighbor.

Detective Ames: Were you particularly close?

Pollitt: What are you asking me?

Detective Ames: Were you having an affair with her?

Pollitt: No.

Detective Ames: Then why did you need a phone?

Pollitt: *(pause of several seconds)* She approached me once, a couple of weeks ago, at a party at her boyfriend's house. I was in the backyard, drinking a beer. She hinted that she would be open to seeing me. I was shocked, frankly, and I said no. I'm happily married, and I had no interest in her. She slipped the phone in my pocket.

Detective Ames: Did she ever approach you again?

Pollitt: Yes. I still said no.

Detective Ames: Why not just throw away the phone and tell your wife?

Pollitt: Danielle played a singular role in our lives, having helped us get our son. I didn't want Iris to know her friend had behaved this way. And keeping the phone around seemed to placate her.

Detective Ames: Or give her hope. Weird how there are no
sexy texts. Usually when you're offering to have an affair,
there's flirting.

Pollitt: We didn't flirt.

Detective Ames: So, she had an unrequited passion for you?

Pollitt: She had a boyfriend who was my friend. I don't know
what their set of issues was.

Detective Ames: Did you tell him about her approaches?

Pollitt: Of course not. Mike Horvath is my friend. So was she.
I assumed there was a rough patch that they could figure
out.

Detective Ames: Where did you keep this phone?

Pollitt: Hidden on a shelf in our garage, behind a box of pipe.

Detective Ponder: I'm going to ask you again. Did you have
any involvement with the death of Danielle Roberts?

Evander: I'd like to confer privately with my client.
    (Break)

Evander: We'd like to cooperate.

42

FROM IRIS POLLITT'S "FROM RUSSIA WITH LOVE" ADOPTION JOURNAL

2002

I made my choice.

Alone.

Without ever telling Kyle or Danielle what I was offered to say no to Grant.

And screw you, lady. His name is Grant. He's mine. Ours.

Feliks was not our driver this time. Pavel, however, was again our interpreter. His arm was still in a cast. I hugged him when I saw him at the hotel. Danielle hugged him, too. Our driver was an older man named Vladimir, balding and spare, with eyes that were always watching.

And I watched for the warning woman. I never called her. I never responded to her.

But she knew we were back. She knew our travel arrangements before; she knew our schedule.

I sounded paranoid. I was paranoid. Russia has that effect on people.

When we get on the plane to go back to America, Sasha will be in my arms and he'll soon enough be Grant Alexander Pollitt. The Russian boy he was will start to fade and a bright American boy will stand in his place. And the warning woman would find a new hobby.

I just hoped the phone she gave me wouldn't ring.

I steeled myself for the day ahead, in case she tried to disrupt our final steps.

Danielle and Pavel guided us to many buildings in Saint Petersburg. There was so much paper: papers to sign and money to give. This was like everyone in Russia exacting a price for taking their beautiful boy away: money, money, and more money. Pavel told Kyle what we were signing and I half listened. I'd sign anything to get this baby. I started thinking of it as the Adoption Obstacle Course. My hand grew a little weary with the signatures. The Russians didn't smile a lot, as if they knew they were selling away a part of their future. I wondered, seeing Kyle hand more bills to the third Russian we met with, why it was fine for me to pay a bribe but so repellent if I had taken the warning woman's bribe.

"Are you OK?" Kyle kept asking me. I nodded. I looked for the warning woman, for the black SUV that had caused us to wreck, but there were only the faceless crowds, the normal traffic as we went from building to building, collecting paperwork and leaving bribes—sorry, payments. We would be here for ten days. It felt like forever already.

The paperwork was done. I forgot to say, earlier, we rode in a van this time, with lots of room, and at first I thought it was because I was nervous about being in a car again and the van was bigger. Like Danielle would worry about my feelings. But after our last signature and our last bribe-slash-gift, we went back to the hotel. It was the same one we stayed at before, which made me uneasy.

"I thought we were going to see Grant." I was done calling him Sasha.

"We are. There's another family riding with us. I hope that's fine. They're here for their first visit. I thought you wouldn't mind."

I did mind. I didn't mind. Kyle said, "Of course." Wonderful, I could ask them if an odd woman offered them a bribe not to adopt a child—it's such a conversation opener.

We went into the hotel; they were waiting for us in the lobby. Vince and Chele Robinette, from Philadelphia, a nice, friendly couple. They were adopting a little girl, also at Volkov, and like us that first trip, they were loaded with gift bags and hope. They also didn't look like anyone had tried to frighten them out of this adoption.

We all got in the van together and Vladimir wended his way through the Saint Petersburg traffic.

"This place," Chele asked me. "Is it wonderful? Or awful?"

"Hasn't Danielle told you?" I said, sounding harsher than I ever could have intended.

"I was curious what you thought of it." Chele was unperturbed by my rudeness. I liked her immediately; she was tough. You have to be to do this.

"I hope our son won't remember it," I said. Pavel glanced back at me; maybe it was impolite to criticize the orphanage, but I didn't care. A country run by billionaire friends of the president, they could make it nicer if they wanted. They didn't care.

"It's not terrible," Kyle, the diplomat, said. "Just depressing."

The Robinettes told us about themselves, and Kyle and Vince talked football, and I reassured Chele that the chicken pox has probably burned through the orphanage and her daughter wouldn't be all spotty for her first pictures with them, but if she was it would be fine, and I thought about holding my boy in my arms.

I hadn't thought this through. I didn't remember there was one "greeting" room of mirrors where families spent time with their future children and so we and the Robinettes couldn't use it at the same time. It would have been inconceivable to ask them to wait a couple of hours to meet their daughter for the first time. So we gave them the room, and Chele gave me this giant hug that nearly made me cry. I felt so on edge, and I couldn't let anyone see. They went in, and Maria, not being their caseworker, gave me and Kyle a short tour. The door to Grant's ward was closed; we'd see him later, but now I knew where his crib was. Older children we saw looked at us with empty eyes, and I realized again how narrow Grant's world was—had he ever been off this property since he was brought here? Had he known a true moment of comfort? We gave the extra gifts I'd brought this time, including more basic supplies, all of which was accepted with a murmured thanks.

Kyle wanted to be sure everything was fine with the paperwork.

Maria agreed. She and Danielle and Kyle went to go check all the necessary and tiresome details again, as the judge we had been assigned was extremely nitpicky about these matters and had a reputation of being difficult. It was why we had given ourselves ten days here (well, one of the reasons).

I couldn't bear to look at more paperwork. I'd handled it all in the US and Kyle had handled it all here (because you could see that the Russians expected the man to take the lead in all this; apparently I was here just to look maternal and hold the baby—and refuse quarter-million-dollar bribes).

"May I go for a walk outside?" I asked Maria, and she nodded and said something in Russian. Pavel was with the Robinettes, and Danielle said, "Yes. Just watch where you go"—like I was a child, but I nodded and left.

I kept wondering if I should tell Danielle about the warning woman's approach. The offer of money. But if I did, what would Danielle do? Report it to the Russian authorities? They might derail the adoption for their own reasons, deem it too dangerous. I couldn't risk it. I would not risk my child's future out of fear. I would not let him be left here. So—I stayed silent.

Outside, the air felt bracing. No sign of the warning woman or the bad guys in the SUV. Our driver sat in the van, drinking from a thermos, reading a thick novel. I ignored him.

The snow had drifted against the buildings. It fell steadily—it had not been snowing on our way in—and the flakes danced. I pulled my knit cap low and breathed in the cold air. I started walking through the snow. I had half an idea that perhaps, at a window, I'd see Grant staring down at me, waiting for his new mom and dad. Of course not. He was ten months old. But the chicken pox had passed, and I was going to get to see him healthy now, and I couldn't wait…

I walked past the main building, toward two smaller buildings— I'm not sure what they were used for—and I saw her. In the shadows. She stepped forward, a figure in a heavy coat. I froze for a moment. Then she gestured to me, and there was something urgent in her wave. My nerves were on edge… There was no one out here but us, and I couldn't ignore her. I walked toward her.

I knew who this might be: the warning woman.

The day was already cloudy, the sky spitting snow. She didn't meet me halfway along the snow-covered path but stayed close to the building.

When I got closer to her, I saw half her face covered by a thick scarf. But I also saw it was not the warning woman. She was younger. Her coat was high-end, expensive. Her hat was fur, like you might expect a Russian princess to wear.

"You are American?" she asked. Her accent was heavy.

"Yes."

"An adopting mother here?"

"Yes."

"I need help. Please. To get inside." She pointed toward the main building.

"There's an entrance at the front," I said.

"I know, but I cannot go in alone." She pulled the scarf down, and I saw a shadow of a fading bruise along her delicate jawline. "You could say I was your translator."

"Why do you need to go in?"

Several seconds passed. "My child was taken from me. And brought here."

"Taken against your will?"

She blinked at these words, and I tried again: "Did you give up your baby? It's all right. I understand."

"I changed my mind. I want my baby back."

Surely they'd just give it back to her. Surely. I couldn't imagine that they wouldn't.

"We can go see the woman in charge," I told her, and she shook her head.

"No. No. They won't give him back."

Him. Something colder than the wind began to creep along my flesh. "Why won't they give the baby back to you?" I asked calmly, thinking she could be a crazy woman who just wants a baby. I was not going to help her kidnap some kid. There had to be a reason, if her story was true, that they have not just given her back her child. She was an addict or unstable or dangerous or... An addict wouldn't have a nice coat like that, and her eyes were clear. But there were plenty of well-dressed mental cases in the world.

"What's your name?" I asked.

"Anya."

"Anya, I want to help you, but I can't. If I break a rule, they won't give me my child."

"Please. Please. You are an American with money. They will listen to you."

I felt sick. I felt torn. As a mother, I couldn't NOT help her. As a mother, I couldn't help her. I couldn't risk the adoption for this. Maybe I could find out, though, where her child was, where he was in the adoption pipeline.

"What is your baby's name?"

I saw her struggle to trust me. She decided.

"Alexander Borisovich Stepurin," she said, very quietly.

Sasha. Grant. My son.

I repeated the name to her, slowly, like I'd not heard it before. She nodded. She pressed a piece of paper into my hand, with a phone number on it. I closed my hand around it.

"I can ask about him," I managed to say.

"You must not tell them you talked to me. You could say that you are interested in a second child. Adopting two. Ask for a boy. He's nine months old."

"Why didn't you ask for him back before?"

"I couldn't," she said, without explanation. Shame flickered in her eyes.

I thought: If I help her, what will they think of me? If I don't help her, what will I think of me?

"You could go inside. Take him to a window. Let me see him. I have not seen him since he was born."

My courage started to desert me. It felt like God was saying I couldn't have this child. "Why have they not given him back to you? Are you ill? Are you an addict? I know nothing about you and you ask me to take this risk." I can't even remember everything that I asked her then.

"There are people...who don't want me to have him," she said.

"Who? Who?" How did the warning woman fit into this?

"To explain would put you in danger," she said. "I cannot. I have tried to get help from inside, from the workers, and no one will help me. I'm up against too much. The money they make."

"He might be better off with a new family. Have you thought of that? The families that come here are so nice. They'll give him the world."

She stared at me. "What baby are you adopting?"

What will she do to me if she realizes I'm going to be her child's mother? So I lied to this beautiful, lost soul. "A girl. Her name is Natasha. She's eight months old." This was the child the Robinettes were adopting, I just borrowed the name.

My lie mollified her. "Will you help me?"

I should say no. But I need to know...what does this have to do with my child? Who might come after him if we take him? I can't ask for another child now. Clearly, clearly something is wrong—being warned off him, being followed, the crash, the bribe, his mother lurking in the snow—and I need to know the whole, sprawling truth. She won't just tell me; I can see that. I have to earn it. I have to deceive her a little.

"Let me go inside and see if I can find him," I told her. "Go to the back window." I pointed to one of the windows, and she nodded. "I'll bribe a nurse to show me your Alexander," I said. She nodded again.

I trudged through the heavy snow. I put my emotions in check. I went inside. The receptionist, Svetlana, who very much liked the chocolates I had given her, told me Kyle and Maria were still checking the mountain of paperwork.

"Could I go see Sasha? Just for a moment?" I asked in my best mommy tone. "I know where his ward is."

She'd seen all the supplies and toys I brought the last trip, and she spoke a bit more English than most of the staff, since she had to deal more with adoptive parents arriving. She nodded and gave me a sticker pass to put on my coat.

I went up two flights of stairs; two staffers glanced at me, but they saw my pass and only nodded. I smiled back.

My heart shuddered in my chest.

I opened the door to his ward and found a room lined with cribs. No wonder the chicken pox tore through here like wildfire. There were ten cribs in this room, all occupied. There was no attendant in here at the moment.

I saw Sasha—I mean Grant—in his crib. The pox was gone. My heart pounded, danced, twirled. He was such a handsome boy.

She can't have him. I won't let her have him. She can't give him what we can. She made her choice. She's not stable. She's not reliable. She doesn't want what's best for him. I...

I took a giant breath and broke into sudden tears.

I cannot take him away from his own mother. I cannot. I'm so many things, but I am not that person. I'll take him and give him to her. I can't live with myself if I don't. Kyle will understand. The money we've spent—I'll write some more songs. I'll make it back. How can I look this sweet boy in the face every day if I don't do the right thing?

And a little voice in my head said: Why is giving him back to this woman you know nothing about the right thing? What if she's mentally ill?

Grant wriggled in his crib, eyes open, bored, but the stuffed dinosaur we brought him was tucked in the crib's corner with him. I picked it up and nuzzled his nose with the toy. He watched me. No smile, no gurgle of recognition.

"Hello, sweet boy," I said to him. "Hello, my boy."

My boy. He won't be my boy. I'm so sorry. I would have loved you so...

"Will you come to me?" I asked, and then I picked him up because he was not going to give an answer. He liked being held, I thought, but he didn't cuddle up to me; he didn't seek that comfort of contact. Because he didn't know I would die for him. Mostly he just looked around.

I took the deepest breath of my life and walked him to the window.

She was out there, twenty feet away and below us two stories, looking up as though she were seeing the sun for the first time in forever. I could see the bright smile come across her face. She raised a hand toward him.

I lifted up her son's—our son's—hand toward her and waved back, very slightly.

I saw Anya was crying. Trying to smile.

I waved his hand again. Sasha…Grant…looked out the window like he'd never seen the view before. The snow. The clouds, from two stories up.

The woman.

The dog.

I saw it loping toward her, a big one, a breed—I don't know breeds, but it was big and sleek, like a police dog, and I was powerless, but I gestured toward her. She just waved harder, and now I cried out in shock as the dog leapt upward.

Did she not hear it? Was she so laser-focused on her child, on seeing him for the first time in nine months, that she didn't hear?

The dog caught her heavily coated arm and knocked her into the snow. I saw two men, I didn't know if they were guards or what, hurrying toward her through the drifts. She was screaming—I saw the bright O of her mouth—and the dog wasn't releasing her arm. He pulled her across the pure white canvas. I could not, would not let Grant see this. I put him back in the crib, and now, happy to have been held, he fussed for me. He wanted me to hold him, for the first time, and my heart tore in two. I rushed back to the window, fearful.

She stood now, thankfully, but wobbly, one of the men having pulled the dog off, the other one having helped her to her feet. The sleeve of her coat was in shreds and I saw blood drops dotting the snow.

The dog was under control though, not attacking her, and a shudder of relief went through me. I watched as they led her not to the main building but…to the road that cuts through the orphanage's compound. They were not even taking her to the infirmary. Or the nurse.

They were just removing her.

I ran from Grant's room, I hurried down the steps. I found a side door and burst out of it. I ran toward the trio in the snow. The dog looked at me and growled.

"What are you doing?" I yelled at the guards, or staffers, or whatever they are. "She needs medical attention."

Anya stared at me, wildness in her eyes. And gratitude. I had showed her Sasha.

One of the guards talked to me in shattered English. "She is problem lady," he said. "Many problem. Not to be here."

"Help me, help me," Anya yelled.

"Stop!" I made them stop and looked at her arm. The heavy fabric of the coat and her sweater protected her, but the arm was badly bruised and there were two narrow marks, oozing blood.

"Doctor," I said. "She needs a doctor!"

"Choice," the guard said. "If doctor come here, police come, too, arrest. If she go to doctor in town, no call police. Her choice."

"Her baby," I said, pointing to the building.

"Not her baby," the guard said. He wiggled a finger near the brain. Anya looked down at the snow.

"Please don't do this," I said. "Think of what your mother would say. Your own mother."

This plea didn't move them.

"You want YOUR baby? Go back into building, lady," the guard told me. They pulled Anya away and I couldn't stop them. I heard the threat in his tone.

I watched them drag her away in the snow. She screamed "Sasha!" twice.

"I'm sorry you had to see that," Danielle said. The three of us were back at the hotel, having dinner. I embraced being in Russia: I downed vodka in steady sips. The Robinettes were off buying supplies for the orphanage, as I did on my first trip, and I was grateful they couldn't hear this conversation.

My lie was a careful one. I told them that I had been in the building and had seen the woman, heard her scream Sasha's name after the dog attacked her, hurried out to help.

Not that I had talked to her before. That I kept to myself.

"Did you know about this?" I asked Danielle.

"That Sasha's mother was being difficult? Not until today."

I wasn't sure I believed her.

"She wants her child back," Kyle said.

"How are we supposed to stand in her way?" I asked. He took my hand and I squeezed his.

"Maybe if we could talk to her, reassure her that we'd be good parents to him," Kyle said.

"Or they should just give her back her child," I said.

But Kyle shook his head. "It's been nine months. Not nine days. She had plenty of time to think this through. Why now? Why has she changed her mind now, once the adoption process started? We're literally a day away from getting him. What happens when she wants him in a year? Do you give him back then?"

"I didn't want to tell you this because it's no reflection on Sasha, but there's an unfortunate history here. Anya gave up an earlier child as well," Danielle said. I remembered the medical file told us she'd given birth once before. "She asked for him back. The orphanage returned him, even though they had concerns, but an adoption process hadn't started. She returned that child to the orphanage four weeks later. He was hungry and neglected. They're not going to give Sasha back to her."

"Danielle," I said, very quietly. "She's standing out in the freezing snow, looking at the building where her child is."

"She's not well. You can't talk to her again. Contact is forbidden. She doesn't get the child back. What would it do to adoption here if the Russians cave on this?"

"I don't care about government policy. This doesn't feel like adoption. It feels like kidnapping."

Danielle started to speak, and I waved her silent. "I got warned in the airport. Our car got run off the road. She wants this child and someone doesn't want us to have him. What is going on here, Danielle?"

"You know as much as I do." Her voice shook. "I've done more than twenty adoptions here and this has never come up."

"She's trying to scare off any adoptive parents," Kyle said.

"They won't give her the baby back, so she's mounted this campaign against us. The woman in the airport, the men who drove us off the road."

And the warning woman, with her quarter-million-dollar offer? It was too late to tell them about that. And maybe that was a lie. That woman could have somehow been helping Anya. I didn't know what to think.

I pulled Kyle's laptop out of his bag and opened it. "Alexander Borisovich Stepurin. That means his father is Boris Stepurin, yes?" I did an internet search on the name. There were several hits, mostly on sites written in Russian. If I needed to drag Pavel down here to translate all night, I would. But then I saw a listing: a biography from a Russian investment firm. A man in his early thirties, blond and handsome like Sasha. Educated in Moscow and London. A senior investment broker.

"Why worry about the father?" Danielle asked. She sounded a little uneasy.

"He might have sway with her," I said. "Maybe he fathered her other child, too."

"I should go see him," Kyle said.

"We don't even know this is the right man," I said. "The bio says he's married to a woman named Irina. Not Anya."

"Maybe Anya was a girlfriend," Kyle said. "A mistress."

"Maybe he doesn't even know there's a baby," Danielle said. "I would not do this."

"If this is his child, he knows. They would have contacted the father when the child was surrendered at the maternity ward. He would have been given the option to claim him, right?"

"If they're not together, she might not listen to him," Danielle said.

"Look, what if he can convince her our adopting him is best for all?" Kyle said. "Then we can adopt him with a clear conscience."

I nodded. "The court hearing is tomorrow afternoon," Danielle said. "After that, he'll be yours."

"Do you think Anya could show up to protest?" I asked. I dreaded the thought. Even if she gave up and took back and gave up an earlier child, she is Sasha's mother. For this to work, she must let him go of her own free will. Out of love for him, to have a better life.

What if the judge sided with her? It could happen. A decision overturned, for the sake of a mother.

Danielle stood up. "I feel like the two of you have decided not to listen to me anymore. I'm telling you, don't go see this man. If the ruling goes your way, then fine, he's yours. If not, he's not."

"But he could be the deciding factor," I said. "I…"

"You asked me to get you a child. I've done that. I want no more part of it."

"Danielle…" I started, but Kyle stopped me.

And let me just say, his indecision was gone. GONE.

"Look, I get maybe she has regrets. But she gave Sasha up. That is a decision she has to live with. She might take him back and then want to give him up again in a month like she did with her first kid. We know nothing about her, her life, her circumstance, her mentality. You said she was well dressed. Well, if she can afford a fur hat, she can afford a lawyer. She's skulking around the orphanage like a criminal, making accusations against the orphanage and the staff, and they've been nothing but fair with us. There's a process and she's failed it, more than once." I just stared at my husband, my mild-mannered man, full of fire for his son. "If she can be reassured that this is the right decision, then that's what we need to do. But not adopting this child isn't an option. We've spent all the time, all this money, and we love him. He's part of us now, and we're not just giving him up because she changed her mind."

I had never heard your father talk like this before. Usually I'm the talker. I took his hand.

"This could be what's best for her as well," Kyle said. I wanted to believe that.

"We'll go see the father?" I asked.

He nodded. "Before the hearing. I'll even stand over his desk while he makes the phone call to her."

We just had to get through the next twenty-four hours and our lives would be wonderful.

43

EXCERPT OF TRANSCRIPT OF TCSO AND LPD INTERVIEW WITH KYLE POLLITT

(Interview continues)

Detective Ponder: And by cooperate you mean what?

Pollitt: I will confess to killing Danielle Roberts. But it was an accident, not on purpose.

Detective Ponder: OK, we're listening. Tell us what happened.

Pollitt: We were having an affair. The phones were to stay in touch. So Mike and Iris would not know.

Detective Ponder: How long had the affair been going on?

Pollitt: Only a couple of weeks. She approached me about it. I shouldn't have done it, but things haven't been great between me and Iris lately. It was obviously a mistake.

Detective Ponder: Where would you meet?

    (Pause)

Pollitt: Her house. When Ned was at school.

Detective Ponder: What, you'd just walk over to her house? Isn't your wife a stay-at-home mom?

Pollitt: Yes, but she has a lot of volunteer duties. She's gone most of the day.

Detective Ponder: OK. Did you ever go to a hotel?

    (Pause)

Pollitt: No.

Detective Ponder: And how many times a week did you see each other?

Pollitt: It had only gone on since she gave me the phone. Maybe we'd seen each other twice.

Detective Ponder: Twice? You don't know?

Pollitt: Twice.

Detective Ponder: Tell me about the night she died.

Pollitt: I wanted to end it. I'm not made for having an affair. We spoke on the phone. I understand Ned heard her arguing about ending it.

Detective Ponder: Ned said she used the phrase "I want out." If you were ending things, why did she say that?

Pollitt: Her pride was hurt, so she decided she did indeed want out.

Detective Ponder: So you broke up. You ended the affair.

Pollitt: Yes.

Detective Ponder: So, if you ended it, why did you meet up with her again? She didn't die at midnight.

Pollitt: She had threatened to tell my wife and kids about it. I walked over to her house.

Detective Ponder: What time?

Pollitt: I don't know. I couldn't sleep. Maybe 4:00 a.m.? She called me on the burner. If you can access the damaged SIM card, you'll see I'm telling you the truth. I went over to her house, and so we wouldn't wake Ned, we walked up to the park.

Detective Ponder: Did you plan to kill her? To silence her?

Pollitt: No, not at all. We got to the park. She said she would tell Iris. We argued.

Detective Ponder: Did you yell?

Pollitt: No. We didn't want to wake anyone in the houses by the park. We spoke in harsh whispers.

Detective Ponder: Harsh whispers.

Pollitt: Yes, that would be accurate.

Detective Ponder: They must have been harsh indeed to escalate to death.

Pollitt: She kept threatening to tell Iris. She was hurt and she
    wanted me to hurt. Finally I hit her, in the throat, I didn't mean
    to hit her so hard. I felt something give; I guess I hit her wind-
    pipe just right. She collapsed. I didn't know what to do. I
    panicked. I was going to call 911, but then…it would all come
    out. She died. I put her on the bench. I couldn't be seen carry-
    ing her back to her house, and I didn't want Ned to find her.

Detective Ponder: You forgot her phone?

Pollitt: I was out of my mind. I ran home. I went to bed; Iris
    woke up for a moment, and I told her that I'd been up late
    working. I have insomnia. She believed me and went back to
    sleep. Then, when I realized you'd find her burner phone, I
    destroyed mine.

Detective Ponder: The injuries to your face. Did that happen
    that night? Did she strike you?

Pollitt: No. I fell while running in the greenbelt.

Detective Ponder: Running? Like for a jog?

Pollitt: Yes.

Detective Ponder: You killed a woman you were intimate
    with, went home, got into bed with your wife, slept a few
    hours, went to the crime scene because your daughter found
    the body, and then went for a jog.

Pollitt: I'm a horrible person.

Detective Ponder: You said you punched her in the throat.

Pollitt: Yes. I'm very sorry about that.

Detective Ponder: Which hand?

Pollitt: My right.

Detective Ponder: Show me the fist you made.

    (Pauses)

Pollitt: I'm not sure I can remember. It happened so quickly.
    I've tried to shut it out.

Detective Ponder: Try. Was it a closed fist? Was it like a karate
    chop with the side of your hand? Was it stiff-fingered?

Pollitt: Closed fist, I think.

Detective Ponder: You used your fist. Not a weapon. Not a
    blunt instrument.

(Pauses)

Pollitt: I didn't have a weapon. It was my fist.

Detective Ponder: You wear a college class ring on your right hand.

Pollitt: Yes. I went to Rice.

Detective Ponder: Your Rice ring's extremely distinctive, isn't it? That square shape of the crest. The chevron. There's no stone. You'd expect it to leave a particular kind of mark with a punch of that force.

Pollitt: Yes. Well. I don't think I had it on though when I went to the park.

Detective Ponder: You don't remember.

(Pauses)

Pollitt: I'm sure I didn't. I didn't wear my wedding ring around Danielle. So I would have taken off both rings.

Detective Ponder: I mean, maybe that was what cracked her windpipe. And not a blunt instrument.

Pollitt: I don't know.

Detective Ponder: So you argued, you killed her, you came home—is that where we are at?

Pollitt: Yes. Are you going to arrest me now?

Detective Ponder: Yes. I am placing you under arrest for the murder of Danielle Roberts.

44

IRIS AND GRANT

Iris calls the attendance office and pulls both kids out of school for the day; Julia drives her brother home.

She meets them out in the driveway, hurries them into the house.

"What's happening?" Julia asks, breathless.

Iris explains to them that their father is being questioned because of the phone that was found in their trash and the phone found near Danielle's body.

They take the news in quiet shock. Grant looks scared, and Julia looks as though something is caught inside her chest. Her palm is pressed over her heart.

"Grant," she says quietly. "I need to talk to Mom alone. Please."

"Why? If this is about Dad, it affects me." He's in tears.

"Please, Grant, please."

He storms outside, to the backyard.

Iris wants to tell him to go upstairs so she can talk to him about the thousand dollars in cash in his drawer, but she keeps her focus on Julia.

"Ned…" Julia doesn't know how to say it. How much to say to her mother. This is going to destroy her mother's image of her: the wonderful daughter, the outstanding student, the bright and spotless future. Of course, it's not worse than her father being a person of interest in a crime. "Ned was acting like he knew who he thought had killed Danielle, and then Gordon texted him, and then he was all upset with Dad. I think he suspected someone else before."

"Who?"

"He won't tell me now. He thinks Dad is guilty. But... " What does she say? If she confesses what she and Ned have done, then it might help her father, but her future is over. It's over.

So, Julia takes a deep breath and tells her mother everything.

Grant's phone pings. It's a text from Peter: my dad just told me to come home. That there are "developments" in the case. Have you heard anything?

Grant wonders what he should do. But Peter has been helping him, so he writes: my dad is being questioned by the police and I don't know what's going on or what I should do.

Peter says: wait I'll come straight over

His mom and Julia are having a long talk. They treat him like a child, when Julia's only two years older and has done plenty of stupid teenager things.

What if his dad's been caught? The Sender knew his dad did something wrong. Maybe the Sender has evidence. The Sender must want something from Grant, to keep reaching out to him, to send him these things. So what is it?

His phone pings again. Email. He opens it. It's from the Sender: No pictures for you today. But go look in the tree for a surprise.

Peter's camera. If the Sender was there, it would have caught him or her.

He closes the email. He decides to wait for Peter. Having a witness is important. And he doesn't know how to get the video off Peter's hidden camera.

He texts Peter: come to my house via the greenbelt, not front door.

Ten minutes later, Julia and Mom are still talking inside and he sees Peter loping up to the house. He's flushed.

"Hey," Peter says.

"Hey. I got another email. Directing me to the tree. I hope your camera worked."

Peter holds up a hand, and with a sinking feeling, Grant can see the iciness in his stare.

"What did your dad do to Danielle?"

"I...I don't know."

"I think it'd be super hard to keep a big secret from your mom," Peter says. "She's just the type to see through that. It was something Danielle liked about her."

Grant bites his lip.

"After my mom died, my dad was sad for a long time, and Danielle made him happy again." His voice shakes. "When we came here from Canada, I was sad, because I couldn't go visit my mom's grave. But hey, I can go visit Danielle's. She wasn't my mom, but she was gonna try. Do you understand that? She was gonna try."

The pain in Peter's voice is real, and Grant doesn't know what to say at first. "Peter, I can't believe my dad would hurt her. And all the stuff that's happened, I haven't made that up. I wouldn't even know how to start."

"I know you deleted that email that talked about the bad thing your dad did. I found it. You can't really delete stuff if I'm looking for it. It's not gone; it's just hidden. You want to tell me what that was?"

"If we go check the camera down by the tree right now, we'll have our answers," Grant pleaded. "Please."

Peter turns and walks out of the backyard and down the trail. Grant follows, catching up to him. They get to the tree. Lying in the trail is Peter's little camera with its USB drive, smashed, the adhesive tape that secured it to the tree in tatters.

"Oh no," Grant says. "Oh no."

He steps forward, and Peter stops him. "Don't touch it. Even if it's damaged, maybe I can get an image off of it."

Peter starts to step around the debris, toward the tree, and he gestures at Grant to stay back. "I'll check the tree, if you don't mind." He kneels and looks into the cleft. From here Grant can see a flash of color.

Peter pulls something out, and he audibly gasps. Grant can see it's a book bag, quilted, imprinted with the logo of the Lakehaven Library. His mom has a similar bag. This one has Danielle's name stitched on it.

Peter looks inside and freezes. "Oh, no, no," he says.

Grant looks inside, too. He sees blood splattered in the lining of the book bag and a metal pipe.

There's blood on the end of the pipe.

45

IRIS

Julia has just finished telling Iris about Ned, the drugs, Marland, and Iris is staring at her daughter as if she's a stranger, someone who slipped into her daughter's straight-A skin.

"Mom?"

"OK. We'll deal with it. That's what we do." She has to extricate her daughter from this mess. A plea deal, turn evidence against Ned and this Marland person.

"Where is this phone of Ned's that has the threat to Danielle in the text?"

"I hid it in a safe place. It's leverage against this Marland guy. We can get him to leave me out of the ring and give me this incriminating evidence he says he has against Dad and then we can show it to the police."

"If we show it to the police, then your involvement in Ned's...drug stuff is going to come out. That cannot happen."

"So?"

"Your father and I won't ruin your future, Julia."

Iris's cell phone rings and she answers. It's Kip Evander. "Iris. He confessed."

The words make no sense. "To what?"

"To Danielle Roberts's murder."

The day is simply happening too fast, too intensely. This should be a day to plan dinner, to help Grant with his homework, to check over Julia's math, to phone the volunteers for the choir musical, to tell Kyle about her day and to hear about his over a little red wine as she finishes preparing dinner. Not all this. Her life, crashing down around her.

"That's not possible," she says. "He couldn't have done it."

"They have arrested him based on the confession. But I'm not sure they're convinced."

"What do you mean?"

Kip's tone becomes cautious. "I think he's protecting someone. I'm not sure everything in his account added up. He said he killed her with a punch. They repeatedly asked him about that, and I'm thinking maybe there's forensic evidence that it wasn't a punch."

Who would he be protecting? Her gaze meets Julia's. Ned and Julia. Maybe each parent protecting their own. Or maybe he was wrong, and he thought someone else had killed her.

Someone like Iris.

"What happens now?"

"He'll be processed into jail. Look, even if they have doubts about some of what he said, he confessed. They'll look to validate that confession, not discount it."

"What do I do?"

"They'll have a press conference shortly. The press is about to descend on you all. I'll see if I can get him to talk to me about who he's shielding. Also, while I'm happy to represent him if you want, I think I want to call a friend who does nothing but criminal law."

Kyle. Kyle. She takes a deep breath. She thanks Kip and hangs up.

"Mom? What?" Julia says.

The doorbell rings. Then a fist, pounding on the door.

46

FROM IRIS POLLITT'S "FROM RUSSIA WITH LOVE" ADOPTION JOURNAL

2002

"I am not sure why you wish to see me," Boris Stepurin said. It was unusual, presumably, for Americans to show up at his office and ask to speak with him about a private matter. We were sitting in a conference room at this investment firm, the door shut, hot coffee in front of us all and Stepurin looking very uncomfortable. He was blandly handsome, dark blondish hair, blue eyes, a square jaw.

"I'm not going to waste time," Kyle said. "You are listed as the biological father on the papers of a boy we are very close to adopting."

"I am married with children of my own. This must be a mistake."

"The mother's name is Anya."

"I do not know an Anya."

"She had the boy at a hospital near Saint Petersburg and then gave it up. He's at the Volkov Infants Home. Our adoption hearing is today."

"Congratulations. I wish you much happiness. This has nothing to do with me." There was fear in his face.

"You talk to Anya," Kyle continued, "and you tell her that it will all be fine. We will give Sasha a great life. He will never lack for love or any material comfort. His future will be bright. We live in a town with a great school, and many kids there go to the best universities in America."

"How fortunate for the child." But he didn't get up and leave.

He didn't open the door and order us out. His gaze flickered between us both.

"So you need to explain this to her, and she needs to stop going to the infants' home. And she needs to stop asking for the baby back. She did that before and it didn't work out."

He stared. "There was an earlier child?"

"Yes. And she asked for him back, and then returned him, neglected."

"Boris," I said. "We don't want to interfere with your domestic life. But we don't want Anya to interfere with ours. It must be so hard. We are so grateful to you both for your courage. But we want her to know in Sasha's case, she need not worry. He will be so loved."

He cleared his throat. "I don't want you to think…badly of us."

"We couldn't," I said, and I meant it.

"I was working on a project in our Paris office and she was working as a model there. Many Russian girls in Paris. My wife and I were separated…having problems. My family was back here and I was lonely in Paris. Anya was like having a friend from home. We were friends, first. Then…it was a mistake. We are not matched for each other, but I care about her. I want her to be happy. Now…my wife and I are back together. Please. My father-in-law owns this firm. I cannot shame them…and Anya promised me that she would give the child up."

"We understand."

"I will call her. You will not have further trouble, Mr. and Mrs. Pollitt. But please don't come back here."

"Are you smart?" I asked.

He blinked at me as he stood for us to leave. "Pardon me?"

"Well, you speak great English and you have what appears to be an excellent job. Are you smart?"

"Yes," he said. "I'm considered smart."

"Any genetic illnesses in your family?" I asked. How often do you get to talk to a birth parent? This was my one chance.

"No. Both my grandfathers died of cancer though. Tell your son not to smoke." He stood up.

"What about Anya?"

"I know little about her family. I'm sorry. She was healthy. But she...she can be impulsive. I'm not sure that is a problem in the blood. He is a handsome baby?" He bit at his lip.

"Yes, he's a wonderful baby," I said.

"May I make a suggestion to you before you go?" he asked. We nodded.

"Once you have my—I mean your—son, home with you...Never come back to Russia. Don't let him ever return to Russia, either. Never. Not once."

We didn't know what to say—was this a warning or a threat?— and the silence grew awkward. Then he gestured us, politely, toward the door.

We thanked him and left.

"That was weird at the end," I said.

"I think it's going to be all right," Kyle said, and took my hand. "I think it was his way of not wanting our son to show up looking for him."

"Maybe," I said. "Or maybe more."

Please let Boris be making that phone call, I thought. For all our sakes.

47

IRIS AND JULIA

Iris opens the door and Ned stumbles inside. His face is wild.

"I want to know what you know," Ned says, his voice shaking, "about Kyle killing my mom."

Iris and Julia stare at him.

"I want to know what was going on between them, and I want to know what you two knew about it. You've been protecting him." Ned's voice breaks.

Julia starts to speak, but Iris holds up a hand and Julia stops. Iris says quietly: "You getting involved with this Marland guy is what killed her."

Julia gasps, and Ned blurts, "Don't you dare blame me! Your husband did this!"

"If he confessed, it's out of a misguided sense of protecting us. And you, Ned, were the last person to see her. You pretended to call back to her when you and Julia were leaving. You didn't want her messing up your drug dealing."

"I would never let anyone hurt my mom!" he screams. "You can't say this to me!" He takes a step forward and Julia takes a step back.

Iris glares him down. "I mean, it makes perfect sense," Iris says, the words like a knife. "She finds out about the drug dealing and freaks out and argues with you. How it's ruining your future. Maybe she says, hey, we'll throw Julia to the cops to save you, although Julia only knew of it because you told her; you abused your friendship with her to drag her into it. And so she calls this Marland guy and tells him she'll expose him, and he kills her. And it's all because of you." She cannot believe the words coming out of her mouth. But this is what desperation for her own family is. This is what fear is.

Ned erupts in a shuddering, shaking howl of grief, of disbelief.

"I don't think normally she'd meet a man like Marland in the park, but she would to protect you. To keep you from knowing what she did. To make a deal with him to save your future..." She doesn't recognize her own voice.

"Mom, stop. Stop!" Julia yells, clutching her arm, but Iris shakes free.

"STOP IT!" Ned screams, and he shoves Iris away from him. She sprawls on the hardwood floor.

"It was Kyle! She argued with Kyle! I heard her!"

"Of course you'd say that. You need to blame someone other than yourself for setting all this in motion..." Iris slowly gets up from the floor, Julia helping her, Julia staring at Ned like she's never seen him before. Or seen this rage and heartbreak inside him. "You told Julia you thought you knew who killed her. But if it's Marland, it's your fault. You can't face that truth."

Ned's hands close into fists. His voice shakes when he speaks. "You liar. You should have kept your own husband happy. Then he wouldn't have come around my mom. And killed her."

"She found out about your drug dealing and that you dragged my poor daughter into your idiotic scheme. Did your mom want to go to the police and cut a deal that would protect you and offer up Julia as a whipping boy to the police, someone you could frame and blame because she'd kept her mouth shut, because she dared to be your friend? Now, I could believe that's what she and Kyle were talking about. Your mother wouldn't have minded hurting us," Iris says, her voice cool, controlled. "Kyle wouldn't kill her. Even if they had an affair. Because he knows I'd forgive him. I'd make him pay for it. But I'd forgive him. He's confessing to protect Julia's future, the one you've nearly ruined. So none of this comes out. But he wouldn't have killed her. Maybe Marland threw the punch, but you set all this in motion, Ned. *You.*"

Ned looks at her like a back corner of his heart knows it's true. His face contorts in grief and guilt.

"Mom…" Julia's voice breaks.

"Shut up, Julia. You're never seeing this boy again. Ned, if I were you…"

The door opens and Gordon storms inside. "I heard what you said to my son. What the hell is wrong with you? Are you insane?"

Shaking with rage, Ned pulls his phone out of his jacket pocket. The screen shows an active call to Gordon's phone. "My father was listening." His voice drips hatred for Iris.

"How dare you accuse my son of any involvement in this?" Gordon yells.

If Iris restrained herself against a kid, she unleashes against an adult. "*Now* he's your son. *Now* he's your son. Suddenly you've found your paternal instinct. You've ignored this boy for years. You're part of this entire mess. You disgust me."

"You'd say anything to protect your husband. He confessed! The police just told us."

She shoves a hand into Gordon's thick chest, and surprised, he stumbles back. "Ned started a drug ring, Gordon. Drugs!"

"Not the bad stuff!" Ned yells.

"This ring of yours, drug dealers want to make it bigger, so yes, you idiot, it's the bad stuff!" Iris yells.

Ned's sobs stop, and his trembling mouth turns to a savage line. "This isn't my fault. What is wrong with you to say that to me?"

"My husband wouldn't do that. My daughter wouldn't do that. It leaves the drug dealer you've pulled into our lives." She pauses. "Or you."

"Mom, please stop. Please," Julia says.

"Wait, what?" Ned says. Gordon just stares at her.

"Maybe she never met Marland. Maybe Ned and Danielle argued about the drug dealing, her telling him he was putting his whole future at stake, and they fought. He hit her. Harder than he meant to."

"Oh, Mom, no," Julia says.

"You horrible bitch," Gordon says.

Ned just stares at her.

Iris's voice is like a judgment. "I mean, the police would consider the possibility. She dies. Ned can't leave her in the house. He takes her to the park, where he knows she'll be found quickly. He leaves the phone he doesn't recognize, that she was using before, because it'll throw suspicion on someone else."

"Are you suggesting I killed my mother?" Ned says, his voice a slow, awful rise. He looks at her with a blind rage and then shoves her into the wall. Julia and Gordon pull him back.

"You see what he's capable of...?" Iris yells, pointing at Ned.

"Is there anything you won't say or do?" Gordon snarls at her. "Kyle confessed. Deal with it and leave my son alone."

The back door opens. Grant hurries in, followed by Peter. "Come see!" Grant cries. "Come see what we found. The murder weapon."

That silences the room. They follow Peter down the trail and to the tree. Mike is standing there, guarding something. Waiting. His phone at his ear.

"The boys called me," Mike says by explanation. "So I called the police. They're on their way. Don't touch it."

Iris looks at Danielle's book bag and the pipe extending from it. "Someone planted that here."

"Yeah, your murdering husband," Ned says. He turns away, kneels down, and vomits into the grass.

Peter leans against his father and starts to cry. Grant takes his mother's hand. Ned stands up and stares at Julia with a hate she's never seen before.

The police sirens approach.

"We say nothing about what our children have done," Gordon whispers to her. Desperate now, the way she was moments ago. Now he's afraid.

"I'm not letting my husband go to prison for this."

"If you talk about the drugs, then you give your husband even more motive," Gordon says. "To silence her. You destroy my child and you destroy yours. He confessed. You ought to think that he might be telling the truth—that he cheated on you and murdered her to keep her quiet. Do you save your daughter or not?"

"What's happening?" Mike says, his voice rising. He has one arm around Peter, the other around Grant, comforting him. "What are you two whispering about?"

Iris stands there, staring at the bag. Lose her husband and her daughter or lose just one?

Choose.

48

TRANSCRIPT FROM INTERVIEWS FOR *A DEATH IN WINDING CREEK* BY ELENA GARCIA

Elena Garcia: You'd known both Danielle Roberts and Iris Pollitt for several years.

Francie Neville: Yes. I referred Iris to Danielle after Iris asked about our adoption experience—my husband and I had adopted three children from Russia. So I was maybe the only one in our mom group who knew Danielle longer than Iris.

Garcia: What was your impression of Iris?

Francie: I liked her. She was semi-famous, you know, but that wasn't something she talked about. Having written songs for such famous people. I'd heard her songs so many times on the radio and I didn't know. If I'd written for NSYNC and Britney Spears, I would have told everyone probably within five minutes of meeting them. That was not Iris. She knew it made her look better if you learned it through a friend or idle talk.

Garcia: And what was your impression of Danielle?

Francie: We used her services with all three of our children— we adopted one to start, and then two together later. So obviously I would have a good opinion of her.

Garcia: Was there ever anything strange or odd about their relationship?

Francie: Most of our little group felt that without Danielle, we might not have had such a good experience in the adoption process. She was good at her job, mostly.

Garcia: Mostly?

Francie: Well, all the way.

Garcia: You seem to be editing yourself a little bit.

Francie: I...well. A little. I don't want to bad-mouth her.

Garcia: I want you to be honest.

Francie: The Russians are never easy to deal with. But both adoption trips—it was like Danielle was a different person than we knew in Texas. Distracted. Like...she had something better to do than shepherd us through getting our kid. It was just odd. Like when your doctor is normally really attentive and the next time you go in, he can't find his stethoscope. Like that.

Garcia: Why would she be distracted?

Francie: I don't know. It was certainly not the experience the other moms had with her. I heard them all—well, not Iris, but she wouldn't talk much about it anyway—say how fantastic she was. Susan and Georgina never mentioned problems in Ghana or China with Danielle. And I remember, once, a mom talking like that, and Iris and I looked at each other like, *Oh yeah?* I asked Iris once: "Was there a problem in Russia?" And Iris looked at me like I'd dumped a bag of vomit on her foot. Seriously, just shock. She was hard to shock. I knew that from volunteering with her at the schools; you hear the things the kids say, and c'mon, she'd worked in entertainment. There was, like, a really painful moment of silence. Us looking at each other. And Iris said, "No. Did you have a problem?" And I told her about what we'd dealt with.

Garcia: Which was what?

Francie: Well. On our first trip, a couple of times, Danielle didn't show up to go to meetings with us. I mean, I know she has other adoptions she's working, but hey, we're her only clients right there in Russia, put the focus on us. She would apologize, say she got pulled into another meeting.

And she didn't have to be there with us, the process moved forward, but then why was she in Russia if not to help us? On the second trip, the morning of our hearing, you know, we don't want to be late, and there's no sign of her in the hotel lobby, where we're supposed to meet. My husband, Hugh, is frantic, and I think maybe she's just out on the street, waiting for the driver. And I see her, but she's walking *away* from the hotel. And I'm thinking: What the hell? She's too far away to hear me yell, but I can see it's her. Leaving, ten minutes before we're supposed to be heading to the adoption hearing. Can you imagine what I'm thinking? I'm thinking something's gone horribly wrong and she's leaving so she doesn't have to tell us, or she's having to go find a new driver, which, I mean, we could just take a taxi—I'm not thinking logically at all.

Then I see a man get out of a car. A really nice car, like a Mercedes SUV, and he speaks to her. He's in a really expensive suit—you don't necessarily see a lot of those in Russia. Dark hair. She hands him something, and he hands her something. They talk for maybe fifteen seconds. Then she walks on.

I'm wondering what the hell is going on.

Then I see her go to a park, and she walks by a trash container and drops what she's carrying into it. She turns; I'm hanging back at this point, glancing at my watch. We're five minutes from the hotel. I follow her back. I don't want to look behind me now. I've seen movies where someone dumps something for pickup. I don't want to see someone maybe pulling that package she tossed into the trash after the man gave it to her.

I don't want to know.

When the hotel is in sight, I catch up with Danielle.

"Hey, Danielle," I say, and she turns and looks at me and says, "Hey." Like, you know, we're not in Russia and we've just bumped into each other at the grocery store.

I say, "What…what were you doing?"

"Some bribes you don't need to know about," she says.

I'm sure you've heard, well, bribery is an ugly word, but it's important to give lots of gifts to everyone you encounter in Russia in the adoption chain.

I'm thinking...that was a bribe? I know I must have had an odd expression on my face, and she was starting to figure out that I'd followed her, and she says: "Francie. You want these babies, yes? Both of them?"

I nod.

"Then keep your mouth shut and don't tell anyone what you saw today and everything will be fine. You can do that for your babies, yes?"

I say then: "I was worried you were taking off right before we have to leave for the hearing. That's all." I keep my mouth shut because if this odd behavior was making the adoption happen, then I was for it, and if it was a problem, it was hers and not mine. I was so anxious about the hearing, I didn't think straight. And the hearing was really long, because they were giving us two babies, so the judge seemed twice as bitter about Russia losing two future citizens, and it was only really when we were on the plane that I thought: Well, it couldn't have been a bribe. Hugh and I are paying the money for all the bribes, and she didn't ask us for money. And she threw it away. A bribe, being passed on. But I had a son and now two babies to take care of, and what did I care what Danielle had been up to? She asked me not to mention it and so I didn't. Until I told Iris a few years ago, and now.

Garcia: What was Iris's reaction to this story?

   (Long pause)

Garcia: Francie?

Francie: She asked me about the man and the car. I tried to describe them as much as I remembered. But why would she ask, unless she'd seen them, too? There was no reason to ask. And then she asked me if anyone had ever tried to...warn us off the adoption. Like, you know, someone approaching us in Russia and saying, "Go home."

Garcia: Did that happen to you?

Francie: No, it didn't. I asked her if that had happened to her
and she said, "Yes, just a crazy lady; it was nothing." But I
wondered how a crazy lady would know that they were
Americans there to adopt. I didn't ask again, though. You
can tell when a question is a bad idea.

Garcia: Did you ever ask Danielle about this? Or about the
Pollitts' experience in Russia?

Francie: Why would I? It's like asking about a business trip.
Iris said it all went fine, no issues. That's what you want to
hear.

Garcia: But Danielle confided in you about Steve and Carrie
Butler.

Francie: Yes, and I feel terrible about that...like I should have
told her to go to the police. She said they were just mad—
heartbroken—and she said she could handle them. That was
months before she died. I didn't know they'd moved in
down the street from her. I think it's really, really odd she
didn't tell me that...but when your kids get into high
school, you get so busy. I'd sometimes see her at choir functions, my middle kiddo is a year younger than Ned but also
in choir. We stood together and handed out programs at the
fall concert as people came into the auditorium and we didn't
have so much to say, other than how our kids were doing.
And she told me she'd started dating a guy in her neighborhood, Mike, and that he was really great. She stopped
coming for coffee nearly a year before she died, and c'mon,
that was her fan club, her Lakehaven moms. She made most
of us into moms. Why would she turn her back on us?

49

GRANT AND IRIS

It's all going to fall apart. Nothing can be saved.

The police have arrived to secure the scene, Ponder and Ames both there, and they are questioned. Iris says nothing about the drugs. Gordon says nothing about the drugs. They stare at each other.

Mike says, "I think they've all been arguing about Kyle's confession. There's something going on between them about the kids, and I do not know what it is." He looks right at Gordon and Iris both, as if his heart is breaking.

"I'm not saying anything more and neither are my children," Iris says. She puts her arms around her children and heads back up the trail to her house. She locks the door behind them. Julia and Grant stare at her.

"What have you done?" Julia says. "Ned will never help us now."

"Ned was never, ever going to help us. We're all on our own," Iris says. "He used you. He used you and you let him use you, and I thought you were smarter than that."

"You had to have the last word, and now Dad will go to prison."

"Ned's father is going to get him out of the country and to the UK or Ghana so fast your head will spin. Don't kid yourself that Ned was about to help us."

"The tree. Dad wouldn't hide that pipe in the tree," Grant says.

"Someone else has been hiding stuff there. The pipe wasn't there before."

They both look at him.

"Someone has been sending me notes. With pictures. Telling me to the go to the tree. They've left me money. They've left jewelry. It makes no sense." He looks at them. "But they keep saying you and Dad have lied to me. And this happened right after Danielle died."

The three of them are silent. "Show me these emails," Iris says.

He gets his laptop. Opens it up and opens the emails.

Iris stares at the first picture, of the woman in the rain. "Peter searched it. It's a stock photo from France."

Iris blinks. "Show me the rest of them."

He shows her the cat looking out in the snow from the house. She stares at it.

"Mom?" Julia asks. Iris seems far away.

Grant says, "They left me money and some jewelry. Why is someone doing this?"

"The thousand dollars in your room?" she asks. "I found it."

Grant nods.

"Who else has seen this? You said Peter."

"He checked my laptop and found a program planted on there. He said it's an old kind of software the CIA once used, but that hackers might have gotten it, and that the emails come from Saint Petersburg. In Russia."

Iris's face is like ice. She is utterly silent, and her children wait.

Julia finally speaks: "Mom?"

"I am going to need you both to do exactly what I say," Iris says very softly. "You stay in the house. You stay off your devices. Don't tell anyone where you are. Don't...Don't go anywhere. We don't talk to the police or the press. I will handle this."

"Mom, what's happening?"

There's a knock at the door. It's Detective Ponder. Iris opens the door and simply says, "I'm not answering your questions. You do not have permission to interview my children."

"Mrs. Pollitt..."

"Kyle didn't kill her," Iris says. "He may have confessed, but he didn't kill her."

"So who did? I'm curious what you think."

The question throws her off. Why would Ponder ask? She has a confession. "I don't know."

"Is he protecting you, then? Or another family member?"

Iris doesn't answer. *Something's wrong with Kyle's confession. There must be holes in it. Because...he didn't do this.*

"I have concerns about his confession," Ponder says. "Do you know what happened, Iris?"

"No."

"Help me help your husband. Why did he confess?"

Iris shuts the door in Ponder's face. She turns off the porch light.

Ponder calls through the shut door. "Mrs. Pollitt, it doesn't work this way. We have a warrant to search the premises. Open up."

She turns to her children. "He confessed to buy us time. Remember that. Your father is innocent. I'll believe nothing else. But say nothing right now. Say nothing."

Iris opens the door and steps aside to let Ponder and the police in.

50

IRIS

Two hours later.

The police have searched the house. They've taken Kyle's computers, they've taken the clothes Kyle wore the past four days, they've taken his coats, and they've searched his car. They found the cash in Grant's room, which Iris lies about, saying it's emergency cash they keep on hand. They've given an inventory list to Iris, and she notices a Chromebook she doesn't remember owning. It was in Kyle's car trunk. But she says nothing, and she hands back the list.

After the police leave, Julia tells Grant about Ned's drug dealing and her involvement; they all need to be on the same page. Grant just looks at her like he doesn't know her. The children have now each retreated to their rooms.

The doorbell rings. She's had on the news, and while there are reports an arrest has been made, they haven't yet announced that it is Kyle or that he's made a confession. Iris wonders what they're waiting on.

I have concerns about his confession, Ponder had said. What did that mean?

She answers the door. A fortyish woman, attractive. "Mrs. Pollitt? I'm Elena Garcia. I'm a reporter with KATX."

"I have nothing to say." Iris starts to shut the door.

"I spoke to your friend Francie Neville," Elena says. "She talked to me about some oddities of the adoption experience with Mrs. Roberts. I'm wondering if that's an angle that should be further explored in this case."

Iris shakes her head. "I have nothing to say." She closes the door.

She leans against it in shock. What her son has shown her, what Kyle has done, what Danielle could have kept... She wonders if she will ever sleep again.

Her phone keeps ringing. Friends, or people she thought were friends. She goes into the bathroom to wash her face. To try to order her thoughts. She doesn't hear Julia go out the back door.

51

JULIA

Julia hears voices on the greenbelt trail.

It's that loosely organized band of neighborhood parents, and under a streetlight she hears them calling to one another, laughing.

She thinks that as soon as news of her father's confession breaks, this so-called patrol won't have a reason to exist. But she can't let them catch her or spot her. She's arranged a meeting and she can't miss it. She sees two of them, both fathers of girls she knows from Lakehaven High, go one way on the road, and then she sees a big redheaded man—that would be Steve Butler, who helped right after they found Danielle's body—head off alone in another direction. The direction she intends to follow. But he's on the street, walking, glancing around, and she sticks to the dark of the greenbelt. She doesn't even turn on the flashlight app on her phone.

The abandoned Carlyle house again.

She supposes the advantage was that one could park near the greenbelt, far away from the house, and walk along the path until reaching the backyard and going into the house. There was no fence—several of the houses on the greenbelt didn't have them. And Winding Creek didn't use resident stickers, even though the greenbelt and the creek were the private property of the collective neighborhood, owned jointly through the home owners' association.

She goes through the backyard, and the back door is unlocked.

Marland sits on the carpet, looking furious. There's a thin glow from a lamp to light the room.

"Well," he said. "It seems like the police have been at your house. I hope you've kept our deal. Otherwise video of your daddy creeping around the neighborhood hits the police servers."

"I'm not working for you," she said. "And I'm wondering exactly why you're so insistent on it. Why me?"

"I heard the investigators are looking at your dad. I guess you've got a lot on your mind." The words were like ice on her spine.

She was scared, but she had to do this. He was underestimating her and maybe she was overestimating herself, but she had no choice.

"You texted a threat to Danielle before she died, on the phone you gave Ned. She found out about the drug deals. She told you no. And you threatened her, and she ended up dead. If you don't leave me and my family alone, I go to the police."

"That's your theory?" He doesn't seem rattled by her announcement. It's not what she expected. "Listen, do you know why I want to work with you? You don't take the pills. I've tried to work in Lakehaven before. You need a sober kid on the ground. Too many of them sample the merchandise. They're unreliable." He seems utterly unfazed by her threat.

"No. Why don't you go find someone who actually wants to work for you? Again: Why me?"

He takes a step toward her. And he loosens the scarf around his throat. Maybe he was warm. Maybe he meant to hurt her.

She takes a step back. "I found the phone in her house, while going through her stuff."

"Where was it?"

"In a blazer jacket pocket in her closet."

He looks almost rueful and Julia realizes: he was in Danielle's house at some point, maybe looking for the phone.

She presses ahead before she loses her nerve. "If anything happens to me, or to Ned, or to his father, or to my family, that phone goes to the police. And I'll tell them it's you on the other side. Being told off by a mother who didn't want her kid in a drug ring.

Maybe you were scared she would talk or cut a deal with the cops. Protect her son from prosecution and put you in jail in trade. But I have Ned's burner phone, and if you don't leave me and Ned alone, that phone will still end up going to the police."

He takes another step toward her.

"You'll never find where the phone is now. Or guess who has it. But they have their instructions. You're going to give me that video of my dad and Danielle. First."

He brings up the video on his phone. She knows he can have copies elsewhere, but that's true of her and his text message, as well. He shows her the video, then trashes it. "There. Happy?"

"Thank you."

"I want us to trust each other, so sure. Get me Ned's phone, now."

She nods. She turns and goes upstairs.

She hears Marland laugh and say, "You smart little thing. I never would have looked here."

She goes into the bathroom of the smallest bedroom upstairs. She shuts the door. She kneels before the sink, opens the cabinet door, and fumbles along the top surface. The key Ned gave her to this house was finally useful: she guessed Marland wouldn't suspect she'd hide something here. She'd secured the phone here, bound with masking tape, after she'd found it, afraid to keep it in her house, and she stares at it for a moment that turns into minutes. If she gives this to him, he'll erase the text messages and her leverage is gone. She takes a deep breath and snaps a picture of the threatening text message with her own phone's camera. It's better than nothing, but it also proves nothing. But if he grabs her phone and inspects it for a backup photo, he'll see it.

She keeps the photos. She decides it's worth the risk. She takes a few moments to gather her courage.

She goes to the top of the stairs.

The lamp downstairs, with its faint glow, is off.

"Marland?" she calls.

No answer.

"This isn't funny. I'm doing what you want." She takes a tentative step down. She puts Ned's burner phone in her pocket and switches on the flashlight app to light her way on the stairs.

Surely he didn't leave. It's a miracle no one has spotted Marland or her at the abandoned house, especially with Steve Butler's stupid patrol working the streets. She should remind him about the patrol. He might get caught if he leaves without being careful.

Now, at the bottom of the steps, she hears a harsh rattling noise, but in the darkness she can't see anything. She flashes the light along the room.

Marland lies on the carpet, five knife wounds in his chest, his life bubbling out of him as she watches. The bloodied knife lies on the floor. Marland raises a hand, pleading for life, and then the hand drops.

Julia thinks: *This just happened. The killer is still in the house.*

Terror washes over her like a wave. She screams, twice, shattering the quiet of the night. She drops her phone, its screen giving the death room an eerie, faint glow. She stumbles out the open door. She can't breathe. She can't see, and then she realizes she dropped the phone in her terror and shock and she can't go back for it. She can't go back in that house. The sky lit by moonlight, she can see well enough to flee. She runs off the deck, stumbling, crashing down to the lawn and hurtling herself into the darkness of the greenbelt, which feels like a safer darkness than the house.

She runs, blindly, back into the greenbelt. But under the canopy of the trees, she can't see the trail. She can't see anything. Because the killer still has to be there. How long was she gone? Five minutes? An eternity? Then she hears it.

Voices. "Hey! Hey! Come back here! Stop! Citizen watch!"

Another voice: "Call the police!"

They know she was there. *They saw me.* Her terror is now like a thing clawing out of her chest.

Julia stumbles into her house, trying not to cry, a strange choked noise coming from her. Grant's in the kitchen. She nearly falls to the floor.

Then through the haze of her panic, she remembers. *Her* phone. The police are coming and her phone is there. And the patrolling dads are there, and the police are coming, and it's too late.

She sobs. Grant closes his arms around her, whispering, "What's wrong? What's wrong?"

Where is Mom?

She's come into the house off the back patio. They're in the breakfast nook next to the kitchen and she gets to her feet, Grant holding her, now she's screaming for her mother. Where is she? And then she sees the clear knife rack, with its steel black blades in an orderly row, and the biggest one, with a Japanese name she can't remember, is missing.

52

FROM IRIS POLLITT'S "FROM RUSSIA WITH LOVE" ADOPTION JOURNAL

2002

It's showtime.

Will Anya show up? Will Boris? I cannot let my nerves show. I have to be steel.

I had thought the hearing would be in a courtroom. Instead it was just in a large room, with a large table, with the judge sitting across from us.

The judge had complete power over our happiness. That's an odd realization to have...that this stranger holds the course of the rest of your life in her hands. That your years to come pivot on the next hour, and you have no control over it.

She was a small woman, with little bolts of gray through her black hair. Her eyes were dark, too, and serious, and inspecting us behind her eyeglasses. She looked tired and irritated. Also in the room were another court official (I assume a clerk; his title was never stated to us); Maria, our caseworker from the Volkov Infants Home; Pavel, our interpreter; and Kyle and me. Danielle waited outside, but she'd explained the all-important ritual:

Judge asked question.

Pavel translated question.

Kyle and I stood up, answered question, sat back down.

Pavel stood up to translate our response.

Repeat, repeat, repeat.

It was like a long play of jack-in-the-box.

Up and down, up and down, like my heart had been this whole process.

But no sign of Anya. No indication from the judge or the orphanage director that she had appealed or that she had sought to attend. Maybe she didn't even know today was the hearing.

"You already have a child?" the judge demanded (as Pavel translated, seated).

We both stand. I can tell every fiber of Kyle's being wants to just keep standing, to stop this silly ruse, but we don't dare. "Yes, Your Honor, a daughter who is three. Her name is Julia."

"And she was diagnosed with cancer as an infant?"

"Yes, ma'am, a very treatable neuroblastoma. She is healthy and doing well."

I felt dizzy even talking about this with this woman.

"I am glad to hear that. So, this Russian baby is an insurance policy? Eh?"

Yes, she actually said that: "Eh?" Like an old man. "Is that how you view him? In case your first child is sick again?" Pavel's voice was steady as he translated the question.

We had been coached—relentlessly—by Danielle that we must be absolutely compliant, show no anger or frustration, and to not ask any questions.

They are giving us a son of Russia. A piece of their future. Show gratitude, shut your mouth.

I wanted to say: "If I just wanted a replacement baby, honey, I would have taken the quarter-million-dollar bribe. But no, I want this one. No other will do." I wondered if my mouth quivered with my unspoken response.

Kyle said, "No, Your Honor, he is not an insurance policy. Our experience with our daughter's illness taught us how precious life is. We found capacities for love we didn't realize we had. We cannot have more biological children of our own. We have love to give and we want to give it to Sasha."

"What if your other child gets sick again?"

"She is in remission, Your Honor, but of course there is that chance. If that happens, we will love her and take care of her and

Sasha will be part of that. He will never be neglected because his sister is sick."

"Mrs. Pollitt." This is the first time the judge has addressed me directly and I stand, having just sat down.

She continued, with Pavel translating in chunks: "You already have a child who might demand extra attention because of her needs. How badly do you want this boy? Why this boy?"

I thought: She must not have been satisfied with Kyle's answer. It's up to me. I can't give the answer rattling in my head. I put all that behind me. I waited for Pavel to be ready; he's gulping a sip of throat-clearing water, since he's doing twice the amount of talking as anyone else.

"Yes, ma'am. I understand your concern. I've wondered the same. Maybe his biological mother wants him back. He's such a wonderful boy, I cannot imagine her sacrifice in giving him up so he can have a better life. Whether he was adopted here in Russia or by us." Everyone looked at me, as apparently one doesn't usually talk about the biological mother, but I want this in the record. "But he has captured my heart. Our hearts. Never ask me what I won't do for Alexander, because I will do anything to give him a wonderful, fulfilling life."

I paused to let Pavel catch up with the translation.

Then I went what Kyle calls full Iris: "Since we began the process, I have been approached by a woman warning me off adopting here, another car rammed into us after we left the orphanage and then fled, and the caseworker can tell you Sasha's biological mother showed up wanting to see him. His mother has an unfortunate history with not being able to care for her children. It has been dramatic. And none of that, not a single moment of it, has swayed us from wanting our son as much as we wanted our daughter. I nearly lost my daughter. I won't lose my son to what feels like an active campaign of harassment. May I ask you a question?"

I had just broken, stomped, shattered every single rule in the book. If Danielle were in the room, she would have erupted like a defense attorney staving off a courtroom confession. Pavel actually gasps, but he gathers himself under the judge's impatient stare and translates. Maria, the caseworker, had an opposite reaction, apparently forgetting how to breathe.

The judge said, steel in her voice: "Ask your one question."

"If Alexander's mother changes her mind, I want to know you will abide by your ruling if you give him to us. That he will be ours forever. That his mother will have no standing to try to claim him. That this...campaign waged against us will not be endorsed by the Russian government."

Pavel translated, with seeming precision and care. The judge listened intently, but her gaze was fixed on me. I stared right back as she answered and Pavel rendered it into wry English.

"Never ask me, Mrs. Pollitt," the judge said, "if I will not stand by my rulings." When Pavel finished the translation, there was a flicker of respect on the judge's face. Barely. Just for me to see.

I said, unbidden, unasked: "Yes, ma'am. We only want to love him. We've already had to deal with far more here than most adoptive parents. We don't want her trying to contact him or us. If when he's older he wants to reach out to her, we will support that. But not now. Not as a matter of custody."

"Help me," Anya had said. *I'm sorry, Anya. I'm sorry.*

The judge took a long, deep breath.

"You. Mrs. Pollitt. I am told you are a songwriter?"

"Yes, Your Honor."

Maria, the caseworker, glanced at me as if embarrassed.

And then the judge started humming a song I wrote for NSYNC, one of their early hits, and tapped out the rhythm on the desk. I got the first smile from her.

We have our son.

53

EXCERPT OF TRANSCRIPT OF TCSO AND LPD INTERVIEW WITH KYLE POLLITT

(Continued from previous session)

Detective Ames: What was your wife's relationship with Danielle Roberts?

Pollitt: Basically, the same as mine. Neighbor, friend, helped us get our son. Where's Detective Ponder?

Detective Ames: Busy.

Pollitt: Why are we still talking? I confessed.

Detective Ames: We need to clear things up on the case. Just tie stuff together.

Pollitt: But I confessed. It's over.

Detective Ames: We have some more questions. Danielle helped you get your son. What all does that cover?

Pollitt: She worked for an adoption consultancy. She helped us navigate the process. She was the liaison with the Russian officials.

Detective Ames: Did she go to Russia with you?

Pollitt: Yes.

Detective Ames: So you traveled with her.

Pollitt: My wife and I, yes.

Detective Ames: I understand that the relationship between your wife and Ms. Roberts was strained.

Pollitt: If you're trying to say Iris had anything to do with this, you're wrong. I've confessed. Stop complicating this stuff.

Detective Ames: What happened in Russia?

Pollitt: We got our son. Nothing else. Lots of paperwork. Judge had a hearing. We gave his caseworkers and the other kids gifts.

Detective Ames: Danielle Roberts told another pair of her clients that you had created problems for her.

Pollitt: *(long pause)* I have no idea what that means.

Detective Ames: What problems?

Pollitt: I don't know. It was years ago. Our son is now a freshman in high school. Who are these people saying this?

Detective Ames: Other clients of hers.

Pollitt: Bull. I want names.

Detective Ames: I can't tell you their names. Was there anything fishy or illegal about your adoption?

Pollitt: No, no, no. What is this? Y'all are going after my son now?

Detective Ames: Does Iris have a reason to wish ill to Danielle?

Pollitt: No. Do you not believe my confession? I told you, look at her phone card. She called me at 4:00 a.m.

Detective Ames: That doesn't mean you had a conversation and then went over there. Or that an affair is what you were discussing.

Pollitt: I've told you the truth.

Detective Ames: Kyle. I just have to say…we think you're lying to us about certain aspects of that evening. We understand your daughter is involved with her son. You're best friends with her boyfriend. You used her services to help find your son. You and your family are more connected to this woman than anyone else.

Pollitt: So what? I killed her.

Detective Ames: We found the murder weapon.

　　(Long pause)

Detective Ames: It was hidden inside the victim's Lakehaven

Library book bag. A metal pipe. You have a similar pipe, stored on the top shelf of your garage, left over from a renovation last year; the part numbers match. There is blood inside the bag. It was found inside a tree where I understand your son used to hide objects as a child, along the Winding Creek greenbelt. You left that out of your confession, sir. You said you killed her with your bare fist.

Pollitt: I did.

Detective Ames: The forensic evidence doesn't match your story. Now, the pipe appears to have come from your house, which means another member of your family, or your circle of friends, could have had access. Are you protecting someone, Kyle? Your wife? One of your children?

(Long pause)

Pollitt: I'd like to speak to my lawyer, please.

(Break)

(Interview resumes)

Pollitt: What the hell? Kip says you've arrested my daughter. She's a child!

Detective Ames: Yes, Julia has been arrested. Her phone was found at a murder scene in the neighborhood. A knife that matches a knife set from your home was used as the weapon. She was seen leaving the murder scene immediately following the crime.

Pollitt: That can't be. It can't. Julia would never hurt anyone.

Detective Ames: Do you know who this man is? For the recording, I'm showing him a photo of the victim found at the Carlyle residence, 2308 Marbletop Road.

(Pause)

Pollitt: I don't know this man. I've never seen him before. Who is he?

Detective Ames: Your daughter says that his name is Marland. She doesn't know if that's his first or last name. Or even his real name.

Pollitt: Who is he?

Detective Ames: We're trying to establish that as well. Two murders in the same posh neighborhood in a week. Your neighbors are going to love you.

Pollitt: I need to speak to my daughter. You cannot keep me from my daughter.

Detective Ames: You're in custody and you're not going to talk to her.

Pollitt: Make it possible. Make it possible and I'll help you however you want.

Detective Ames: Is it Julia you're protecting? Did she have a reason to want to kill Danielle as well?

Pollitt: I…I…will never believe Julia could hurt someone. Please. You have me. Just leave her alone.

Detective Ames: You can't talk to her right now. I'm sure she's talking. Telling everything she knows. You should do the same. Just come clean.

Pollitt: The blood in that library bag isn't Danielle's. It's mine. Your tests will tell you that. You see my face? Someone attacked me.

Detective Ames: How? What happened?

Pollitt: You let me talk to my daughter and I'll tell you.

54

IRIS

Iris pulls into the driveway past midnight, exhausted, beaten.

Her daughter is spending the night in jail. With Kyle arrested, the judge has decided to keep Julia as well.

She sees the front door open and Grant appear on the porch...and then Mike appear in the doorway.

Grant runs toward her, embraces her in the driveway. His hug is like solace.

Mike stands on the porch, watching.

"Where is Julia?" Grant asks.

"She's at the detention center. I think we can get her out tomorrow." Iris isn't at all sure of that, but she has to give Grant hope. "It's late. You should go to bed, baby."

"I can't sleep," he says, but exhaustion slurs his voice.

She turns him back toward the house and walks him up to the porch.

"I didn't think he should be alone," Mike says quietly.

"Thank you," she says. She's surprised the press aren't here, but they were at the detention center and she had to push through them. Maybe they've decided now that half her family is in custody to give her some space. It seems unlikely.

Mike follows them in and shuts the front door behind them. Grant leans against Iris, and she tries not to collapse. She has to be strong right now.

"Did you get something to eat?" she asks her son.

"Mom, did Julia kill this guy? Like self-defense?"

"No. Of course not," she says. That he can even ask the question shows how their lives have spun out of control. "It's late. Tomorrow will be a long day. Go upstairs and go to bed."

"Are we not going to talk about this?" he asks.

This. Your father and your sister are under arrest for two murders. What words do I say to tell you everything is going to be all right? That—snap of the fingers—life will be back to normal? Where is this in the parent manual? She takes a deep breath.

"I can't tell you much. We will be putting together a legal strategy with their lawyers tomorrow; Julia's arrest changes everything. But we know they're not guilty, right? You and I know that."

Grant nods.

"And so we're going to find a way to make the police understand they're not guilty. That they couldn't have done this. The police are very good at their job, but they can make mistakes, and they've made a mistake here."

"But Dad..."

"I know. I know. Go to bed. Sleep if you can. If you can't, play video games, whatever makes you feel better. But sleep if you can."

He turns to Mike. "Thanks for staying with me."

"You are welcome," Mike says. He and Iris both watch Grant trudge up the stairs.

"You didn't have to stay," she says.

"I didn't want him to be alone. And I suppose it sends a message to the neighborhood that I am standing by my friends. For now."

"For now."

"I don't want to believe Kyle did it," Mike says. "Danielle loved your family..."

"No, she didn't. She loved Grant and Julia. Let's just cast away all the illusions that we were still close." Saying it is a relief.

"I can only say what she told me. The regard she held for your family."

"When we started working together, I thought I had a friend for life," Iris says. "You…you go through a lot together, adopting a child."

"I'm sure," Mike says. "You've had a long day. I'll go. But…Grant cannot hear us right now."

She turns to him.

"Did Kyle kill her?" Mike asks, very softly.

Iris is silent.

"Or is he protecting you?" Mike's voice is still soft.

Iris says nothing.

"I have been so grateful for your family. It was hard when Peter and I came here—we wanted a fresh start and you welcomed us." For a moment he stops. "I don't want to believe it of you. Either of you. That one could kill her and the other could keep it secret."

Now she finds the words. "I don't know why this is happening, but we are innocent of this."

"Ned. Ned brought this into our lives," Mike says. "You think I don't know what you and Gordon whispered about? You are trying to protect Julia and Ned. I found prescription drugs in Ned's backpack one night. I will search it—Danielle never would. This man Julia found dead, he has some drug involvement? I heard the police talking."

Iris says, "I don't know, honestly."

"I think you are lying to me. I think you better start telling the truth, for Grant's sake. You know what it is to conceal evidence? To interfere in a police investigation? What happens to Grant if you go to jail, too?"

She hears a creak on a stair; she suspects Grant is listening. "I've done nothing."

"But you say that about Kyle and Julia, too."

"Did Danielle ever tell…ever say to you that she had reason to be afraid of someone?"

"You mean that someone threatened her?" His voice rose slightly.

"Yes."

"No. What do you know, Iris?"

Silence.

"Who has come after her, Iris?"

"Maybe the Butlers."

"Those two? Steve Butler is a clown."

"They were unhappy with her. They moved close to her. I think they're capable of anything." She doesn't add that she thinks that because she saw something of herself in them: Iris is capable of far more than people think.

Mike waits for her to say more. "Have you said anything to the police about them?"

"No. I have no proof. Except they say they're getting a baby from a cousin, and if that were true they wouldn't need Danielle."

"Babies. You're all so obsessed with babies." Mike shakes his head. "Becoming a father changed a lot of my life, but it didn't define me. You all...live through your kids too much."

Iris hates him for saying this but she's exhausted, so she just says: "That's a valid point."

"What will you do with Grant tomorrow? He can come over and stay with Peter. He shouldn't be alone."

"That's not appropriate, given..."

"If Kyle killed her, Kyle can burn in hell. And if you know he did and you're covering for him, you can burn in hell, too. But I won't turn my back on Grant. He's not responsible for your choices."

Iris doesn't know what to say. She hears the creak of the step; Grant has left his eavesdropping post. "I didn't kill her and neither did my husband. I appreciate your offer of help. But Grant will be just fine."

"If you tell me this, I'm going to believe you," Mike says, his voice breaking. "I'll believe you. But you really have to say it to me."

"We're innocent," she says. "We could never kill someone."

Mike wipes his eyes with the back of his hand. She's never seen him cry. "OK," he says, gruff. "You deal with your lawyers tomorrow. Grant can stay at our house if he wants."

"Go sleep if you can," she says. She wants to give him a hug, but she doesn't. She doesn't want to touch anyone right now, except for her children.

Mike leaves. From the window she watches him walk down the street in the darkness, a pale, broad figure in the moonlight.

She goes to bed, alone, listening to the quiet. No sound from Julia's room. No sound from Grant's. And the other side of the bed is a new kind of empty.

55

JULIA

They didn't put Julia in the regular jail where her father was, as she was a minor, but instead they placed her in a juvenile detention center in South Austin, alone in her cell, wondering where her mother was, wondering what would happen next.

She had been seen. Her phone was by the body. The knife was from their house.

And Julia keeps thinking and saying: *No, this is wrong. It's wrong.*

At some point after midnight she falls asleep, and for one awful, delicious moment when she wakes up, she thinks she is in her bed, snug at home, with her books and her photos of her friends acting goofy and the key Ned gave her tucked under her pillow where she'd put it so she'd feel close to him during this horrible time. But the light in the room is too bright, and she can hear sobbing and arguing from strange voices, nor far away.

This isn't home. This is a nightmare.

She lies curled up on the bed, waiting for the tears to come, but trying to think now that sleep had wiped away the shock.

Marland is dead.

She thinks it through, because this is real and she has to deal with the reality, find the proof that she couldn't have killed this man. Whoever killed him had killed him in a matter of moments — very quickly. Five stab wounds, she remembers seeing. Done quickly. Which meant…the murderer was in the house already when she and Marland arrived.

And Marland either knew and trusted that person, or Marland didn't know he or she was in the house.

But Marland had not cried out. Marland had faced this person and gotten knifed. Or had been grabbed from behind and knifed, although to Julia, well versed in crime shows on streaming channels, that seemed a harder sell.

Marland knew his killer. He had not been surprised to see him. Maybe they had planned together to get the phone from Julia and then kill her. But the killer turned on Marland and left Julia holding the knife…

…which had been in her family's kitchen. A fancy black blade, not silver-colored like most blades. They'd had the knives for a few years. But that meant that whoever got the knife had had access to their house. It would take only a second to hide the knife, and if it wasn't in the rack, one would assume it was in the dishwasher. It wouldn't be missed right away.

Who'd been there?

Ned. Gordon. Mike. Peter. Any of the neighbors who had brought food or comfort.

Her parents. Grant.

Even Danielle.

But the world was full of knives. You only took one from a house when you wanted to frame someone. So someone had known she was talking with Marland, knew she would talk again with him, and knew she had access to the abandoned house.

That was Ned. No one else knew, except her mom.

And Gordon. If Ned had told him everything.

What would Gordon do to protect his son? Kill the man who could link his son to the drug ring? Blame the girl who stood on the edge of it? Marland had been pressuring her to join; was that the only reason?

Had Gordon put Marland up to this and then killed him, solving two problems with one blow?

The door to her room opens. A woman she hasn't seen before

enters. Pretty, in her thirties, Julia guesses. She wears a paramedic uniform.

"Hello," the woman says. She smiles, checks a clipboard. "Julia Pollitt?"

"Yes."

"Hi. They have you listed for…a mild sedative." She has a slight, odd accent.

"Who does? I haven't seen a doctor."

"It was ordered, sweetie. You want left arm or right arm?"

"I don't want it at all. I want to see my mom."

"She'll be here later." The paramedic steps forward; she already holds the syringe. "Left or right arm?"

"I don't want it!" Now Julia's voice rises.

"I understand," the paramedic says. "If you refuse it and I have to call the guards to hold you down, you get a disciplinary mark. Loss of privileges."

For a moment Julia thinks a shot to make her sleepy sounds great—numb this awful experience. But the thought passes. "I want my lawyer here. I do not want to be medicated."

The woman shuts the door. She flicks the needle guard off the syringe with her thumb. She rushes forward, dropping the clipboard. Julia cries out, but the needle is through her sleeve and in her arm before she can stop the woman. She tries to twist away as the woman's thumb gropes for the plunger. Her other hand clamps over Julia's mouth.

The chemical wave hits her like a tsunami. Numbness, then a feeling like she can't move.

"It's just enough," the woman says.

Julia falls back on the floor. She can't move. Her hands, her feet, feel like anchors. She tries to make a sound.

The woman starts to hum as she works quickly, gathering up the sheet from the cot, twisting it tight, shaping it into a rope, smiling at her.

The woman ties one end into a noose and slips it over Julia's head.

"It won't hurt," the woman says softly in her breathy accent.

56

FROM IRIS POLLITT'S "FROM RUSSIA WITH LOVE" ADOPTION JOURNAL

2002

Grant is ours, and no one can take him away from us.

The judge congratulated us and signed documents and we signed the final papers that needed to be signed. Danielle looked nearly faint with relief. Pavel smiled at us, shook our hands.

"Let's go get your boy," Danielle said.

I nodded, feeling stunned. Kyle was silent though. I hadn't told him I might say what I was going to say. I didn't think he was angry with me, maybe just shocked that I had broken the main rule laid down to us when we started this journey.

"Kyle?" I said. I took his hand.

"Yes?"

"Are you all right?"

"You're a fighter," he said. "I don't know that I ever knew what a fighter you were. Even when Julia got diagnosed, this was something different from that. She was ours; we were just making sure she got what she needed. This was you fighting to have him." He swallowed.

"I didn't know I'd go quite that far."

"You read the room. I'm glad she was a fan."

"We have him. Despite everything. We have him."

We were so happy. We put our foreheads together, moved closer, kissed and hugged.

Today our driver was a woman named Tatiana, early forties, kind smile. She told us her sister worked at Volkov as a caretaker and she was always happy of a chance to visit. Pavel sat in the front with her, and the three of us sat in the back. Maria was in her own car and would meet us at the orphanage. On the drive, I thought Kyle was going to crush my hand.

We had a son.

Forget you, warning woman. Thank you, Anya. I hope you find some peace and happiness.

At Volkov, they stripped Grant of his orphanage-issued clothes—even his diaper, which was still clean. We had clothes and a fresh diaper ready for him. It was as if he were shedding the skin of his old life and putting on his American life. My hands shook a little bit as I dressed him. He was fussy, having been woken from a nap, and I just kept saying "Mommy and Daddy are here. We love you and everything is going to be OK." I thought: You went to sleep as Alexander Stepurin and you've woken up as Grant Pollitt. Welcome to your new life.

His new onesie had a little Texan flag on it, and maybe that was gauche, but he was going to be an American child now. I put him in his coat and a warm hat; the snow still came down outside. I really, really wanted to be gone from this place and never look back at it.

The goodbyes were short and fueled by Maria ensuring that we had all the paperwork, double-checking we had his Russian-issued passport. I wanted to say, "Any other paperwork we haven't signed, you can scan and email to us or fax to us," but I didn't. Everything checked.

We said a thankful goodbye to Pavel, who was staying on at the orphanage to help another family whose translator had canceled at the last moment. He shook our hands and wished us well.

The snow came down like a curtain; I was really getting anxious about the weather. Danielle, Kyle, and I trudged through the snow to the parking lot, where Tatiana and the car waited, and opened the doors. I had already set up your baby seat in the back because I didn't want to fiddle with it as we were leaving the orphanage. Get in and go. I settled you in, and Kyle and I shut the doors and buckled up and I felt the weight of a stare. I looked up to meet eyes in the rearview mirror and realized the woman in the driver's seat in Tatiana's coat and hat wasn't Tatiana.

It was Anya.

Danielle, in the front seat, was staring at her and not moving.

"Anya," I said.

"She has a gun," Danielle said, very calmly. "Aimed at me."

"You are not taking my baby," Anya said. "Danielle, you drive. Get out of the car and come around to driver's seat while I slide over. If you run, if you yell, I will shoot both of these Americans."

Her English had improved.

"You wouldn't. Not in front of the baby," I said.

"I will," she said, and I believed her.

"You would hurt his ears with a gunshot," Kyle said calmly.

"Then don't make me shoot," she said.

Danielle got out of the car, Anya slid over while keeping the gun aimed at Kyle, and Danielle got back in the car. She was sweating despite the cold.

"Anya, don't. Don't do this. It will never work," Danielle said. "Let them go and we'll go talk about this."

"Drive. I will tell you where."

Danielle pulled out of the lot, tentatively, as one would driving with a gun aimed at you and with icy conditions. "Where is Tatiana?"

"Visiting her sister. I took her coat, with the car keys in the pocket, and hat off the rack at the service entrance." She stumbled over her English here. She risked a glance at our baby; I realized this might be the closest she'd been to him since giving birth.

"Anya, do not do this. There is time to stop this, right now," Kyle said. "If something happens to us, Boris will know you did it."

"Boris won't care what I do now."

We reached the main road. "Turn left," she ordered.

We drove into the increasing whiteness. I held on to Grant's hand.

Danielle was silent. Anya was silent. Kyle tried to reason with

Anya again and she said, "Shut up or I'll shoot you in knee," and he shut up.

Grant fussed. His toys were in the bag, now in the trunk. "He needs something to play with," I said.

Anya frowned. Then she unclasped a bracelet from her wrist and tossed it to me. It was lovely, silver and small emeralds. I danged it above Grant and he thought it was a toy. The crying stopped. I could see Anya fighting back tears at the sight of this baby playing with her jewelry.

"If you love Sasha," I said to her, "you'll stop this right now and let us go."

"Don't try and talk love to me," Anya said. Her English was better than when she'd asked me for help. She'd been playing on my sympathies then, but not now.

"You could have come to the court. You didn't. Your boyfriend is married. He's not going to help you. This isn't the solution." If you had ever told me I'd be trying to talk a distraught mother into giving up her child, I would not have believed you. But here we were.

"Give me his passport," she said. We couldn't take Grant out of the country without that.

She guessed correctly that Kyle had it and gestured at him with the gun. Then she told Danielle to take the next right.

Kyle didn't produce the passport.

"Now," she said, putting the gun up to Danielle's head, "as there will be no adoption, consultant not needed." Danielle gave out a little shriek.

I thought: She'll do it.

Kyle handed her our baby's passport. My throat felt thick as she tucked it into her own coat. She gave Danielle some more directions—we were off the main road now, and we pulled into a town that looked abandoned. There were signs in Russian, a bright yellow.

How many abandoned towns have you seen outside of movies? Well, in Russia, they have them. Either because the land around them gets bought up by oligarchs or the government moves everyone or the town dies for all the reasons towns have died throughout time. For one awful second I thought, "What if this is like Chernobyl, radioactive or something?" But then I knew they wouldn't have the orphanage close to it. It was just two streets and a dozen small houses left behind. This town appeared to have died a natural death.

"Stop the car. Park by that car." She pointed to a car parked farther down the street. It sat next to a cozy-looking house, where a cat peered out from the window, watching our little drama. Is this where she'd been living, with only a cat for company?

"You walked from here," Danielle said.

"Yes. The roads wind, but going by the fields, it's only a few kilometers on foot."

"You know this will never work. You know us taking the baby is the only way this works," Danielle said.

"Give me your mobile phones," Anya said. We handed them to her.

"Get out of the car. And you"—she looked at me—"you take out the car seat while he holds my child."

"He's not yours anymore. You made your choice," I said.

"You are going to destroy both your lives," Danielle said. "Stop this, and it's forgotten. And forgiven. You can go back to your life and no one will know."

"I'm saving us both," she said. "You would use us."

It was like there was another conversation happening and I was hearing only part of it.

"Anya," I said. "I didn't lie to you. I brought him to the window. So you could see him. So you could say goodbye to him. Because your country has given him, legally, to us. Because you gave him up. You made your choice just like you made it before. He is not yours, not anymore. Please. You cannot have that gun around him and be telling me you are going to take good care of him."

"I want you to shut up now, lady," Anya said. "You know nothing about me."

"I know you are trying to take this poor child from a wonderful life," I said.

"I can give him a better life than you can. He will have everything, now."

She made no sense, so I pressed my argument. "You are putting him in danger, waving that gun around. He is precious."

"He is valuable. To her," Anya answered. Indicating Danielle.

"Adoption is a business, yes," I said. "But…"

"Shut. Up. Now."

I've freed the car seat from the buckles. We're all out of the car now, Kyle holding Grant. I have the car seat. Danielle is by the driver's side, Anya by the passenger side.

Waving the gun, she gestured us all away from the car. Toward the parked car. We moved toward it, a small group of very nervous people. The snow still flew; the wind picked up.

"Put the child seat in back seat of that car," Anya orders me.

"They'll never let you get away with this," Danielle said. "Anya. You know this. You know this won't work."

"I know it will."

She was going to kill the three of us, I realized. Alone in this deserted town, with the cat in the window as the only witness. We will just have vanished. The police will look for us, but no one will be looking here, not for a while. And she will be long gone, certain she is right.

"I can't get it to work," I called to Anya, my voice in rising hysterics of frustration. I held the car seat up in front of me.

"Danielle, help her," Anya said.

"I don't know how those work," Danielle said.

Danielle has a kid. Of course she can work one. She looked at me.

"Try again. Fix it." Anya took a step forward toward me, anger flashing on her face.

And I threw the car seat at her. Hard. Straight at her face. "RUN, KYLE!" I screamed, but Kyle didn't run. He just spun, putting his body between that gun and Grant, holding him close. Anya managed to get her arm partially up, but the car seat still hit her full in the face. I ran toward her, and Danielle ran toward her. Both of us grabbed at Anya's arm, her nose bloodied from the car seat impacting her face. It was all a blur, Danielle grabbing at the gun and me grabbing at Anya and Anya saying clearly to me, "You don't understand," and then the gun fired, the sound awful in the cold quiet of the snowfall. But not so loud because the gun was aimed not at the sky but into her coat.

Anya jerked and Danielle and I looked at each other, each of us thinking, "You're shot," but it wasn't either of us. Anya fell to the snow. It seemed to take forever, and then the blood was bright against the white.

And then a terrible silence.

Broken when you started crying, Grant, Kyle holding you, staring at the dead woman. Your dead mother who was never going to be your mother.

I touched her throat, but there was no pulse, no thrum of life.

Danielle had killed her. Danielle had grabbed the gun and turned it back toward Anya, trying to pull it out of her grip, but it had been HER hands on the gun. While my hands had been on Anya's arm, pulling her off-balance. But I hadn't touched the gun. It was Danielle. I want to be clear about that.

Danielle's mouth moved at me, but in the aftermath of the gun blast I couldn't hear. I just stood, watching. Anya was dead. There was nothing to be done. It had been over in an instant. She lay on her back, eyes toward the endless gray sky, the snow beneath her, and I stared and saw snowfall settling on her open eyes. I stared and stared, like my eyes were dead as well.

Danielle grabbed my arm. She mouthed words I couldn't quite hear. Shoving me back toward the car.

We had to get out of here.

It was a strange numbness. I was in shock, so Kyle sat me down in the snow and I held Grant while Kyle put the baby seat back in our car. Danielle walked away, behind the green house.

The cat in the window had fled. A few minutes later I saw it in the snow and thought for a horrifying second that someone in the green house had let it out and I got up and walked around and saw there was a cat door at the back. This must have been where Anya was living. Hiding.

Danielle came around the corner, on her mobile phone, whispering urgently. I couldn't hear what she said and she turned and walked away from me.

Later, when the shock subsided, I would wonder who the hell Danielle was calling.

I still had the warning woman's phone in my pocket. How had she been connected to Anya? I'd been too terrified to ask, to confess in front of Danielle and Kyle that I'd been offered a fortune to decline this baby. I held Grant closer to me.

"We have to tell the police. We can't leave her here," I said in a daze. Grant was looking up at me as I held him, eyes bright from the cold, sleepy. He had finally stopped crying after the shock and scare of the gunshot.

Danielle knelt before me. "You cannot tell anyone this happened, Iris. Ever. Do you understand me?"

"But…"

"Listen. They will take Grant away from you and Kyle. We have to go back to Saint Petersburg. Then to Moscow, just like we planned, and fly home. We do everything just like we planned after we picked up your son. We do not alter plans or deviate. We don't leave early. Because this did not happen. Do you understand me? This. Did. Not. Happen. The Russians won't care that she was in the wrong. She's a Russian citizen and she's dead because of us."

"Because of you," I wanted to say, but I couldn't say that. I nodded.

I wasn't scared of the Russian government. Well, I was, but I thought of the warning woman and her massive bribe and what she would do if she'd approached us for Anya and then learned Anya was dead. We could get back to America and this could come crashing down on us.

We had been so happy just minutes before. It was so unfair. I steadied myself.

"What do we do?" I said.

"It looks like she's been camping out here. When she's found, it will look like a woman living alone out here who ran into a bad guy. That's what it will look like."

Kyle knelt next to me. He enclosed me in his arms. "We can do this. You can do this, Iris. For our children we can do anything."

I decided then to believe him. Yes, I could be steel. The steeliest steel.

I stood with my son in my arms. I looked down at the body of the dead stranger. That's what she had to be to me now. A dead stranger. A sad, broken woman I'd never really known, who for all intents and purposes took her own life.

We put the body in her car she'd parked next to the green house. Left the car door open. Wiped down any place we touched on the car. Turned the bloody snow over so the red didn't show. I took the emerald and silver bracelet she'd let Grant play with and put it back on her wrist. Put our son in the baby seat and drove the car to Saint Petersburg.

I didn't look back when we left the abandoned village. I never looked back, because there was nothing to see.

This never happened. This never happened. This never happened.

Appended to the journal page here, a handwritten note:
This never happened this way.—Danielle Roberts

57

IRIS

Iris is up long before the dawn, thinking. The quiet—the awful quiet of half her family being in custody—has cleared her head. She has to think now.

And she's been thinking about what her husband could have done.

Two things haven't sat right with her. Someone beat up Kyle (she no longer believes he just fell down to the creek), and he had that computer in his trunk that she'd never seen before.

What do those things mean?

Kyle went somewhere, in the chaos of the bodies being found. On the greenbelt. Well, he could have gone to Danielle's house that way if he didn't want to be seen. And he had a phone she'd given him. Was he afraid of something else that could point at him? Or did he want to see if she had leverage against him or Iris?

Kyle could have gone to her house. And he could have gotten beaten up there.

Because someone else was there, looking. Someone else who had a reason to want her dead.

And then, what? He went and bought a computer? Why?

Because whatever he found needed a computer to be read. So. A CD or a flash drive. And he was scared to read it on a computer that they owned.

She starts searching their room. She goes through bureaus,

drawers. Nothing. She goes up and searches his office. An hour passes. Still nothing. She sits and tries to think like Kyle.

He goes to Danielle's house. He finds something. He gets punched, repeatedly.

He would change clothes. He was in his running clothes, and the police took them.

She stands in her husband's closet. Where would he hide something in here?

On his dusty top shelf there are shoeboxes. She searches them, all empty. There is a duffel bag he rarely uses. She starts unzipping the compartments.

In a side pocket she finds lint, expired breath mints, and a flash drive. Holds it up to the light.

She plugs it into her computer. Spreadsheets, with payments to "Firebird" and to "Lark." They mean nothing to her. These payments were made years ago. What does that have to do with now?

Firebird, though. That's the name of the company that called and left the voicemail at the Butler house.

She opens another folder. Photos of adoptions in Russia. She finds a folder named Pollitt. She clicks through. Pictures of them, in front of the hotel in Saint Petersburg, at the orphanage. Looking happy but stressed.

A photo of drops of blood on snow.

She stops. She stares. She goes on to the next picture. It's fuzzy, looking lifted from a traffic camera. A man, getting out of a car. An SUV, with damage to its passenger side. He's in a suit and dark glasses and a silver tie. But she can see his face, the high cheekbones, the small scar near his mouth.

The police showed her a picture of Marland last night, just his face, calm in death, to see if she recognized him. She didn't. But now she does.

That was the SUV that hit them when they left the orphanage the first time.

That was the man she saw talking, animatedly, with Danielle in the hotel that first morning.

Iris stares at the pictures. She tries to gather her thoughts. Why is this happening? Why would this man step back into their lives? Who is he?

She can't just show this to the police. It ties them even further to Marland. She can imagine telling Ponder and Ames: Well, you see, he tried to wreck our car once years ago. But we don't *know* him.

She goes and she makes coffee, thinking how to handle this without tearing the rest of their world down. Then, as she is stirring sugar into her cup, she hears car doors slam, voices raised in anger.

Iris goes to the window. She sees, two houses down, Ned standing by Danielle's car, apparently having slammed a door, and Gordon on a phone in the driveway, pacing, angry.

By Gordon's feet she sees a suitcase, which Ned picks up and puts into the trunk while Gordon raises his voice.

She heads out the front door, coffee cup in hand. Down to the circle, across the pavement.

Ned sees her coming and freezes. Gordon has his back to her. "I am asking you to help my boy. You helped us before…I'll pay, even. Double. I'm just…"

And then he senses her approach, like Iris's anger is a shock wave traveling ahead of her. He says, "I'll call you back." He listens for a moment, then disconnects the phone.

"Going somewhere?" she asks, her voice calm.

"To a hotel," Gordon says. "It was a mistake to stay here. It's too emotional for Ned."

"Not the airport? Not running to London, or Ghana, ahead of the law?"

"We have no reason to run."

"My daughter's in jail because she tried to help Ned. And of course he's abandoning her." She glances at Ned. "You're nearly a man. It's time for you to decide what kind of man you want to be."

His gaze meets hers, and then he looks away.

"Who was Marland? How did you get involved with him?" She tries to keep the fury out of her voice.

"He's not answering your questions."

Ned looks at her. "He approached me."

"Who was he, though? Did she know him in Russia?"

"Russia? What does he have to do with Russia?"

"But why you? Why?"

"I don't know. He was a friend of a friend."

"But who was he? Where did he live?" Ned tries to look away from her again, and she gently but firmly puts her hand on his chin and turns his face back toward her. "Please. If you ever cared about Julia, ever, show me now. Please tell me."

Ned looks at her and takes a deep breath. His voice shakes. "Marland asked me once if things got hot, did I have a plan B? I think he wanted to be sure I wouldn't turn on him. Or give him access and then abandon him. I told him my dad was from Ghana and I'd probably go there if we had to run. I never really thought it would happen. I asked him what he would do. He shrugged. But it made me wonder, like he knew my plan but I didn't know his. So I asked a friend—a customer—who was already on his way to my house and who didn't know anything about Marland or who he was to follow him and as payment I'd double his order at no cost. He was blocks away, and I called him when Marland left and he found him and followed him. Marland turned into an old neighborhood off Old Travis. He pulled into the parking lot of an apartment complex called Marble Hills. Now, maybe he spotted my friend and he just pulled in there and waited until he passed. Or maybe he's got a backup place to hide if he has to, and that's it. That's all I know."

Ned starts to get into the car.

"Who is Firebird? Or Lark?"

"What?" He freezes.

"Do those names mean something to you?"

"Firebird Investments owns Danielle's house," Gordon says. "How did you know that?"

Danielle's house. And the Butlers' house. The same company. What did that mean? "What is Firebird?"

"I don't know. We can't find who the owners are," Gordon says.

"Doesn't that strike you as distinctly odd?" she asks.

"My mother's dead and you're asking stupid questions," Ned says.

Iris stares at him. "You're too young to realize what you've lost. Your mother. You'll miss her every day. You'll pick up the phone to tell her something and you'll realize she's not there to hear your good news or lift you up after your bad day. You never get over it. You just learn to live with it."

Ned stares at her. Gordon says, "Iris," but she ignores him.

"But you've lost your best friend. You threw Julia away. For what? Because you got involved in something stupid to prove how cool you were? You figured if you got in trouble, your mom and your friends would dig you out. Well. That worked out." She stops as she sees the enormity of it all weigh in his eyes. It's sinking in, everything he's lost. Suddenly he can't look at her and he gets in the car.

"Don't speak to him again," Gordon says. "Tend to yourself."

She realizes Mike was the person on the other end of that call, refusing use of his friend's private plane Gordon used to get here. They'll have to fly commercial. There are daily direct flights from Austin to London, but she doesn't know when they are. They can't run so fast right now.

She dials Detective Ponder as they drive away, in case they're not supposed to be leaving the country. They're the police's problem now.

She leaves a long message for Ponder. As she does she gets another call: the juvenile detention center. She quickly finishes her voicemail to Ponder and then listens to the center's voicemail insisting she call back immediately, and she dials the phone with a hot, sharp fear in her heart.

58

IRIS

It's the same hospital that Julia was in when she first got sick, before they knew it was cancer. The hallways are the same, even when Iris is taken to a different ward.

Her daughter lies in bed, unconscious, her throat bruised, but breathing steadily, her heart rate echoed by a faint beep.

All of the words the officers said swirled around Iris's head when she first got there: Found her in the cell. Looks like she tried to hang herself. The closet hook broke, though. But she's taken something; she's sedated. They're running tests.

"Julia would never hurt herself," she says again and again, and the officers and the doctors and the nurses all give her that typical patronizing look of endless understanding.

"No. She survived cancer as a child. She would never do it." And then she thinks about wondering what Kyle was capable of, of what she was capable, and maybe Julia could do this.

The day becomes a haze. She holds Julia's hand and waits for her to wake up. She makes phone calls. Grant has stayed home from school. She doesn't want him here at the hospital seeing his sister like this. Hearing the words "suicide attempt." Not yet. She asks Mike to check in on him and he offers to bring Grant to the hospital. She says no.

Ponder and Ames come in, and she stands. "I need to know who this man is. This Marland. Who is he?"

"He doesn't seem to have a criminal background. Or any background. We believe Marland was an alias."

"Ned must know."

"Ned Frimpong is not talking," Ponder says. "Neither is his father. They've gotten the Ghanaian ambassador involved now." She leaves to make some phone calls.

Iris could tell them about the apartment Ned mentioned to her. But what other secrets still lurk there, secrets that could inflict further destruction on her family?

* * *

Her troops arrive. Francie, and Susan, and Georgina, bringing coffee and food, bringing love and encouragement. She nearly cries when she sees them. They stay in the room with her for a few minutes and then go into the hallway when Ponder returns.

Soon after that, Julia wakes. Her eyes open and then lock in on her mother. Iris squeezes her hand. Ponder takes a deep breath.

"Baby, it's OK," Iris says.

Julia just looks at her, confused, dopey.

"Julia," Ponder says, "can you tell us what happened?"

Julia tries to speak, but her throat is too bruised. Ponder hands her paper and a pen.

WOMAN, she writes in a shaky hand. MEDIC. GAVE ME SHOT.

"She came in your cell and gave you a shot?" Ponder asks.

Julia nods.

"Did she say why?"

SHE SAID SHE WAS SORRY, Julia writes.

Ponder gestures, and she and Iris step outside. Her friends all fall silent.

"There was no medical order to sedate her," Ponder says.

"Someone did this to her. I want her under guard," Iris says. "Kyle, too. No one can get near him."

"I agree," Ponder says. "You want to tell me why this is happening?"

Iris doesn't answer. She goes back into Julia's room. She kisses her daughter's cheek; Julia is groggy with drugs to ease her pain, and she tries to smile at her mother. "Mama is going to take care of everything," Iris says. "Everything."

"Accent," Julia whispers. "She had accent."

The words are a knife in Iris's heart. "Was she older? Graying hair?" Iris asks.

But Julia is asleep.

Iris goes back out and asks her friends to stay with Julia for a few hours. They all agree.

"Where are you going?" Ponder asks.

"You find whoever this woman was. Go look at the security footage. She wasn't supposed to be there and she was. Someone got her access; someone bribed someone. Figure it out. You protect my daughter," Iris says. "I have to go check on my son."

But she knows Grant is safe, under orders to stay at home and not answer the door or the phone. She has someone to stop first.

59

GRANT

Grant walks out of the house. They still haven't announced that his father and sister were arrested in separate incidents, so right now there's no press lined up in front of their house, but word has started to spread in the neighborhood. He can tell: the man puttering in his garage who stops to stare, the woman who turns away from him as she is walking her dog, and that odd Mrs. Butler, who watches him the whole time she's coming back from the mail station as he walks past her.

He goes to Mike's house. Mike's car is in the driveway; so is Peter's. He knocks on the door.

Mike answers it. He just stares at Grant for a moment.

"I'm sorry," Grant says. "I'm sorry, I'm sorry, I'm sorry." He can't say more, the tears welling up inside him, and suddenly big Mike is hugging him, holding him close, saying, "It's not your fault, Grant. It is not your fault."

They step inside to the foyer, and Mike shuts the door.

"Everything that happened with Danielle..." Mike starts to say.

Grant says, "I didn't know anything."

"I know. Of course not." Mike doesn't seem to know what else to say. "It's not your fault."

"Can I talk to Peter, please?"

"I'm not sure he's up for a visitor. Finding what looks to be the murder weapon, it upset him."

"I understand."

"Hold on." He pats Grant on the shoulder and goes upstairs. Grant can hear soft talking and Peter clearly saying "no," and he closes his eyes. He hears more talking, Mike pleading his case. After a few more moments, Mike reappears at the top of the stairs and gestures Grant up.

Grant walks up the stairs.

"Grant, does your mom know you're here?" Mike asks quietly.

"She's at the hospital with Julia. I just wanted to talk with you and Peter."

"You shouldn't be alone."

"I don't need a babysitter." And he wasn't sure he could bear for Mike to worry about him. "She'll be back soon. Can I ask you a question?"

"Yes."

"Did Danielle ever talk to you about my adoption?"

He hesitates. "Not really. What would there be to say?"

"I just thought maybe she said something. If it was weird in any way."

"She said your mom kept a journal about the adoption."

"Yeah. I've never seen it." Grant wonders where this journal is now. "But Mom says she didn't keep one."

"Huh. Danielle said she wrote a note to you in it. I remember her telling me that."

Grant stares, thinking.

Peter appears in the doorway of his room. He looks like he hasn't slept. "Can we talk for a minute?" Grant asks.

"Do you need me here?" Mike asks, and Peter shakes his head. He nods and goes downstairs.

"What?"

Grant says, "I guess you think it was my dad who tore down your camera and put that bag and pipe in the tree."

"It seems likely."

"But that's all happening here, so why is someone emailing me from Russia?"

"I don't know. I don't want to do this anymore, Grant."

"But I have to know."

"I understand. But Danielle is dead. This Marland guy is dead and I tried googling him and there's, like, nothing that matches what we know about this guy. His name is Patrick Marland, but the Patrick Marlands who come up in every search aren't him. I think this is dangerous. Leave it alone. Let the police handle it."

Grant bites his lip. "I go back to Russia and the CIA software. You think this has something to do with me being from Russia? How? I was a baby then. The CIA wouldn't be interested in Russian adoptions. And let's say they were. Why wait all these years? Why contact me this way? Why not come to the front door and knock?" He shook his head. "I'm a kid. The CIA doesn't do this."

"Maybe Danielle was a CIA agent," Peter says. "I mean, she went to Russia a bunch, right? And China? That would be a good cover, wouldn't it, for a spy? An adoption consultant."

Peter's words shift something in the room. Grant and Peter look at each other like he blurted out an uncomfortable truth.

"But spies want military secrets and financial information and stuff like that. How would she get that? All she went to was hotels and orphanages. I know that much."

"People with the secrets to give to the CIA could meet her there and give them to her," Peter says. "No one would be watching her."

Grant feels cold. "So, she's not a spy. More like a courier, bringing back secrets?"

"Yeah."

"OK. So let's say your guess is the right one. She worked for the CIA during the time she was going to Russia. What does that have to do with my family and me? Did my parents know that? Or did they see something that they shouldn't have seen?"

"Wouldn't you have to ask your mom?" Peter says quietly. "We're just guessing here."

Peter is right and Grant knows it. "Thanks, Peter. For everything you tried to help me with."

"Don't talk to my dad about this."

Probably because it sounds crazy. Grant nods.

After a moment, Peter offers his hand and Grant shakes it. Peter pulls him into a quick hug and then turns away.

Grant goes downstairs. Mike is in the kitchen. Grant can hear him puttering around and he doesn't know what else to say. He opens the door to leave and Mike hurries to him.

"Your dad is my best friend here. I adore your sister. I don't want to believe this of either of them. But."

"But," Grant says. "Thanks for the times you took me fishing."

Mike looks like he might cry. "If I could help you, *chlapec*, I would."

"If all this is true, then it's Ned's fault," Grant says, unable to keep the bitterness down. "My mom told me he started this drug thing. He drew in my sister. His mother found out and maybe that's why she and my dad fought, or whatever. It goes back to him. I wouldn't loan him your friend's plane again to make it easy for him to get out of the country as fast as his dad got here. But I know you'll help him if he asks. You're just too nice."

He walks away, and when he looks back, once, Mike is still watching him.

Then he heads toward home. That journal. It has to be some-where where no one would find it and Danielle could get to it to write him a note, like Mike said. The police have already gone through the house after his father's arrest. So where might it be?

60

FROM IRIS POLLITT'S "FROM RUSSIA WITH LOVE" ADOPTION JOURNAL

2002

I didn't relax when we boarded the plane eight days later. We had flown first class over but flew economy back; I felt people would be more understanding about a baby in the back. Grant fussed and cried, and that kept me busy. People looked at me as if wondering why I would be flying transcontinental with such a young child. I ignored them. He would quiet down for Kyle more than me, so he became more Kyle's problem. (This bothered me, and I wondered if it was because, at some deep level, he felt more protected with Kyle…considering what had happened.)

We were ten minutes late pulling away from the gate, me thinking the whole time that the police will come onto the plane and arrest us for murder. I was having second thoughts about our reaction. If we'd called the police immediately, well, the orphanage already knew Anya had tried to see her child at Volkov. Her kidnapping us would have sounded plausible. The Russians would have had to understand the shooting was an accident, a horrible tragedy, not a murder. Not a murder.

But we hadn't played it that way.

The next few days, in Moscow, had been a nightmare. I constantly glanced over my shoulder, looking for the warning woman, looking for Anya's ghost to materialize in the snow like a winter's specter from a dreadful fairy tale. Grant was restless, shocked to be away from the only world he knew. The caretakers might not miss him, but he missed them; Kyle and I were strangers. I felt like a stranger. I kept waiting for the deeper bonding to kick in, that thread between mother and child that no force of nature or man could break. He writhed in my arms, he frowned, he cried, he reached for Kyle (Julia had rarely done that as an infant, but now she was a daddy's girl), and I felt vaguely abandoned.

What were we doing with this baby? Would he ever love us? We'd chosen for him.

By blood and violence.

How had I let Danielle talk us into turning this awful tragedy into this permanent secret? Now we could never tell. Me writing this down is the only telling, my own way to process it, my own way to rebel against Danielle's order, my only way to chronicle for my child what we saved him from.

My only way to convince Grant that he must never, ever come back here.

Kyle had gone to the airplane lavatory as our fellow passengers continued to board. I pulled the warning woman's phone out of my purse. Powered it on. Selected the one number.

It rang.

"Yes, Mrs. Pollitt?" Her voice, calm.

"No," I said, just the one word. She told me I'd find out what would happen if I said no to her.

Silence, for a moment. Then she hung up.

I tossed the phone back into my purse. Kyle returned to his seat and Grant gurgled and fussed, but I wanted to hold him right then, not hand him over to Kyle. I got a bottle ready to help him with the stress of takeoff.

The plane took off. Grant cried harder. I'd nursed Julia, and it had always seemed a comfort to her, a way to quiet her, but I couldn't nurse with Grant. The bottle didn't ease his burdens.

I waited for the "OK to stand up" light to click on, and I stood up and surveyed the other passengers around us. "I'm sorry," I said, in the tone of a public announcement. "I'm sorry our baby is crying. We've just adopted him. He's not used to me or my husband. He just isn't. So, he may cry a lot of the flight. I apologize in advance and we'll do our best to keep it to a minimum. Thank you for your understanding."

An older couple clapped and smiled at me; several others looked blankly at me and then went back to their books or tablets or screens. A man with an English accent joked, "Buy me a beer and I won't complain," and so Kyle did, and the man toasted our handsome new son, to long life for him and much happiness.

From her seat, across the aisle, Danielle just watched me. Then gave me a slight smile, like everything was normal.

I tried to curl the crying Grant into my arms, get him comfortable. I didn't look at the screen in the back of the seat in front of me. But Kyle had his on and instead of a movie or a TV show like a normal person, he was watching our flight path.

He was watching to see when we left Russian airspace.

Grant settled down slightly against my shoulder; I patted his back and he eased down, letting me comfort him. Danielle got out a novel to read, losing herself in a Harlan Coben paperback. She'd canceled her longer stay; it seemed prudent to leave when we did. I couldn't imagine she'd ever come back to Russia.

I stared at the flight path on Kyle's screen, forgetting to breathe, holding Kyle's hand, feeling my son shift into sleep on my shoulder, and waited and watched until we were clear of Russian airspace.

I just had to hope that we weren't met by police while changing planes in London.

We landed at the same terminal we came through the first time in London. No police waiting for us.

I went to the same bathroom where the warning woman spoke to me. I washed my hands in the same sink. Looked again in the same mirror.

The warning woman. What did she know? Did Anya send her? What did Anya know?

A quarter million dollars for our child. Who would offer such a thing, and what would they do when they found out Anya was dead?

And another question pricked at me: How did Anya know Danielle's name? She called her by name. I hadn't thought of it at the time, but there it was.

Danielle told us what to do, but not why it had happened. We were two people so frightened of losing our son, we stayed quiet. We did as we were told.

Danielle came into the restroom; she'd stopped to make a phone call. Kyle was out in the terminal with Grant. Our gazes met in the mirror. We had a thousand things to discuss and hardly anything to say.

"How did Anya know your name?"

Danielle washed her hands thoroughly, and I thought of Lady Macbeth lathering up. "Never ask me. I'm stealing your line, Iris."

But there was no smile on her face.

Never ask me. It wasn't so cute when it was directed at you. When it closed a door that you needed to see what was behind.

"Are you ever going to tell me?"

"No," she said. "It's better you do not know." Her gaze held steady against mine.

Those final days in Moscow, I watched English-language news sites for Russia obsessively, to see if there was a body found in the abandoned village. There was not. No one had driven through. No one had found her.

Who had Danielle been on the phone with when we were dealing with the body, me sitting in shock in the snow?

"Who did you call...?"

"Never ask me," she repeated.

Because she was right. If we were caught, we all had so much to lose. We would be considered unfit parents; no decent people would conceal the death of a desperate young woman who only wanted her baby back. We were monsters. If I had just grabbed her arm first, maybe we could have subdued her. Detained her. Called the police.

But that wasn't what happened.

Of course they killed her to keep that baby, it would be said. I could imagine the whispers, the headlines, the outright accusations. It would destroy our family. Even though Danielle had killed her, although accidentally. Danielle might get extradited back to Russia; even if not, it would end her work there, perhaps mean the end of Global Adoption Consultants. What if social services back in America took Grant from us? They could decide our cover-up—of murder—made us unfit. They wouldn't have to return him to Russia. They could just give him to a more worthy family here in the United States. The whole thought pressed like an avalanche upon me.

If anyone knew about Anya, we could lose everything.

We left London. Grant, you had been horrible on the flight from Moscow, fussy for nearly all of it, and now you settled against Kyle's shoulder like it was the safest place on earth. You acted like you weren't thrilled to have me for a mother. I knew that would pass, that I would come to love you and you would come to love me. But as we settled into our seats and Danielle licked her finger and turned a page in her novel and studiously avoided looking at me and acted like a normal person who hadn't accidentally killed another person (I mean, she did the killing, and I was the mental case in shock and dismay), I couldn't bear to look at her, and so I looked at you, sleeping in your father's arms, and I thought: You can never know.

How will the carrying of this secret shape you and me?

61

TRANSCRIPT FROM INTERVIEWS
FOR *A DEATH IN WINDING CREEK*
BY ELENA GARCIA

(Via phone)

Elena Garcia: I appreciate you talking to me. Can you hear me OK?

Boris Stepurin: I really have nothing to say, and I don't understand what you think I can tell you about the Pollitt family.

Garcia: Are you familiar with the story? Your English is fantastic, by the way.

Boris: I read the news article links you sent me.

Garcia: I want to talk to you because this father is accused of murdering the woman who got them their child because there was a crime being committed between the families. And since your biological son's adoption was the foundation of the friendship, I wanted to talk to you.

Boris: I cannot tell you anything of interest.

Garcia: I went through the paperwork, which is public record. You are listed as the birth father of Grant Pollitt, who was born in Russia as Alexander Stepurin.

Boris: I have nothing to say. I am a happily married man with children.

Garcia: But you are his biological father.

Boris: Yes. There was a brief friendship with his mother dur-

ing a separation from my wife, while I was living in Paris and
Anya was modeling there. A mistake.

Garcia: Anna Averina is his biological mother, yes? She is
listed on the adoption form. Are you in touch with her?

Boris: No. Not since she decided to give up the baby. We
parted. It seemed the best decision for all.

Garcia: The Pollitts came to see you in Russia when they
were adopting your biological son. Is that true? I have their
adoption consultant's notes here; her company shared them
with me. Her name was Danielle Roberts and she's the murder victim.

Boris: Yes, so I read in what you sent me.

Garcia: She advised the Pollitts not to meet with you.

Boris: If you say so. I would not know.

Garcia: But later that week, according to her notes, she met
with you. Why? She didn't need to. You had made no claim
on the child. Custody had already been awarded to the Pollitts. They hadn't left Russia yet, but she came to see you.
Without them.

Boris: I do not remember meeting any Danielle Roberts. I'm
sorry. I must go now. I cannot help you, and please do not
call again.

Garcia: How do I reach Anna Averina?

Boris: I have no idea. Look, she gave up a child before. I
would think she does not want to be found by the children
she gave up. Can you not respect that? What business is it of
yours?

Garcia: Do you have any desire to see your son?

Boris: He is their son now. I wish him well. Goodbye.

Garcia: Why did Danielle meet with you again before leaving
Russia? Sir? Sir?

62

ROM IRIS POLLITT'S "FROM RUSSIA WITH LOVE" ADOPTION JOURNAL

2002

Home with our son. And our beautiful daughter.

Ready to build our lives together.

Waiting for the sword to fall.

We settled back into what was our new life. The change was not just you becoming ours, Grant.

It was what we had seen. What we had done.

I routinely checked the English-language news stories from Russia. Nowhere could I find mention of a dead woman found in an abandoned village outside Saint Petersburg. Had it simply not made the news? Or at least the English-language news feed from Russia? That was my suspicion—it wasn't about the government, or business, or something bad happening to a foreigner, so it didn't rate the English feeds out of Moscow. And I could hardly recruit a Russian speaker here at home to ask.

I didn't tell Kyle about the bribe offer. He would have tried to go back to Russia, hire investigators, see if he could find who it was and "fix" the problem. And just no. They could have come after us when we were in Russia. They didn't. Why poke the hornet's nest? We'd won; they'd lost.

It didn't always feel like we'd won.

Danielle would not discuss it with me, because It Had Never Happened. I could hardly blame her. She focused more on adoptions from Africa and China—I don't think she ever went back to Russia. If she did, she never told me.

I thought of emailing Anya's boyfriend, Boris the investment banker, but…if her body had been found, I didn't want to raise suspicion. Her boyfriend knew us. Knew our names. Knew how desperate we were to dissuade Anya from fighting the adoption. If she was found dead, wouldn't he speak up? But he was married. He might not want to jeopardize his happy life.

I couldn't wait for the anvil to fall. We lived our lives. I was the mother Julia and Grant needed. Grant, you got older, started walking, started learning English words, played with your sister, who gave you hugs and kisses, turned into an American boy who stared at the stars at night and loved the Houston Texans and the Houston Astros and soccer and video games and hip-hop and superhero movies.

From Russia, only a long silence.

We didn't see Danielle much after we got home. Death makes things awkward. We did not enjoy each other's company. Julia and Ned had become playmates during the adoption process, and sometimes they still asked to play together. The only reminder that Danielle had touched our lives was Grant. And the moms group, where I went because I genuinely liked the other moms, but it was also a way to keep track of Danielle. Keep an eye on her, make sure she wasn't cracking under the pressure. Sometimes killers just up and confess to a friend, and I could not have that. She joined us sometimes, and it was like a neutral ground between us, where we could observe each other. Take each other's pulse on how well secrets were being kept. Danielle lived in a different neighborhood in West Austin; we didn't see her around very much. Playdates with Ned and Julia (after her illness I was very reluctant to cut off Julia from any friends), dinners and barbecues and birthday parties with the Mommy Club and their kids.

Until the day she moved to Lakehaven, two doors down from us.

It was like a cruel joke. *Hi, new neighbor! Remember that time we covered up a murder? I'll see you at the community picnic. Bring your chocolate chip cookies—everyone loves those!*

Why would she even want to be near us? We were radioactive to each other. There was no reason for us to interact now. Our business was concluded. Our lives, moving on.

Yet here she was, walking onto our stage.

She hadn't even told us in advance that she was becoming our newest neighbor. The house was sold (the former neighbor was a widow who spent a lot of time visiting her grown children who had moved to California). The moving van for the new residents arrived. And then a car, with Danielle getting out of it (and Ned coolly strolling toward our house to surprise Julia).

It made my blood run cold. Danielle, flexing her fake smile, and me thinking: You better be a real estate agent now, because there is no other reason for you to be on this street.

I walked out to meet her in the yard. I wasn't sure I wanted her in my house, and then Grant's rushing past me to go greet her. Of course he loved her. He thought she was the reason he got paired with us.

Grant hugged Danielle and she hugged him back and watched me over Grant's head. (This was before the human beanpole caught up and passed both me and Danielle on height.)

"You're moving in? Here? Really? That's awesome!" Grant said.

I managed to put on a smile. If Grant was a daily reminder of what had happened, then I could deal with Danielle. "I want Ned at Lakehaven High when the time comes," she said. "And his father agrees it'll be best for him." But she couldn't meet my gaze.

So that was how she could afford the house. Gordon, helping out. I had wondered.

"The schools are great," I agreed. Grant moved on to go see the house's interior and its backyard with Ned and Julia.

"Iced tea?" My tone made it sound like I was offering arsenic.

"Sure."

We went inside my house and I closed the door. I kept my voice friendly but low. "There must be dozens of houses for sale in Lakehaven, yet you pick the one closest to us. Really?"

"It's a great house. We each have our own lives. And...It. Never. Happened."

I felt sick. Tired. "I dreamed about her the other night. It happens less often now, but I worry, what about when I'm old and losing my mind in the nursing home? What if I trip up and say something to Grant. What if he finds out?"

"You're the only mother he's ever known."

"Because of what happened." I shook my head. "Of all the cul-de-sacs in Lakehaven, she walks into mine." I tried to make it light, ease the tension. It was wrong, thoughtless. There is no way to do that.

"I gave you this great life," she said suddenly. "And you dare to stand there and judge me. To look down on me. If we hadn't done what we did, then either we'd both be dead, or she'd have your son. And you'd be in a Russian prison."

"We?"

"Both our hands were on the gun."

"Whatever you need to tell yourself to sleep well at night."

"Whatever you need to tell yourself to raise that boy. You'll never tell him the truth. Of what you did or who you are. You're too scared he'd turn away from you."

"You'll never tell either."

Were we testing each other, then? Wondering if either would tell? Nothing to be gained by it. It was mutually assured destruction.

"Was her body ever found?"

"No."

"But we left her in that town." The abandoned town, where no one apparently went, not even drug addicts looking for a place to rest and hide and shoot up. It wasn't that far from Saint Petersburg. It made me wonder. "What was the name of the town?" There had been a sign but only in Russian. She knew enough Russian.

"Bukharin," she said, as if reluctant to say the name aloud.

"You never told me," I said.

"Why would you need to know? You were never there. None of us were."

I had no answer to that. "I don't think you moving here is a coincidence, Danielle."

"I just want a better life for my son." Her voice shook a little.

"It's a really expensive house."

"My finances are fine."

"Big for the two of you."

"I consider a home in the Lakehaven school district to be an investment." Danielle crossed her arms. "We don't have to be friends, although I don't think you've ever once thanked me for saving your life or saving Kyle or even saving Grant." A hint of bitterness now.

The silence between us deepened. "Thank you," I said. I meant it. But I'm not sure how it sounded. Both our hands on the gun. Ignoring that it was her who turned the weapon into Anya and fired. I was having to thank a liar for my life.

"I'm not here to remind you of the past," she said. "I'm all about the future. I hope both of ours are bright."

She didn't look good; she looked tired, haggard. Gray was making an early debut in her hair, one streak widening. Guilt wore at her. Even if she didn't act guilty.

"Let's make the best of it," she said. "I'm your neighbor. For better or worse."

"All right," I said.

"Does it scare you?" she asked suddenly. "Me being here?"

"Of course not," I said. "We'll always be connected." Not friends now. But connected.

"I just want us all to be happy now," she said.

But she didn't seem happy. I believed she had to be here for a reason. What could she want from us?

Nothing.

Yet here she was.

I have a vaguely fake yet convincing smile Kyle calls my volunteer smile. "Do you need anything? Help unpacking? Meeting the neighbors?"

"I'll be fine. And I'll be a good neighbor, Iris. Tell Kyle I said hello, I'll see him later. Your kids are welcome to hang out over at the house as we get unpacked." She left and shut the door behind her.

I went to the computer, logged into Faceplace, and wrote on the Winding Creek Neighborhood page: I'm beside myself with excitement! Our longtime friend (who helped us with our adoption in Russia) is now our neighbor. Please welcome the wonderful Danielle Roberts and her son, Ned (grade 7), to Winding Creek!

And I sat there and watched the "welcome, neighbor, so glad to have you here" messages start to pour in, and I wondered what it would be like if Danielle were dead.

You might wonder why I've written this down. And kept it. Because if anything happens to me or your father, the police need to look at Danielle. We have her secret. We are nuclear weapons aimed at each other. We will never fire ours. But she might fire hers. And whatever we've done, we did out of love and we did it for you. She cannot say the same.

And, Grant, if you ever decide to go back to Russia and look for your mother: this journal is why you cannot. You must not. Ever.

63

GRANT

No sign of a journal, but the file with his adoption paperwork is right where it's always been. There have been times in the past when Grant has gotten it out and paged through it, thinking, *This was my start.* Once he had to look at it all for a school project on family background. He had wanted to write about where his four grandparents' families came from—Dad was English and Czech, Pollitt a name originally from Lancashire, and Mom was Scottish, Irish, and Swedish. But his teacher had said, "Well, but it's just *so interesting* that you are from Russia originally"—(he later figured out that someone had told her about all the international adoptions at that school)—"you should write about that." Like he'd had some golden childhood in Saint Petersburg full of Russian traditions and charming customs before he accidentally wandered into the loving arms of his American family. So instead he said he'd been born in Saint Petersburg, shared a bunch of pictures that showed off the city in a charming way, then said he'd been adopted from an orphanage and the only thing he remembered was a Russian lullaby, "Tilly Tilly Bom," a horrifying song about a mysterious man in the house who would kidnap you if you didn't fall asleep soon. He said nothing showed the contrast in culture between home and Russia more than a threatening lullaby, and he played a bone-chilling rendition of it he'd found on YouTube and left the class sitting in shocked silence. Then he said, in defiance,

"I'm an American boy now." He got an A and didn't have the nerve to tell the teacher (who never, ever asked him about Russia again) that the rendition he played came from a Russian horror movie made a couple of years before and wasn't exactly a traditional lullaby as presented.

But, on the legal form from the Volkov Infants Home, he had looked at the name of his birth mother, Anna Alexandrovna Averina. His birth father, Boris Vladimirovich Stepurin.

He had never googled them. But he must now: the strange emails, the pictures, the accusations, the knowledge of his personal history, the use of the tree—now to leave him both enticing objects and a murder weapon. Why was anyone bothering to send him pictures of a stock photo of a woman dancing and a cat in the snow and a cozy house?

He looks first for Anna Averina. There are a number of them— Averina is not an unusual name. There are a few women with that name in the West: in Canada, in Australia. He clicks through. None of them appears to have lived in Russia for a while, or ever. Most of the other results are in Russian and he can't read it. A few results are dead web pages, no longer active, and he wonders what that means.

Then he starts looking for Boris Stepurin. Here he gets an English-language result. Boris works for an investment firm that assists Western investors in finding opportunities in Russia, the Baltic states, and much of Eastern Europe. The photo shows a man in his forties, with blond hair starting to gray. The bio says he is married to an art history professor and that he has two sons, both a few years older than Grant.

He closes his eyes, thinking backward, about the few times he asked about his biological parents: What were they like?

Iris, or Kyle, depending on who he asked: *You understand that we never met them. Your mother had you at this hospital*—Mom would point at the paperwork—*in Saint Petersburg and she never took you home with her. She came there alone, and she left alone.* No one but Grant seemed to understand how sad that sentence was.

Once, he had asked: *She didn't hand me over to you?* As if that somehow would have made it easier, as if his birth mother chose the Pollitts.

No, she didn't. She gave you to the hospital and then the hospital gave you to the orphanage.

What about my father?

And every time he asked, he could see the smallest crinkle in his mother's mouth. *We don't know anything but his name, sweetie. I don't think they were a couple.*

Maybe he would have wanted me when she didn't.

He could see the pain in her eyes when he theorized about this alternate set of parents, but he couldn't help himself. He was a kid grappling with this basic concept of his identity. *Listen, I'm glad he decided to give you a better life*, Mom would say. She would never in a million years say the phrase "they gave you up." Grant knew she never wanted him to feel as though he'd been unwanted. It was always as if his parents were sending him to a better life. Never surrendering him, never thinking to themselves, *Thank God we got rid of that baby neither of us wanted.*

But they hadn't wanted him. And it was OK, because he loves his mom and dad so much he can literally not imagine life without them. People expect him to be curious about Russia, to like Russian things, and he doesn't even want to watch TV or movies set there. He doesn't like to watch anything about Russia. It means nothing to him.

He stares at the picture of Boris Stepurin.

There are certainly other Boris Stepurins in Russia. But here is one who has a bio written in Russian and English on the website and lists his spoken languages as Russian, English, and French. He has worked in his firm's Paris, Saint Petersburg, and Moscow offices.

Paris. Hadn't the stock photo of the woman in the rain been from France? It was in the first email the Sender sent him.

Grant finds an email link on Stepurin's bio. He presses it and writes, quickly, before he can talk himself out of it:

Dear Mr. Stepurin:

My name is Grant Alexander Pollitt. I was born Alexander
Stepurin and adopted from Russia. I think you might be my biological father. My mother was listed on my papers as Anna Averina.
I don't want to bother you and I don't want anything from you—
you have your own life and your wife and your kids and I bet we're
probably both happy in our lives. But someone has been sending
me weird emails and I traced the emails to Saint Petersburg and I
think it has to do with me being from Russia, like there's a secret
connected to it.

He attaches the pictures he's gotten. The woman in the rain, the
cat in the house.

If you are my father I won't bother you again, but please could you
answer one question for me? Do these photos mean anything to you?
I hope you have a nice life. I really do. I have had a good life; my mom
and dad and sister here love me so much and I'm happy, so I hope
that puts your mind at ease. I am sorry to have bothered you.

Best, Grant Pollitt

He wonders if the man might delete the email as soon as he reads
it, as the laughter of his legitimate children sounds in the background. The soft voice of his wife asking him when he'd be done
on the computer, to come curl up on the couch together with them,
to watch a movie. Or he'd read it in his office or on his phone and,
embarrassed, trash it immediately and never answer.

Grant presses send. The little stupid whooshing sound does its
business, and he stares at his in-box, waiting for an answer. After a
moment he shuts down the screen.

* * *

The alert comes, waking him from a deep sleep where he dreams of
snow. An email notification on his phone screen. He taps it.

Hello, Grant. Yes, I am your biological father. It's nice to hear from
you, but as I am sure you understand, you are still legally a child and
so I cannot just contact you without your parents knowing or permission. But I hope they will forgive me as I can tell you are scared or

tense in your email and I want to put your mind at ease. One of the pictures you sent does mean something to me.

The photo of the woman in the rain is Anya, as I called her. Your birth mother, Anna Averina. She was a model in Saint Petersburg and then Paris for a short while, where I met her and knew her well. Yes, it's a stock photo, but it is her in it. That was the work she did there. Then she came home to Russia. She was homesick and had problems. She was sick in the mind. I don't know who the pictures of the house and of the cat belong to. Those mean nothing to me. They are not of places where I knew Anya to live, but I only knew her in Saint Petersburg and a little in Paris where I met her and my work took me. She came back to Russia when I did, but I was married, and my wife and I worked out our problems and got back together. This made Anya sad especially after she found out she was pregnant. She decided to have the baby (you) and to give it up. I was not part of her decision, but I do believe she did the right thing and am glad you were taken by an American family. It was all for the best. I wish you well.

Grant reads the email and then writes back: Where is Anya my mother now? Why would she send me these pictures with no explanation?

He almost does not expect an answer, but he gets one five minutes later: I do not know answers to your question and we cannot talk again.

Something cold snaps in Grant. He writes: Yes, you will tell me. If I can find you, I can find your wife and your sons—my brothers. Do they know about me? Maybe they would like to know. I want to know who would send me these pictures. Is it her?

The email comes faster than he expects: My wife knows about you. I did not send those pictures. I can't think of anyone who would.

Grant responds: What about my mother?

I don't know where she is and I cannot contact her. She asked me to never contact her again. I have respected that.

Did you ever meet my American parents? he asks suddenly. After all, the Sender said his parents were lying to him. What could they have lied to him about except his adoption? Everything else pales.

The in-box stays empty for five minutes, and he feels his nerves

begin to tense up. Then the answer comes: Yes. Briefly. They came
to see me one time. Before your hearing. They were concerned your
mother Anya wanted you back. They wanted me to help them complete the adoption by keeping Anya away.

They had seen her, Grant guesses. He types that.

Yes. They saw her. She had caused problems at the orphanage.
They were afraid of her changing her mind. She had an earlier child,
had given it up, wanted it back, and gave it up again. They were afraid
she would do the same to you.

Somehow, although it was forbidden, his parents had encoun-
tered his birth mother and father both in Russia. And lied about
that to him. And now Danielle is dead. He feels a sick twist settle
into his stomach. He stares out into the darkness beyond the window.

He types and sends: So she wouldn't send these pictures to me?
You say one is of her. Is she trying to find me?

A terrible dark thought comes to him. Danielle is dead. Someone, maybe his biological mother, is sending pictures to him from
a Russian server. And his family is, at the same time, completely
falling apart. Is it that Danielle's death is unraveling them, or is
there a deeper danger? But that can't be. All of the terrible things
that have befallen his family cannot be under the control of a
woman back in Russia.

*What if she's not back in Russia? What if she's here? Putting gifts
for you in the tree.*

Grant's throat feels thick. No answering email yet. He writes
again: Would she try to hurt us? Is she angry?

The longest two minutes of his life tick by. He is about to give
up when the message appears: I called her the day of the court hearing for your adoption and she told me she was not going to give you
up and she would stop you from being taken to America. But then I
never heard from her again. I decided she changed her mind or lost
her courage.

Something in the answer…in the words…frightens him. What
would his parents have done?

I can't be involved. She was never well. She gave up the first child

TWICE because she was unstable and she should have never had another one. I don't mean that against you. It was just how it was with her. She would say unwell things to me. People were after her. People were coming for her. All in her imagination. I have to go now. We cannot talk again.

Grant writes: Can you put me in touch with her family? Her parents?

He sends the message, and he sits and waits, but there is no answer. There is never an answer.

So Grant sends a note to the Sender: Is this Anya? Are you my mother?

64

IRIS

The Marble Hills apartment complex is so 1970s in its look, Iris thinks it could be named Macrame Hills. Two stories, built of dark stone and arched wooden doors all facing the parking lot, with old-fashioned numbers on brass plates. Maybe twenty apartments, ten on each floor. She parks and stands by her car, wondering if the police have already connected Marland to this place. Did he even rent it under his name?

There's a manager's office, but a sign says no one's in at the moment.

Iris waits ten minutes and then a car pulls in cautiously to the steep parking lot, a young woman finding a spot for her truck. She glances at Iris with a moment of curiosity.

Iris puts on a friendly smile. "Excuse me. I'm looking for a friend who lives here. I don't know which unit is his."

The young woman raises an eyebrow. "I'm kind of new. I don't know everyone."

"He's tall, handsome, early forties, dark haired, professor glasses."

"Ah. The night owl. He lives in number ten." She points to the far end of the apartment wing.

"Oh. Thanks."

The woman gives her another glance and Iris walks to number ten. She waits for the woman to go inside her apartment.

She hopes the new neighbor is right. There's no key hidden under the mat or on the doorframe. Of course not. She walks past the corner of the building, heading toward the back. Each apartment has a small balcony and his, being on the end, means she can crawl over the railing without being noticed. Beyond his patio the ground gives way to a further slope and downward to a creek that leads down to the lakeshore, so no one will see her unless they're walking to the lake.

She glances, but there's no one on the other balconies. She kneels by the balcony door. It's locked. She grabs a rock and smashes the glass. And then again and again. It gives way. It's hugely loud. Anyone who is home in this wing is probably going to hear it. She doesn't care. Enough of the glass gives way that she crawls through, taking care not to cut herself.

The apartment is empty. It doesn't look as though the police have been here yet. There's a compact living room, with a small flat-screen TV. Cheap furniture that doesn't match, and not much of it. Like a waystation. She goes past the extremely tidy kitchen, past the dining nook with its one chair at the small table. She finds the bedroom—also immaculately tidy. The bed is made. The closet has three changes of clothing, all hanging together. Organized. She searches the nightstand and its drawers. In the bottom is a Glock nine-millimeter pistol. She doesn't touch it. She peers under the mattress. Nothing. Back to the closet. Nothing. She goes into the kitchen. It's spotless. A single skillet, only a couple of plates. For a man who ran drugs, this is very sparse. That means it's here for a purpose. But there's no laptop, no convenient folder of papers or receipts to show her Marland's associates.

She keeps searching. The police might be on their way if someone heard her breaking the glass; but so far no one has come to investigate either.

The refrigerator is also painfully tidy and bare; a carton of milk, pimento cheese spread, a loaf of bread, butter, packaged salad. The freezer has a neat stack of frozen dinners. And on the bottom of the stack, a box of waffles.

She starts to shut the door, then stops. She can see the expiration date on the waffles: three months ago. She has a thing for expiration dates, as Julia refuses to eat anything that's past one. She reaches in for the package. Inside aren't waffles but another Glock and two tidy stacks of cash and a phone. And three passports. All with Marland's picture, but under three different names and countries: Belgium, Canada, Panama. She takes it all, even the money, stuffing the gun, cash, and phone into her coat pocket.

Who *was* this man? She feels cold, and not from the open freezer.

There's nothing else for her here.

She goes back through the broken door, careful not to cut herself.

She climbs the slope back to her car. Two women are standing by the truck that pulled in, one was the woman who told her which apartment was Marland's.

"Were you down there? Did you hear glass breaking?" the woman asks.

"Yes. I did." Iris doesn't stop. She gets in her car, and the two women are looking at her. One lifts her phone and takes a picture.

Iris waves and drives off.

65

KYLE

Kyle's in the interview room again, waiting for Ponder and Ames. Or his lawyer. Or his wife. He's not sure. No one has told him why he is back here.

He's scared they're going to tell him that Julia is dead.

They've told him about Julia's apparent suicide attempt. He cannot believe it, that their lives have fallen apart so completely so quickly. They let him talk briefly to his lawyer, who updated him on Julia regaining consciousness, but he doesn't know any more.

And now they've pulled him from his cell and made him wait, when a woman comes in.

Alone. The woman sits down across from him. He glances at the door and sees Ames standing there. Then the detective shuts the door.

This woman looks vaguely familiar but he can't place her. Grayish blue eyes, tiny mole on her cheek, slightly crooked front tooth.

"Hello, Mr. Pollitt. It's been a long time."

"Do I know you?"

"We never formally met. I spoke to your wife, not to you." Her voice is soft, with a slight New England accent. She's in a somber gray suit, l   hair pulled back, minimal jewelry.

Now he sees it. He knows her.

Iris called her "the warning woman." The one who made Iris nearly lose her mind in the London airport. The one who told them to go home.

"In London," he says, stunned.

"Yes. And also in Saint Petersburg, but I don't think Iris ever told you about our meeting there, did she?"

"No, she didn't."

"Things might have been so different if she had."

"What—what are you doing here?"

"I'm here to help you. But I need to know information."

"Who are you?"

"If you want to help your family, we won't spend time on your questions. Do you understand me?"

"No! What is going on…?"

"Do you understand me?"

He stops. He looks at her. Somehow she has gotten into this room, with the blessing of the police. "Yes."

"Did you kill Danielle? There is nothing to gain from a lie."

He wonders if Ponder is watching. "No. I didn't."

"Why did you say you did?"

"I thought…I thought I would be protecting someone."

"Iris?"

"Yes."

"She had a motive to kill Danielle, as did you. You've had a motive for a while."

He doesn't want to say it, but finally he does. "But we didn't."

"Did Danielle ever tell you what really happened in Russia?"

"What really…?" He stops, waits for her to say more, but she doesn't. So he can only give one answer. "No. I guess she didn't."

She slides a phone to him. "Call your wife. Tell her to collect your son and go to an address I'm going to give you. We will meet them there."

He slides the phone back. "I'm not telling her to go anywhere with you until you tell me what is happening."

"I can do that, but I cannot do it here. Not here." He realizes she means not here in the jail.

"Well, I can't go anywhere right now," he says.

"They will release you into my custody."

"Who *are* you?" Kyle asks.

She doesn't answer him. She waits. She glances at the phone she's tried to give him.

Kyle takes a deep breath. "I need you to explain."

"And I need you to trust me and to call your wife." The warning woman's voice is even and strong.

Kyle stares at her, trying to decide. Realizing this might be the most important decision of his life.

66

IRIS

"He says you know how to break into computers and stuff," Iris says to Peter. "Can you break into this phone?"

She's phoned Peter and he's reluctantly let her come over to his house. At the front door she gives him an awkward hug, and she notices he doesn't hug her back.

"Grant was here a bit ago. Dad's been checking in on him. But he went back home."

"Can you do this quickly?"

"Yes. I don't like sounding like a criminal," Peter says. But he examines the phone, turning it over on its back.

"What?"

"I'm looking to see if it's modified in any way," Peter says. "Whose is it?"

She can't say *It belongs to the man Julia is accused of killing.* "Someone who I think could clear my daughter's name."

His eyes widen. "Then this is police evidence. Take it to them."

"Well, here's the deal, Peter. I stole it."

Peter stares at her for a moment. "This is a mistake."

"Those people, whoever's behind this, this is who killed Danielle. Please help me with this."

Peter sighs but takes the phone and disappears into a back room. He pauses at the door and says, "It's better you don't know what I do." And then the door closes and Iris sits down to wait.

She texts Grant. There's no immediate answer, and considering that half her family is in dire trouble, this unsettles her.

She wishes she could talk to Kyle and Julia just in that moment. To let them know she is fighting for them, fighting against whatever darkness spread its wings across their lives.

Grant texts her back: I'm fine. Where are you?

She says back: OK I'll be home soon.

Grant says: something's wrong with my phone battery.

And then nothing more.

She waits for a few more minutes.

Her phone rings, but it's not a number she recognizes, so she doesn't answer it, and she tucks her phone away as Peter comes back down the hall.

"I got into it," he simply says. "There's no email on it, and only a few contacts and texts. I don't know any of these names. Do they mean anything to you?"

She looks at the text list. A note Marland sent to NF—presumably Ned Frimpong. Asking for a meeting, making promises. Things they wouldn't have said in the game because that might have been on the game companies' servers.

And another series of texts.

To ANYA.

The name freezes her on the spot. She stares at it, as though it is a ghost that has taken form. It can't be. Anya is dead, killed by Danielle, left dead and cold in the Russian winter. She makes a noise in her throat and her chest, and Peter reaches out and touches her. Iris flinches. She turns away from him.

To Anya: I've made contact with NF. Have a sense now of the size of the operation he's running. It's small, just trading prescription drugs among friends. R U sure you're interested?

Anya, to Marland: Yes. Make his operation bigger. Supply him. I want it to start to attract attention.

Marland, to Anya: All right it's your money. Will see how JP is involved.

Anya, to Marland: If she's not involved, make her involved. Draw her in. Or make it look like she's involved.

JP, Iris thinks. *Julia Pollitt.* A few days later, another spate of texts:

Marland, to Anya: JP knows about NF's operation, he told her; I listened in via the microphone on his regular cell. She tried to talk him out of doing this, he didn't listen, and he tried to get her involved because I told NF I'd double the payments if he got a student no one would suspect to be involved, as a front. She said no. But she hasn't called the police, Ned and she were at a movie, he asked to borrow her phone to make a call, passed it to me outside the theater, I hacked it to monitor her calls. She has not called the police on him. He uses this game so many of the kids play as a code and a messenger system. Various drugs have nicknames tied to the game "Critterscape." I'm sure he thinks he's being super clever but it's generating a record of communications we can use.

Anya, to Marland: Whatever it takes. Does his mother know about his activities?

Marland: Not that I can determine.

Anya: Good. I want to tell her myself, perhaps. Let her know her son has no future.

Marland: I'll let you know what I find.

Iris forgets to breathe until there's a tightness in her chest. Anya. Here. Watching Danielle. Watching Julia. Which meant she was watching…

Anya: The younger child. Grant. Is he involved with Julia and Ned's dealings?

Marland: No indication of it.

Anya: Good. Other than Julia, stay away from that family as much as you can. Other plans for them. I'll send you instructions.

Other plans for them. Instructions. It feels like a punch to the throat, the heart, the gut.

She can't be here. She's dead. But she clearly wasn't. Could she have survived? Maybe she had a pulse and Iris, in her panic, thought she didn't. And did Marland sound like a drug entrepreneur? No. He sounded like a hired muscle, not some drug kingpin taking over a territory.

And Anya…she killed Danielle. Or had her killed, perhaps by

Marland. And she set in motion a terrible vengeance, a hand from the grave, cold, closing its grip on their happy lives.

"Mrs. Pollitt?" Peter sounds nervous.

Iris finds her voice. "Did you...? Did you copy any of this to your computer when you broke into it?"

"No," Peter says after a moment.

"I have to go," she says. "Don't call the police. Please. Please don't. I..." What could she say? How could she explain? This was something else. She could not tell the police the why of this. *This woman whose death we covered up has come after us.* Because it was more than that. It was mother versus mother.

What does she want?

Well, vengeance, but what would that mean when the Pollitts were destroyed?

That woman wants Grant. He'll never go with her. Never with some stranger.

She imagines the words, spoken in the soft broken English: *Grant, I am your real mother. Your true blood. Look what has happened to your family. Let me help you. But I need to tell you the truth about what your parents did to me. You deserve to know the truth. They stole you from me.*

Iris runs out the door.

67

GRANT

Grant's phone is dead. Something's wrong with it. He just charged it recently. He goes into the den. The TV is still on. The national news media has picked up that an Austin-area man and his daughter have both been detained for questioning in a pair of murders. Wait, he thinks, until they hear that his mother is a well-known songwriter. Then it will be on the entertainment channels.

Within minutes the local press have set up again outside his house. He keeps the curtains drawn, stays away from the windows. They've rung the doorbell and he ignores it.

Grant sits down on the floor. His sister is arrested. His father is arrested. His mother has lost her mind, trying to do something to find a way to clear them both when she should be hiring more lawyers. He doesn't know what to do. He can't talk to his friends about this, or their parents. With his friends he talks sports and video games and homework, and this is so far beyond that.

He turns off the TV as soon as they show a picture of his father. His face feels hot, like he needs to cry. He goes to his computer.

There's an email there. From the Sender. He'd last asked if she was Anya. The only answer is:

Are you ready?

Grant feels a strange surge, a mix of fear and excitement. Like the Sender has been some stranger he's repeatedly played against in an online video game, giving him hints, clues, all to solve the ultimate puzzle. For a moment he feels like he's won…something valuable—what he needs to win the whole game. The Sender knows what's happening. So he writes: Ready for what?

To help your family. To help the people who love you.

YES, he writes.

Your mother says she'll tell the truth. I'm going to send someone you know to bring you to me. You can trust them.

He doesn't trust anyone right now. But he writes: OK who is coming?

There's no immediate answer. Then: go to our tree.

At least he'll get his answer as to who this is. He's scared. He goes to the kitchen, and after a moment's thought he takes a steak knife, the kind his parents use only when they actually serve steak, and he carefully tapes it just above his sock, hidden by his jeans. This feels foolish and silly, but it feels stupid to go defenseless.

He slips out the back door, down to the greenbelt. The quiet among the trees is nearly deafening. He heads toward the tree, which still has ribbons of yellow police tape around it.

Then a strong hand closes on his arm. He looks up to see Steve Butler, a smile trying to creep onto his craggy face. "It's all right, Grant. I'm Mr. Butler. I live down the street at 3308. It's OK."

"I don't know you."

"My wife and I know Iris. And we knew Ms. Roberts. It's OK." He eases his grip on Grant's arm, which doesn't reassure Grant. "We're supposed to take you to your mother. She really wants to see you."

"My phone's not working," he says, and then Steve Butler says, "I know," which in the moment strikes Grant as so odd. "We have to get you past the press, past the police out there in front of your house."

Grant nods. This makes sense.

"This is my wife," Mr. Butler says as an introduction. Now Grant sees the woman, bundled in a coat, stepping out from behind a tree, flicking on a smile for him. "We're going to take you to your mother."

"Are you the ones leaving stuff for me in the tree?"

"We were asked to do that," Mrs. Butler says. Now they've both got ahold of him and they're hurrying him along, deeper into the greenbelt. Past his house. "Your mother is at our house and we'll figure out how to get you out of here without the press and police seeing."

"Why...?"

"Grant, Iris is taking you out of the country," Mr. Butler says.

"Why?"

"Because she can't stay here. She can't. She'll be arrested soon."

Grant's mind whirls. His mother. Running from the police and not wanting to leave him behind. She did it, then. She did it. She killed Danielle. Not Dad. Or Julia. His mom, his wonderful, fiery mom would take on the entire world for him. Running from the police. For only one reason.

Grant pulls free of both the Butlers. He's stronger than he looks, and Steve Butler releases his hold on him. Grant runs forward, because the Butlers are moving too slowly.

They hurry after him.

He stays on the greenbelt, panting, nerves screaming, mind racing. If he and Mom run, what happens to Julia and Dad? They cannot just leave them. What if both his parents were involved in the murder? What happens if they both go to jail? What will he do? He cannot imagine his world. He has to talk Mom out of this. He has to get her to see reason. But if Mom killed Danielle, what can he say? What can he do except go with her? He can't let her go alone. He can't.

Mr. Butler catches him, grabs his arm. "You'll run past our house if you're not careful."

Now Grant stops, panting. He allows Mr. Butler to lead him into a backyard that needs mowing, into the brick two-story that is a few down from his house and Danielle's house.

They go inside. He calls, "Mom! Mom!"

"Grant," a low voice rumbles. He sees Mike Horvath step from the shadows. "Are you all right?"

"Where's my mom?"

"Change of plans. She couldn't get here, not with the press

around and the police coming. She'd be arrested immediately. I'm going to take you to her." He looks at the Butlers. "I'll take it from here."

"OK," the Butlers both say, in unison.

Mike's car is in the Butlers' garage and the door powers up. Peter is in the back seat, looking pale. Mike pushes Grant down in the back seat so the press throng won't see him, then backs out of the driveway. Mr. Butler obligingly closes the garage door.

"Stay down," Mike says.

"Where is my mom?"

"I'm taking you to her right now."

Peter puts his hand on Grant's back, and Grant feels a little reassured. "Are the police looking for her?"

"Yes. I talked to your dad's lawyer." Mike's voice is hard.

The feeling in his chest is so tight, Grant can't breathe. He clenches his eyes closed. "Are you helping Mom get out? Where would we go?"

"Canada first. Then elsewhere."

"You'll like Canada," Peter says. "We still have a house there. I have a great game system."

Grant lies there, quiet. He can tell from the increased speed that the car is on Old Travis now, and he can see from the signs that they're getting close to one of the highways on the western side that loop around Austin. It's the loop that would take you to 71 and then the airport.

The shock wears off and logic crowds into his brain. "If you think my mom or my dad killed Danielle, why are you helping her?"

"I think it's this drug dealer Marland guy who killed Danielle and he knew enough about your family from Ned to try to frame your dad. We know now he threatened Danielle. Your sister has it on a cell phone that he gave Ned to use. I can't let your parents go to jail for something they didn't do. That's not justice. We will get this worked out."

"But, Mike…"

"Right now we just need to get you to a safe place and we can talk with your mother, all right?"

"All right," Grant says, because he can tell that the car is driving at sixty miles an hour and when he tests the door handle, it's locked with the childproof mode. But then he thinks about all this: the tree, the messages, all coming on the heels of Danielle's murder, and it's all too soon. It all happened too soon.

Maybe someone else is lying to him. Not just his parents. And sometimes parents tell lies for good reasons, not bad ones, and Mike has always been good to him. But he sits up, and sees Mike's gaze on him for a moment in the back seat, and now he's afraid.

"I want to call my mom. Give me your phone. Something's wrong with mine."

"She's driving to meet us right now, Grant," Peter says quietly.

"She'll pull over and take my call."

Mike says, "I have access to a friend's private plane—you know that. I got Ned's dad here from London faster. It's going to take you and your mom to Canada. We have friends there who will help you."

"Won't you get in trouble?"

"Maybe. But we'll see about getting you somewhere else where she can't be extradited until this is over. You don't want your whole family in jail, Grant."

Extradited. Grant doesn't know what that means. But no, he doesn't want his whole family in jail.

"You trust me, don't you, Grant?"

"Yes," he says finally. He does. Mike has always been there for him.

68

IRIS

Iris pulls into her driveway, inching past the press vans that are there, honking at them. Iris ignores their questions as she hurries into the house.

"Grant! Grant!"

She runs through the house. *Anya, Anya, has Anya already been here? Where is my son?* Then she sees his open laptop on the kitchen table. On the screen is the email, telling him to go down to the tree; she'll send someone he knows.

The tree. She runs out of the house, down the yard, to the greenbelt. No press here yet; it is private property, unlike the public street in front of her house. She runs down to the tree. No one is there.

Who is helping Anya destroy Danielle's and Iris's families?

Marland. The Butlers? Their house is owned by the same company as Danielle's. Firebird. Did Anya find discredited clients of Danielle's, give them information to blackmail Danielle with, and buy the house for them? How deep does her revenge run?

She runs back up the greenbelt. To the Butler house.

The back door is unlocked; the Butlers stand in the kitchen, drinking champagne. They are toasting each other, clinking flutes. Carrie stares at her; Steve turns, and the joy on his face vanishes and turns to stone.

"Where is my son?" Iris says. The tone of her voice is one she's never heard before. Not even in the cold of an abandoned Russian village.

"Get the hell out of our house."

"Where is he?"

"He's not here," Carrie says. "We haven't seen him." Her voice is sharp and harsh. "You seem to have a real issue with keeping track of your children. Why they gave you one is beyond me."

"I will go outside and start screaming at the press that are outside my home that my son is missing," Iris says, "if you don't tell me where he is."

"He's not here," Steve says, and so Iris pulls Marland's gun from her purse. She aims it squarely at Steve.

"I will use this," she says slowly, carefully. "Where is my son?"

They don't answer, staring at the gun. "Now, put that down," Steve says in a calm voice. "Grant is fine. No one's going to hurt him. But he's not here. Did he tell you he was coming here?"

"You met him at the tree," she bluffs.

"Well, he didn't meet us. He surely didn't. So let's just calm down and—"

She fires, and the bullet shatters the cabinet behind him. She hears the breaking of glass, the splintering of wood. Carrie screams. Steve drops his champagne flute, and it shatters on the floor.

"What are you celebrating, a job well done?"

They're silent. Breathless with shock.

"You moved here just to scare Danielle. She wasn't going to give you a child. She told you no. You couldn't possibly choose to see the woman who denied your dreams on a regular basis as a neighbor. So, why are you here? Who is Firebird? Why did someone buy you this house?"

Their faces go pale.

"I mean, Steve, here you are. Right on the scene after Danielle's body is found. Was that on purpose, so you could make sure all went to plan? And then your so-called patrol, so you could be out in the neighborhood, conveniently, to call the police on my daughter."

They are silent, Steve reddening.

"Someone bought you this house under a front company to be close to her." Then the realization. "Or, equally, to be close to us. To spy on us? To scare us? Was it Anya?"

The name is like a grenade landing in the room. She sees their startled reaction. "Where is Anya?"

"No one is harming your son. I promise you, as a mother," Carrie says.

"Your nursery that you got ready," Iris says. "Is that why you did this? There is no generous pregnant distant cousin. This is how you're somehow getting a baby? By helping to steal mine?"

"You're not going to kill us," Steve says with confidence. He takes a step toward her, hands up, voice cooled to reason. "But the police are going to be very interested that you shot at us in our house after your family's other crimes. Your whole family's going to be in jail. Is that what you want for Grant?"

"That's what Anya wants. A clear path to my son. Where. Is. He?" She aims the gun straight at Steve's head. "Carrie. I will make you a widow, I swear to God, if you don't tell me where my child is."

"The airport," Carrie says immediately. Steve gives her a look of absolute loathing.

"Airport," Iris repeats, nearly dizzy with shock. No. Can't be. Couldn't be. Anya can't be taking him. He wouldn't go with a stranger.

"We don't know any more, all right? We don't know any more!" Carrie says.

"Give me your phones and car keys," Iris orders. She has to think this through. For her son's sake. She can't make a mistake now.

The Butlers comply. She sees the house phone and demands the cordless as well. She orders them into their walk-in pantry, slams the door, and jams a chair from the breakfast nook hard up under the handle.

Weirdly, the garage is empty, but she sees an Audi parked in the street, and one of the keys is for an Audi. She takes it; the press down the street don't seem to notice her. She roars away.

She doesn't see one woman break away from the crowd, get in a car, and start to follow her.

Stoplights and red lights are for other people, and screaming apologies and trying to be careful, she races through them when there are gaps in the traffic, warning all by laying on her horn.

She thinks as she drives. She talks aloud to herself as she drives, sorting it out.

Anya can't just whisk Grant onto a plane. And she thinks of Gordon, flown here faster on a private jet that Mike said he arranged through a friend.

Could Anya force Mike to help her that way? Using Grant as leverage? She can't race up to the terminal and just tear through it looking for her son. The private jets, though…

She floors the car, weaving like a madwoman in and out of the Highway 71 traffic, roaring toward Austin-Bergstrom International Airport.

Iris makes a noise deep in her throat. She can feel her family, the reality of her loved ones, slipping away from her. Forever.

69

GRANT

The car stops near one of the private jets. "Your mom's on my plane."

"Have her come out to the car and talk to me," Grant says.

Mike turns around in the seat. "I don't think it's a good idea for the people around here to see her. Remember her. The police are looking for her right now." He fixes his gaze on Grant. "I need you to be a brave kiddo, the one I know you are, and come with me. I need you to trust me. Just stick close to Peter, all right?"

"I don't have my passport."

"Your mom kept it just in case she needed it."

"I don't have clothes."

"We can get all that in Canada," Peter says.

Grant gets out of the car. Mike wouldn't lie to him. Mike will never lie to him. Mike has been there for him all those times. Grant, Peter, and Mike walk to the stepladder going up into the private jet. Normally he'd be all excited about boarding a private plane, snapping selfies and texting his friends about how awesome it would be, but now he just wants to see his mother.

He climbs into the passenger section, Mike behind him. Two columns of plush leather seats, on either side of the plane; halfway down, a large table.

He sees a woman step out from the back of the plane. Long hair, pretty, soft eyes, nice smile. Dressed nicely. It's not Mom.

"Where is she?" Grant says.

"Back there is a really small bedroom. She's resting back there."

The woman tries to say something to Grant, but he ignores her. He pushes past her and hurries into the bedroom. It's empty.

He turns back and Peter has followed him into the small room.

Mike fills the door, tears in his eyes, gesturing gently with his big hands.

"Where is my mother?" Grant asks.

"I need you to listen to me, Sasha."

For a moment the name, unexpected, freezes him. "That's not my name."

"It has always been your name. Your true name."

"Sasha," Peter says, as though testing the word.

"Mike, where is my mother?" Now his voice is quavering.

"Her name was Anya. Once I loved her very much," Mike says.

"What? Mike?"

"I am your father," Mike says, and he tries to smile again at Grant.

70

IRIS AND GRANT

Iris pulls her car onto a side road that leads to cargo and private jet operations. She's never been here before and she's trying to remember the times Mike mentioned this plane—he mentioned it as a friend's, but one where "he had access." During massive Austin events like the music and film festivals, there would be dozens of private planes arriving and departing, and Mike once joked about his friend charging business associates in Canada high fees for the private jet. She drives along the access road and then she sees Mike's car. Parked, and between the buildings, near the access runway for private jets, she sees a jet. Parked. Just the one at the moment.

She screeches to a stop behind Mike's car. Nothing matters right now except finding her child.

She still has the gun, now tucked into the back of her jeans. She hopes the Butlers haven't broken down the door and called him. The plane is still on the ground. She runs up the access stairs and enters the cabin.

There's a woman there, with an open medical bag. She stares at Iris.

"Where is he? My son?"

The woman doesn't answer, and then the door opens and she sees Mike.

"Where is Grant?" she yells.

"Mom!" she hears Grant call behind Mike. He's in the back room or hold or whatever it is. Mike slams the room's door shut behind him.

"Grant?"

"Aren't you looking for Anya?" Mike says.

Her name, spoken by him, staggers her. "Where is Anya?"

"She's dead. Of course, you knew that already." A coldness in Mike's tone, none of the hearty warmth she's always known from him. But of course everything about him is a lie. Everything. The past two years of friendship were all a falsehood. She can hardly wrap her head around it.

"No...Anya was in touch with Danielle. And with Marland, that drug dealer. Where is she?"

"Dead, where you left her. Where I found her, when I went looking."

Iris hears Grant screaming in the room, pounding on the door.

* * *

Peter pulls Grant away from the door. Peter's tall and rangy but not athletic, and Grant dodges away from him.

"Are y'all crazy? He's not my dad. I talked to my Russian dad."

"You talked to Boris Stepurin. He's an old friend of our mama's. Mama told him he was the father and he believed her. She needed someone else's name on the birth certificate so Papa wouldn't know."

For a moment the phrase doesn't register with him. *Our mama.* "What...?"

Peter smiles. "Mama gave me up, too, for a little while, till Papa found me. I don't want to hurt you, but you're going to sit down on that bed. The nurse will give you a shot if you feel anxious. We won't be in Canada long. Then we'll fly home."

Home. Grant stares at him. Then he drops to one knee, as if shuddering in shock and dismay, his fingers searching for the knife he tucked in his sock.

* * *

Iris pulls the gun from her waistband and aims it at Mike.

"Are you going to shoot me, Iris? The way you did Anya, when all she wanted was her child back?"

"It wasn't like that…She was going to kill us…"

"Well, you *were* taking her child from her. You were in the way. No jury would have convicted her."

"He was ours! She gave him up!"

"Could you ever give up Grant? If it was what was best for him?"

She stares at him.

"Your husband killed Danielle. Your daughter killed Marland. It's likely that you personally concealed evidence in both cases—in fact, that will be found to be so, very soon. You're felons, all of you. What future does Sasha have with such a family? None. None at all. I'm his father, and I'm taking him home."

"Who *are* you?"

"My name would be meaningful to you if you followed Russian politics, but I don't expect that of a woman who writes forgettable pop songs. I'm a man with some means. A man who was betrayed by Anya, a young woman he loved. A man who was spied on by Anya for your friend Danielle, and so Anya left me and hid and found out she was pregnant with my child and gave up the baby. Then she changed her mind. I never knew until I went looking for her. And found her."

"The village."

"I'd bought Bukharin, you see. The whole village was to be cut down so I could build my estate on it. She went there because she felt safe; she could hide and wait for me there. No one would look for her there. And there she would be, with my child. A bargaining chip to ask my forgiveness for betraying me to the CIA."

She remembered what Danielle had said: these places get bought by oligarchs and millionaires and torn down for estates. More than an idle speculation, a statement of fact.

"Danielle and Anya spied on you."

"Danielle was a CIA courier. Perfect cover, right? She goes to Russia often on business. Material could be given to her that she could take out of the country. Documents you would not want transmitted through the internet. Or photos. She picked up material from agents the CIA had recruited. Anya was my girlfriend, and the CIA turned her against me with lies and deceptions. She stopped when she realized she was pregnant. But she made the mistake of telling Danielle, her handler. And Danielle talked her into giving up the baby. She'd done it once before. I didn't even know she was pregnant, but I had told her, no babies. Back then I didn't want kids. Anya was afraid of angering me, so she left me; she went off to model, she said, as she'd done before. And she had Sasha. But Danielle had told her CIA bosses about my baby, and they decided that baby was valuable. That baby was leverage to be used against me, my own blood, safely adopted by an American family and held out as a carrot to me to get me to give them what they wanted on the Russian president, his inner circle, the most powerful men and women in Russia.

"But after you all killed Anya, they abandoned that plan. No one wanted to have to explain where Anya was when the question would come up. Danielle told the Agency that Anya had died, killed by you and your husband, and the CIA decided not to use my child as leverage against me. And once Russia stopped allowing adoptions, Danielle became less useful to them."

The people following Danielle in Moscow—the men in the fancy cars. Conduits to Anya, or other informants. "The woman who warned me off adopting Grant..."

"The CIA division that Danielle worked for was torn. One side felt it was wrong to use a child as a tool—or that it was too risky, that I could simply go to the Russian press and say the CIA helped get my child adopted by an American family and I never knew. They did not want you to adopt Sasha. They wanted Anya to return to spying on me, and with a child in her arms, she and I would be even closer, they thought. She had been a steady source of important information." His voice was bitter.

The warning woman, Iris thinks. The bribe. The CIA would pay that much to keep an informant close to one of the most powerful men in Russia. It was a pittance to them.

"The other side wanted the adoption to go through—so Sasha could be leverage if ever needed, kept close to a family near Danielle. But they abandoned that, of course, after Anya vanished." Mike shrugs. "Does it matter? You and Kyle and Danielle killed my woman and took my child."

"Why would Danielle help you now?"

"Do you think I gave her a choice? If my child was going to be leverage used against me, he could be used against her. Danielle didn't want to be exposed as complicit in a murder. It wrecked her work for the CIA, having been involved in the death of an asset. They terminated her employment, disavowed her. And linking her to the CIA would destroy her adoption work, China would never let her in again or let her agency work in the country. When I came to Lakehaven, she knew who I was and she knew what would happen to her and her son if she didn't play along. I bugged her house. I routinely hacked her phones. She had no way out from under my watch. If she talked about our arrangement to anyone, her son would be dead. I guaranteed that. Even if I was caught, arrested, and she and Ned were put into witness protection, her son would be dead. I have many friends in Russia who owe me many favors." Now he smiles, shrugs. "Plus, I think she felt just a little guilty. I told her I only wanted a chance to know my boy. Like any good papa."

Iris thinks: *She pretended to be your girlfriend, so you'd be more readily accepted. Living in an endless trap, to protect herself and her son, so mine could be stolen.* She tried to imagine Danielle's terror. Her fear. She'd given a phone to Kyle not for an affair…but maybe as a first step of escape or warning. Even then she'd been too terrified to tell Kyle the truth, unwilling to risk her son's life.

"Mike…"

"Mike was a deep cover identity I used in my intelligence career, long before I made my billions working for our president and his friends. I just stepped back into Mike's shoes. Back in Russia they think I'm a recluse in my estate, or off on a yacht in Monaco, or whatever. You can run your business from wherever you are."

A former intelligence agent. A billionaire. An oligarch. "You did this to our family. You coerced Danielle into helping you. You killed her, then framed my husband for it, killed Marland and framed my daughter."

The slightest smile. "Your family is clearly unfit for the boy. He sees what you all truly are."

"He'll never love you. He'll never accept you. He'll never forget about us."

"I can give him everything he needs and anything he wants. You can give him visiting hours at the local prison." His contempt is thick.

"This is kidnapping."

Mike smiles, and it is, to her horror, the same crooked grin that Grant has. It is the one resemblance between them. "That's the thing about truth these days—we all get to define it. I'm one of the most powerful men in Russia, when I'm home. The Russian press will take my side—that my son was wrongly stolen from me years ago, that you bribed the judge, then murdered his poor mother, that I have simply taken back my son rightfully. Sasha and I will issue a statement saying that he came willingly because of what you and your murdering husband did. The Russian government will never send him back to you."

"He'll be an adult in four years. He won't stay."

"Perhaps. Of course, you may all still be in prison, and he may have gotten used to the lifestyle my son is entitled to enjoy. I can give him a life of comfort and luxury you can scarcely imagine. You can give him nothing."

"You launched a war against us. Against my family."

"More like an intelligence operation. To show Sasha what you really are. Murderers." The smile vanishes. "Am I wrong? Did you not leave Anya dead?"

Her voice quivers. "Punish me and Kyle, fine. But my daughter did nothing to you."

"Sasha doesn't need any ties here. Plus, you took my child. Do you understand that? You are nothing, and you took something that belonged to me." Mike pats his own chest. "So, it's important to me that you understand what kind of special hell that is, Iris." The flicker again, of the smile. "That is the hell I have made for you."

"Grant!" she screams. "Mom is here, baby!"

"Mom!" Grant screams on the other side of the door.

"Pilot! Take off now!" Mike yells. "Peter! Tell Sasha it will be all right."

Both of them hear Peter scream.

And then Iris aims the gun right toward Mike.

Mike shakes his head. "How many people are you going to kill for your son, Iris? Do you think this will make him love you? Or will it just make him afraid of you?"

Iris stares at him.

"Danielle told me how you always insisted *she* had killed Anya. But she said it was you. You turning the gun close to Anya's heart, you pulling the trigger." He looks at the gun, unafraid of it in her shaking hand. "Are you going to kill both of Sasha's parents?"

"Danielle was lying."

"Danielle is dead. Take off!" he yells at the pilot. And she hasn't even noticed the pilot in the cockpit, presumably going through some preflight configurations or whatever they do.

She lowers the gun.

"Now, that's reasonable," Mike says. "I'm going to tell you how this works, because you've inspired me. We're flying to London for refueling. You and Sasha don't get off the plane in Britain. We fly to Saint Petersburg, and you will be my guest at the estate I've built where you killed Anya. Guessing you don't have your passport with you, but that's fine; the Russian government will welcome you temporarily. You will help my son transition. If you provide me that help, and behave yourself, evidence will be produced by my people here that clears Kyle and Julia of their crimes. You go home then, and you get your family back, Iris." His smile is an awful thing, a final twist of the knife.

"But my son…"

He pauses, watching her, and she realizes he has waited nearly two years to savor this moment. "Not all your family. Not the one you stole from me. Not the one you murdered a young woman to get. Sasha was never truly yours. He never could be."

"Mom, Mom!" Iris hears Grant on the other side of the door, his voice fading.

"The nurse here will give him a sedative. You will tell him that it's all going to be OK. Or your husband and daughter…"

"It's going to be all right, Grant," she says. Mom voice on, like a switch has been flicked. Reassuring, calm.

"Sasha. You will call him Sasha from now on. That's his name."

"It's going to be all right—Grant," and then Iris turns and fires two bullets wild into the cockpit, hitting random instrumentation, and there are sparks, then screams from the pilot and the nurse. Iris feels Mike lumber into her, wrapping his arm around her throat from behind and tackling her. They crash into the airplane's deck, Mike screaming in rage and Iris closing both her hands around the gun so he can't pull it away from her. Not making the mistake Anya made.

"Grant!" she screams. "Run!" The door to the plane is still open.

Mike lifts and slams Iris into the plane's deck again. She feels the carpet scrape her face. Yelling behind her, Grant's voice loud again. Mike slams her into the deck again. She feels her nose break.

"Run!" she screams.

Grant, screaming, now atop Mike, somehow with a bloodied steak knife in his hand, slashing at Mike's shoulder. Mike shrugs him off. "Sasha, no!"

Then Grant, kneeling before them both, dropping the knife, pulling the gun from his mother's hands, raising it toward his father's face, fumbling for a grip on it. "Let my mom go! Now!"

"Grant," she screams. "Don't! Don't!"

"Sasha…" Mike begins.

The gun fires.

71

AFTERWORD OF *A DEATH IN WINDING CREEK* BY ELENA GARCIA

A journalist should never be part of the story, but when I spotted a frantic Iris Pollitt coming out of the Butler home and roaring off in her car, I followed. She drove like a maniac and so did I. Sometimes you have the sense of when a story is drawing to a close, and yet with this unusual American family, one could feel, even after everything they survived, that their story was just beginning.

I was the first person to call the police after the gunshots rang out in the private jet that Iris boarded, and I was there when Iris Pollitt and her son, Grant, and the others aboard the plane were brought out by airport officers and Austin police. And even not knowing fully what the story was at that point, I remembered thinking: *This man went to war with the wrong family.*

What makes a family in our modern world where people can feel hyper-connected and yet so alone? It is more than the connection of blood and DNA.

Is it sacrifice, like Kyle Pollitt was willing to do to protect those he loved? Could you face life in prison to shield another person?

Is it determination, like Julia Pollitt, a teenager who took on a dangerous and vicious criminal—and got in entirely over her head, yet did not flinch?

Is it transcendent love, like Iris Pollitt showed to her son, charging into a life-threatening situation without knowing what she would face and taking a life to save her child?

Or is it simply choice? Grant Pollitt was given a choice and he chose his family. His real family: the mother, father, and sister who had given him love and loyalty.

We choose to love. We choose to stand together as a family. In the case of the Pollitts, I believe that is what defines a family. And you don't want to go to war with a family like that.

72

THE POLLITT FAMILY

RURAL VIRGINIA, TWO WEEKS LATER

When Iris thought about that dark day, she would focus on a few images: leading her son off the plane, her arm around Grant, murmuring reassurances. She had thought of racing to the park on that morning of Danielle's murder, shifting into mom mode for her daughter. Staggering away from that private jet was mom mode times a thousand: seeing that reporter Elena Garcia with a cell phone pressed to her ear and steering Grant away from her. She knelt and hugged Grant and kicked the gun away so the police could see her hands were empty. Behind her, back on the plane, she had heard Peter howling in either pain or grief. But pushing past all the chaos was the weight of her child, *her* son, leaning against her, needing her, drawing strength from her.

"Mom, Mom," Grant kept whispering, his voice broken, and she told him it was over; it would be all right.

Now she'd find out if she'd told him the truth.

* * *

"As deals go, it's not bad," the warning woman explains. Her name is Jill, so she says, and Iris has not seen her since Grant was a baby. Before all this, Iris last saw Jill in a Saint Petersburg café, faking a slight Russian accent, whispering a warning not to proceed with the adoption. "The evidence and the statements from his accomplices clear both your husband and your daughter; the blame is laid on this man known as Patrick Marland, whom Horvath hired as an accomplice. You all move from Austin, drop out of sight for a few years, it's forgotten. News cycles are measured in minutes now. But we think it's best you be here, close to the Agency, where the government can offer you protection."

"And what about Mike? Does his story get buried along with him?"

"The late Mikhail Vladimirovich Ivanov, as we know him. The Russian government isn't keen on acknowledging that one of their president's billionaire inner circle and former intelligence officers went back to his active espionage background to exact a personal revenge. And then helped murder American citizens. The Russians will paint him as not close to the president, using criminals like Marland for his scheme and having gone rogue."

"I just want to understand it..." Iris begins, but then she realizes she understands, at some level, what drove Mike. He wanted his child back. "If he was the father, why didn't he just say so?"

"Because he knew you would never surrender Grant, and Grant would not go willingly with him. And he wanted to make you pay for Anya's death. And also because if he had, certain... activities in his past would have come to light, and he couldn't maintain his billions or his position if they had." Jill clears her throat. "Years ago, Danielle worked for the CIA as a courier. One of her contacts that she received information from was... Mike. One of the others was Anya, who spied on Mike and his close friends for us."

"And if he announced we had his son... that would have come out?"

"Yes. Most of the trusted advisers around the Russian president share his background of having worked for the KGB and then becoming powerful leaders of business in Russia. Mike was no different. Except he had shared information with us. He could only gain his son through treachery. So he forced Danielle to help him destroy your family."

Iris closes her eyes for a moment.

"The flash drive Kyle found in Danielle's house? It was insurance she thought she could keep to protect herself from Mike. A record of payments made to two Russian agents in the employ of the CIA from years ago, who passed along information to Danielle when she would come to Russia for adoption visits. She used their CIA code names: Lark and Firebird."

"Anya and Mike—I mean Mikhail."

"Yes."

"They *both* were on the CIA payroll?"

"Mikhail was one of our key assets. He'd been identified as a possible successor to the president. You can imagine our interest in him, and our desire to protect him as a source. Anya we paid to keep an eye on him, to make sure he didn't lie to us, but he didn't know that, at least then."

"That was why you offered us money not to adopt Grant. To keep him in Russia, so she could go back to Mike with a child and be closer to him than ever."

She nods. "We tried everything to dissuade you."

"You could have killed us."

"The operative assigned to follow you...went rogue that day."

"I saw a picture of him on that flash drive. The man called Marland, standing next to a damaged SUV, just like the one that hit us. Marland was CIA."

Jill looks uncomfortable for a moment, then takes a deep breath. "Yes. He was very protective of Ivanov. An asset like Ivanov was unique. What if the Russian president has a heart attack? Ivanov was one of the five top contenders to be next in line back then. But Anya had already burned her bridges with the orphanage system the first time. They weren't going to give her back Sasha when she decided she'd be better off going back to Ivanov."

Iris stares at her.

Jill shakes her head. "They were really a pair. The high-placed Russian billionaire whom we couldn't bribe, but we could let him invest and grow his money in the West, where other Russians couldn't get ahold of it if he fell from power, and the poor young model who loved him but became increasingly unstable under the pressure. You know, Danielle could never meet directly with Mike.

He'd send people to her hotel. Those guys going to hotels full of Western business types wasn't suspicious."

"And Marland was CIA. But here he was working for Mike..."

"Yes. Marland was a former field operative in Russia who became Mike's handler after we dropped Danielle when Anya died. His real name was Patrick Crawford. He got close...too close, too chummy with Mike. Marland was greedy. Marland would keep him informed of certain CIA activities in Russia or neighboring countries, and Mike used the information to stay in power, to expand his influence. And he set up very nice financial accounts for Marland under a range of names. Marland left the CIA with no crimes proven, but under a cloud. Before he left, he managed to get the Agency's forensic file with photos and details of the team's processing of the scene in the abandoned town after Danielle reported that Anya was dead—a murder she blamed on you and Kyle."

"That's who Danielle called...a CIA team. To clean up the mess."

"And to document it. When Marland finally acquired the CIA file a couple of years ago, he sold it to Mikhail, who decided he wanted his biological son back...but was not going to risk asking you for permission to see him. I'm not sure if he was driven more by love or a sense of outrage that you had taken something that should have been his. He blamed you for Anya's death, hence you had to suffer. The photos of the cat in the window, the snow, all of that was from the CIA file. Danielle called us to clean up the scene, but we had little time—he owned that land. He'd bought the village to tear it down and build a complex there. I think Anya planned to wait for Mike there, with their child that he didn't even know about yet. When he saw the CIA report, he must have dug and found her body buried on the edge of the property, and retrieved the bracelet you put back on her wrist."

"So armed with the CIA report on how Anya had been killed while kidnapping us, he came here under an old Russian intel cover and co-opted Danielle?"

"Yes. He showed up in Austin as Mike Horvath, Canadian investor, with a teenage son in tow and conclusive proof of her involvement in Anya's death. Obviously that would have destroyed her business and her life here. And we believe, from what Peter told us, that he threatened to kill Ned if she didn't cooperate. He had her under close surveillance and control. Her phone had been compromised by Russian hackers to monitor her constantly. So she did as he asked. He bought her a house close to you, via this Firebird front company, so you would be neighbors, as he did later for the Butlers. Danielle, under coercion, helped establish Mike as the friendly, trustworthy neighbor. Helped him befriend your family. Helped him get access to your house so he could surveil you either through tampering with your phones or computers or listening devices—it won't surprise me if we find your house is bugged. He had a long game, and having help—Danielle, Marland, and the Butlers—was key to his operation."

"She could have told us. Warned us."

"We think she was preparing to…That was why she gave Kyle the burner phone recently. But she never got up her courage to tell Kyle. Her and her son's lives were at risk."

"It must have been very lonely for her," Iris says. For all her anger toward Danielle…this is horrifying to hear. To live this way, in constant fear.

"We think that Mike ordered Marland to kill Danielle when she finally rebelled against his control. We think the burner phone she gave Kyle was to communicate with him where Mike couldn't know. She didn't want to have an affair with Kyle; when she found out that her son was enmeshed in a drug scheme, she could see it was a revenge play not against just your family, but hers as well. She wanted to find a way to warn you all without putting your family and hers in mortal danger. If she warned Kyle, she risked her son's death. She was trying to figure out how to do it, how to contact him, how to tell him without him freaking out that Sasha's father was mounting an intelligence operation against your family. I believe when she threatened to go to the police to protect Ned—then her usefulness was done. She may not have even known her old colleague Marland was the drug dealer. He killed her, using pipe Mike had stolen from your house at some point. He must have called the one number in the burner phone he found in her pocket and realized it belonged to Kyle. Kyle told the police the truth, that he got an early-morning call from her burner...but not that Marland hung up when he realized it was Kyle on the other end. Then they knew they had to escalate the attack against your family."

Iris feels cold in a way she hasn't felt since the awful moments in Bukharin, with Anya dying in the snow.

"But they couldn't remove the listening devices in her house until Ned left the house with your daughter. That's what Marland was doing when your husband went inside Danielle's house—cleaning up the evidence, making sure nothing could point to them because they still had to destroy your family. Marland beat Kyle and then told Mike about bloodying him in the bag, and that was a perfect way for the murder weapon to be produced. They planned long term, but they took advantage of sudden opportunities. Very good at his job."

Iris can't quite bear the admiration in Jill's voice and she looks away.

"What about Peter?" She hates Mike, Marland, the Butlers...but she feels sorry for Peter.

Jill takes a deep breath. "What Peter told Grant on the plane is true. He is Anya's older son. Your child's half brother. We just confirmed it with DNA testing."

Iris takes a deep breath. All this time...his own brother, right there. Grant had slashed Peter's arm to get free from the room.

"Anya had a series of tumultuous relationships among the Russian elite before Mike. She was his mistress who made his unhappy marriage bearable. She had Peter, fathered in another relationship, and she gave him up for adoption as the father would give no support. She got Peter back, then got cold feet again and returned him. But Peter was never adopted by a family. After Anya's death, we believe Mike learned about Peter and adopted him, as a way of honoring Anya. But he did so under his Mike Horvath name, which he had used in intelligence operations against Canada. Peter Horvath was raised by Mike in Toronto, where Mike established a second household that his Russian wife didn't know about. After his wife unexpectedly died, he was free to move between both lives as Mike and Mikhail as he liked. But he got Russian intelligence hackers to train Peter and used Peter to reach out via email to your son, as Anya, sending those pictures and messages to slowly break down Grant. Peter was helping his adoptive father destroy your lives. His loyalty to Mike was absolute and unquestioning."

"But Peter talked about losing his mother."

"He has very few memories of Anya, but I know he felt her loss." Jill clears her throat. "That so many images and details of Anya's life were scrubbed off the internet—Peter told us his father asked him to do that. To help erase his mother's presence."

Iris feels ill. "Grant asked Peter for help."

"Of course. He was a trusted fellow teenager with the know-how; Grant probably wouldn't have gone to an adult. Peter was the perfect confidant—actively hacking your family's computers and phone, and better yet, Peter could tell Grant any lie or truth about the hacking that helped their cause, and Grant would believe him. Peter told Grant what their father wanted Grant told. Bits and pieces of the story—emails from Saint Petersburg, hints of lies told by you—to warm Grant up to the idea of his Russian father."

"What will happen to Peter?"

"The Russians don't want him; he's no longer a citizen, and they've frozen all of Mike's financial accounts that they can reach. Grant is his sole relative. He has no one else. He'll face charges here and probably be deported back to Canada."

Iris closes her eyes. "He did the same to me with my phone. Pretended to break into that phone of Marland's and shattered my world with those texts supposedly from Anya."

"All communications to Marland and the Butlers from 'Anya' were from Mike. That was Mike's alias in the operation, one designed to unnerve you if you discovered it."

"I don't think they thought I would do anything but run."

"And that way they could have easily gotten rid of you. They didn't need to frame you for a crime."

"So who killed Marland? One of the Butlers? Peter?" The thought that Mike would order his own son to commit murder chills her.

"The Butlers say it was Mike himself. He knew the neighborhood; it was easy for Butler to direct the patrols away from the house while Marland and Julia were there. Plus, we've seen his Russian intel files. Mike was skilled in using a knife for assassination. Marland got used. The video on his phone that he had of Kyle and Danielle leaving that so frightened your daughter? The time stamp had been digitally stripped, but it was from last Halloween. The two of them went out to walk the neighborhood and hang out with other parents supervising the trick-or-treating."

It was a Winding Creek tradition—parents walking, sometimes drinking a glass of wine, keeping a distant eye on the kids. "Yes. I remember that. I left before Kyle did. Neither wore a costume. Mike was there that evening, too. A big group of us."

"Mike must have filmed them walking then and tried to make Julia think it was from the night of the murder. He had Steve Butler primed to 'discover' Julia at the scene of the crime. That was the actual purpose of his neighborhood watch—to catch Julia as soon as Marland was killed and make her look guilty."

"He killed him in the few minutes Julia was upstairs?"

"He was a pro and he knew that was his chance. He eliminates someone who could testify against him and takes another huge step in his revenge."

Iris meets Jill's gaze with her own. "A pointless revenge. Anya's death was an accident."

"But who really pulled that trigger? You or Danielle?"

"Does it matter?"

"Your husband was very ready to sacrifice himself for you, Iris. Kyle put everything on the line to protect you all."

"I know. I love him so much."

"That's sweet. But it makes me wonder. Was that devotion because Kyle knew something you'd done in the past for the whole family, something that he felt he owed you for?"

Iris dares a smile and says, "We're a team. Always."

"This journal that 'Anya' mentions in the emails. Danielle must have told him about it. I'm sure he wanted to read it."

Iris won't look at Jill. "I don't know what you mean. If I *had* kept a journal, it would have been to give to my son if I ever had to dissuade him from going back to Russia. To help him understand why he absolutely could not. What the stakes would be."

Jill waits for her to say more, but Iris doesn't. Finally Jill says: "But *you* shot Mike."

"Yes," Iris says immediately. "I feared for my life and my son's life."

"The pilot and the Russian nurse aboard didn't see that."

"That nurse drugged and tried to hang my daughter on Mike's orders. She's not exactly a credible source."

Jill shrugs. "The pilot had shut the cockpit door to protect himself, and the nurse says she was prepping a syringe to sedate you. No one saw the shooting but you and Grant." Jill says this, like she hasn't already read it in the report, like saying it aloud in front of Iris might pry off new information.

"I shot him dead," Iris says. "Never ask me again."

*　*　*

The safe house is in the Virginia countryside. The morning mist burns away and the January sunshine is bright. Iris likes to sit on the porch (she never thought a safe house could have a porch, but this one does, enclosed with bulletproof glass) and drink her coffee and think about what her family will do next.

For now, the kids are being privately tutored by a teacher provided by the Agency, and Kyle is taking a break from work. Iris stands on the porch, watching her two children on the lawn below the backyard deck. Julia looks healthy again, her cheeks flushed as she and her brother toss a football between them. Grant looks…Grant looks like Anya, that poor lost soul, misled by Danielle, used by people higher than her both here and in Russia. The woman who changed her mind, who maybe was scared to leave Mike, or scared to stay and keep spying on him and wasn't afraid to kill to get her baby back. She aches for Anya now. Mike had been assessed as a potential heir to the Russian president. The pressure on Anya must have been intense. Grant's going to look more and more Anya's son the older he gets, her loveliness strong in his face.

She loves both her children so much.

Kyle brings her coffee, and they stand together at the railing. It's been hard to talk, shell-shocked as they both are by the truth about their child, about their friends, about the past.

"He understands why you lied. To protect him. But you can't protect him from the aftereffects."

She glances at him. "What?"

"That he shot Mike."

"He didn't," she says, steady, now staring at Kyle. "I did."

"You don't have to lie, Iris."

"Grant had the steak knife and wounded Mike. So I took the gun and shot Mike. That's what happened. Grant and I agree. I feel like you always talking about it is just unnecessary."

"It's not Anya all over again. We don't have to lie."

She won't look at him, and then she does, straight-on, staring. "Grant believes Danielle killed his birth mother. Let him believe that. Please."

Kyle starts to speak and then stops. What is there to say? Nothing.

Grant makes a leaping catch, and Iris sets down her coffee to clap, to yell encouragement, to give her children all the love and attention they need. Her face is flushed with happiness.

She has kept one secret this long. She can keep another.

Never ask her how long she can keep a secret.

ACKNOWLEDGMENTS

Heartfelt thanks to Wes Miller, Lucy Dauman, Peter Ginsberg, Ed Wood, Lindsey Rose, Callum Kenny, Ben Sevier, Karen Kozstolnyik, David Shelley, Beth de Guzman, Matthew Ballast, Holly Frederick, Jordan Rubenstein, Andy Dodds, Millie Seaward, Jeff Holt, Carmel Shaka, Joe Benincase, Morgan Swift, Nidhi Pugalia, Jonathan Lyons, Sarah Perillo, Madeline Tavis, Shirley Stewart, Eliane Benisti, Lieutenant Robert Mills, Juraj Slavik, Nick Slavik, Chip Evans, Sam Richardson, Will Graham, Richard Shaw, Toni McGee Causey, Meg Gardiner, and J. T. Ellison.

Special thanks to Vince and Chele Robinette and Bo and Colleen Brewer, for sharing their adoption experiences with me.

As always, my greatest thanks to Leslie, Charles, and William for their love and support.

ABOUT THE AUTHOR

@ Leslie Abbott

Jeff Abbott is the *New York Times* bestselling author of eighteen novels. He is the winner of an International Thriller Writers Award (for the Sam Capra thriller *The Last Minute*) and is a three-time nominee for the Edgar Award. He lives in Austin with his family. You can visit his website at www.JeffAbbott.com.